WITH EVERY YARD HE ADVANCED THE SHOUTS BEHIND HIM INCREASED.

THE
BRAVOS OF ALSATIA;

OR,

THE FORTUNES OF FELIX FERDINAND.

BEAUTIFULLY ILLUSTRATED.

COMPLETE.

LONDON:

"BOYS OF ENGLAND" OFFICE, 173, FLEET STREET, E.C.,

AND ALL BOOKSELLERS,

THE BRAVOS OF ALSATIA;

OR, THE FORTUNES OF FELIX FERDINAND.

"'FELIX, THE SECRET OF YOUR BIRTH—QUICK, THE SECRET!' GASPED NICHOLAS."

THE BRAVOS OF ALSATIA;

OR,

THE FORTUNES OF FELIX FERDINAND.

———————

CHAPTER I.

OF THE LOSS OF A GREAT SECRET—OF HOW FELIX STARTS FOR THE " GREAT CITY."

STRATFORD, in Essex, in the year 1610, which is the period at which our story commences, was a small—very small village indeed. It could hardly be called a village, for the number of houses, or, more properly speaking, huts, did not number two-score, and these were scattered, at unequal distances, all over the place.

What the inhabitants did for a living was a perfect mystery; probably they themselves could not have told how they really existed. If there was a person in Stratford who was considered better off than his fellows, and who was, consequently, considered of more importance than the others, it was Nicholas Fielding, who was known as the " Mysterious Old Miser of Stratford."

It was somewhat difficult to understand why Nicholas Fielding should have been thought a miser.

Very often he had been told that that was the name given him, but his only reply was a grim smile and a shake of the head.

Nicholas Fielding, some seventeen years previous to the opening of our romance, resided in the heart of London, but what occupation he had there followed no one knew.

He came, with his wife, and an infant of a year old, one dark night to Stratford, accompanied by the proprietor of the cottage, who, before he left Stratford, was loud in his expressions of admiration for Nicholas Fielding, who had paid every penny for the cottage without a murmur.

When Nicholas first came to reside at Stratford, he was reckoned to be about fifty years of age, and his wife thirty-five, and that they were, though of that age, only a newly-married couple, since they had a child, a boy of a year old, and since Mrs. Fielding had (laughingly, however) said that was the only one they ever had.

When, however, the Fieldings had resided at Stratford some ten years, the neighbours became aware of the fact that there was some peculiar mystery connected with them.

They learned that " the only son of the Fieldings," as he had been considered, was, in fact, no son at all.

The boy, at ten years of age, was sent to a school some five miles from Stratford, and he was sent there in the name of Felix Ferdinand, and the boxes which accompanied him were so labelled.

So here, at least, was a mystery connected with the Fieldings, and the neighbours found it to be an impenetrable one.

Time passed on.

When Felix had just turned his fifteenth birthday, and while at school, he learned of the death of the good lady whom, during the first years of his life, he had called " mother."

He attended her funeral with Nicholas, they being the only mourners, and on their return, he begged the old man to allow him to remain at home to keep him company.

But the old man replied with a sad smile.

"Nay, my lad," he said, "you must return to school and learn all you can. Do not forget to try and become a good scholar, for it will be of service to you in the time to come. Yet, though at school, be always ready for instant departure. You may be suddenly taken away from me, and then—then, maybe, we should part for ever."

In vain, during this meeting, did Felix endeavour to persuade Nicholas to tell him who his parents were, and if Felix Ferdinand was his proper name.

"That has been a secret with him who gave you to me as an infant," said the old man, "and a secret it will remain until you are claimed. If Heaven wills it that I should follow my dear wife before you can be claimed, then I will tell you, on my death-bed, where are ample proofs of your parentage."

So Felix returned to school, visiting old Nicholas only at rare intervals, and each time finding him declining in health.

Felix had nearly reached his twentieth birthday, and was still at school, when we again introduce the cottage of Nicholas Fielding to the notice of the reader.

It was a wild night in December, and the Stratford fields were coated with a thick layer of snow. Around the cottage-door stood about a dozen men and women conversing in whispers.

In the front room of the cottage a dim light was burning, and its sickly rays fell upon the pale, emaciated, and eager face of Nicholas Fielding, who was lying upon a low truckle-bed near the fireplace.

At the head of the bed, his watch in his hand, stood a physician, while at the foot stood the old minister of Bow Church, who had been brought to Nicholas by the neighbours.

"What is the hour?" asked Nicholas, in low, hoarse tones.

"Near upon ten," replied the physician.

"And you give me how long to live?"

"One hour—I can no longer deceive you."

"You do quite right—quite right. It is most important that 1 should know. And it is still snowing?"

"Fast!"

"Lord help me!" ejaculated Nicholas, as he glanced despairingly round the room. "Will he come? Will he come?"

"Do you think that the messenger you sent to the school arrived there safely?"

"I think so—yes, I think so. He was a trusty man; he always faithfully fulfilled my wishes."

"It is somewhat strange he has not returned to the village," observed the physician.

"Pray Heaven," said the minister, "that he is safe, and that your ward, this youth whom you have had in your custody for so many years is safe also, and already on the road. But, alas! there is not much time left to you, Nicholas Fielding. Think over what I said but a short time ago. You have a load upon your mind, and you will die easier if you make me your confidant."

"It is impossible," replied Nicholas, emphatically. "Would you have me break an oath which I made upon God's holy Bible?"

"Nay, nay; but under the circumstances, when——"

"I repeat, it is *impossible!*"

"Listen. You have less than an hour to live. If you die before the lad arrives——"

"I shall not die before he comes—no—no!" interrupted Nicholas. "Tell them to watch—to watch—and to shout when a horseman is seen descending the hill. Oh, Felix, Felix! hasten, hasten!" he moaned, clasping his hands nervously together.

The time passed on; the physician stood near the bedside, the watch in his hand; the minister sat by the side of Nicholas, reading passages of Scripture which he considered suitable to the occasion.

Presently the clasped hands of Nicholas parted and fell helplessly to his sides; the unnatural brightness of his eyes began rapidly to die out, and his breathing became heavy.

The physician replaced his watch and beckoned to the minister, who, falling upon his knees, commenced a prayer.

But suddenly a loud shout was heard without.

The cottage door was pushed open, and one of the neighbours cried out—

"Here they be. Here comes the lad

and the man as fetched him, at a rattling pace down the hill."

The eyes of the dying man opened wider, his wasted hands nervously clenched the quilt of the bed.

"Raise me—raise me!" he gasped; "so that I may tell him where—where——"

The physician and the minister sprang to him and raised him on his pillows, as the long-expected youth, Felix Ferdinand, dashed into the cottage.

He was tall—remarkably tall for his age, and undoubtedly possessed an active and muscular frame.

A finer specimen of the "old school" could hardly have been found.

Snatching off his hat, and thereby revealing a finely-formed head adorned with a magnificent mass of curly hair, the youth stood still for a moment, spellbound at what he beheld.

"Heaven!" he cried; "why was I not sent for before?"

"Because your guardian did not believe that death hovered so near him," replied the minister, solemnly; "but you have arrived just in time."

"Oh, father," cried Felix, throwing himself on his knees by the bedside, "am I then to be quite alone in the world?"

"Felix," gasped the old man, wildly; "Felix—the secret of your birth—quick—the secret. Put your ear to my lips—quick!"

"I have, I have!" sobbed Felix.

"The secret—the——"

Nicholas paused, he gasped for breath, clutched Felix with one hand, and with the other pointed to the floor.

The physician raised him still higher, but no sound issued from the lips of the dying man.

Felix now saw how important it was that he should become the possessor of the secret which Nicholas Fielding for so many years had held.

Frantically did the old man try to speak again, but all his efforts were in vain.

With his right hand pointing to the floor, and with his eyes affectionately fixed upon the eager, handsome face of the youth who had been as a son to him since his infancy, Nicholas Fielding died.

Felix burst into a passionate flood of tears.

"My only friend," he moaned. "The only one who cared for me—gone! I am now indeed alone in the wide world!"

"The secret of your birth," said the minister, "evidently lies hidden beneath the floor, and since it is now of the utmost importance that you should know who you really are, I would suggest summoning the men without and having the flooring at once taken up."

"Nay, nay," said Felix; "not until he lies in the churchyard."

The mission of the physician and the minister being concluded, they soon took their departure, leaving Felix alone with the dead.

* * * *

On the third day after his death, Nicholas Fielding was laid to rest by the side of his wife.

Though many of the inhabitants accompanied the coffin to the grave, Felix was the only mourner. After the funeral the cottage was thoroughly searched, in the presence of the minister, physician, and Felix, and the sum of fifty guineas found between the mattress and the bed.

Wrapped around this money was a paper bearing these words, "All the money I have."

The flooring was next taken up, but nothing whatever was discovered.

"It is certainly extraordinary," said the minister.

"The man was evidently labouring under a delusion," observed the physician.

"Then the delusion was of many years' standing," replied the minister, "for on many occasions old Fielding hinted that Felix was of high birth."

Again and again the place was searched, the walls sounded, articles of furniture taken to pieces, but nothing came to light.

The men, after replacing the flooring, took their departure.

The day after the funeral, Felix sold what the little cottage contained, and the next night he turned his back on the village of Stratford.

At one place only he called, and that was at the house of the minister at Bow, where he received some good advice, and a promise of assistance should he ever need it.

With tearful eyes and a heart full of sadness, Felix bade good-bye to the poor, but good-hearted minister, and turned his face in the direction of what, even at that time, was known as the " Great City."

It is our intention, in this romance, to follow him there, and to give a faithful account of the many and startling adventures which befell him

*   *   *   *

Felix made up his mind to walk to the City; but in the period of which we write, it was hardly safe to be abroad of a night without some means of defence, in case of attack by robbers, who infested almost every part of the kingdom.

A short distance from Bow Church, Felix came to the shop of an armourer.

In the window he beheld a goodly array of pistols, swords, and other weapons.

With all kinds of arms he had been made thoroughly acquainted at school, but he thought of the large price asked for pistols, so he determined to purchase a sword only.

For what, at the present time, would have been considered a ridiculously small sum, he purchased a first-class sword, buckled it about his waist, and concealed it by the cloak he wore, and again set off.

He walked slowly, for he had many sad, bitter things to think over, and the clock had struck ten when he came to " The Cross Keys," a hostelry at the farther end of Aldgate.

It being a dark night, and the snow lying upon the ground very thickly in some places, lighted lanterns were slung from many parts of the balcony.

Just as Felix entered the courtyard, loud voices shouted to him to stand aside.

As he drew back, an elaborately-painted coach, drawn by four horses, rattled up to the principal door of the hostelry.

The arrival of a coach, to which four horses were attached, on such a night as this, was a somewhat surprising occurrence, and, as may be supposed, a large number of persons, male and female, turned out, anxious to learn to whom the coach belonged.

Felix was also curious, for this was the first time he had ever beheld such an elaborate vehicle.

Eevryone was soon satisfied.

" Run Bartolph ! " cried the hostess. " Can't you ? 'Tis Master Walker, the goldsmith of Fleet Street, and his pretty daughter."

" Lord ! " exclaimed the host, as he dropped a quart measure and dashed down the passage leading to the entrance with such impetuosity that he sent three or four of his customers rolling over like ninepins.

When he reached the entrance, he found that Master Walker—for he it was—had already left his coach and was handing out his daughter, a gloriously beautiful girl of some seventeen summers.

Rosamund Walker, at this time, was considered one of the most beautiful girls in England.

The title given to her was " The Pride of the City," and, having in view the fact that Master Walker was reputed to be one of the wealthiest men in the City, it was only a matter of course that Rosamund should already have had numerous offers of marriage—offers which came from the Court as well as from the City.

But at present she had no idea of contracting marriage.

The heart of Felix Ferdinand almost leapt into his mouth as he beheld this beautiful creature. The whole affair was more like a dream to him than anything else.

" Allow me, sir ! " cried the host, bowing and scraping as fast as he was able ; " allow me to conduct the young lady to my wife, who shall see her comfortably installed in the best rooms our hostelry contains."

" You are very kind," replied Master Walker, as he placed his daughter's tiny white hand in the brawny one of the host ; " and if you will see that she is comfortably placed, I shall be extremely obliged.   But, host——"

" Your servant, sir ! "

" See," whispered the goldsmith, " see that she is not only *comfortably* placed, but *safely*.   You understand ? "

" Perfectly," returned the host, as he placed his finger to his nose in a significant manner.   " Your worship, no doubt, would like a room next to your lovely daughter ? "

" By all means, host."

" You will join me directly, father ? " asked Rosamund, in clear, silvery tones.

" Almost immediately, my dear," replied the goldsmith.

The host led Rosamund to his wife,

gave her some instructions, and then returned to the goldsmith.

"Whom have you in your hostelry, Bartolph?" asked the goldsmith.

"No one of any note, your worship, has honoured our house with a call since this morning."

"And who came then?"

"The Lord Mayor, your worship."

"Hem! Are your rooms now empty?"

"Oh, no. I thank goodness they never are. No, your worship, two rooms are engaged by four poor travellers—at least, that is what I take them for, since it is certain that they have not much money in their purses. But may I ask why your worship enquires?"

"Because, Bartolph," whispered the goldsmith, "I am bound to be careful. You are an honest man, Bartolph, and we have known each other for years, so I can tell you with safety that I have notes about me to the value of over two thousand pounds."

The host expressed no surprise.

"Marry!" he said; "'tis a large sum: But—why—who can your worship be afraid of?"

"You can guess if you think, Bartolph."

The host shook his head.

"You don't know? Let me tell you. I am afraid of the Bravos of Alsatia!"

"Why, but, your worship, they never come here."

"Ha! so far as *you* know. *I* know better. They go *everywhere* in search of plunder. Why, Bartolph, one had the impudence to seek an audience with the king a week ago."

"Lord!"

"Yes; I was present, and despite the disguise he had assumed, I recognised the villain."

"And you informed his majesty?"

"Immediately."

"Quite right; and he was kicked out of the royal presence?"

"Immediately."

"Soh! Good, good! Ah, well, Master Walker, I am a pretty good hand, like yourself, at penetrating disguises; and none of the accursed bravos would enter *my* house, if I knew it—nay, not even if they paid like princes."

"Quite right, Bartolph," said the goldsmith, patting the short, fat host on the shoulder! "you are indeed a careful man. But you see, Bartolph, I have under my charge something of higher value than all the money I possess—my daughter."

"True, true. Ah, well Master Walker, rest satisfied that while at 'The Cross Keys,' both money and your daughter are safe."

Little did Bartolph Bently, the careful and scrupulously honest host of "The Cross Keys" dream, that even while he was speaking, four of the most notorious characters that ever walked the back slums of Alsatia were actually beneath his roof!

But so it was.

Felix, during the foregoing conversation, of which he had overheard every word, was standing in a recess behind the host.

He would have moved out, but he was afraid that if he did so, it might be thought that he had placed himself in that position so that he might overhear what was being said.

But as the goldsmith and the host moved off, Felix came forth and entered the hostelry.

The vast dimensions of the place startled him.

The grandness of the place caused him to think of the small amount of money he carried.

He hesitated whether he should enter, but as the snow began once more to descend, he thought it would be better to stay there the night.

Entering he met the hostess, who had just returned from seeing that the goldsmith's daughter had been made comfortable.

"And who are you, my lad?" she asked, as she gave a rapid look first at Felix's clothes, and then at his handsome, but sad-looking face.

"Madame, I seek a lodging for the night."

"Well, well, you can be accomodated here, my lad, if you are an honest person, and if you have the wherewithal to pay for a lodging."

"I am honest, I thank Heaven, madame," replied Felix, "and, moreover, I am provided with the money to pay for a lodging—that is, if the price is reasonable."

"Well, we shall not ask you too much. But what are you?"

"Nothing at present."

"Nothing ? " laughed the hostess— and a better-hearted woman never lived. "Well, *who* are you ? "

"Heaven knows ! Don't laugh at me. I am an unfortunate youth, madame ; and I have resolved to try my fortunes in London," said Felix, simply.

"You are an orphan, perhaps ? "

"I am."

Felix, of course, could not reply that he was anything else.

"An orphan lad in search of a fortune —yes, that is it. Well, well, it shall not be said that I did not assist a youth who had set out to seek his fortune. Listen. We charge heavily for the use of our rooms, but if you choose to accept it, you shall be shown to a little bedroom, where you can make yourself comfortable enough."

"I accept it with many thanks, madame. And pray how much will that be ? "

"Nothing."

Before Felix could renew his thanks, the hostess called to an attendant, and directed him to show Felix the room.

Close by the door was a staircase, which communicated with the visitors' apartments upstairs.

Felix found it very comfortable—there being a clean, snug-looking little bed, and useful articles of furniture.

The hearth was also well-piled with faggots, which the attendant told him he was at liberty to light.

Felix gave him a small sum, and begged him to bring him some refreshment.

This being done, a lantern was left with him, and having lit the fire, Felix bolted the door and took a seat, thankful that he had got on so well.

Having finished his meal he was about to retire, when he noticed a curtain hanging from the ceiling at the farther end of the room.

Curiosity at once prompted him to draw this aside, and he saw just beside the curtain a small ladder.

Looking up, he noticed an iron ring fixed in a square piece of board, which appeared to be let into the ceiling.

"Curious," he thought, " but perhaps it leads into one of the lofts."

Undressing himself, he extinguished the light in the lantern and went to bed.

But try how he would, sleep would not visit his eyes.

His brain was too fully charged for him to sleep.

More than an hour must have passed when, from the many and various noises which reached his ears, he became aware of the fact that "The Cross Keys" was being closed.

Soon all was hushed in silence.

For some time no sound, save the wild shrieking of the wind, which told him what a terrible night it was, met his ears.

Of the logs he had lighted, only a few embers remained.

He began to doze, and probably would have fallen off to sleep had not a noise, as of something falling overhead, caused him to start up.

The sound was followed by low, chuckling laughter, and this, in turn, was followed by the chink of money.

There was no doubt about it—it was distinct enough.

Still, there was nothing very peculiar about that, as Felix thought these might be visitors who had just arrived, or who were amusing themselves with cards.

Yet the noise made had thoroughly aroused Felix, and he found himself quite unable to doze again.

The sounds above increased, and it became evident to our hero that there were three or four, or perhaps half-a-dozen persons above.

He listened intently, and was able to make out, now and again, a few words of what was said.

The conversation, to Felix, was of a most extraordinary description—never before, in all his life, had he heard the like.

He became restless, and at last he arose and attired himself.

"I wonder," he thought, " if I can hear more distinctly what is being said if I ascend that ladder ? Yet," he added, after a moment's reflection, " why should I do that, since the conversation of those above concerns me not ? "

Yet some irresistible impulse seemed to urge him on.

He did not light the lantern. There was sufficient light from the dying embers to enable him to ascend the ladder.

Very slowly and carefully he crept up.

On the last step but one he paused abruptly.

There was a long, but very narrow chink by the side of the trap-door, caused, of course, by the trap not fitting exactly.

Through this streamed a light.

Still higher went Felix, and placed his eye to the crack.

What he beheld almost caused him to utter an exclamation of astonishment.

Seated at a table in the centre of the apartment were four men.

Felix could plainly see their faces, and assuredly his eyes had never rested upon more repulsive ones.

They were attired as ordinary citizens, but they wore thick, heavy cloaks as a protection against the severe weather.

These, however, were thrown back over their shoulders, revealing a number of weapons, including pistols, in their belts.

On the table lay a few pairs of false beards and other articles evidently used as disguises.

As Felix looked, one of them rose.

Our hero took more notice of this man than the others, owing to the fact that the awful ugliness of his face was considerably increased by his only having *one eye.*

" Well, my friends," he said, in hoarse tones, " one glass more, and then to business. This shall be a toast which should meet with your approval. Let us drink it upstanding."

The others rose, took their filled glasses in their hands and held them aloft.

" Here's to the goldsmith and his pretty daughter," said the man with the one eye, " and may we find his bags as full as we imagine ! "

The toast was drunk.

" Quietness is everything now," continued the man with the one eye, " for by this time, I should imagine, everyone has retired. Ah, ah ! Even if we got nothing, my friends, we have done a fine bit of work to-night. Yes, we have deceived old Bartolph. How often has he been heard to boast that he could penetrate any disguise ? Ah ! little does he think that some of the Bravos of Alsatia are actually beneath his roof, and that they have a plan cut and dried for the possession of the goldsmith's money-

bags ! By my soul, it is the finest job I ever had to do with ! "

" True ! " muttered the men.

" And if we get as much as we think," said one, " we ought to divide it and make ourselves scarce for a time."

" Zounds ! " growled the man with one eye, " do you mean to turn traitor—eh ? Make ourselves scarce for a time ? Never fear it ! The spoil must be equally divided among all the boys. We shall have nothing to fear, my lads, even if it became known that we stole the money. We shall be safe enough in Alsatia—eh, *Parson ?* "

" Yes," growled a short, bloated, almost hairless individual at the right hand of the one-eyed man ; " but since we are about to do one job, why not do the other ? "

" What other ? "

" You know what Master Melton said when he was last in Alsatia ? "

" About the goldsmith's daughter ? "

" Aye."

" Oh—what ? That he would be willing to pay a hundred crowns to me if I could arrange to carry her off. Well, I must admit that a hundred crowns is sometimes an important sum with us. But it is not *now.* Another time we will see about that—especially if Master Melton trebles the amount. Now listen to me. We are, as I said before, exactly beneath the chamber in which the goldsmith's daughter is sleeping.

" Next to her room is the chamber occupied by the goldsmith. Now, as I am, I flatter myself, about the cleverest with the false keys, my duty be it to gain an entrance to the goldsmith's chamber. Your duty be it to guard the landing while I effect the robbery. And do not forget this—that we are determined, if we once have the money, not to let go of it. Therefore, if our movements awake the goldsmith, and his cries attract that old fool Bartolph, or his men—cut your way through them with pistol and sword. Soh ! now you know what you have to do, be prepared for anything. Now, put the lantern under your cloak, one of you, and lead the way."

The very blood of Felix Ferdinand turned cold as he listened to the words which fell from the lips of this hardened ruffian.

His experience of life was, at present,

very limited, but he knew that a robbery was contemplated, and that, perhaps, in carrying it out, murder would be committed !

Had he not heard the goldsmith say that he had the large sum of two thousand pounds in his possession? Certainly.

And if the goldsmith awoke and attempted to defend his property, was it not likely enough that he would be attacked and, perhaps, assassinated ?

Yes, he considered it quite likely.

" And this lovely girl," thought Felix; 'Heaven only knows what might happen to her, if, attracted by the cries of her father, she came forth."

Felix descended the ladder as the four men cautiously crossed the floor, and for some few moments he stood still, considering what he should do.

He thought he would alarm the house, but that was dismissed as soon as thought of.

" For," he considered, " if I attempt to arouse the house I shall alarm these bravos, who would quickly return to their room, and in the result I should be laughed at. I must, however, do something to foil them in their designs. I have it—I will follow them."

Down on his knees went Felix, and blowing the embers into a blaze, he placed a few more pieces of wood upon them.

Then he buckled on his sword and again ascended the ladder.

The light from the fire was sufficient to enable him to see the bolts of the trap-door.

Very carefully, so as to avoid the least noise, he pulled the bolts back from their sockets.

He then pushed up the trap with ease.

The bravos having taken the lantern with them, the room above was in darkness. Felix, however, did not hesitate.

Placing his hands on the woodwork of the trap, he drew himself up, and was soon in the room.

Closing the trap-door after him, he listened.

But no sound met his ears.

He crept across the floor to the door, and pausing on the threshold for a moment, he distinctly caught the sound of whispering.

Looking out of the door he saw the four men, and they were not ten feet away from him.

Felix saw that the landing was a very large one, richly carpeted, and there were four or five doors upon it, showing that these were five or more rooms for the use of visitors.

" Now," whispered the man with the one eye, as he pointed, first to one recess, and then the other, " place yourselves there and wait. As we never know what may happen, draw your blades ; and don't forget—we are determined to have this money, if we have to kill. So, if old Walker wakes and offers any resistance—well, there will be one goldsmith the less in the City of London."

" Stay," whispered the one who had been called " Parson," " which is the girl's room, eh ? "

" There," replied the one-eyed wretch, pointing to it; " but attempt nothing, or I shall begin to fancy that *you* are in love with the girl, and you would not like that spread all over Alsatia, I'll warrant it."

With this he took the lantern, produced a key, and on tip-toe crossed to the room in which, unconscious of danger, lay the goldsmith.

In a scientific manner the one-eyed villain placed the key in the lock, and after a few seconds the key on the inside of the door was turned round—a fact which caused the man to utter a quiet chuckle of satisfaction.

Pushing the door noiselessly open, he allowed a faint ray of light to issue from the lantern beneath his cloak, and entered the room.

The position of the bed was favourable to his movements, for it was at some distance from the door, and was almost entirely surrounded by heavy curtains.

On the table lay a pile of documents.

In a marvellously calm and collected manner, the man turned over the documents.

But he found nothing of importance.

A diamond ring next caught his eye, and this he placed on one of his fingers.

Next he turned over the goldsmith's clothes, and rapidly turned out the pockets.

He found nothing.

He paused a moment to give vent to

his feelings, which took the shape of an oath.

Approaching the head of the bed, he drew aside the curtains and looked at the pillows.

Just peeping from beneath the one on which lay the grey head of the respected goldsmith was a leathern strap, and the corner of what the man at once recognised as a pocket-book.

"That's it, sure enough," he muttered. "But how to get it out?"

He placed his hand on the strap and began to wriggle it to and fro.

The movement at once caused the goldsmith to move, and the man, drawing back hastily to conceal himself, his cloak was drawn back by the bedpost, the lantern was shifted, and its rays fell full upon the face of the goldsmith, who at once started up.

He was about to shout for help, when the man snatched up the pocket-book, and, with the lantern, dealt the goldsmith a stunning blow on the face.

The goldsmith leapt from his bed and made a frantic grab at the villain, and caught him by the collar of his cloak.

"Villain!" he cried. "Villain! my money! Return it, or——"

The man's accomplices hastened forward, and one would have plunged his blade into the goldsmith's body, had not Felix at this moment dashed across the landing.

Drawing his sword from its sheath, he struck up the blade levelled at the goldsmith's body, and snatched the pocket-book from the hand of the thief.

There was a moment's pause of astonishment on the part of the thieves, but it was *only* a moment.

"Cut the cub down!" cried the one-eyed man. "Cut him down, I say!"

The one-eyed man pulled the long sword he carried from its sheath, and commenced to attack Felix with extraordinary ferocity.

Two of his comrades came to his assistance, but the one called "Parson" slunk away.

The goldsmith, who had now recovered his pocket-book, fearful that the person who had come to his rescue would speedily meet with his death at the hands of the enraged thieves, shouted for help as loud as he was able.

The first to hear and answer his cries was the beautiful Rosamund.

Flinging open the door of her room, she appeared on the threshold, a small night-lamp in her hand.

How gloriously beautiful she looked, her splendid black hair streaming down the white cloak she had hastily thrown about her shoulders!

The cries of alarm she was about to utter stuck in her throat as her eyes caught sight of the savage-looking bravos with their naked blades in their hands.

It instantly struck her, however, that the youth covering her father, and who was wielding his sword against three opposing weapons with such extraordinary dexterity, must be the preserver of her father, and though she herself was powerless to assist him, she watched his movements with admiration, though it was mingled with horror and fear lest harm should befall him.

The sharp rattle of steel rose high above the cries of the terrified goldsmith.

The fight waxed fast and furious, for the bravos, in their desire to slay the one who had thus unexpectedly baulked them, appeared to forget that there was such a thing as the possibility of being captured by the inmates of the house.

In a few moments the opening and shutting of doors could be heard; and the shouts of men and women, the hurrying of footsteps up and down stairs, showed that everyone was aroused.

We have said that the Parson had slunk away, and it was now seen that by so doing he had saved his companions.

He had crept down the stairs and had opened the front door, and when the tramping of footsteps told him that his companions were in danger, he shouted to them to fly.

This was hardly necessary, for the one-eyed villain, with a bitter curse, turned, and, calling to his comrades to follow him, rushed down the stairs just as the host, carrying a heavy bludgeon in one hand and a lantern in the other, and followed by his wife and a score of domestics, men and women, armed with whatever they could seize on the spur of the moment, appeared on the scene.

"Ho!" shrieked Bartolph, "ho, what can this mean? Wife, wife, come hither! —here—here!—thieves—thieves! But" —here his eye rested on Felix—"this surely cannot be one of them, Master Walker?"

"Nay," replied the goldsmith, warmly. "This noble youth has not only saved my property, but my life."

"Oh, father, father, thank Heaven you are safe!" cried Rosamund, as she ran forward and threw herself into her father's arms.

The voice of the one-eyed villain came up the stairs—

"*Look to yourself, Master Walker; look to yourself! And let your boyish champion look to himself! For, if ever we come across him, he will pay with his life the penalty of interfering with us!*"

"Bring the pistols!" roared the host, as he frantically stamped his feet; "bring the pistols, I say!"

Just as one of the terrified attendants handed him a pair, the door was closed with a crash.

But the host rushed down a few stairs and flung up a window which commanded a view of the courtyard.

By the aid of the fire, which still burned in the centre of the yard, he was enabled to see four dark figures hurrying away.

With trembling hands he cocked one of the weapons, pointed it at the retreating figures and fired.

One of the figures—it was the villain with the one eye—turned at the sound of the shot, shook his fist fiercely at the house, and shouted, "I'll have revenge on you some day!"

"A ball wasted, Master Walker," said the host, as he slammed down the window; "well, no matter. If he ever comes here again I will not give him the chance to get very far ere I let fly at him, the rogue—the villain—the——"

"The monster!" added the excited hostess.

"Certainly, my dear—the monster!" said the host; "but there is no doubt Master Walker recognised the scamp."

"Recognised him?" said the goldsmith in great astonishment. "That I certainly did not."

"Good gracious! Why I thought everyone would have recognised the wretch. That was the chief of the Alsatians—one of the depraved 'Copper Captains.' You know, Master Walker."

"His name?"

"He calls himself, and is called by his associates, Captain White. Is that not right, wife?"

"Yes, quite right," replied the hostess; "he is called Captain *White*, sure enough, though why the *black* looking villain should be called *White* I don't know. And so, Bartolph, with *all* your cleverness, they've outwitted you."

"I must admit that they *have*, my dear. Well, well, who would have thought that four such harmless-looking travellers were in reality nothing less than four of these bravos in disguise?"

"I should," replied the hostess, who, like a great many of her sex, was very brave now that all danger was over; "*I* should! And had I seen them when they first came I would have torn them limb from limb!"

"I haven't any doubt of it," replied her husband, meekly; "and they would have stood still while you did it. And now, Master Walker, let me express my thanks to this youth for rescuing you."

"Oh, let me do that," cried Rosamund, as turning from her father she placed her little hands in Felix's; "but alas!" she said, "I have no words which are sufficiently strong enough to express my thanks."

"The pressure of your hands conveys more to my heart than volumes of words," replied Felix, gallantly.

"You have forgotten to ask whether the lad has been injured," said the hostess.

"I thank Heaven I am not!" said Felix.

"And that is owing to his splendid swordmanship," said the goldsmith; "for never before did I see the sword so dexterously handled. The person who can handle a weapon with such consummate coolness and cleverness should be a person of some distinction."

Felix smiled sadly.

"I am not a person of any distinction, your worship," he said.

"Are you attached to the Court in any capacity?"

"My dress is sufficient to show you, sir, that I am not."

"Hum, well said! Well, then, my lad, who and what are you?"

Felix looked at Rosamund.

Her bright eyes were fixed upon his face.

"'HO! WHAT DO YOU MEAN BY HIDING YOURSELF IN THAT DOORWAY?' CRIED THE MAN."

He turned to the hostess, and she perfectly understood what he meant.

"He is an orphan lad," said the hostess, "and has come to London to seek his fortune. I gave him a bed in one of the ostler's rooms, and that, now that I think of it, is immediately beneath the room in which those four men were."

"Yes," said Felix; "I was awake, and thinking all was not as it should be, I crept up the ladder and listened to what was being said."

"Father," said Rosamund, "you can return the service this brave youth has done you. You have both influence and money."

"Very true, my dear," said the benevolent goldsmith; "if he would accept of it I would offer him an engagement in my own house."

"Sir!" cried Felix, eagerly, "such generosity——"

"Wait, wait, my lad," interrupted the goldsmith. "First, let me ask you this —have you received a good education? for on this would depend the position in which I place you."

"I am proud to say, your worship," replied Felix, "that I possess an education far in advance of many of my age."

The words of old Nicholas Fielding recurred to him at this moment: "Try and become a good scholar, for it will be of service to you in the time to come."

"Then," said the goldsmith, "if your references prove——"

"Sir," interrupted Felix, "I have no references. I am alone in the world."

"Father," said Rosamund, "his face and the events of this night should be sufficient references."

"You are right, my child," said the goldsmith, "and they shall be. I will instal him in the vacant office of under-secretary. If he is careful, a bright future and fortune await him."

Felix warmly thanked his new-found friend as well as his daughter.

The host and hostess were delighted at this display of generosity on the part of Master Walker.

So were the servants, who, led by Bartolph, gave the goldsmith three hearty cheers.

"Come to me as soon as it is daylight," said the goldsmith, "and we will then talk over matters."

In another few moments Felix was again in his little room.

But he could not sleep.

He had suddenly and unexpectedly been lifted on to the first rung in the ladder of fortune.

But what struggles—what adventures would he have ere he reached the *last*?

CHAPTER II.

SHOWS HOW FELIX IS DISPATCHED ON A MOST IMPORTANT MISSION—OF HOW HE WAS ASSAILED AT CHARING CROSS, CAPTURED, AND CARRIED OFF TO ALSATIA.

THE residence of the worthy goldsmith was in Fleet Street, close by Temple Bar.

It was a very large house, indeed, one of the largest houses in the City.

Anyone passing under Temple Bar would at once have their attention drawn to it, because of its rich and brilliant decorations.

Projecting from the centre of the house was a huge gilt hand, and this was the sign of the goldsmith's business.

Above that was the Royal Arms, and underneath, in enormous letters, were the words:

"By Royal Command."

This signifying that Master Christopher Walker was one of the goldsmiths to the Court of his Majesty James I.

But though the exterior of the goldsmith's mansion was so magnificent, the same cannot be said of the interior.

Certainly the ground-floor of the goldsmith's residence did not show any signs of a business being carried on.

In an inner office, during the day, three or four elderly individuals could be seen, busy either with piles of documents of various shapes and sizes, or examining the setting of this or that costly article of jewellery entrusted to, or purchased by, Master Walker.

Amid the noise and bustle of Fleet

Street, silence—deep, solemn silence—reigned within Master Walker's mansion.

Even when a costly equipage drove up to the door, and a titled lady or gentleman sought an audience of the wealthy goldsmith, no ceremonious ushering in was made by the fat old porter whose duty it was to waddle from his chair and open the door whenever a knock was heard.

It was to this huge and, as some people were pleased to think, mysterious residence, that Felix accompanied the goldsmith some few hours after the events recorded in the previous chapter.

When we say that he rode in the goldsmith's own carriage, and that he was seated next to the beautiful Rosamund, his feelings will be better imagined than described.

In the first place he was conducted to the secretary of the establishment, and then to the others engaged, and these were made acquainted with all that had happened.

Felix was overjoyed to find that he was warmly welcomed by all, and more especially by Mistress Walker, who, made acquainted by her daughter with the particulars of her husband's narrow escape, embraced and thanked Felix with tears in her eyes.

So, as the under-secretary to the wealthy Fleet Street goldsmith, Felix was duly installed.

Six days passed away.

The goldsmith was delighted beyond measure that chance had thrown in his way such a well-educated youth.

And Rosamund—but no, we must not betray her secret at present.

One evening, some two hours after all engaged by the goldsmith had departed to their homes, Master Walker called Felix into his private room.

"Felix," he said, "though we have been acquainted so short a time, I am happy to be able to say that I have every confidence in you. I feel that no matter what errand I may entrust you with, you would perform it to my satisfaction."

Felix bowed.

"Sir," he said, "I will try my utmost to carry out your commands."

"I am sure of it. Now, look here."

The goldsmith opened a small case, and displayed a magnificent diamond necklace.

Felix started at the sight.

"This necklace," continued the goldsmith, "is really my property until the money I advanced upon it be paid. The person who deposited it with me is the Countess of Rothburn. She is about to go to a ball to-night, and has begged of me to allow her to have the use of it for this occasion. Her address is The Willows, near St. James's Park. Anyone will direct you when you reach Charing Cross."

"Sir," cried Felix, in astonishment, "you surely do not intend me to take that to the countess?"

"Certainly I do. I have said that I can trust you. So here is the necklace, Felix; place it in your breast. So! that is it. And now wrap yourself in your cloak, for 'tis very cold, and the snow is still on the ground. Give the countess my compliments, and say that you will call for the trinket on the morrow."

Felix left the goldsmith's presence, ascended to his room and proceeded to attire himself.

The generous goldsmith had provided him with the best of clothes, as well as money.

Felix donned a long, black cloak and a low-crowned hat.

Then he buckled on his sword, and placed a pistol in his belt.

"'Tis the first time I have ever been entrusted with jewels to such a large amount," he thought, "and 'tis as well to go armed, in case of being attacked by the bands of ruffians who take possession of the streets after nightfall."

Leaving the house, he commenced his journey with a beating heart and a fervent hope that he would not be molested, for he felt that if anything happened to him and he lost the jewels which had been given into his custody, he could never face the goldsmith again.

It was a wild and bitterly cold night.

The snow still lay upon the ground.

In some parts it was ankle-deep, and Felix had the greatest difficulty in getting along.

Perhaps it was the wild night which caused the streets to be so deserted.

Certain it is that not a solitary soul

did Felix encounter all the way from Temple Bar to Charing Cross.

He was congratulating himself on this fact and was thinking of rousing some-one at one of the houses in order to learn the whereabouts of the residence of the countess, when he heard voices.

Indistinct they were for a few moments but the sounds got nearer and nearer.

Some men were rounding a corner near him.

He drew himself in the shadow of a shop, and as he did so, a loud and bitter curse fell upon his ears.

In another instant three men came into view.

All three wore long cloaks after the style of the one he wore himself, tremendously broad-brimmed hats, and high boots, armed with enormous spurs.

"There!" cried one, pausing within ten feet of where Felix stood; "what did I say? I said it was all a pack of lies. Bah! just as if Master Walker would be such a fool as to send off a diamond necklace without first having the money which was advanced upon it! Soh, my men. Soh, my jolly blades! Ho, ho! we are fairly done—fairly done! But I pity the poor devil of a footman when we tell the captain that we have been on a wild-goose chase. He will slit his tongue and nail his ears to the wall."

"And we shall amuse ourselves with pelting him with empty bottles!" said another, with a hoarse laugh.

"But," said the third man, "let us wait a little longer. The messenger *may* pass, you know."

The blood seemed frozen in Felix's veins.

His heart seemed to cease its beating.

"How," he thought, "did they get to know that the necklace was to be sent? They mentioned a footman. I am in a daze! If they see me, they——"

At this very instant one of the three men turned.

He looked for a moment, and then cautiously approached him.

"Hallo!" he chuckled. "Why, what are you doing here? Quick, pals! come hither."

The men approached and looked.

"Ho!" roared one, as he seized Felix by the cloak and dragged him out. "What do you mean by hiding yourself in that doorway? Come out! Come out, or my sword shall be through your body!"

And he pulled Felix forward with such violence that his hat was displaced, and fell upon the snow.

"By all the incarnate fiends!" shouted one of the ruffians, starting back in amazement, "what do I see before me? Ho! Why, 'tis the very cursed youth who stopped us at "The Cross Keys.""

"The Bravos of Alsatia," muttered Felix, "*again!* Heaven! The necklace! Rather would I lose my life than that! If they know that I am in the service of the goldsmith, they will search me."

"Ha, ha!" laughed the ruffian, who had recognised Felix. "'Tis certain, comrades, that we shall not go back empty-handed. This prize our noble captain has been searching for for the past week. If we take him a prisoner to the captain, he will think more of it than the possession of a diamond necklace."

"Well, then," was the answer of the others, "let us seize him!"

"At your peril!" cried Felix, stepping back a pace. "At your peril."

"Eh, do you dare us?"

"Advance at your peril!"

And instantaneously Felix's bright blade flashed from its sheath.

The bravos paused, but it was only for one moment.

"Disarm the cub!" yelled one; "disarm the cub, I say, but don't kill him, if you can help it. Slay him, and you spoil the captain's sport and our own, too."

Simultaneously the long and heavy weapons of the bravos left their sheaths, and fell with a loud clang upon Felix's sword.

"I warn you," exclaimed Felix fiercely, "that I will defend myself. I would sooner part with my life than be made a prisoner by such infamous ruffians as you are."

"Ruffians—eh?" shrieked the bravos. "We shall see, you cub! we shall see. At him, men."

The attack was commenced, the three bravos plying their blades with extraordinary ferocity, and trying every possible way to break the weapon in two, or tear it from our hero's grasp.

But it seemed as if they would prove unsuccessful.

It was an undoubted fact that Felix was a perfect master in the art of fencing; but he got no chance of disabling either of these cowards, for he had as much as ever he could do to ward off the desperate lunges aimed at every part of his body.

As the bravos warmed to their work, their mutterings, expressive of rage and disappointment, increased.

The oaths they uttered would have appalled the stoutest heart.

Suddenly one of the men stooped and picked up a heavy stone.

Raising it over his head, he, with a foul expression, hurled it with all his force at Felix's head.

But our hero was too quick for him.

He bobbed his head, and the result was that it struck the door behind him, splintering the woodwork, and sending the glass down in showers.

It was the last stone that villain ever threw.

Felix snatched the pistol from his belt, and aiming it at the fellow, pulled the trigger.

The flash and the stunning report were followed by a blood-curdling shriek from the man, who, throwing up his arms, staggered backwards and forwards for a few moments, and then fell with his face on the snow—Dead.

As soon as he had fired, and while the sulphurous smoke still hung in the air, Felix glided away a few paces hoping to make his escape ere the bravos could recover from their horror and astonishment.

But that hope, alas! was a vain one.

One of the men—the one who had recognised him—perceived the movement, and as quick as thought he pounced upon our hero, seized him by the collar of his cloak with one hand, and with the other seized the hilt of his sword, while at the same time he yelled to his companion to assist him.

This, however, was hardly necessary, for his comrade, perceiving the advantage gained, was quickly at his side, and snatching the sword from Felix's grasp, he broke it in half across his knee and hurled it aside.

Then he seized the pistol by the muzzle, raised it aloft, and brought the heavy butt on Felix's bare head.

It was a tremendous blow, and the effect was instantaneous, for Felix, with a low cry, dropped down like a stone.

"Now then!" chuckled one; "we have you at last. And——"

"And," said the other, raising his sword, "I propose that we have our revenge. We will kill him, and——"

"Go away, you fool," cried the other pushing him on one side. "We will *not* kill him—at least, we will not *at present*, though I admit he deserves death for slaying Paul Pelrone. But he is our captain's prize, and therefore must go to Alsatia."

"As you will," replied the other, with an oath; "but unless I am much mistaken," and here he leaned over and looked into Felix's face, now nearly covered with blood—"unless I am much mistaken, he will be dead ere we can reach the captain, so——"

"Pah! No doubt he has as thick a skull as either of us, and we have had more than one clout like that in our time. He must take his chance. I have a drop of brandy here, for myself and then for you. Here! Take a dram."

The villains refreshed themselves from a flask, and then one suggested that before Felix was taken to Alsatia he should be searched, and the articles found upon him equally divided.

This was agreed upon.

Felix's pockets were turned inside out, and what few articles they contained were divided.

But they did not open his breast.

Had they done so, oh, what a prize would have been theirs!

We need hardly say that had they found the necklace, it would have been divided between them.

The captain would probably not have received a crown as his share, since he could not prove that Felix was the messenger, who had been despatched from the goldsmith's.

The next thing the villains did was to produce a couple of straps.

With these they bound our hero's hands firmly together.

Next they turned their attention to their dead comrade.

The first thing they did was—as might be expected—to turn out *his* pockets.

They found a few pence and a flask of brandy, and *these* they equally divided.

"It's a sad end for one so young," sighed one. "Parson Pearman prophesied that poor Paul would be a subject for the hangman. So once again he is wrong. Well, we must see that he is decently buried. We are some distance from the Thames, or we might give the watermen a chance of earning a crown. Let me see, the best way of disposing of Paul is——"

"Not much hesitation is necessary," interrupted the other; "let us force open yonder sewer and put him down. Since he is dead, it is a matter of indifference to him where he is placed."

"Ha! Good idea. Come."

The two men went into the centre of the road, where stood one of the entrances to a sewer, then in course of construction.

The brickwork of it was raised about three feet from the ground, and the top was protected by beams of wood.

The two men removed the beams of wood, then returned, and, picking up the body of their dead comrade, carried it to the aperture, resting it for a moment on the brickwork, then pushed it down the black hole.

"Poor Paul!" said one; "and so many times merry together. So many times we have shared our—our fortunes. Farewell, Paul," he added, as he listened to the body bumping and thumping against the sides of the deep hole in the descent; "farewell."

And then the pair of ruffians turned from the spot, laughing loudly.

The death of a companion in one way or another was a matter of everyday occurrence, and they thought but little of it.

There were plenty more ruffians to be found in Alsatia.

As soon as one was dead, another was easily found to fill his place.

Having disposed of their comrade, they took another draw from the flask, and then attended to our hero.

He had not recovered consciousness, so that our readers, when they consider that snow or ice frequently restores in a short time an insensible person to consciousness, will easily understand that the force of the blow he received was terrific.

"Let us hasten," said one, "or we may be interrupted. There——"

"Hold!" interrupted the other; "what have we yonder?"

And he pointed to a black-looking object moving across the snow at some little distance.

The pair watched a few moments, then both simultaneously cried in exultant tones—

"A sedan-chair!"

Again they watched.

Nearer came the object, until at last it got within fifty yards of them.

"Aye, aye," said one, "there is not much mistake about that. It is a sedan-chair, sure enough. And from the way they are carrying it there is no one within. Come along, comrade. Have you got the pistol still?"

"Yes, here in my belt."

"Well, use the butt-end, as you did just now, on the head of one of these bearers, while I tackle the other. We must have that sedan-chair."

Then the pair crept round to the corner of a house past which the bearers would carry the chair.

Slowly, and totally unconscious of any danger, the bearers walked along with their burden, a magnificent sedan-chair, and, strangely enough, this very chair was the property of the Countess of Rothburn, at whose residence our hero should, ere now, have delivered the diamond necklace.

The man with the pistol dashed forward directly the first bearer appeared, and dealt him a tremendous blow on the forehead.

He fell, stunned and bleeding.

But the end man dodged the blow aimed at him by the other bravo, and with wild cries, darted off as fast as his legs would carry, and the snow permit, him.

Having placed the unconscious bearer in a doorway, the ruffians, laughing loudly at the manner in which the other bearer had run away, placed themselves within the handles of the chair, and carried it to where Felix was lying.

Paying no heed either to the decoration of the chair or the magnificent cushions within, the two bravos lifted Felix up and unceremoniously flung him into the chair, slammed the door to, and seizing the handles, set off for Alsatia.

CHAPTER III.

CONDUCTS OUR READERS TO ALSATIA, AND INTRODUCES THEM TO THE "FOUNTAIN OF LIFE," TO THE EXTRAORDINARY INDIVIDUALS THERE ASSEMBLED, AND SHOWS WHAT HAPPENED TO FELIX.

ALMOST every reader of history, and historical romances, must have read of Alsatia, but it is our intention in this work to show our readers Alsatia and the Alsatians, in a manner which we may affirm without fear of contradiction, has never before been attempted, and which is the result of a long course of study undertaken specially with the view of making this work as complete as possible.

Alsatia, or, more properly speaking, Whitefriars, lay exactly along the edge of the Thames, and could be approached either from the Temple or Fleet Street, from which places it was shut off by huge gates.

It was a series of narrow lanes, after the manner of a honeycomb, and dirty, foul-smelling lanes they were.

The houses, of various heights, and of all shapes, were built, some of wood, some ot stone, but wood principally.

Almost every house was surrounded by a wooden balcony at a height of about twelve feet from the ground, these balconies being principally used as "drying grounds" by the women, or as "smoking kens," or "plotting shops," by the swaggering, bullying, drunken bravos.

Every sixth house was a tavern. And every tavern was the resort of debtors, thieves, aye, and of murderers, who, so long as they kept within the precincts of Alsatia, or the "Holy Sanctuary," as the bravos were pleased to call it, appeared to be perfectly free from molestation.

When Whitefriars first became the hiding-place and refuge for the scum of London—and, indeed, elsewhere—is not known with certainty, but it is a positive fact that it was at the height of its hideousness during the reign of James I., the period of which we are writing.

It is also a positive fact that Alsatia continued to flourish until the latter end of the reign of King William, when the privileges of Sanctuary were taken away, and the occupants of the foul dens and slums were swept away at the point of the swords of the king's troops.

The crimes committed in Alsatia were many, frequent, and horrible. Here, too, were the headquarters of a terrible and desperate set of ruffians, who called themselves "The Bravos of Alsatia," commanded by "Captain" White, who, if anything, was a far greater villain than the notorious Colonel Blood, who came after him (Charles II.)

The headquarters of Captain White were at a tavern, called "The Fountain of Life."

The owner of it, a man entirely "under the thumb" of the scoundrel White, was named Paul Bruckley, but he was called Bruckley Bacchus, and those who used his house were called the "Worshippers of Bacchus."

Below the "bar" of this tavern and quite underground, was a series of vaults.

The largest of these vaults was converted into what was called "the captain's reception-room."

The walls were concealed with heavy drapery; the floor was covered with the remains of a magnificent Turkey carpet.

The night on which we introduce "The Fountain of Life" to the notice of our readers was a special one with the denizens of Alsatia.

A great riot had taken place owing to a number of officers of justice having obtained an entry to the "sacred" precints without the necessary permission.

And the riot had ended with the death of two officers and four Alsatians.

So the denizens made merry over their success in driving off the officers at every tavern in Alsatia.

Captain White's reception-room was crowded.

There were men and women of all ages, but the men predominated.

But the men who were most prominent were the well-known Alsatian Bravos.

There was no mistaking the greasy, blood-stained doublets.

Their trunk breeches, their broad and discoloured shoulder and waist belts.

Their huge, heavy swords, their repulsive faces adorned by enormous pairs of moustaches, which the majority of them wore curled up to their very ears.

The room was illuminated with lamps hanging from the ceiling, and through the clouds of tobacco* smoke you could occasionally obtain a glimpse of the principal persons.

At the farther end of the room, in a raised and well-cushioned chair, was seated a man of about fifty years of age.

He was of the middle height, and somewhat stout.

His red, pimpled, and bloated face was made still more hideous owing to the fact that he had an enormous "mulberry nose" and *one eye*—the right one.

The left he had lost in a quarrel over a game at dice, his opponent in the game having snatched his dagger from his girdle and plunged it into his eye.

Over this, when he thought proper, as he did on this occasion, he wore a black patch.

At his left side hung a long sword, at his right a jewelled dagger, while in his broad waist-belt he carried a couple of large pistols.

This formidable and ferocious-looking villain was Captain White, to whom all Alsatians, great and small, bowed the knee—whom all the Alsatians obeyed.

At the right hand of Captain White sat a somewhat shorter man, though quite as stout.

He was attired after the fashion of the clergymen of the period.

His face was more bloated than Captain White's, his nose was just as red, and he was the possessor of a couple of small rat-like eyes.

A more depraved - looking wretch surely never walked the streets of London.

This man was known as "Parson Pearman," and was one of the many "hedge parsons" who scandalised England in those days.

---

* Then gradually coming into use, much to the disgust of King James.

On his left was seated a lean, lanky individual, called Long Lock, and this man was Captain White's "lieutenant" (?).

The hour of ten had chimed upon the cracked bell of a cranky-looking clock at the back of the captain, when Parson Pearman said—

"Observe the hour, and they have not returned, and we may therefore conclude that their errand has proved useless."

"Not so fast," answered Captain White; "they would not return in a hurry if they thought there was a chance of getting such a thing as a diamond necklace! Oh, that I could feast my eyes on it! Well, parson, it would be much better in our pockets than round the neck of the beautiful countess, or in Master Walker's safe."

"Oh, truly, truly," replied the parson, turning up the whites of his eyes, and fiddling with his fingers and thumbs. "It seems almost too good that such a valuable trinket should come into our possession."

"*My* possession!" growled the captain.

"I beg your pardon, *your* possession."

"Yes, but it is past ten. Well, I must admit that I am getting anxious. Let us have that powdered monkey out again, Lock."

"Right," cried Long Lock, starting up in great haste, and thereby overturning a huge bowl of punch. "Right; I'll have him out in the twinkling of a thunder-clap!"

"Ah, let us look at the countess's pet!" was the cry on all sides; "let us look at her ladyship's lap-dog. Out with him!"

Amid loud cries and shouts of laughter, Long Lock drew aside a pair of curtains on one side of the room, unlocked a small but heavy oaken door, and in a moment more emerged, dragging out by the collar of his magnificently laced jerkin, a footman.

It was the Countess of Rothburn's pet footman.

He was a good-looking young fellow, but terror had so distorted his features that it is doubtful whether the countess would have recognised him at this moment.

Dragging him forward, Long Lock

commanded silence while the captain spoke.

"Get a chair," said Captain White, "and place him on the table so that all can have a good look at him."

This order was greeted with cries of approval and loud laughter.

A chair was brought, and the unfortunate footman thrust into it.

He was then lifted up by three of the bravos, and deposited on the table.

"Silence!" roared the captain; "silence, I command ye all. Let the lacquey answer my questions. Soh! knave, did you not say when you were captured and brought here, that a messenger would be dispatched to the countess with the necklace?"

"I did," groaned the lacquey.

"Soh! You had then just returned from the goldsmith?"

"I had, worshipful sir."

"And the goldsmith himself told you that he would send a messenger?"

"He did."

"And he did not describe him?"

"He did not."

"Well, look you, master footman. The messengers *we* dispatched to intercept the messenger sent with the necklace have not returned. Now if what you have said turns out to be false, you will have your ears nailed to yonder door, your tongue slit, and——"

"Generally he will be much disfigured," put in the parson in a mincing tone of voice.

"Yes, generally disfigured is the proper way of putting it," said the captain grimly.

"And it is *such* a pity to waste *such* a *nice* man!" cried a painted female.

"I swear that what I said was true!" moaned the footman, looking fearfully round.

"Well, we shall see," said Captain White, "if what you have——"

At this moment such a tremendous shouting above was heard, that almost everyone present leapt to their feet, and the vaults rang with loud cries of

"Tipstaff! Tipstaff! An arrest! An arrest! Bailiffs! Bailiffs! On to them."

Swords, daggers, and pistols at the same moment were plucked from their hiding-places.

"Hold! Hold, ye fools!" yelled Captain White, as he jumped upon his chair, and wildly waved his sword. "Hold! There can be no more officers to-day, unless we are warned in time. The guard is fixed at all points. Down with you! Let us hear what the noise is all about. By all the saints, Bruckley Bacchus is letting them do as they like; I——"

Long Lock the lieutenant rushed into the vault.

"What is it, Lock?" asked Captain White.

"A most important arrival, captain," was the reply. "Faulkley and Grafton have returned, and——"

"Well, where is Paul?"

"Dead and buried."

A roar of astonishment greeted this.

"Yes, he's dead," continued the lieutenant, "but you'll know all about it in a few moments. Faulkley and Grafton have returned, I say, and——"

"Brought the prize with them," interrupted the parson.

"No such thing. They have brought with them a splendid sedan-chair, and in it is a person you much want, captain."

"Hum!" growled the dissatisfied captain. "Curse the sedan-chair! But who is within it?"

"The youth who prevented you from relieving the goldsmith at 'The Cross Keys.'"

"He is!" exclaimed the captain as his one eye brightened considerably. "How do they know he is the same——"

"Why, Faulkley recognised him."

"Oh, ah! Of course Faulkley was with us at 'The Cross Keys,' parson."

"He was," replied the parson; "a brave boy is Faulkley, and a cunning one to boot. Ha, should it turn out to be without doubt this youth, we can nail *his* ears to the wall, and slit his tongue instead of the footman's."

"You wait!" replied the captain with a ghastly grin; "something more than that will happen to him, unless I am much mistaken. Down with him!"

But Felix was already down.

The two men who had almost killed him brought him down between them, and as soon as they appeared on the threshold of the vault, they were greeted with a wild savage cheer.

Another instant, and our hero stood in the centre of the horrible crew, and facing the one-eyed captain, who, despite the state he was in, instantly recognised him.

Poor Felix!

The upper part of him was covered with blood, and the wound he had received was still bleeding.

Did he have any difficulty in recognising in Captain White the wretch with whom he fought at 'The Cross Keys?'

Despite the black patch, despite the fact that he was more elaborately dressed, despite the insolent swaggering manner, he at once called to mind the man from whose hand he had snatched the goldsmith's property.

He also recognised Parson Pearman.

For a few moments a hush fell upon the whole assembly of ruffians.

Notwithstanding the intense pain he was undergoing, Felix remained facing the captain, firm and erect.

"Soh!" growled Captain White, placing his thumbs under his armpits, and his legs asunder. "Soh, the bird I have been looking for is caged at last? You know me, you cub, don't you?"

"None but a fool could mistake your villainous face after seeing it once," replied Felix, calmly.

The captain's one eye opened very wide indeed at this.

A growl of anger left the lips of the villains present.

"The lad is demented surely," said Parson Pearman, "or he would never dare to utter those words."

"He is not demented," replied White, "but he is an insolent young braggart. Had we not been interfered with at "The Cross Keys" he would have been in his coffin ere now."

"You are a liar!" cried Felix, "and also you are a cowardly bully. Place a sword in my hand and let us have space, and you will see—weak as I now am— who will be placed in his coffin first."

A tremendous roar of astonishment was the reply to this.

"I am not likely to fool away my time," said White; "but I will tell you what is about to happen to you. You will have your ears nailed to yonder door; your hands and feet will be securely fastened; your tongue slit; and in that condition you will remain until I choose to order your release."

This met with a loud shout of approval.

"Since all hope of our obtaining possession of the valuable property we expected is vain," resumed the captain, "we will let the countess's lap-dog loose, in the hope that, at no distant date, he will give us better and more accurate information. Do you hear that, sirrah?"

"I do—I do!" gasped the footman, clasping his hands.

"Are you grateful?"

"Oh, honoured sir! Oh, kind gentleman! How could I be otherwise than grateful? I return you my most——"

"Wait a moment, wait a moment— don't be too fast. We cannot possibly let such a gorgeous and pretty creature as you go without you bear some Alsatian mark. Down with him!"

A dozen violent hands were laid on the unlucky footman.

"Now then," said the captain, "razors."

"Oh!" shrieked the footman, falling on his knees, "don't—don't! Think of my poor widowed mother. Don't kill me!"

A pair of razors were brought, and while several held him firmly down, Parson Pearman deliberately shaved off every bit of hair on the footman's head.

The poor wretch's screams of horror were awful to listen to.

His hair being cut completely off, the footman, entirely transformed, was dragged to his feet.

But he was not done with yet.

"The *dregs!*" cried Captain White.

Instantly every man and woman caught up his or her goblet or tankard, and before the footman had time to realise what was about to happen, he was deluged with the vile stuff remaining in the goblets.

The result was days and days of intense suffering, for a great deal of the wines and spirits went into his eyes, nearly blinding him—indeed, he could not see for hours after.

His gorgeous livery presented the appearance of having been dipped in dyes of various colours.

In vain he appealed for mercy.

"*Keepsakes!*" yelled Captain White.

Long Lock snatched his dagger from its sheath, and in an instant the footman's gilt buttons, bearing the monogram of the proud Countess of Rothburn, were cut off and divided among those around.

"Now out with him," shouted White. "Two of you take hold of him, and conduct him outside the boundary."

Two of the bravos seized the footman and dragged him out.

He was taken beyond the precincts of Alsatia and there left.

"Now for this accursed wretch!" cried Captain White. "Oh, how I have longed to get a chance at him! I have most important business to transact tonight, but I will delay it on purpose to carry out my intentions towards this cub. What is thy name?"

No answer.

"What is thy name?" thundered White.

"Find out!" answered Felix, looking hard at the villain.

Little did the captain think that Felix had worked his hands free.

He had been working away at the straps for some time, and fortunately his cloak had concealed his movements.

"Do you hear what the noble captain says?" said Long Lock, poking his ugly nose into our hero's face. "Answer him directly."

"Brain him!" yelled the men.

"Tear him limb from limb!" shrieked the women.

"You may brain me, or tear me limb from limb," said Felix, with provoking coolness, "but you shall not wring an answer from me."

"I will ask you once more," said Captain White, whose bloated face had actually become almost white with rage. "Give your *name!*"

And down on the table he brought his ponderous fist.

No answer.

"Curse you, give your name!" cried Long Lock.

The brutal lieutenant raised his hand and dealt our hero a blow on the face, and this had the effect of causing the wound in his head to bleed afresh.

Felix stifled the cry of pain which rose to his lips, but still he did not answer.

The howls of rage at his obstinacy were now loud in the extreme.

Swords and daggers were snatched from their sheaths, and our hero certainly thought that his last moment had come.

"Answer!" shouted Long Lock. "Answer!"

He again raised his hand, but ere he could strike another blow, Felix drew suddenly back, raised his clenched fist and struck the lieutenant a blow exactly under the left ear.

Long Lock fell like an ox, in the centre of his companions.

This daring deed was the signal for a general shout of vengeance.

One of the bravos more than half intoxicated, caught hold of a bottle and dealt Felix such a heavy blow on the head that he fell, without one single groan, to the floor.

"You have killed him, you infernal idiot!" yelled Captain White, rushing forward, "and, therefore, you have baulked all of us. Had he been spared so that we could have tortured him, we might have had a little enjoyment. Turn him over, Lock."

Long Lock, who had been assisted to his feet, took hold of Felix and brutally hurled him upon his back.

"Now keep clear," said Captain White, "and we will search him. Maybe he has something about him, by means of which we shall ascertain his name. Parson, to you I entrust the task of searching him."

"And you could not have selected a better person," chuckled the hypocritical wretch, as he advanced and fell upon his knees by the side of Felix. "My nature, like my hands——"

"Which were made for *picking and stealing*," interrupted the captain.

"Not so," replied the parson, with a hideous leer. "I was about to observe that my nature, like my hands, are gentle, and I will treat him as carefully as a child. Ho, ho!"

He soon turned out every pocket, but they had already been cleared.

"Very *peculiar!*" ejaculated the captain. "*Very* strange that he should have nothing about him."

"Yes, *very* strange," repeated the parson.

"Loosen his dress!" cried the captain. "Quick! By all the fiends! I thought he was dead, but he is regaining consciousness. Here, Faulkley, stand by him—so, and if he attempts to raise his head, strike him down with this bar of iron."

"'HOLD!' CRIED THE COUNTESS, 'FOR THE LOVE OF HEAVEN, FORBEAR!'"

"'HOLD!' CRIED THE COUNTESS, 'FOR THE LOVE OF HEAVEN, FORBEAR!'"

"YOU KNOW ME? ONCE SEEN I AM NOT EASILY FORGOTTEN!" CRIED CAPTAIN WHITE."——*See No. 4.*

"Fear it not," grinned Faulkley. "I will strike him hard enough."

The parson tore open our hero's doublet, and the case rolled forth.

Captain White darted upon it with the rapidity of a vulture on its prey, and in an instant it was forced open.

The brilliant, the gorgeous, the magnificent diamond necklace—the pride of the Rothburn family, in whose possession it had been for generations—the countess's precious jewel, the counterpart of one lost years ago, which, reluctanlty, she had pawned with the goldsmith, in order to raise money for a certain purpose, was before the eyes of the bravos; the trembling hands of Captain White clutched it as a miser clutches his hoarded gold.

A great, a mighty shout of admiration, wonder, and surprise escaped the lips of all who looked upon the treasure.

Dozens of hands itched to grasp it.

Captain White, on his knees, appeared to be spellbound—riveted to the spot.

"Holy Virgin!" he cried, in hoarse, trembling tones, "here is value! *This is the necklace*—this is the necklace, by——"

"It is—it is!" murmured the parson; "let me hold it—if but for one single moment!"

"Thou fool!" cried Captain White, quickly closing the case and starting up, "*you* hold it! Pshaw! 'twould melt in thy hands! Ha, ha! No one shall hold it but *me*—that I swear!"

And he placed the precious jewel in his pocket.

A mighty shout arose.

"Shares! Shares!"

"You *shall* have shares," answered White, "if you will allow time for the sale. Old Merrywell will buy it, and we will share the money. Do I not always equally divide whatever is obtained? Of course. Then rely upon it you shall have a fair share of this. And *this is* the goldsmith's messenger. Hum. 'Tis a wonder I did not guess it long ago."

"What is to be done with the youth?" asked Long Lock ?

"Well, we cannot amuse ourselves with him in his present state, that is very certain. He, no doubt will require careful attention, or he will die ere morning dawns. Let us save him until to-morrow night, and——"

"By which time you will have sold the necklace," interrupted the parson.

"I never said so!" answered the captain sharply; "it will take time to dispose of it. Well, now let the youth be carried upstairs and placed in the long room. We will then summon an apothecary, and bring him round if 'tis possible."

Little did the horrible wretches dream that our hero had overheard all that had been said.

"My life," he thought—"my life before the necklace!"

Oh, little did he think of *what actual value to himself* was that very necklace.

Directed by Captain White and the parson, Long Lock and half-a-dozen of the men raised and carried our hero up the stairs.

They passed through several long, narrow passages, traversed two or three balconies, and finally paused on a small landing.

Captain White took a key from his pocket, and, opening one of half-a-dozen doors, said—

"Now, in with him!"

CHAPTER IV.

OF THE MANNER IN WHICH FELIX REGAINS POSSESSION OF THE NECKLACE—OF HIS DARING LEAP—OF HIS FLIGHT ACROSS THE TEMPLE—OF HIS BOLD PLUNGE INTO THE THAMES, AND OF HOW AND BY WHOM HE WAS PICKED UP.

THE men bore Felix into a long narrow room almost destitute of furniture.

On one side were two fairly-sized windows, both of them being wide open, probably to admit a little fresh air.

At the farther end of the room was a truckle-bed, on which was laid a ragged mattress.

To this Felix was carried, and as he passed one of the windows, which was at some considerable distance from the ground, he observed a large hay-waggon drawn up beneath it.

A thrill of joy ran through him as he saw this, but it immediately afterwards passed away.

"I am too well guarded to escape," he thought; "ere I could attempt to drop it half-a-dozen balls would have penetrated my body."

Down on the truckle-bed they flung him.

"Now," said White, "we will see about an apothecary, and then to business. We have important work to-night, parson—eh?"

"We have. Shall I get an apothecary?"

"Aye, do."

"Good. And—but do, oh, do let me have just one look more at the necklace!"

"You idiot!" cried White, "what is your object in wanting to look at it?"

"Only a desire to note the exquisite glitter of the diamonds," replied the parson.

"Your desire shall be gratified for this once, but look out for yourself if you touch it. Here, bring the lantern."

One of the men carrying a lantern advanced to where the captain stood, and raised the lantern aloft.

The others, with the exception of one who stood by the window, crowded round, and prepared, for a second time, to feast their eyes on the necklace.

Felix opened his eyes cautiously, and looked at the man at the window.

He saw that he was apparently watching something going on below.

"Shall I dare it?" thought Felix. "Shall I dare it? The necklace and a chance of escape, or certain death—'tis one or the other! I am so weak—so weak. Oh, Heaven, give me strength but for a few moments. Oh let me restore that jewel to that kind, generous goldsmith, and I shall be willing to die!"

Another look he directed at the bravo standing moodily watching what was going on below; and just as Captain White opened the case, he drew himself up, unfastened his cloak, and let it fall on the bedstead.

Then he placed one foot on the floor, then the other.

He stooped, noiselessly took off his shoes, and seized a heavy, three-legged stool.

But he need not have been so careful, for the bravos in their admiration of the necklace, were making sufficient noise to drown any movements he might make.

Creeping cautiously behind the villains Felix again paused.

Captain White, with all the effrontery in the world, was explaining this and that part of the necklace to his associates, explaining what he knew absolutely nothing about.

Felix, standing on tip-toe, stretched forth his hand, and making a sudden dash, snatched the jewel from the captain's hand.

A wild cry left the bravos' lips. The cry caused the man at the window to turn.

"Bar the window!" yelled White, as he frantically endeavoured to disengage his pistols. "Stop him! Stop him!"

Across the floor darted Felix, the fierce look in his eyes showing only too plainly that he was determined to sacrifice his life, if necessary, to save the goldsmith's property.

Hastily the man at the window drew his long rusty blade, and placed himself in a half stooping position.

But had there been twenty men before him, Felix would at this moment have attempted to pass through them.

Dashing boldly at the blackguard, he raised the heavy stool just as the bravo made a plunge at him with his blade.

Round his head Felix whirled the stool, and then let it go.

It struck the man on the temple, and with a wild gasping cry, he fell forward, receiving in his breast the contents of Captain White's pistol, which at this instant he had discharged.

Closing his eyes, and uttering a cry to heaven for safety, Felix grasped the necklace tightly in his hand, gave one terrific spring, and bounded clean through the window.

As he took the leap two or three shots were fired in quick succession at him.

All the harm they did, however, was to damage the windows and splinter the woodwork.

Down through the darkness with awful velocity sped our hero.

Over and over he went, for the distance

as we have before remarked was considerable.

But he did not release his hold of the necklace.

He held it with the tenacity of a vice.

Captain White and his villainous associates stood for an instant looking alternately at the open window and at their dead comrade.

Then with loud cries they rushed to the window and looked out.

Felix had disappeared.

He alighted on the load of hay, rebounded, and toppled over into the arms of a drunken bravo, who, laughing loudly at what he considered was a joke on the part of one of his friends, placed his arms firmly about him.

Felix, however, was well aware of the fact that every second was a precious moment to him, and he disengaged himself from the man's embrace, by throwing him down.

As he fell, his sword clanked on the stones, and this reminded Felix that he was unarmed.

Stooping, he drew the man's blade from its sheath and sped away, just as loud shouts warned him that the pursuit after him was commenced.

A horn was blown and instantaneously it was answered by a dozen others.

Loud shouts filled the air, lanterns by dozens were hung out from the balconies, the clash of arms was heard, and the hoarse roar of scores of men who, hurrying from the taverns, were crying out—

"Tipstaff! Tipstaff! A bailiff! Down with them! Tear them limb from limb! An arrest! An arrest!"

The lights from the flaming links and the lanterns fell upon Felix as he sped along, and even the Alsatians paused in wonder and astonishment.

"A madman! A madman!" shouted the bravos, and so loud were the shouts that, fortunately for Felix, they drowned the cries of Captain White and his men, who, at no great distance, were behind our hero.

Certainly Felix looked like a madman.

In what direction he was going, of course he had not the remotest idea, and to him the lanes seemed interminable.

With every yard he advanced the shouts behind him increased.

At last Felix got into a lane, from one side of which he could here and there see the Thames.

Straight along he ran, and at the end of the lane he saw on one side of him a broad passage, before him a short flight of stone steps, and at the bottom of them an enormous gate.

Should he turn down the passage?

No, he decided to descend the steps.

And it was well for him that he did so decide, for had he ventured down that passage he would have been caught like a rat in a trap.

Before descending the steps, he paused and locked behind him.

He saw a vast crowd advancing at a rapid rate—a vast crowd of men, women, and children, their savage faces being made wonderfully distinct by aid of the links and lanterns they carried.

A violent and instant death would be Felix's fate did they overtake him.

Many of the villains carried loaded pistols in their hands, and they would have fired had it not been for the fact that every moment some denizen of the slums made his or her appearance, and so stood a good chance of being shot down in mistake.

At the bottom of the steps Felix encountered one of the gaurds or "Friars," who in his turn was watching the gate in order to give warning on the approach of "the enemy"—officers of justice—at that gate.

Seeing Felix flying down the steps, and hearing loud shouts of "Stop him!" the man snatched a pistol from his belt, and without a moment's hesitation fired.

Here again, singular to say, the ball proved fatal.

It missed Felix, but very narrowly, and struck a woman, who, with a child at her breast, was looking from a balcony a few yards away.

The unlucky wretch dropped dead, the child still clasped in her arms.

Hurling his pistol away with a curse, the man attempted to draw his sword.

But he had no time, for Felix, raising the heavy sword on high, brought it down on his head, which was nearly cloven in twain.

The sword, too, snapped off at the hilt.

Set in the massive, iron-bound gate was a narrow door, with a heavy ring for a handle.

This Felix seized, and pulling at it with all his might, it yielded.

Our hero bounded through it, and the door closed with a loud clash.

And now Felix found himself in almost utter darkness.

Before him loomed a mass of large, irregular-shaped buildings, and here and there were enormous oaks, now leafless and partly covered with snow.

An exclamation of surprise burst from his lips as he recognised where he was.

He was in the Temple—and a part of the Temple was at the very back of the goldsmith's residence.

And he knew also how strict were the laws of the Templars as to who invaded their sacred precincts.

He looked to the left, and the faint glimmer of a light on the water met his eyes.

"The Thames!" he muttered. "The Thames! It is my only chance."

Securing the precious necklace within his breast, he started off in the direction of the river.

Just as he crossed the terrace leading to Temple Stairs, the horns of the Alsatians broke out afresh.

The gate was again forced open, and the motley, savage crew crowded through.

Lights appeared in the rooms of the dark, gloomy-looking buildings of the Temple as if by magic, and in a few more moments the hurried tramping of feet and the clash of weapons showed that the Templars were alarmed, and were issuing from their chambers to repel the invasion by the Alsatians.

The young students, armed with rapiers and other weapons began to crowd into the open space in front of the gate.

The Alsatians, now headed by the panting and enraged Captain White, paused.

They had had many a bitter lesson from the Templars, and they did well to pause and consider before they attempted to advance too far into the Temple.

The prompt action on the part of the young Templars was of the utmost importance to our hero, since he was no longer followed.

Remembering the glimpses of the Thames he had had ere he passed the gate, he considered it quite likely that the Alsatians, if they thought he would

take to the river, would take boats and meet him in a very short space of time.

Rushing down the narrow pathway which led to the Temple Stairs, Felix arrived panting and breathless at the edge of the broad river.

The shouting had ceased for a few moments, but, nevertheless, a subdued murmer of many voices met his ears.

Had the Alsatians abandoned the chase? he thought.

Suppose they had? Should he turn back?

Suddenly the report of a single shot rang out.

Instantly it was followed by a dozen others.

Then arose a roar far louder than any Felix had previously heard.

Above the shouts rose the clash of weapons.

What could the sounds that fell on Felix's ears mean?

It meant that the Templars and the Alsatians were hard at it—that a fight, a fearful fight was in progress between them —a fight which would not terminate until probably some dozen on either side were lying mortally wounded or still in death!

Felix considered, after a few moments' reflection, that the Alsatians had quarrelled among themselves, and that they were fighting it out.

Back he could not turn—to do so would be only to rush into the midst of the danger from which he had been fleeing.

Forward—into the broad black river he must go, for, after all, there was a chance of being rescued.

Walking along the piles which stood by the side of the steps, Felix sprang forward and plunged into the river.

Directly he touched the water he felt his spirits revive, and it was with a hopeful heart that he struck out into the middle of the stream.

Before he had got far the sounds of strife proceeding from the Friars grew fainter and fainter, and at last he heard nothing whatever, save the faint sighing of the wind and the rippling of the water on either side of him.

Our hero was a good swimmer, and he struck out firmly and boldly.

Before he had taken the plunge he had noticed the ghostly objects we have spoken of, floating by, and guessed they were barges laden with merchandise, but now not one passed him

On and on he went, still hopeful of being picked up, but by degrees he began to despair.

He would have made his way to the opposite side of the river, but he had heard that in many parts it swarmed with desperate characters.

Reckless and daring smugglers and river-pirates had possession of many parts of the river, and they did very much as they liked.

However, at last exhausted nature warned Felix that unless he obtained rest and proper attention, his life would be forfeited, and he was about to make an effort to reach one side or the other when he heard the slow measured stroke of oars behind him.

Looking back, he saw a wherry advancing.

Raising himself, he shouted with all his might—

"Help, help!"

"Hold!" cried a deep voice, as a dark figure rose in the wherry's stern. "Hold! Lay to! Hark!"

The watermen—there were four of them—rested upon their oars, while the person in the stern cried—

"Who cries 'help'?"

"Help!" answered Felix. "Help! here —here!"

The person in the stern caught sight of our hero as he raised himself.

"Pull away," he said. "Gently —gently. Soh! Hold!"

Down upon his knees he went, and, stretching forth his hand, grasped Felix by the collar.

And not one moment too soon, for our hero almost instantly became insensible.

Assisted by the watermen, the person in the stern pulled Felix into the wherry.

"Hum!" he said; "only a youth. Good Heavens, what a state he is in! Why, he has been almost murdered, I should say. How on earth could he have got into the water?"

"Perhaps he has escaped from the clutches of the Alsatians," suggested one.

"Probably. Well, here is brandy," and he took a flask from inside the ample cloak he wore—a cloak which concealed a magnificent costume—and poured some of the contents down our hero's throat.

But apparently it had no effect.

The dose was repeated, but no result followed.

"He is in a dangerous condition, your lordship," said one of the men.

"He is," was the reply. "Row with all speed to Whitehall Stairs."

And, seating himself in the stern, he supported our hero's head on his knees.

The watermen resumed their oars, and the wherry again shot forward.

Whitehall Stairs was soon reached.

Directly the boat touched the steps a man, whose figure was almost entirely concealed by a thick, heavy cloak, stepped forward, and, touching his broad beaver, said in a low tone of voice—

"Lord Clinton?"

"Right!" was the reply, as his lordship—for Lord Clinton it was—stepped from the wherry.

"Your lordship's coach awaits you."

"Good. Well, show——" Ho! stop. Dominic!"

"Your lordship's servant," replied the man, pausing and bowing low.

"Send hither the footmen—or *bring* them hither, Dominic, and assist yourself, in conveying the youth you see in the wherry to my coach."

The man went and procured the footmen as directed, and Felix, under the eye of Lord Clinton, was conveyed to the coach.

A pair of cushions were placed on the floor of the coach, and on them Felix was laid.

"Now, quick!" cried Lord Clinton. "Jump in with me, Dominic. Now," he said to the footmen, "home like the wind! and as you pass Dr. Blake's house, jump down, one of you, and tell the doctor to hurry along to me."

With this Lord Clinton jumped into the coach, Dominic followed, and away dashed the horses to Clinton House, St. James's Park.

No doubt the man, Dominic, was under the impression that Lord Clinton was about to give some information as to how he had picked up the youth.

If so, he made a great mistake.

Lord Clinton sat in a corner of the coach, gloomy and silent.

His eyes were fixed upon the blood-stained face of Felix Ferdinand, and these thoughts were running through his mind—

"What a strange fate is mine! I am continually doing something extraordinary—something entirely out of the common. Great heaven! here is the realisation of my dream. The cry of despair coming from the very middle of the Thames—the blood-stained but finely-shaped face! Heavens! this youth is a dreadful-looking object, and yet I feel irresistibly attracted towards him. Drive on—faster! faster!" he shouted, as a succession of severe quivers passed through our hero's frame.

"My lord," said Dominic, "would it not be better to place him in charge of Dr. Blake until——"

"No," interrupted his lordship; "no, no, I tell you!"

At the house of Dr. Blake one of the footmen dismounted, and left his message as directed.

In about five minutes afterwards the coach halted at the great gates of Clinton House, which stood at the edge of St. James's Park.

The porter at the lodge drew back the gates.

Up a beautiful avenue rolled the coach, and the next instant stood beside the magnificent marble staircase leading to the front entrance.

"Dominic," said Lord Clinton, "call some of the men, and have this youth carefully conveyed to the Red Room. Mind, let it be done carefully, and take great pains not to alarm the household."

"Never fear, your lordship," replied Dominic.

In but a few short moments our hero was lying upon a splendid couch in the Red Room, one of the principal bedrooms in Clinton House, which was then one of the grandest houses in London.

With great care he was washed by some of the men-servants, his lordship standing by watching the operation.

Hardly had this been done, ere Dr. Blake and his assistant arrived, and very fortunately the assistant carried a case of surgical appliances.

The worthy doctor was startled when he looked upon Felix, and he gravely shook his head.

"Attend to him, Dr. Blake," said Lord Clinton sharply, "and do not stare at him or at me."

"Your lordship's pardon" said Dr. Blake meekly, "but I fancy I am summoned too late."

"Pshaw!" cried Lord Clinton impatiently, "what care I what you *fancy?* Attend to him, I say. He is in a sad state, I must admit, but I have seen worse cases than that, Dr. Blake. With proper attention he will recover."

Dr. Blake proceeded to do as he was ordered.

"We will give him some dry clothes first." he said.

"You will do nothing of the kind," said Lord Clinton; "he is going to bed, and, for the present, will not require fresh clothes. Let him be undressed, his wounds bandaged, and at once put to bed."

Waving his hand, all with the exception of the doctor and his assistant retired from the room.

Dr. Blake proceeded rapidly with his task.

Suddenly an exclamation of surprise escaped his lips.

"What is it?" asked Lord Clinton, starting forward.

"This was beneath his shirt," said Dr. Blake, handing the case containing the necklace to his lordship.

Directly Lord Clinton beheld the case, he turned as pale as death.

His hands trembled violently as he looked upon the monogram on the case.

"Yes, yes," he said, "it is quite right. Proceed—proceed—quick. For the love of Heaven, quick!"

Withdrawing into the shadow of the bed-curtains, he opened the case.

A great sob escaped his lips as he looked upon the necklace.

"How on earth did this come into *his* possession," he muttered. "Here indeed is a great mystery. Who and what can this youth be? Lord, my brain seems on fire! I am beset by a thousand grave apprehensions. This I must reserve—I must keep this a secret. He must fancy he has lost it. I will——"

His reflections were interrupted by Dr. Blake.

"Your lordship," he said, "I have now done for the youth all that can be done at present. Medicine shall be at once sent in, with the necessary directions. I have only to urge on you the necessity of keeping the patient perfectly quiet."

"Fear it not. He shall have perfect

quiet. I will see to it myself. But listen to me. When do you suppose that he will be sufficiently strong for me to put a few questions to him?"

"He will not be able to answer any questions, your lordship, nor, probably, will he be able to recognise anyone or anything for at least a week."

"Heavens! So long?"

"Aye—longer, perhaps. Your lordship, it is quite evident, is not aware of the extent to which the youth has been injured. Brain-fever will follow unless I am much mistaken. I shall be here again directly morning dawns."

"Fail not. And mark it, Dr. Blake —never mind the expense," said the nobleman.

The doctor bowed, and, with his assistant withdrew, chuckling over the fact that there was not much fear of *him* "minding the expense."

For some few minutes after their departure Lord Clinton stood in the centre of that grand apartment, alternately looking at the necklace and at Felix.

Then he commenced to pace the apartment with rapid strides, muttering to himself, and wondrous strange were those mutterings!

Before he left the room for the night —or rather morning—a nurse was placed at the bedside of our hero.

So another adventure, and a strange one this time, was added to "the fortunes of Felix Ferdinand."

CHAPTER V.

SHOWS HOW LORD CLINTON VISITS THE COUNTESS OF ROTHBURN, AND OF THE DUEL FOUGHT BETWEEN CLINTON AND LORD STRETTON.

DR. BLAKE'S words proved prophetic.

Felix, before the middle of the next day, was attacked with brain-fever.

Lord Clinton, however, summoned two of the most skilful physicians from the Court to attend upon him, and promised them an enormous fee, provided they would bring him safely through.

Lord Clinton knew how highly the countess prized her diamond necklace, and the fact of a stranger having it in his possession was a perfect mystery.

Hours upon hours his lordship waited, hoping that Felix would so far recover as to be able to give a few collected replies to the questions he might put to him.

Delusive hope!

Every hour Felix grew worse.

Such a height did the fever attain that the physicians looked grave indeed.

The wild ravings of our unfortunate hero were heard in almost every part of that extensive mansion.

Of every matter of importance, which had occurred to him during his young life, he raved.

Of Nicholas Fielding, of the cottage, and of the LOST SECRET.

A secret which he had begun to fancy had been buried with its holder in the silent churchyard.

But it was of the diamond necklace, and of Captain White, Felix principally raved.

And Lord Clinton, who recognised the name of the blackguardly leader of the Alsatians only too well, became more mystified than ever.

At last, on the third morning after the discovery, he resolved to wait upon the countess.

Securing the necklace about him, he attired himself and set out on foot.

Reaching the countess's residence, a large and noble mansion, he was instantly admitted and shown into the drawing-room.

"Is the countess at home?" he asked.

"She is, your lordship," replied the footman. "The countess has been in the library for the past two hours. I will say——"

"Stop, stop!" interrupted his lordship; "do not interrupt her. I will go myself to the library."

The footman bowed and held open the door.

Along the broad and highly polished oak floor walked Lord Clinton, and presently he halted before the library.

The door was partly open, and Lord Clinton was enabled to see within the room.

Seated at a table in the centre of the lofty and magnificently-appointed library, sat the Countess of Rothburn.

She was a lady of about forty, but not more—probably a year or two less.

Despite her somewhat grave looks, and the fact that a grey hair or two might have been found amid her splendid black tresses, she was still a most lovely woman.

A thrill of rapture pierced the breast of Lord Clinton as he looked upon her, and a sigh—a deep sigh—was it regret? —escaped his lips.

Coughing slightly, so as to make his presence known, he walked slowly into the room.

The countess started up, thus showing off her graceful figure, her lovely bust, to perfection.

"Your lordship has taken me quite by surprise," she said ; "it is not often now that your lordship honours me with a visit."

"Pray do not disturb yourself, your ladyship.   This time——"

"You have come on business," interrupted the countess with a sad smile. "Well, well, times are altered.   You look grave, my lord ; I trust nothing has occurred to upset your usual equanimity."

"Something unusual *has* occurred, and it is of the utmost importance to *you.*"

"To me ?" cried the countess, considerably surprised.

Lord Clinton nodded.

"Ah," sighed the countess, "misfortunes never come alone.   *That* I have, to my sorrow, repeatedly discovered ; and now I am to learn something else. Ah, me !   Proceed, my lord, tell me what has happened."

"From what you have just said, your ladyship," said Lord Clinton, "I infer that you have lately received some bad news ?"

"Alas, I have !"

"May I ask the nature of that news ?"

"Oh, yes, for by this time, since large rewards have been offered, all London must know the misfortune which has overtaken me."

"I am surprised, then, that nothing has reached me."

"Well, it *is* strange.   My lord, you have on several occasions seen my diamond necklace."

"Many times—yes, around your ladyship's exquisitely-shaped throat and——"

"Spare your compliments.   And your lordship knows, from what you have heard me say, that that necklace is of the utmost value to me."

"I have."

"For one day, should Heaven be merciful, it will aid me to discover my long lost son."

"What reward has your ladyship offered ?"

"At present my means are limited, so that I have been unable to offer a very large sum.   I have offered five thousand crowns, and another person has offered a like amount."

"*Another* person ?"

"Yes."

"May I ask who that is."

"Oh, simply a—a—friend—a City goldsmith, who——"

"I understand.   Total reward, ten thousand crowns.   Now listen to me, countess.   Suppose—only suppose—that *I* brought you this precious trinket, what reward would you give *me ?* "

"Cease—oh, cease this talk !   Does not your lordship see in what a state of mind I am ?"

"Your pardon.   I repeat, what reward would you give me if I restored to you this diamond necklace ?"

"Torment me not, I implore you."

"I will not torment you ; I——"

"*Can* you restore the necklace—that is the question ?" cried the countess, stamping her little foot.

"I can."

"Ah !"

"Aye, I can !"

"You are an accomplished courtier, Lord Clinton, but you are not a magician."

"Yet I can restore to you this necklace."

"Do so then !" cried the countess, incredulously : "and *then* talk of reward."

Lord Clinton placed his hand beneath his cloak, brought forth the case, and laid it by his side on the table.

"There, my lady," he said, "is the diamond necklace !"

So completely astounded was the countess, that for some few moments she stood perfectly speechless.

Her hands were clasped tightly together, her beautiful eyes fixed upon that treasure which she had begun to fancy was lost to her for ever.

At last she burst out—

"In the name of Heaven, my lord, how came you in possession of that?"

"I will tell you anon. First, however, my reward."

"At the risk of offending you, I feel bound to say that you are entitled to the ten thousand crowns."

Lord Clinton smiled.

"What are ten thousand crowns to me, your ladyship?" he asked. "Or what, indeed, would be *thrice* ten thousand crowns?"

"I might have known that King James's proud and favourite courtier would never condescend to stoop to——"

"Nay, nay, do not——"

"Well, well," cried the countess, impatiently; "thy reward?"

"Your hand!" cried Lord Clinton, sinking upon one knee, seizing the countess's hand, and pressing a burning kiss upon it. "This hand, for which, on so many occasions, I have pleaded in vain."

"It cannot—*cannot* be!" cried the countess.

"Say not so, countess—say not so. Pause—reflect for a few moments. Why am I so constantly refused?"

"Why do you so continually ask for my hand, Lord Clinton, when there are hundreds of far more beautiful, far more wealthy ladies who would be only too ready to be yours? There are many whose highest ambition would be attained did the handsome, the wealthy, and the petted Lord Clinton condescend to say, 'Be my wife.'"

"Why do I so continually ask you for your hand? Because I love you—because in you I behold the one who should be the sharer of my wealth and my honours. Oh, countess, refuse me not this time!"

There was now a painful pause of some moments.

The countess appeared to be buried in thought, while Lord Clinton remained upon his knee, still holding the white, jewelled hand, still having his eyes eagerly fixed upon the lovely face, as if endeavouring to read her thoughts.

This pause gave him hope; his heart beat loudly and rapidly.

"Rise, my lord," said the countess, "and listen to me."

Lord Clinton rose, and folding his arms prepared to listen.

"My lord," said the countess, "we are neither of us young."

"Nay; but then both of us are in the prime of life," said Clinton.

"Truly so," resumed the countess; "and so we are enabled the better to consider matters calmly and deliberately. Now, my lord, you must know, if you think a moment, why it is that I have so often refused you—*you*, in whom, to speak the truth, I behold all that is good in man! I have watched your career with great attention, and with pride and satisfaction. I have taken a vast interest in you because—because—"here her voice faltered—"because you were my husband's friend. I repeat, my lord, that if you think a moment, you must know why it is I have so often refused you."

"Because of Lord Stretton?"

The countess bowed her head.

"Think no more of him, your ladyship. Forbid him ever again to darken——"

"Stop, stop. You know not what you say. My lord, if I gave you my hand while Stretton lives, *I should be answerable for your death!*"

"Great Heaven!" cried Clinton; "what mean you?"

"That Stretton or his rascally bravos would slay you."

Clinton smiled contemptuously.

"I am willing to risk it," he said; "I fear Lord Stretton no more than I do the worm grovelling in the earth."

"And that is not all," continued the countess; "Lord Stretton holds the secret as to my son."

"I do not understand you."

"Well, Stretton could, so he says, place my son in my arms ere four-and-twenty hours have passed."

"Then why does he not do so?"

"Because I have not consented to become his wife."

This the countess said calmly and firmly.

"He has made a bargain, then?"

"He has. That as soon as we are married he will restore to me my long-lost son."

As she uttered these words, the countess covered her face with her hands, and burst into a passionate flood of tears.

"As soon as you are married," said Lord Clinton; "not on your *promise* of your hand."

"Nay."

"Then I believe what he says would be found to be an infamous falsehood. Has not your ladyship so considered this?"

"Many times. But I have dispelled the idea as soon as considered, for I am now fully persuaded that he knows something as to my lost son."

"Countess," said Clinton, in low, ominous tones, "*does he also know how your husband met with his death?*"

A wild shriek escaped the countess.

She started back, clutching the table for support.

Lord Clinton thought that the reason of this agitation was the result of the question he had asked, but when he saw the eyes of the countess fixed upon the door, he partly moved, and lo! standing in the shadow of the heavy curtains, was the tall figure of Lord Stretton.

A savage expression rested upon his swarthy face, his small grey eyes glittered with deadly hate.

If he were under the impression that his unexpected presence and his fierce looks would startle and disconcert Lord Clinton, he was mistaken.

Lord Clinton surveyed him with a look of calm indifference.

"Soh!" said Lord Stretton, "it is thus I am spoken of when my back is turned!"

Recovering her composure by a supreme effort, the countess cried—

"By what right, my lord, do you dare enter my house uninvited?"

"By *every* right."

"Mention one."

"I refuse; and——"

"Speak not so to——"

"Silence!" thundered Stretton.

"Lord Stretton," said Lord Clinton, "your words show your mind when you so far forget yourself."

"Are you the Countess of Rothburn's champion?" sneered Stretton.

"I am not her *champion*, but I am a *gentleman*, Lord Stretton, and as such would have no hesitation in becoming the champion of the poorest woman on aerth, were she threatened or interfered with, and did she call on me."

"Pshaw! Your observations are but the outpourings of a breast filled with pride, and vanity, and——"

"Seek not to insult *me*, Lord Stretton or you will find that my sword is for use, as well as for ornament."

Stretton bestowed upon Clinton a look of fiendish contempt, then he turned to the countess, and pointing to the case, he said, in hoarse tones—

"I see you have recovered it."

"I have."

"From whom? Who had it?"

"That, my lord, is *my* business, and not *yours*."

"Will you be pleased to tell me the reason Lord Clinton has honoured you with a call?"

"Certainly *not!*"

Stretton was baffled.

"My lord," said the countess, directing a disdainful look upon Lord Stretton, "I must again request you to leave us, as I have business of importance to transact."

"*Business!*" cried Stretton, elevating his eyebrows; "*business!* Ha, ha!"

"I repeat my request that you will retire," said the countess, firmly.

"I refuse, until you tell me who brought you this necklace."

"That I *swear* I will not tell you."

"You shall tell me!" hissed Stretton.

And, taking a few rapid steps forward, he, utterly ignoring Lord Clinton's presence, seized the countess by the wrist.

This was too much for Clinton, who seized Stretton by the collar, and hurled him with terrific force against one of the bookcases.

The villain lay where he fell for a few seconds, but suddenly starting up, and uttering a howl of rage, he snatched his sword from its sheath.

"Draw, dastard—draw!" he shrieked, "or I will kill you as you stand!"

"This is neither the time nor place to fight," replied Clinton calmly. "The presence of a lady——"

"Draw, villain—draw!" thundered Stretton, now boiling over with rage.

And he made a thrust at Clinton, which, had not his lordship moved, would have proved fatal.

Instantaneously Clinton's blade flashed in the weak sunlight.

"Hold!" cried the countess, darting with a wild shriek between the two; 'forbear! forbear!—for the love of Heaven, forbear!"

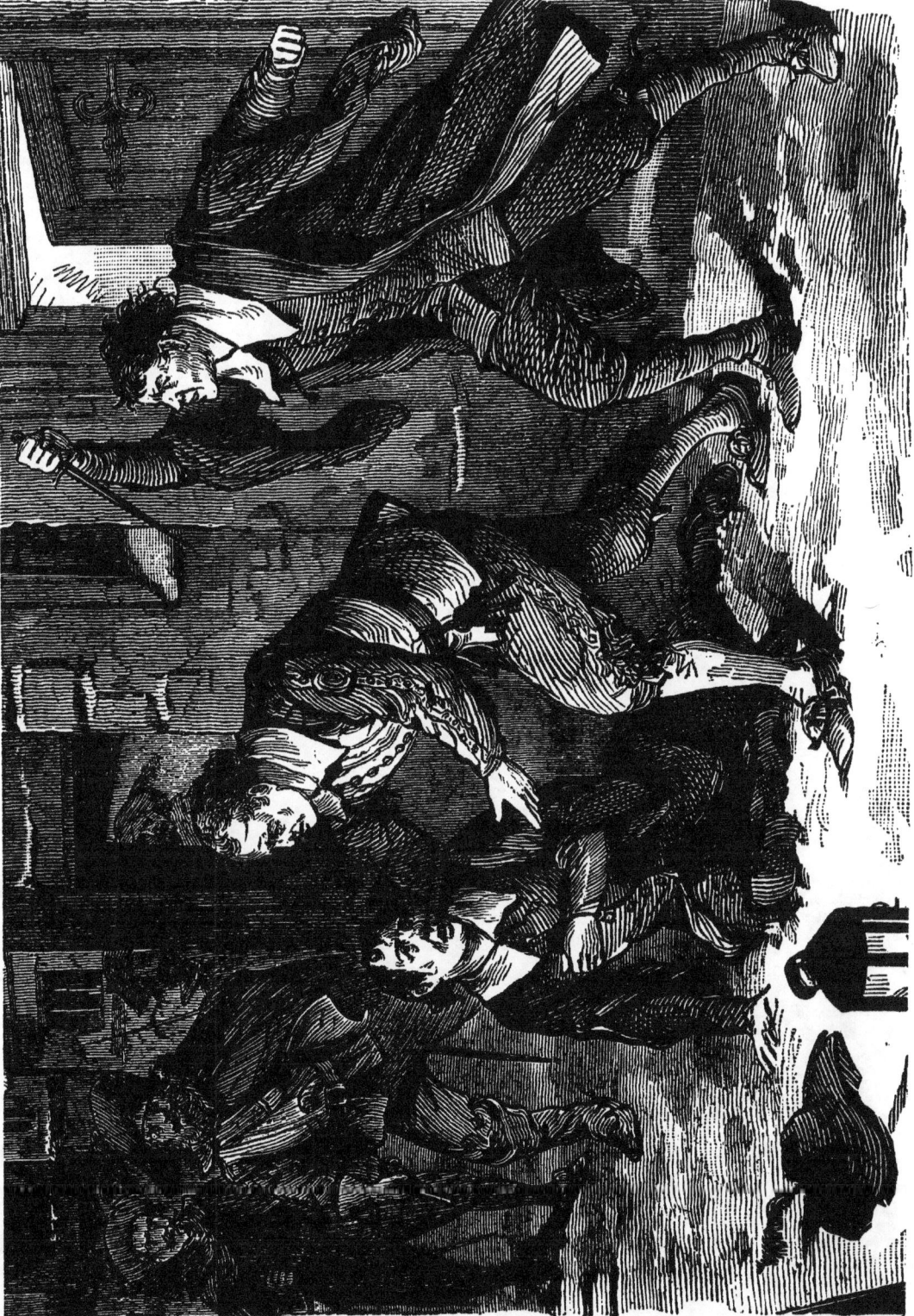

"SHARPLEY, GLIDING TOWARDS THE PORTER, RAISED HIS DAGGER."—See No. 5.

"Stand out of my path!" roared Stretton, in his blind fury raising his sword on a level with the countess's breast; "stand back, or to reach him I may have to slay *you!*"

"Thou brutal coward!" said Clinton. "Those words, if I live, shall reach the ears of the king. By Heaven's grace, he shall know what sort of man my lord of Stretton is. Your ladyship," he said, and he gently placed his hand on the countess's wrist, "I pray you retire, and leave this villain to me and my good sword."

"Oh, no, Clinton, dear Clinton! fight not—oh, fight not! You may fall, and then—oh, Heaven! I cannot bear to look upon these naked weapons. Clinton, you said, a little while ago, you loved me. By that love I charge you—sheath your blade!"

"He said he loved you!" screamed Stretton; "then hades itself should not stay me from trying to slay him!"

And savagely pushing the countess aside, he advanced.

The swords crossed.

Both lords were experienced swordsmen, but Clinton had the advantage in skill, and therefore it is not to be wondered at that Stretton failed to slay him.

Frantic and furious in the extreme were Stretton's passes, but every movement he made was met with a steady hand.

Clinton stood as firm as a rock, with his bright sword firmly gripped in hand.

The Countess of Rothburn had sunk into a chair.

For a time she buried her face in her hands, but the ring of the steel possessed an irresistible attraction for her, and she sat looking at the rapid flashing of the weapons in a state of dreamy fascination.

Every moment Stretton was becoming more maddened with rage.

No opening could he find to deal Clinton a fatal blow.

While he fought he cursed in a truly appalling manner, utterly ignoring the presence of the beautiful and outraged countess.

Presently Clinton said, in a tone of voice which there was no mistaking—

"I am allowing you most excellent practise; anon *I* shall commence, and then you may feel that my sword-point is sharp."

"Idiot! dastard! fool!" yelled Stretton, "anon I shall spit thee as my servants spit a fowl."

"Boasting fool, you lie!" cried Clinton, "as *this* proves."

Stretton's sword was dashed from his hand, and went crashing into a bookcase.

Then, before he could draw back, Clinton's sword passed completely through his left arm.

And now the sealed lips of the countess were opened, and a terrible scream escaped them.

She rushed forward, but Clinton raised his arm.

"Stay, my lady," he said; "I have not slain him, though I could easily have done so, for it would have been quite as simple for me to pass my sword through his heart as his arm. I have merely disabled him. The sting of the wound he has received will remind him, for some time to come, of the undeserved insults he heaped upon you."

"And upon you, noble Clinton," replied the countess, with a bitter sob.

"Nay; so far as I am concerned, my lady, his insults might just as well have been addressed to yonder piece of marble."

Stretton had cowered back against the window, writhing in agony.

Where he had stood was a large pool of blood, and this was slowly trickling towards the fireplace.

Clinton was about to summon the servants, but, on approaching the library door, he found several had assembled.

No doubt they had heard the terrified shriek of their mistress.

They certainly looked frightened enough, as they stood trembling on the threshold.

"Summon a surgeon to attend here at once," said Clinton, not allowing either of the servants to look into the apartment, "and let him bring surgical appliances."

The servants hastily withdrew.

Turning, Clinton saw that consciousness had left Lord Stretton.

He lay now upon the floor, and the countess was standing over him, wringing her hands in great alarm.

"Do not fear," said Clinton, " I took care not to wound him to death. He has simply fainted from loss of blood. The surgeon will soon restore him."

In a short time the surgeon came.

"Attend to him," whispered Clinton, "and mark—not a word of what you see; preserve silence, and I will give you ten times the amount of your fee."

The surgeon nodded and proceeded to attend to Stretton.

He had soon dressed his wound, and then he administered a restorative cordial.

"He will recover consciousness in a few minutes," he said.

"Then begone," replied Clinton, "and call on me to-night at Clinton House."

The surgeon bowed and withdrew.

Sure enough, in two minutes Stretton recovered.

Raising himself, he looked first at his bandaged arm, and then at the blood on the floor, but he made no remark.

In a few moments he tottered, like a drunken man, towards the door.

On the threshold he paused, and, glaring fiercely at Clinton and the countess, he said, hoarsely—

"From now—from this moment—we are deadly enemies—remember that. Think, countess, *of your son!* I have said time after time that he lives. *He does live.* You shall see him, and I will produce before you the proofs you know so well. Then, when you are convinced that it is your son, you shall see him *die*—slowly die—yes, inch by inch —before your eyes! You shall see him die, I say, and yet you will not have the power to raise your hand to save him!"

"Monster!" gasped the countess.

"His words are idle," said Clinton.

"As for *you*, Lord Clinton," continued Stretton, savagely, "you will see that, despite your great wealth and influence, I can cause you to fall. Soon you shall be in my power, and then—— But, wait. My time shall come, and then I will take my deadly revenge!"

With a parting shake of his fist he turned and walked off down the corridor.

"This is all through me!" cried the unfortunate countess, bursting into tears.

"Nay, nay," replied Clinton soothingly; "say not so. Treat his threats with contempt and scorn. After all, he is but a jealous suitor—or he *was.*"

"For years and years! Before my husband married me, and after his death, he has pestered me with offers of marriage. But I could never wed such a monster! Yet, I have more than once wavered, for, oh, I so long to clasp my long-lost son in my arms!" cried the countess.

"Then you *do* really believe he lives?" said Clinton.

"Certainly. When an infant he was stolen from this house. A month after that my husband was murdered. You remember the strange and awful circumstances?" she said.

"Of your husband's murder? Yes, only too well. And my firm belief is that this Stretton was the murderer!"

"Alas, the thought is horrible! but I have more than once thought he knew how my husband was murdered, but I dared not openly say so."

"Listen, dear countess. Does he admit that *he* stole the child?"

"No; only that he knows where the boy is to be found."

Lord Clinton paced the floor for a few seconds.

Suddenly he halted, and, looking earnestly into the countess's face, said—

"Shall we make a bargain?"

"Speak."

"I will search for your son. If I find him and restore him to you, on that very day you will give me your hand?"

"And my heart. Oh, how willingly! But, alas, my lord, such a thing would be impossible!"

"We shall see. Your ladyship knows that I have successfully carried out many things which seemed impossible," said Clinton.

"Truly—truly," exclaimed the countess. "Oh, that Heaven would guide you in your endeavours, and bring your quest to a successful termination!"

"No stone shall be left unturned," said Clinton, firmly; "I swear it!"

"My hand and heart, Clinton, are yours directly you have found my son."

"My dear countess, I——"

He stopped abruptly.

"Go on, Clinton," said the countess.

"You will assure me that I have not been an indifferent object to you?"

"Ah, Clinton, I have loved you for years," she exclaimed.

Uttering a cry of joy, Clinton held out his arms, and in an instant the countess was folded to his breast.

After another pause, Clinton told the countess of the singular manner in which he had become possessed of the necklace.

The countess was overjoyed.

"All doubts as to the safety of the goldsmith's messenger are now set at rest," she said, after Clinton had described our hero ; "only an hour before you came, the goldsmith, Master Walker, was here for the twentieth time, and he, like myself, was under the impression that he had been waylaid and robbed. Anon you will learn how he came into the river."

"No doubt."

"Another mystery is that my favourite servant has disappeared."

"What had he to do with the necklace?" asked Clinton.

"'Twas he I sent to the goldsmith, with the request for the loan of the jewel."

"Now, my dear countess, will you tell me why you placed your property in the hands of the goldsmith?"

"I will answer you candidly — it was because I wanted some ready money."

"For what purpose, may I ask?"

"I required the money to pursue the enquiries I have been making for years as to my lost son."

"A most unwise plan. For there is no doubt that Stretton has been aware of what you were doing, and he could foil you at every turn. Forget not, countess ; leave all to me, and one day, by the blessing of God, I may restore your son to you!"

So a great bargain was made between the Countess of Rothburn and the Court favourite, Lord Clinton.

CHAPTER VI.

SHOWS HOW FELIX RECOVERED, HOW CLINTON MAKES HIM AN OFFER, AND HOW IT WAS DECLINED—OF THE TERRIBLE MURDER COMMITTED IN GUNPOWDER ALLEY BY ORDERS OF CAPTAIN WHITE—OF HOW THE GOLDSMITH'S HOUSE WAS ATTACKED BY THE ALSATIANS—HOW MASTER WALKER WAS BRUTALLY MURDERED—HOW FELIX ESCAPED, AND HOW ROSAMUND WAS CAPTURED.

ANOTHER week passed away, and during that time Felix made considerable progress towards complete recovery.

He had been visited many times by the goldsmith and the fair Rosamund, who, having learned to love him with all the power of her young heart, was overjoyed when the physicians declared that he was entirely out of danger.

On the morning of the twelfth day he was provided with a suitable outfit, and assisted to attire himself by his lordship's own valet.

He was then conducted to the magnificent reception-room, where he found Lord Clinton and the goldsmith awaiting him.

There was a look of great uneasiness on the latter's face.

"Now," said Clinton, "we want you, Felix, to tell us the whole of the adventures which befell you. You have, as yet, only given them to us in a very disconnected manner."

Thereupon Felix told all.

Lord Clinton looked grave, and so, indeed, did the goldsmith.

Both of them knew only too well how much was to be feared from Captain White and his villainous associates.

When Felix had concluded, Lord Clinton said—

"I have been speaking to Master Walker as to your future prospects. I have arrived at the conclusion that you are a brave and fearless lad, and I should like you to remain under my protection. Place yourself under my charge, and you are likely to rise in the world. From what the goldsmith says, the secret of your birth is buried in obscurity, like the birth of a great many men who have attained the highest positions ; but that would affect you not at all at the Court.

Leave it all to me, and I will get the king himself to take an interest in you."

"My lord," replied Felix, without hesitation, "I am exceedingly grateful to you for the way you rescued me from certain death, for the way I have been treated in your house, and for the offer you have made, but I must respectfully decline it."

A sigh of relief escaped the goldsmith's lips.

Lord Clinton was surprised.

He bit his lip with vexation.

"You will, of course, give me a reason?" he said.

"Certainly, your lordship," answered Felix. "It is this: When I came to London for the first time, not long ago, Master Walker——"

"Has told me all about that," interrupted Lord Clinton, "and I have been admiring his generosity."

"Well, your lordship, since that time Master Walker has proved a true friend to me. Never could I repay him the services he, his wife, and his daughter have rendered me. My desire is to stop with him and to prove myself a true and faithful servant, unless, indeed, Master Walker wishes me to go under your protection. In such a case I should have no hesitation in acceding to his wishes."

"No, no!" cried the goldsmith; "no, no; I have no such wish. Thank Heaven you have decided to stay with me!"

"So let it be," said Clinton, who, there could be no doubt, was deeply disappointed at Felix's decision.

"You are offended, my lord?" observed Felix.

"Nay, nay; do not think that. I am not at all offended. On the contrary, I cannot but admire your decision, for it shows that your heart is as grateful as it is brave."

And he held out his hand, which Felix warmly grasped.

"If anything should happen to you at any time, Felix," continued Clinton, "forget not that I am your firm friend. Indirectly, you have rendered me a service."

"I have?" cried Felix, startled.

"Ay, you have."

The goldsmith knew that he referred to the countess.

"Yes," said Clinton; "you have rendered me a service. Now do not forget that if ever you want a friend, you will find one in Lord Clinton; and now farewell."

"Farewell, your lordship. I can only reiterate my thanks."

"Farewell, my lord," said the goldsmith; "I too thank you."

"Do not mention it, Master Walker. We have met each other frequently; I know you as an honest and generous man——"

"And I know you, your lordship," said Master Walker, "as an upright and honourable gentleman, who is deserving of the high honours he has and will yet attain. Would to Heaven I could say the same of many who are enabled to stand and argue with King James I."

Clinton bowed gravely.

Only too well he knew what the worthy goldsmith meant.

In a few more moments Felix was seated by the goldsmith's side in his carriage, which was soon well on the road to Fleet-street.

The joy of Mistress Walker and the lovely Rosamund on beholding Felix was, as may be supposed, very great.

The goldsmith's employés, too, were loud in their expressions of welcome.

It was indeed a joyous reunion, and the remainder of the day was spent in amusements.

And while the amusements were at their height a letter arrived from the Countess of Rothhurn.

It was addressed to Master Walker, and on that gentleman opening it another packet rolled out.

This was addressed—

"*To the brave lad,*
"FELIX FERDINAND,

"*A present from the Countess of Rothburn.*"

On opening the packet, a splendid diamond ring was revealed.

* * * *

At the period of which we write, there stood at the Holborn end of shoe-lane (then a filthy, ditchlike, narrow, and crooked thoroughfare) a couple of sheds called the "Nest of the Pens."

At the top, connecting the two, was an iron rod, and in the centre of that was a sort of shield on which was daubed the figure (or what was supposed to be the figure) of a lion rampant, and over that an eccentric crown.

Underneath, in flaming red characters, were the words:

"𝕿𝖍𝖊 𝕸𝖔𝖗𝖓𝖎𝖓𝖌 𝕲𝖆𝖟𝖊𝖙𝖙𝖊."

These sheds were the "offices" of the only London newspaper—except the official gazette.

The colour of the paper it was printed upon was a dirty red, the type of all shapes and sizes, and the ink was nearly all oil, so that the letters and words ran into each other in quite a comical state of utter confusion.

The "editor" of this "paper" was a man named Stephen Fantenoy, an individual who had a great dread of the Bravos of Alsatia who herded near to him.

Stephen Fantenoy had been absent from his "offices" for a few days, and by some means or another the gentleman who acted as his deputy had allowed an article which gave a terrible account of the doings of the bravos to appear.

Besides this there was a "true" account of all that had befallen our hero.

On the evening of the day on which Felix had returned to Fleet-street, Stephen Fantenoy was seated at a desk in one of the sheds.

In one corner of the desk was stuck a link, the sickly glare from which threw a strange light around the place, and upon the red, but anxious-looking face of Fantenoy, who was bending over a number of documents.

Not a soul was near him; the whole neighbourhood appeared to be buried in profound silence.

So deeply interested was Fantenoy in the matters before him that he did not hear the latch of the shed lifted.

Certainly it was lifted with the utmost caution, but nevertheless a slight "click" followed the lifting of it.

Very slowly the door moved back on its hinges, and a man wearing a long black cloak, a broad beaver hat, and whose face was masked to the lips, slowly entered.

He was followed by another, and then another, dressed exactly alike.

Thus three extraordinary-looking persons had entered the shed without attracting the attention of the studious editor.

Presently, without looking up, Fantenoy stretched forth his hand to take up a pen, and his hand received a terrific blow from the lead-weighed butt-end of a pistol.

Uttering a wild cry of terror, Fantenoy started from his seat, and ran back a few paces, shrieking like a terrified woman.

"In the name of Heaven!" he gasped, who are you?"

"You will see in a moment," growled the first comer. "Come forward."

"No—no—spare me. What have I done that I should be thus molested."

"By the thunder of Heaven!" was the answer delivered in fierce tones, "if you do not instantly come forward, I will send a ball through your attenuated carcass!"

And the glittering muzzle of a pistol was directed full at Fantenoy's breast.

With a bitter sigh Fantenoy crept forward.

He trembled in every limb, and his red face had changed to a ghastly white.

"Look at me!" said the first comer, as he drew himself erect, and snatched the black mask from his face.

"Captain White!" cried Fantenoy, a thrill of horror pervading his body as he remembered the article which without his consent had been inserted in the paper.

"Aye, you know me, that is well. Once seen I am not easily forgotten. Ho, ho! Now then, answer me. Whose hand wrote that article about Alsatia?"

"I——"

"Who wrote it?" thundered White.

"I didn't——"

"Who did. Answer!"

And again the pistol was pointed at the unfortunate editor and so close to his breast that the muzzle nearly touched it.

"My deputy, whose name is Weedon."

"Ah! Let him wait then. Now mark me, you will close this place, or leave it open as it pleases you, and come with us."

"Where—where?"

"Close by. I cannot interrogate you

in a place where we are likely to be disturbed."

"But where do you wish me to go?"

"You will see in a moment. Get ready!"

The trembling Fantenoy placed his hat upon his head.

"You will not murder me," he groaned. "Oh, say you will not murder me!"

"Who ever heard of Captain White committing a murder. Ha, ha! Ho, ho! No, we will not murder you if you answer correctly—*correctly*, mind! the questions I shall put to you. Come!"

Led by Captain White's companions, who were Faulkley and Grafton, Fantenoy went first.

Directly he had crossed the threshold, Captain White lifted up the lid of the desk, seized the torch, and looked within.

A few coins were all the valuables he could see, and these he soon seized upon.

Then looking round the dismal shed a moment, his eyes—we beg pardon his *eye*—rested upon a pile of paper.

With a terrible oath and a hideous laugh he threw the torch among it.

Then he stepped out of the shed, and banged the door to after him.

We have only to say that in a very few moments the offices of the *Morning Gazette* were a mass of flames.

Catching up his companions, Captain White led the way to Gunpowder-alley. On the right, at the sign of "The Pestle and Mortar," was a small and dirty-looking shop, kept by a man named Sharpley Sharp, and there the business of a barber and a "letter of blood, either with cupping or with lancet" was supposed to be carried on.

But Sharpley Sharp did very little business with his razor—at least in the way of shaving.

A sharp-nosed, keen, cunning-eyed, and skinny wretch was Sharpley Sharp, a man always ready to do a dastardly deed in return for the gold of those who thought proper to hire him.

His house was a house of mystery.

It was full of those secret passages, subterranean and otherwise, which, at the period of this history, were to be met with in many houses which disgraced the City of London, and many

a dark and horrible deed was here committed.

Captain White whistled in a peculiar manner, and he was answered by a hand being thrust through a broken pane of glass.

This hand held a key, and Captain White, taking it, opened the door.

"Enter!" he said.

Fantenoy was thrust forward, the two bravos entered, and White brought up the rear.

Threading a long narrow passage a small room on the ground floor was reached.

Hardly any furniture was in the room.

There were three or four forms, and a large square deal table, this being placed exactly in the middle of the room.

For a purpose.

Underneath it, an iron ring could be seen, as well as the outlines of a trap door.

The apartment was illuminated by an oil-lamp, suspended from the dilapidated ceiling.

Sharpley Sharp was soon in attendance, but Captain White majestically waved him aside.

"Be seated," he said to the trembling Fantenoy, "and pay attention to what I say."

"Oh, for the love of——" cried Fantenoy, whose trembling limbs and agonised looks were really pitiful to behold.

"Silence!" shouted White, "or I will strangle you! Now, you are on intimate terms with Master Walker and his family?"

"I am—I am!"

"Soh! What are they up to, to-night?"

"Eh—what are they—— I don't understand you."

"You *do* understand, and if you try to evade my questions, it shall go hard with you."

"Oh, honourable sir, pray explain your meaning."

"I say, what are they up to? The whole place is illuminated, and sounds of revelry can be heard." All this is unusual with the goldsmith—that *I* know —so, I say, what are they up to?"

"Good sir, pardon me, how should I know?"

"Ha, ha! Good, good! Excellent! But you cannot hoobwink *me!* I can see more with my one eye than most people think. You *should* know, for just one hour before we entered your shed, which——"

At this moment the hurried tramping of many feet and loud cries were heard.

The barber cautiously opened the window, and the nature of the cries was distinctly heard.

They were—

"Fire! Fire!"

"There is a fire near us," cried Sharpley. "Look—just look at the tongues of flame over here. Why——"

"Silence!" cried Captain White, "and put down that window. We know all about it," he said, unconcernedly; "the offices of the *Morning Gazette* are blazing away right merrily. Ho, ho, ho!"

And "Ho, ho, ho!" roared Faulkley and Grafton.

Fantenoy turned still paler; great beads of perspiration rolled down his face; his tongue clove to the roof of his mouth.

"Never mind the fire, I say," continued the villainous White. "Answer my question. I was about to say that just one hour before we entered your shed, we saw you leave the goldsmith's residence, which we have been watching; so you see you can't deceive *me* Now answer."

"The goldsmith and his family," replied Fantenoy in hoarse, trembling tones, "are making merry because the youth who preserved the necklace has returned home."

"Oh, returned home—has he! Then to-night we will have him! We will have him this night, even if we pull down the house to get at him!"

"Oh, noble sir——"

"Silence, catiff — silence!" shouted White, who, too excited to sit down, commenced to pace the shaky apartment with rapid strides, his heavy boots and clanking sword striking terror into the heart of Fantenoy.

Suddenly he paused.

"Now," he said, "where does Master Walker keep the keys of the bullion vaults?"

"Constantly about his person."

"Oh, indeed—*does* he? Will you swear to that?"

"I will—he has told me so."

"Ah! Now Sharpley."

"Here, noble captain."

"Bring pens, ink, and paper."

"Good!" replied Sharpley, rushing out of the room.

During Sharpley's absence, Captain White strode fiercely up and down, twirling his enormous moustache and blinking his bloodshot eye.

It is needless to say that his movements were watched with terror by Fantenoy, who, had he known what terrible secrets that room contained, would probably have died from sheer fright.

Pens, ink, and paper having been placed upon the table, Captain White motioned Fantenoy to draw up to them.

"Take the pen in your hand," he growled, "and write as I shall dictate. The goldsmith knows your handwriting?"

"He does—he does!" answered Fantenoy.

"Perfectly?"

"Perfectly."

"Good. Excellent! Now, write thus: '*Dear Master Walker.*' Have you got that down?"

"I have, noble sir," groaned Fantenoy, whose fingers had scarcely sufficient power in them to drive the pen.

"Go on, then. '*The bearer, a particular friend of mine, requests the loan of ten guineas. I have not so much about me, or I would not trouble you for the amount. Pray look to me for the repayment of the loan, which I will liquidate to-morrow without fail.— Greeting you kindly,*

"'STEPHEN FANTENOY.'"

When this precious document only wanted the signature, Fantenoy hesitated.

He fairly gasped with horror, for he saw for what it was required.

Fantenoy was really an honest man, and his soul revolted at this shocking imposition.

"Sign!" thundered White, placing the muzzle of his pistol within an inch of Fantenoy's head. "Sign or I will fire!"

Slowly, laboriously, and with more than one bitter groan of agony, Fantenoy traced his signature on the paper.

Then White snatched it up and carefully scanned it.

He was not much of a scholar, and it

took him some considerable time to read it.

However, he made out that it was all right.

"And now, noble sir," said Fantenoy, "may I be allowed to go?"

"Fool! And give information of all that has passed? No!"

With his left hand Captain White made a series of rapid movements with his finger and thumb.

They were understood by Sharpley, who nodded and grinned hideously.

The two bravos were seated near the window, smoking their pipes—which in itself was a lawless act, for King James had publicly forbidden the use of a "dirty, foul-smelling, and noxious weed —to wit, tobacco"—and apparently watching the reflection of the fire, now fast dying out.

Yet it is perfectly certain that they well knew all that was about to happen.

Captain White got before the now thoroughly alarmed editor, and, holding the paper in his hand, he said—

"Now just listen to me. Look at me —*look* at me, I say!"

"Oh, I am—I am."

"That's well. Now I say many things, but when I say 'Sharp's the word——'"

"Sharp's the word," was a signal.

While Fantenoy had been looking into Captain White's face, Sharpley Sharp, a fiendish grin on his parchment face, had crept up behind his chair.

As White uttered the words "Sharp's the word!" Sharpley started up, leaned over, and drove a gleaming dagger into the neck of the unfortunate man.

With a loud, appalling shriek, he started up, the blood gushing from a gaping cut, and with his eyes seeming as if about to start from his head, he commenced to dash frantically about the room.

Captain White instantly seized hold of a heavy brandy-bottle, and brought it down with all his might on Fantenoy's head, and he fell a bleeding lifeless mass.

"An old saying," chuckled White, "dead men tell no tales.'"

"We have proved the truth of the saying many times, captain?" whined Sharpley.

"Silence, you withered-up old scare-crow!" growled White. "Now, *down with him!*"

The bravos rose, and, assisted by Sharpley, pulled the table on one side.

Then White stooped, placed his hand in the ring we have mentioned, and threw back the trap-door.

Sharpley and the bravos now seized the murdered man and threw him down.

Not the slightest sound did the body make in its descent.

Then the trap-door was closed, and another horrible deed was added to the mysteries of that old house.

That trap-door was directly over a channel which communicated with the Fleet Ditch (of horrible fame), and a body, or anything else, thrown down there would speedily be carried away by the swift-running, nauseous stream, or, if stopped by any projecting point, all hopes of identity would be effectually extinguished by the legions of monstrous water-rats, which beastly vermin made the Fleet Ditch and the outlet, the Thames, their quarters.

Terrible as it is to think of, Fantenoy was not the first who had been hurled down the trap.

"Another gone to swell the number of *strange discoveries!*" half screamed a voice, and turning, Captain White and the bravos beheld the attenuated frame of the barber's wife.

She stood in the doorway, and the bright gleam in her eyes, and the grin upon her thin, bloodless lips, showed how delighted she was at what had been done.

"Away with you, fiend!" shouted White, as he seized upon a dish, and held it as if about to hurl it at her head: "away with you at once, or by Heaven you share his fate!"

Mother Sharpley chuckled derisively.

"Gently," she said. "You don't think you'll intimidate *me* with your looks, do you? No! I'm not such a fool as Sharpley—am I, Sharpley?—eh, eh!"

Bang! went the dish at her head.

But Mother Sharpley was too *sharp* for the captain.

She withdrew her ugly body before the dish could reach her.

"Look you, Sharpley," said White, severely, "you allow your wife to see too many things which should be kept secret, and one of these days you'll repent it."

"Hum! Well, she does *pry*—she

does *pry*," replied Sharpley, uneasily; "but how am I to stop her from——"

"Stop her, you fool!" hissed White in Sharpley's ear; "what is to prevent you from bringing her in here one night when there is no light; bring her in here on some pretence—have the trap open, and push against her, and——"

"I see, I see!" nodded Sharpley; "a very good notion. Yes, yes, a very good notion indeed, and it could easily be carried out. But then—er—who is to see to the business during my absence?"

"*Business?* Ha! ha! Silence, or I'll strangle you, you infernal hypocrite—I will. Now then—get yourself ready for going out."

"Certainly, at once. And——"

"Hold, not so fast, or you will make a mistake, and you know what the result of that will be. Look you; you remember the old gentleman whom you some six months ago made away with?"

Sharpley turned.

"I?" he whispered. "No captain, it was *you*; *I* only——"

"Well, well," chuckled White, "I only say *you* just for the say-so of the thing. Well, you saved his clothes as I told you—at least, some of them."

"Yes, some of them."

"A nice wig, pretty cravat, nice pair of shoes, silk hose, and a nice doublet?"

"Yes, yes."

"And a cloak cut in the clerical style?"

"Yes, yes."

"Put them all on then."

"But they are all too big for me, remember."

"Never mind them being too big. Put them on, I tell you!" thundered White, "and wherever they are too big, make them smaller."

"Suppose anyone should recognise the clothes?"

"Eh? Oh, then you can say you are the old gentleman himself, only you have got thinner. Ho, ho!"

"Ho, ho!" cried the two bravos. "Fancy Sharpley being taken for a respectable old gentleman! Oh the notion's too good."

"Go, Sharpley," said White, "and do as I tell you. You have not far to go."

Sharpley disappeared, and in ten minutes returned, wearing the clothes of one of his and the captain's victims.

Such an object did he look that the two bravos nearly rolled on the floor with laughter.

Even White was inclined to grin.

"Here," he said, as he handed Sharpley the note written by Fantenoy, "take this and go to the goldsmith's. Knock at the door, and you will be admitted by the porter, who will take this note to the goldsmith. Master Walker will read it, admit you to his presence, and will no doubt proceed to the vault to get the money. Your object is to see from where he takes the key. Understand?"

"Perfectly."

"Good. Then be off with you."

"Will you not accompany me?"

"Fool! No; go and be quick."

Sharpley folded up the note and departed.

It was not without much fear and trembling that the wretch travelled Fleet Street.

How did he know but what some friend of the murdered old gentleman might be near and recognise the clothes?

Every now and then he paused, ostensibly to fasten the shoes (which were any amount too large), but really to look about him, for there was a vast number of people in the street all eagerly discussing the fire, which, in such a short time, had totally destroyed the offices of the *Morning Gazette*.

Then, again, Sharpley thought, suppose the goldsmith had heard of the fire? In that case it would be singular indeed that he should have received such a note from Fantenoy.

But Sharpley soon decided what to do in that case.

"I will say that Fantenoy wrote this some hours before the fire," he chuckled.

Having had a good look on both sides of the Bar, and all about him, the villainous old man walked boldly up to the massive door of the goldsmith's mansion and knocked.

In a few moments the door was slowly drawn back and the porter appeared.

"Well?" he said, as he surveyed Sharpley with no good grace. "What do you want?"

"The goldsmith, if you please."

"Hem! he is not transacting business at the present moment."

"Is he at home, might I ask?" asked Sharpley, in mincing tones.

"He is."

"Ah, and will you say that a gentleman desires——"

"What name?"

"Er—"—Sharpley had not thought of this—"er—Master Smith. Here is a letter of introduction. I shall not detain Master Walker more than a few minutes."

The porter took the note, saying abruptly—

"Wait without."

And instantly he closed the door.

"The pig!" hissed Sharpley, grinding the stumps of what had been his teeth, I should like to get him into my hands."

In a brief space the porter returned.

"This way," he said; "follow me, and I will lead you to Master Walker."

Sharpley followed quickly enough, but as he again thought of whose clothes he was wearing, he felt rather shaky.

Through several passages and rooms he was led, until a small room on the first floor was reached.

It was one of the offices used by the goldsmith himself, and a room in which our hero sometimes transacted his share in the business.

By the fireplace stood the goldsmith. Sharpley bowed low, and his salutation was answered in a like manner by the goldsmith, who was a man in the habit of treating both depositor and lender with an equal amount of courtesy.

"Your name, sir?" he said, "is Smith?"

"At your service, sir," replied Sharpley, bowing.

"And you are the gentleman referred to in this letter from my esteemed and clever friend, Stephen Fantenoy!"

"The same, sir."

"Ten guineas, Master Smith are at your immediate service. I trust you left Master Fantenoy quite well?"

From this it was evident that if the goldsmith knew of the *fire*, he did not know at whose place it was.

"I am happy to say, sir," replied Sharpley, with all the effrontery in the world, "that I left him *perfectly* well."

"Good. 'Tis not a very great while since he was here, and I was sorry that he had business of importance to transact, for, I wanted him to join our party. A fine brain has Fantenoy, Master Smith."

"Er—yes—a very fine brain."

"If he is spared for a few more years he will be a great man, Master Smith."

"No doubt of it, your worship. Let us hope he will live many years."

And the scraggy villain cast his eyes up in a splendidly sanctimonious manner.

"Amen!" replied the goldsmith, who placing his hand beneath his doublet, drew forth a small leathern case.

This he opened and took out a key.

Sharpley's eyes, though appearing to be looking at nothing in particular, were, in reality, keenly watching the goldsmith's movements.

"I must go below for the money," said Master Walker, "for I have not so much with me. But I will not detain you long, Master Smith."

"Oh," replied Sharpley, "my time is of *no* importance. I am only too happy to await your pleasure."

The goldsmith retired, leaving "Mr. Smith" in possession of the room.

"Beneath his doublet," chuckled Sharpley; "well there can't be much difficulty about that, anyway."

Then he looked around the room in order to ascertain whether there was anything of value which he could conveniently carry away.

The goldsmith soon returned, bringing with him the ten guineas.

"There, my friend," said the benevolent old gentleman; "there are ten guineas, and much good may they do you."

"Sir, my thanks——"

"Don't speak of them, Master Smith. I am only too glad to be able to serve a friend of Stephen Fantenoy, to whom you will, if you please, convey my regards."

Sharpley bowed—and was escorted by the goldsmith to the shop.

The porter, not observing Master Walker, opened the door with a growl.

"Thou cursed scarecrow!" he muttered as Sharpley passed out. "May the foul fiends claim thy imfamous face —well, well, if he *has* a face. And yet, by the saints his face is wonderfully like —let me see—like—I have it—like that mysterious barber, Sharpley. Yes, yes, very much like. Hum!"

Crash went the door, and the porter resumed his seat in the massive chair, and soon dropped off to sleep.

IMPORTANT.—With next week's Number will be Given Away a Splendid Coloured Picture for binding with the work.

"'OH, FELIX! FLY, FLY! MASTER HAS BEEN MURDERED!' CRIED THE MAID."

Sharpley hurried back to his shop.

The fire which had consumed the offices of the *Morning Gazette* had quite burnt itself out. The ruins were left to smoke as they pleased, and the curious crowds had wended their way homewards.

Fleet Street and the surrounding neighbourhood was again buried in silence.

As Sharpley turned into Shoe-lane, the deep-toned bell of Old St. Paul's chimed the hour of twelve.

He found Captain White and his companions seated at the table, smoking and partaking of the contents of a bottle of brandy which one of them had been out and purchased.

"Oh," said White, "so you *have* returned? Why, we thought you had met with some accident. Hem! You have been long enough."

"I had to wait."

"For what?"

"While he got the money."

"Everything all right?"

"Everything."

"The old man was completely hoodwinked?"

"Completely."

"Good—very good!" cried White, dealing Sharpley such a stunning clap on the shoulder that he nearly went headlong into the fire-place. "You are cleverness and cunning rolled into one, Sharpley; and if that and your razor don't get you a living, then nothing will. So that's certain. Here take a nip."

And he handed Sharpley the very smallest drop of brandy.

This, however, was very acceptable.

"Now," said White, "the ten guineas?"

"Oh," replied Sharpley, opening his eyes in astonishment, "I thought they were for me."

"Oh, *did* you—eh?" answered White, mimicking the tone of his voice. "What do you take me for, Sharpley Sharp? Hand the coin here, or I will chop your fingers off! What we get will be equally divided."

Sharpley, with very bad grace, pulled out the money and placed it upon the table.

White gave him one guinea, each of his companions two, and kept the remainder for himself.

"I should have the most," he chuckled; "because I am the biggest, and because, having only one eye, I can't count correctly, and am therefore likely to make a mistake."

"On your own side," said Sharpley.

"Of course—not on yours. Now, Sharpley, you know the errand we are bent upon to-night?"

"I can guess."

"Good! Will you accompany us?"

"In these clothes?"

"Yes, in those. It will save you time in changing. Come; we are off to Alsatia first, to select the boys, then on to the goldsmith's. A better night could not have been found had we waited for months. And why? Because the goldsmith and everyone in the house will be tired out with their amusements, or whatever foolery they call it, and, consequently, will sleep soundly."

"But you have forgotten the porter," said Sharpley; "he is not to be despised. The big, burly pig! He treated me with utter contempt, though *why*, I——"

Captain White pointed to Sharpley's clothes in so significant a manner that the bravos burst into a roar of ironical laughter, which had the effect of greatly disconcerting the barber.

Sharpley having decided to accompany the villains, took down his keys from a nail, and shouted to his wife.

"Catch these," he said, flinging the keys up the stairs; "and if anybody comes, attend to them."

"Not I," was the answer. "Not I, you midnight prowler!"

Off went Captain White at a good pace, followed by the barber and the bravos.

Reaching "The Fountain of Life," he soon had Pearman at work, and in less than five minutes a number of notes written in cypher were dispatched to various parts of Alsatia.

The result was that in less than half an hour there were assembled in Captain White's "reception-room" about a score of the most desperate ruffians to be met with in all Whitefriars.

Horrible they looked, roused as they had been from their drunken sleep at short notice.

At first the majority of them appeared to be sullen and surly.

But when White, with much swaggering and pomposity, told them why they had been summoned, when, in fact, he unfolded the plot to them, and told them how much *he* (not Sharpley) had done towards carrying it to a proper termination, their sullen looks changed to looks of joy; a cheer of admiration at White's cleverness burst from their soddened lips, and their dull, bloodshot eyes gleamed with savage delight.

The next things seen to were the arms.

They proved to be all right.

Sharpley was provided with a long, terrible-looking dagger, for no amount of persuasion on the captain's side would make him put on a sword.

"The toothpicks," he said, "have such a knack of getting between my legs and throwing me down."

All were now in readiness for departure.

"Listen, all of you," said White. "The youth is to be slain, don't forget that. Kill him as you would kill a dog! But you are to spare the girl; injure her not on any account. *Master Melton* will settle with us as to her, if we can carry her off."

"And the goldsmith?" asked one of the villains.

"If it is necessary, kill him! A vast quantity of treasure must be in his vaults. and nothing must prevent us from getting at it. Now on!"

*   *   *   *

St. Paul's struck one.

Slowly and solemnly the sound floated over the City, now wrapped in slumber.

And slowly and silently descended the white snow, for another snowstorm had commenced, and appeared likely to last for some hours.

The striking of the hour of one was heard by no one in the goldsmith's residence but Felix Ferdinand.

All were in bed and asleep.

The porter below, who should have been wide-awake (for it was his duty to promenade the place every hour), was fast asleep in his chair.

The flickering light from a lantern, on a sideboard by his side, fell upon his face, and upon a pistol, a rattle, and other articles near him.

Felix was seated at his bedside, and his attitude was that of a person buried in profound thought.

And it is easy for our readers to guess what his thoughts were.

Captain White, with Pearman at his side, walked slowly up Fleet Street.

But they did not walk openly.

Their movements were such as might have been made by two men dogging another's footsteps—that is to say, they darted from house to house, pausing every now and then to ascertain whether all was right.

The deep recesses of the shop-doorways, and the immense balconies overhead, did much to conceal their extraordinary and eratic movements.

The score or more of Captain White's rascally companions came up in precisely the same way, Sharpley Sharp being somewhat in advance.

At last Captain White and Pearman reached the Bell Tavern, between Bell Yard and Temple Bar.

On one side of this tavern (closed at this hour) was a long low archway, called the "Passage of Apollo" (afterwards, and, we believe to this very day, called Apollo Court), and just the very spot for a dark deed to be committed.

At the side of the passage was a small moveable wooden house.

It was a watch-box, and was kept there at the expense of the Templars.

Within it were two watchmen, distinguished by wearing upon their arms a leaden badge, with the sign of a lamb and flag.

One was supposed to be promenading that part of Fleet Street, between the Temple entrance and the Bar, but the bitter coldness of the night had caused both of them to shut themselves in the box and get what warmth they could out of a miserable lantern.

With cautious footsteps, Captain White crept up to the box, stooped down, took hold of the little door or flap, banged it to, and fastened the catch.

"Ho!" shouted the men, starting to their feet, and no doubt thinking that some young gallants were playing the fool with them. "What are you doing? Open the door—open the door!"

And they violently shook the door.

"Silence!" hissed Captain White; "half-a-dozen pistols are levelled at the place where your heads are most likely to be, and if you attempt to get out, we shall fire."

A scream of terror escaped the watchmen's lips.

"What have we done?" cried one.

"Nothing."

"Well, why are we to be boxed up here and have half-a-dozen pistols levelled at our heads?"

"Silence!"

"What are you?"

"Silence, I say!"

"You infernal——"

"Silence, I tell you, for the last time!" said White, fiercely.

"Who are you that tell us to preserve silence? Who the——"

"I will tell you. Mark it! I am *Captain White!* So beware!"

A low cry of horror was the watchmen's reply.

"Oh," said one to the other, "we are to be murdered—no doubt of it."

"No harm shall befall you if you preserve silence," said Pearman.

"Now we've trapped the old men," said White. "The next difficulty to get over is the porter within the house"

Sharpley Sharp by this time had come up, and he overheard what White had said.

"Captain," said Sharpley, "let *me* reckon with him. I told you that he insulted me."

"So you did, Sharpley, and that is not to be tolerated, is it, by a gentleman of your sort?"

One by one the bravos crept up.

Two of them were ordered to stand by the watch-box.

"And," said White, loud enough to be heard by the unlucky wretches within the box, "if they cry out, or if you hear them moving, let them have four shots—that will effectually silence them. Where is Long Lock?"

"Here," whispered that lanky lump of humanity.

"Keep the men in hand and follow me."

Turning he gave some whispered directions to Pearman, who crossed the road with him.

Sharpley kept close to them, and the rest of the bravos, with Long Lock at their head, followed at a distance of ten paces.

When in front of the great door of the goldsmith's, Pearman suddenly threw himself on the ground, and then commenced moaning and whining like a person in great pain.

In the shadow of the house on the one side stood White, a drawn sword in his hand, on the other, Sharpley, the long gleaming dagger clutched nervously in his bony hand.

"I'll have my revenge on the porter?" he muttered. "He insulted me. I will not give him time to do it again!"

The effect of the Pearman's ruse was soon seen.

The sleeping porter opened his eyes, rubbed them, and listened.

"Someone met with an accident," he muttered; "serve him right for being abroad at such an hour. All *honest* men are in bed. But, nevertheless, the noise has awakened me, and that is something. I will soon move him on."

Taking the lantern in his hand, he undid the locks, bolts, and bars, and stepped over the threshold of the door.

"Ho," he said as he bent over the prostrate figure of Pearman; "ho, I say! Are you hurt? What ails thee, man, and why did you fall here?"

"Pick me up, friend," moaned Pearman; "I am hurt."

The porter placed the lantern at his side, stooped, and laid his hands on the shoulders of the fallen man.

Instantly Captain White motioned to Sharpley, who, gliding towards the porter, raised his long dagger on high. exerted all the strength he had in his skinny carcase, and brought it down fair in the middle of the man's back.

So fearful was the blow, that the blade was buried to the haft in the man's body, and could not be withdrawn by Sharpley.

The unfortunate porter drew himself nearly erect, his hands tightly clenched and beating the air.

For an instant his eyes seemed as if about to start from their sockets.

His lips opened, but the great cry he was about to give was stifled by a rush of blood from his mouth.

He staggered back as if with the intention of giving some alarm, but a dreadful blow on the back of his head from one of Captain White's lead-weighted pistols effectually prevented this.

The man dropped like an ox to the ground.

"Pull him in with you," whispered White.

All being in readiness, Captain White, turning his pistol and cocking it, and having his sword in his right hand, entered the house, being noiselessly followed by all the bravos, with the exception of the two guarding the watch-house.

The ponderous door was then cautiously closed; and so, for the first time since the foundation of the firm—two hundred years before the commencement of this history—the house of Walker held a parcel of the biggest and most desperate ruffians, who made London their hunting-ground, and Alsatia their home.

Several of them were provided with torches, but they had orders not to light them for the present.

The ghastly rays of the porter's lantern fell upon a score of eager, drink-besotted faces, and its rays were also reflected in the shining steel swords, and the bright muzzles of the pistols they held in their hands.

It was quite a study to look at those villains as the door was carefully closed.

Aye, it was indeed a study to watch the glitter of their eyes, the eager penetrating looks they directed in this and that spot, in the hopes of seeing something of value.

"Come here, you scarecrow!" whispered White to Sharpley; "place yourself in front, and take us the way the porter took *you*."

"No, I will not," answered Sharpley, drawing back.

"What are you afraid of?"

"Nothing, But I have already done *my* share in the business."

"You will have to do *more* or you will not take a share of what we get. Go on first."

"I tell you I won't. I——"

"Will not?"

"Hist!" said Long Lock. "I will go first. Delay is dangerous. Let Sharpley follow me with the lantern. He can tell me which way to go."

"Go on, then. Ah! What is that? *Stop it!*"

Pearman had crossed the threshold of the first doorway, and had touched the spring of a secret bell, which commenced to ring.

Lock saw it swaying, and pouncing upon it, he seized the clapper, and so stopped its clamour of alarm.

But the ringing of that bell had been heard by one person.

And that person was Felix Ferdinand.

Only too well he had been instructed in the use of that bell.

The spring, a small knob, was let into the threshold, and when trod upon, caused the bell above to ring.

Of course, those unacquainted with the position of it would certainly tread upon the spot.

It was taken away in the daytime, being placed there only when all within the house had retired.

Felix, still sitting at his bedside, started up as if shot.

A cold perspiration broke out all over him.

"The *alarm-bell*, as I live," he muttered. "Yes, there it is—once—twice—thrice. Ah, it has been stopped! Great Heaven! what can have happened? Something, or that bell would never ring."

He listened intently.

But he heard nothing more.

The entire house seemed buried in profound silence.

He crept to an office next to his bedroom—the one above the room in which Sharpley saw the goldsmith, and which looked out upon Fleet Street—and noiselessly opening the window, looked into the street.

He saw nothing.

He looked across at the watch-box, and saw two men standing by it.

Of course, he took these men to be the watchmen.

"Nothing can have happened in front," he muttered, "or the watchmen would not be at their box. Can the porter have trod on the bell by accident? Hardly. Well, I *must* see that all is safe, for I could not rest in that bed unless I knew what caused the bell to ring."

From the mantelpiece he reached down his sword, and buckled it upon him.

Then opening a drawer he took out a pair of pistols.

These he cocked and placed in his sword-belt.

Having thus prepared himself against surprise, he took off his shoes, and without a light, went out upon the landing.

On the landing below slept the goldsmith, his wife, and the beautiful Rosamund.

In the meantime Captain White and his comrades, with Lock at their head, and Sharpley at his side with the lantern, crept up the stairs.

The staircases at the residence of the goldsmith were constructed in a very different manner to what staircases are made at the present day.

Where the modern builder sets up a staircase which could almost be blown away by a puff of wind, and which are nearly always minus half their supports, the builder at the period of which we write, made the staircases as strong and as firm as any other part of the house.

Consequently, as Captain White and his men crept upstairs, not a solitary creak was heard from any part of the staircase.

Round and round went the vagabonds, and at last, near the first landing, a halt was made.

And then it was that the rays of the lantern fell upon the face of Long Lock.

Felix, who saw this, was for a moment or so almost paralysed.

It seemed *impossible* that these villains could so easily have obtained admittance.

"Almighty powers!" gasped Felix, clasping his hands fervently together, "what is to be done? If that lantern and my eyes deceive me not, there are at least a score of the bravos on the staircase. Their object? Ha! *Twofold!* Yes, I see it. To rob the vaults and to effect my capture, or, perchance, to kill me. And will I allow them to rob and plunder undisturbed? No!—by Heaven, no! not if the whole tribe of Alsatians were here this moment!"

Drawing one of his pistols from his belt, Felix with a calm and steady hand covered Long Lock, who, unconscious of danger, was listening to the whispered directions of Captain White.

"Another step," muttered Felix through his clenched teeth, "and a ball shall end the scoundrel's career; and unless they turn and fly, so, also, will my career be ended this night, for I could not contend against such long odds. Still, ere I fell, I should have the satisfaction of knowing that I alarmed the household."

On again went Long Lock.

But his foot had scarcely touched the next stair ere a sudden blaze of light was seen, a thundering report rang out, and Long Lock, with an ear-piercing scream of mortal agony, leaped high in the air, bounded forward, and fell, with a ball in his brain.

"Thunder and lightning!" yelled White, starting back; "we have been watched after all."

"I know you, Captain White!" cried Felix, "and let me tell you that no mercy will be shown you."

Again came a flash and a stunning report.

But White had thought another shot was to be fired, and he dropped on his knees one-twentieth part of a second ere the report rang out.

The result of the shot was that it splintered to atoms a little wooden figure fixed on the banisters, and within a tenth part of an inch of the captain's head.

At the same moment the door of the goldsmith's room was flung open, and Master Walker and his wife, in their nightdresses, made their appearance.

The door of Rosamund's chamber, too, was pulled open, and Rosamund's maid, Alice (who slept with her young and lovely mistress), peered from it.

"What is this?" gasped the goldsmith in excited, horror-stricken tones; "what is this? what is the——"

"We are attacked by the bravos!" cried Felix. "Master Walker, close your door while I give the alarm."

"No, no, Felix, I implore! My child—my child—is she safe? Oh, Heaven, shield my child!"

The goldsmith clasped his hands together and wrung them excitedly.

"Be calm," cried Felix; "your child is safe at present, yet——"

"It is the cub who escaped from us, sure enough," muttered Captain White, as he arose. "Look you," he said to the goldsmith, "I will tell you the truth. We did come to rob the house, but if you will hand over to us that cursed youth who has just shot one of my best men dead, I swear that we will go quietly away."

"Never!" cried Master Walker. "This is not the first time he has defended me and mine, and from *you*—whom I recognise as the notorious Captain White—and I will defend *him* while I have life ! "

"Oh, you will, will you ? " sneered White ; " well, then let me——"

"Ah," cried the goldsmith, who at this instant caught sight of the rascally face of Sharpley, " I see it all now ! I see it all ! "

Turning to his wife, who stood at the back of him wildly wringing her hands, he whispered—

" Margaret, go by the secret staircase round to the front, open the door, and cry aloud for help. Fear not—pause not an instant ! Think of Rosamund."

Mistress Walker did *not* hesitate.

Wheeling aside a cabinet, she pulled open a small door let into the wall, and passed through it ; first, however, taking a lamp in her hand.

The door communicated with a narrow staircase leading to one of the reception-rooms, thence to the front door of the mansion.

She traversed this narrow passage rapidly—so rapidly, indeed, that the light she carried was blown wildly about, and once or twice it nearly went out.

The front was reached at last.

On towards the great doors rushed Mistress Margaret, but suddenly she nearly fell to the floor.

Some large object at her feet had stayed her further progress, and holding down the light, she saw the body of the unfortunate porter.

Truly, it was a great wonder a loud scream of terror had not escaped her lips, but she checked the cry by biting her lips until the blood seemed about to start forth.

With hasty fingers she unfastened the door, and then, indeed, a wild scream escaped her.

"Help ! " she shrieked ; "help ! In the name of Heaven come to our assistance ! "

Across the road rushed two men.

Mistress Walker, naturally enough, took them to be the two Temple watchmen.

Alas ! how grievously mistaken she was.

" What's the matter ? " asked one.

"Thieves are in the house," cried Mistress Walker, excitedly—"the Bravos of Alsatia——"

" Are *here* ! " growled one of the men, who, suddenly raising his pistol, brought down the heavy butt-end on the head of the goldsmith's wife, who, poor lady ! could only utter the names of her beloved husband and daughter, ere she sank senseless and bleeding on the threshold of the door.

"That settles *her* ! " said the villain, "and now let us join the others."

In the meantime there had been a brief pause upstairs.

Captain White knew well enough that the goldsmith had given his wife some directions for making an alarm, and when he saw her retire into the room he guessed that there was a secret passage somewhere in it.

As he thought of what would happen did the two bullies he had left below cross the road to her, a fiendish grin spread o'er his ugly features.

" Don't think of turning back," said Pearman ; "think—only think what it would be to turn back—loss of all the treasure, and a chance of some of us being captured. Let us make a bold dash for it."

" All right," said Sharpley in a hoarse trembling whisper (the wretch was afraid a ball might end his career with the same rapidity as it did Lock's). "And since you have suggested that we make a bold dash, do you go first."

" Listen ! " cried Felix ; " listen to me, Captain White—listen to me, thou leader of a host of accursed bloodhounds. Withdraw at once from this house—withdraw ! "

" When I have you in my power ! " replied White, gnashing his teeth with rage.

One of the bravos behind the captain had, quite unperceived by Felix, or indeed, anyone else, drawn a pistol.

He took aim at Felix, whose figure could now be indistinctly seen, and fired.

Truly, another quarter of an inch and our hero would have been stricken dead. The ball crashed into a part of the woodwork, splintering it.

White took advantage of the smoke caused by the shot.

"Follow ! " he roared.

With this he dashed upon the goldsmith, Sharpley holding the lantern.

Captain White seized the goldsmith by the throat with one hand, while he struck him about the head with the butt-end of his pistol.

These blows, however, did not kill the noble goldsmith, but he fell to the ground, and Sharpley plunged his dagger into the heart of the brave old man, who died with the name of his daughter on his lips.

Hearing the cries of her unfortunate father, Rosamund, in defiance of the earnest entreaties of her maid, rushed from her apartment and into the very arms of Pearman, who, at once clutching her with a firm grip, chuckled—

"Soh, my pretty maid! Soh, my angelic creature! I have you at last."

"Release me, monster!" cried Rosamund, frantically struggling to free herself.

But her struggles were useless—Pearman soon had the assistance of one or two men, and in less time than it takes to write, Rosamund was gagged and bound.

Down the stairs, sword in hand, ran Felix, and without hesitation he attacked the man nearest him, for now, without cutting his way through them, he could not hope to reach Captain White.

But the bravos had now quite regained their confidence, and Felix found half-a-dozen weapons opposed to his.

"Oh, Felix!" cried the maid, "fly—fly. Master has been murdered, and Mistress Rosamund has been captured—there she is—there—there—they are passing her down the stairs!"

"Dear unfortunate girl!" cried Felix, as with one sudden and slashing blow he sent one of the wretches to the ground to rise no more. "I fear I cannot rescue her now."

"Fly, Felix," repeated the maid, as she saw Felix's opponents being joined by others; "fly; if at another time you would save Mistress Rosamund—fly!"

Felix saw that the advice was good; it was utterly impossible to cope single-handed as he was with such a number of desperate ruffians, who were now determined not to leave the house without plunder and killing him, if possible.

While Captain White and Sharpley were rifling the bedroom of the unlucky goldsmith, the former continued to shout to his men to "cut the boy down."

Suddenly Felix, drawing a pistol from his belt, hurled it with all the force he could muster at the man in front of him.

Then he turned, and the maid holding open the door of her apartment, he dashed through it to the window, and pulled open the shutters.

He was not followed.

The men paid no heed to what Captain White had said.

They did not want to *fight*, they wanted *plunder*, therefore they did not attempt to force the door.

Felix saw that just below the parapet was a long and narrow ledge. It was covered with a thick layer of crisp white snow.

"Leave the door, Alice, to itself," said Felix; "have you locked it?"

"I have. Oh, my poor young mistress!"

"Console yourself with the reflection, Alice, that as soon as it is possible I will do all I can to effect her rescue. I would ere this have attempted to drag her from the arms of these infamous wretches, only I knew that to attempt such a thing was only to court certain death. Listen to me, Alice—you have said that good Master Walker is murdered."

"Yes, yes—he is—he is? Oh, I am sure of it, for I saw the man with the patch over his eye strike him so hard, again and again, that his head was terribly battered, and then another man at his side stabbed him."

"Great Heaven!" ejaculated Felix with a shudder, "is it possible!"

"Oh, yes—yes," said the maid, now bursting into tears.

"Captain White is the man with the patch over his eye," said Felix, and he added solemnly: "I swear to avenge the death of poor Master Walker! A day of reckoning shall surely come, Captain White—a day of reckoning between you and I! Alice, where is Mistress Walker?"

"Heaven only knows!" was the agonised reply.

"Well, 'tis useless to waste time. These men, besides seeking the goldsmith's treasure, are seeking my life, and if they catch you, Alice, *your* life would not be worth one moment's purchase, for if they put you to death, as undoubtedly they would, another witness of what has transpired would be placed beyond the power of giving evidence against them. You must attempt to escape with me, Alice."

"How—oh, how?"

"This is the only way."

And Felix pointed to the snow-covered ridge, which shone out of the blackness of the night like the silver lining in a black cloud.

Alice shuddered as she looked at the ledge.

"I feel that I can never attempt it," she said. "I am a woman—you a man nearly—no, no! I should become giddy —fall—and be dashed to pieces. Besides, my presence would only hinder you."

"Nay, nay, talk not so! You *must* come with me, Alice. I insist upon it. Never, under any consideration, would I leave you here. Do you know where the ledge leads to?"

"I do not. It is of great length. I have often looked at it. But my impression is that it leads to somewhere in the Temple."

"Well, where it leads must be a matter of indifference to us. Anywhere is safer than is this house at present. Oh, if I could run along that ridge and at once summon assistance!"

"Even then you would be too late. Hark! the villains have distributed themselves all over the house."

"Come, Alice. Listen to me; I will get outside on to the ledge. Then do you take this piece of link"—and Felix lit a piece of link—"creep cautiously out, get on to the ridge, and hold me firmly. We shall have to go like snails, but by the blessing of Heaven we may reach some place of shelter in safety."

"I will hesitate no longer," said Alice, "for after all I would rather a thousand times fall over that projection than into the hands of those villains."

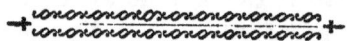

CHAPTER VII.

INTRODUCES MASTER FILLIPY FALLORY, AND SHOWS HOW HE TOOK FELIX AND ALICE UNDER HIS PROTECTION.

OUR hero got carefully out of the window, and then on to the ledge.

He was now enabled to look over, and, so far as he could make out, for he could just see the faint glitter of the snow on the ground below—so far as he could make out, we say—the distance down appeared to be very great.

At any rate he saw that if either of them made one false movement and fell, it was almost a certainty that they would be dashed to atoms.

Felix trembled as he thought that if Alice's courage gave way she might loose her hold and fall, or, if she found herself slipping, she might, in her terror, clutch him, and drag him over.

But Alice appeared to be quite brave and steady, as she prepared to follow Felix's directions.

Her hands trembled not at all as she raised her dress, and clambered out of the window.

Her face, however, was deathly pale, and Felix's keen eyes detected a slight quiver of her lips, as she whispered—

"I come—I come!"

"Quick, then," said Felix, "for if those bloodthirsty wretches observe us from any of the windows, they will not hesitate to send a few bullets at us."

Alice handed the link to Felix, who was now upon his hands and knees on the ridge, and then she got out.

Our hero then handed her the link, and again imploring her to keep firm and steady, he set off.

At a snail's pace they went, as our readers may easily guess, for every moment Felix had to pause and brush away the snow which impeded his progress.

Alice remained firm, and Felix loudly praised her courage.

But the ledge—the ledge!

Verily it seemed as if there was no end to it.

There were yards and yards of it, not a bit of it being perfectly straight, but all of a serpentine form.

At last, after ten minutes had been passed on this terribly dangerous spot, a dim light appeared at no great distance.

Felix halted, and watched it.

It flitted from spot to spot for a few minutes, and then was stationary.

"In what house can that be?" said Felix.

"Alas, I know not," replied Alice.

"You are cold, Alice?"

"Terribly cold. My limbs are becoming quite numbed."

"And mine. Let us go forward, for——"

He paused abruptly, for from the spot where shone the light, came the sound of a person singing the chorus of a drinking song.

The tones were low and somewhat harsh; but nevertheless it was evident that the singer was in a merry mood.

The sound put fresh courage into Felix and poor Alice, and on again they went.

In a few moments they reached the small window of an attic.

The blind was drawn up, and looking into the apartment Felix saw seated before a small but bright fire the figure of a young man.

That he was tall and thin could be seen at glance.

He had stretched his lanky legs on either side of the fireplace; a pipe—then a rare "luxury"—was stuck in his mouth, and a measure of steaming spirits was on the mantelpiece before him.

It seemed to Felix as if this young man had just returned home, and had prepared to enjoy himself before retiring.

When the last notes of the chorus had died away, and while the young man was placing the spirits to his lips, Felix tapped on the window-pane.

Instantly the occupant of the room started up, nearly choking himself with hot spirits, and cried out—

"Ho! *Ho!* I say! Who's there? Speak up, for I am nervous. Ho! I say, who dares to knock at my window-panes? Ha! I will see!"

With this he replaced his glass on the mantelpiece, advanced to a corner of the room, and brought out a rapier.

But this he immediately flung from him in disgust.

"Not long enough," he muttered.

From another corner he brought out a sword.

A rusty blade it was, of about five feet in length, and with a weight of iron at the hilt.

Having poised this in his hand to his satisfaction, he advanced to the window.

"Now knock again!" he shouted. "I say, knock again! And by all the—— Eh?"—here his voice sank into a whisper and his sword to the ground—"eh? What is this I see before me? Two faces peering at me in this my miserable garret near the sky. Oh, they are the faces of the long, long past. I'll see. They *may* be *spirits*—if so, they are certainly not *hot.*"

Raising his hand, he drew back the catch, and as the little window flew open, he stepped back a few paces, and again raising his sword cried—

"I say, who are you?"

"Good sir," interrupted Felix, "I pray you lower your blade. We are no man's enemies."

"Eh? But in the name of all the blessed saints, how came you in this position, and at this hour of the morning? Gracious goodness! A female with you! Is it possible!"

The sword dropped from the young man's hand, and his somewhat large eyes opened to their fullest extent in wonder.

"Are you *aware*," he cried—"I say, young sir, are you *aware* that the slightest oscillation on your or your companion's part might bring you both to the ground."

"I am only too well aware of it."

"This is no doubt a love affair. Well, young sir, I sympathise with you, for I have been in love myself. Ah, yes!" and the singular young man placed his long thin fingers on his heart; "but if you will take the advice of an experienced love-maker like myself, why then, I say, make love while the sun shines, and not while snow is descending, and icicles hang from the roof. Well, I bid you adieu, and——".

"Sir," pleaded Felix, "I entreat you to give us shelter—if only for an hour. This, I can assure you, is no love-affair."

"No."

"No—something terrible has occurred. We, sir, are escaping from the clutches of the Bravos of Alsatia."

"Indeed? From the bravos? Well,

well, come along, young sir, and you, madam. Let the lady come first—soh! Gently—fall into my arms, lady. That is right. Now—jump—ha! There you are."

And taking the almost frozen Alice in his arms, he lifted her through the window, and placed her near the fire.

Then he assisted Felix through, and re-closed the window.

"Well," he said, "this is indeed an adventure. You have, you say——"

Felix pointed to Alice.

Poor girl! What she had gone through had been too much for her; though all through she had maintained her self-possession, the knowledge that at last she was safe had been too much for her.

Her head had fallen forward on her lap, and she was now quite unconscious.

Felix's limbs were so numbed that he felt he could not raise a finger to assist her.

The occupant of the attic bounded forward, seized his glass of hot spirits, threw himself on his knees, and while with one hand he raised the drooping head, with the other he placed the steaming liquor to Alice's lips.

"Drink, my girl," he said in really tender tones, "drink—'twill do you good, I swear. 'Tis the very best that —I was about to say that money would buy—but that would be a falsehood. Drink! Ah, she is quite insensible."

"Pray force some between her lips," said Felix.

This the young man, after some difficulty, succeeded in doing.

The effect of the liquor—brandy-punch—on Alice was wonderful.

After a few wild gasps and many bitter sighs, she somewhat recovered.

"This is a serious affair, sir," said Felix. "We are from the gold-smith's——"

"What from Master Walker?"

"Aye, sir, from Master Walker."

"I know him right well; he——"

"You will never again behold him," said Felix, in broken tones.

"What? Great Heaven! What do you mean? Speak, I pray you."

"I will tell you all in a moment, sir —but—oh, if this poor girl could only be placed in the hands of some kind woman who would attend to her."

"Wait—wait!" interrupted the young man. "I know of such a person—the housekeeper here, but, of course, she is in bed. Whether she will take kindly to being awakened I know not."

"Will you allow me to ask where we are?" said Felix.

"Certainly. You don't know? Strange! Why, my good young sir, you are in no less a place than Pump Court, Temple, and you are at this very moment in the rooms and in the presence of no less a person than Master Fillipy Fallory, of whom, doubtless, you have heard."

"I have not before had the honour, sir."

"Hem! Strange! Well, sir, I am —— But the young lady—the young lady."

And the singular young man was off out of the room like a shot.

Felix could hear him descending the stairs two or three at a time.

"Alice," said Felix; "Alice!"

"Yes, yes."

"How do you feel?"

"Bad—so very bad about my heart, Felix; 'tis breaking—oh, 'tis breaking! My poor young mistress, what will become of her?"

"Mine be the task to rescue her! And rescue her from the clutches of these monsters I will—aye, though it cost me my life!" said Felix.

"Aye, you are the one that *should* rescue her, Felix, for she loves you so dearly."

"Ha!" said Felix, eagerly; "has she said so?"

"She has said as much. And you, Felix—you love her?"

"With all my heart and soul!" cried Felix, fervently. "And therefore—— But hist!—I hear voices; no doubt attention and a good bed will be yours, Alice. Look, here are ten guineas; take them—no—hesitate not an instant, nothing can be done without money."

"But you, Felix—you require as much attention as do I."

"Leave me to myself. Probably I can make some arrangements with this young man."

Another moment and Master Fillipy Fallory entered the room, followed by a stout elderly woman.

"'WHAT IS THAT ABOUT HER NECK?' CRIED THE JEW. —(See No. 7).

The look on the woman's face was not a pleasant one.

"Dame Clattap—*Clap-trap* we call her," said Master Fillipy, "a most estimable person when you don't offend her, and to whom I have the honour to be indebted in a small sum, for the cleansing of my etceteras. Dame Clattap, I have told you how I admitted these unfortunate persons, and——"

"Ah," interrupted dame Clattap sharply, as she placed her brawny hands on her enormous hips, and looked hard at Alice; "ah, unfortunate, and so am I, to be dragged out of my warm bed on such a night as this. But that is the worst of being housekeeper where there is a host of single young gentlemen. There——"

"Madam," interrupted Felix, "if you have a spark of feeling about you, I implore you to provide this young woman with a bed and a little attention. She does not expect you to do it for nothing; she is provided with money, and will pay you what you may demand."

The words "provided with money" made a great impression on Dame Clattap.

The severe expression in her eyes changed now to one of pleasure.

"Heigho, young sir!" she said, "of course I have a spark of feeling about me. I am, I am proud to say, a most charitable woman, to the which Master Fallory can testify. Of *course* I will provide the young woman with attention. The money, let me tell you, is a *secondary* consideration."

"Hem!" said Master Fillipy, "I am proud to hear that money *is* a secondary consideration to you, Dame Clattap, for it relieves my mind of the anxiety I was beginning to feel about the little bill I have the honour to owe you."

Dame Clattap answered him with a look only—it was a look which said—

"I will settle with you anon."

Raising Alice, she escorted her to the door.

Then Alice turned.

"I shall see you in a few hours, Felix?" she asked.

"I think not, Alice," replied Felix, "for I must set about my task. You know to what I refer. But I will not fail to let you know how affairs prosper, and if I effect the rescue of your unfortunate young mistress, be assured that you shall be the first person summoned to her side."

"I implore you to spare a little time in finding out what has become of her mother."

"I will do so Alice; and now farewell."

"Farewell. Heaven be with you!"

"And with you."

And the door closed on Dame Clattap and Alice.

No sooner had they gone, than Master Fillipy pulled open a cupboard-door at his side, took out a large black bottle, and stood it on the table.

"There," he said, "this is for us. I will make it steaming hot, young sir. By the way, you have not told me your name."

"Felix Ferdinand."

"Ha, Felix Bird-in-hand! a very——"

"*Ferdinand*!" said Felix emphatically.

"I beg your pardon—Ferdinand. And a very nice name it is, too. Far better than mine, which I told you is Fillipy Fallory. Yet, despite my name, I am, though perhaps you wouldn't believe it, a most successful courtier."

"Indeed?"

"Yes. Here in these chambers, here in this Temple, sir, I am simply Master Fillipy Fallory, the law-student—some have the impudence to call me the '*lanky* law-student,' but as I am of a forgiving nature, I pass it over. Here, drink this; 'twill warm the cockles of your heart, which I should say are almost, if not quite, covered with icicles."

And he handed a glass of steaming spirits to Felix, who took it with many heartfelt thanks.

Master Fillipy then dragged a huge arm-chair to the fireplace for him, and told him to make himself comfortable.

Then he looked about for some wood to replenish the fire, but not finding any he deliberately placed a heavy oak stool on the fire, with the remark that he could get another below by-and-by.

Then he seated himself by the side of Felix and resumed the pipe, in the enjoyment of which our hero had, as our readers will remember, interrupted him.

Felix then told him all that had occurred.

Master Fallory was nearly petrified with amazement and horror.

"And all this," he said, " has occurred within a stone's-throw of the Temple, where reside the most determined enemies of the bravos! It is certainly extraordinary. I am no longer surprised at the news I heard to-night."

"What was that?"

"That the bravos have been quieter to-night than they have been for months. This, of course, accounts for it. Young man—Felix—you love the daughter?"

"I do."

"Hem! Well, that is not to be wondered at. I have had the pleasure of seeing her, and can say she is one of the most lovely girls I ever came across, In fact, she is *the* Pearl of the City. To you, then, Master Felix, remains the task of avenging the goldsmith's death, and rescuing the daughter."

"And both I will undertake."

"Of course. But let me assure you you will find it far from an easy task; yet, if I mistake not, the Templars would be ready and willing to assist you. They know the goldsmith, for that gentleman has, at various times, transacted a great deal of business with them. Directly morning dawns, I will lay the facts before them. I suppose you do not know the amount of property the goldsmith had on the premises?"

"Nay, but it was a large amount."

"Who knows, then?—we may secure a portion of it. Captain White is sure to have all plunder taken to his place in Alsatia; there, I believe it remains for a week or so, after which it is divided."

"You may depend upon it," said Feilx, "that if I see an opportunity of recovering a part of the property I shall do so for the sake of the unfortunate daughter."

"And now," said Master Fallory, rising, "here you will observe," and he pushed open a small door at the back of him—"ycu will observe that this is a small room—not much larger than a rat-trap, in fact, but nevertheless there is a bed—such as it is—in there, and it is at your service."

"You are indeed kindness itself," answered Felix; "but I cannot accept——"

"Pshaw! no ceremony, young sir—no ceremony. The bed, I say, such as it is—for that villainous Mother Clap-trap never properly makes it—is at your service, and I wish that you use it. As for me, why, bless your heart! I can sleep here as soundly as an over-fed dog. Here, take the lamp and retire; I will call you as soon—well, as soon as I awake."

"Well, since you insist, I will thankfully accept your offer; though I feel certain I shall find it impossible to sleep, I may, at least, rest my weary limbs."

"Aye, true. Well, a good-morning to you. Fear nothing, for while I am here, and this good sword is by my side " and he laid the monstrous blade by the fireplace—"no one can disturb you."

Felix retired, and Master Fallory, having drank up the remainder of his spirits, secured the door of the chamber.

The position of the sword not suiting him, he stuck the point of it between the boards, and so the rusty weapon stood bolt upright.

Then he sat in his chair, crossed his lanky legs in an easy manner, folded his arms, and in a few seconds he was sleeping as soundly as a child.

CHAPTER VIII.

LORD STRETTON AND "MASTER MELTON"—THE LETTER TO MASTER MELTON FROM CAPTAIN WHITE—HOW MASTER MELTON DISPATCHES A MESSENGER IN ANSWER TO IT, AND WHAT HAPPENED TO HIM IN ALSATIA.

BEFORE the hour of ten on the following day, all London was ringing with the news of the foul murder of the goldsmith, Master Walker.

The murder appeared all the more horrible from the fact that the goldsmith was so highly respected, and was such a benevolent man.

Besides that, there was his beautiful daughter to be considered.

What had become of her?

No one could guess, for up to the hour of ten nothing had been heard of Felix.

Then, too, what had become of Mistress Walker, the goldsmith's wife?

That was soon made known.

She was in the house of the Countess of Rothburn, and how she got there was in the following manner:

The two watchmen at length ventured to shout for assistance.

At last, however, a link-boy happened to pass near the box, and hearing the shouts of the men within, he opened the trap.

Then the men were enabled to get out.

The first thing they did was to rush across the road to the goldsmith's.

A terrible sight met their eyes.

Near the threshold lay the insensible figure of Mistress Walker, and not far from her the lifeless body of the faithful porter.

So terrified were the men that they touched neither Mistress Walker nor the porter.

With wild ear-piercing cries they rushed from the house, and commenced to hammer at the doors of the surrounding premises.

Before long a number of neighbours, only partially dressed, hurried to the goldsmith's.

The upper part of Fleet Street was instantaneously converted into a place of lamentation.

Men shouted for vengeance; women fell upon their knees; but above all other cries the ominous one of "The bravos! The bravos!" was the plainest heard.

One woman taking the initiative, others joined her, and poor Mistress Walker was tenderly raised from the ground.

Water was fetched, her temples bathed, her face washed, her matted hair placed gently back, and brandy poured between her bleeding lips.

Oh, what a terrible sight this unfortunate creature presented!

The effect of the brandy was to cause her to open her eyes, and the vacant stare with which she surveyed those around her caused many a strong man to burst into tears.

While the women were getting her round, a man, attired in a shabby suit, wearing a rough wig, and whose face was as pale as the face of the goldsmith's wife, pushed his way through the throng.

This man was no less a person than the unlucky footman to the Countess of Rothburn.

In Fetter Lane, at the house of a friend, he had been ever since his experiences in "Filthy Alsatia," and only this very morning he had set off to the Willows, the countess's residence.

As he came along he had heard what had happened, and knowing the connection between the goldsmith and his mistress, he had resolved to see what he could do in the matter.

"Poor lady!" he said. "And this, too, they say is the work of the bravos! Oh, friends, pray—pray earnestly all of you—that the king's idea of sanctuary be changed, and that he sends his troops to root out this vile crew from the heart of the City of London!"

"We will—we will!" was the emphatic cry.

"Listen to me, friends," continued the footman; "I am one of the principal servants of the Countess of Rothburn, who is a great friend of the goldsmith's. I would take this poor lady to her, for you may rest assured that at the countess's house she will receive every attention."

"A most happy suggestion," said a neighbour. "In my yard is a litter. I will fetch it, and Mistress Walker can be placed within it. There are plenty of us willing to assist in carrying her."

So a litter was procured, and Mistress Walker placed within it.

Four sturdy neighbours seized the handles, and, led by the footmen, they carried it to the house of the Countess of Rothburn, and by that noble lady Mistress Walker was received, and physicians summoned.

Thus it was that Mistress Walker came to be at the countess's house.

Our readers will now be pleased to accompany us to another great mansion.

This is to the residence of the haughty, proud, and, we may add, insolvent nobleman, Lord Stretton—Stretton House, Pall Mall.

It is not necessary to describe either the interior or exterior of this grand house; it is sufficient if we say that it was as grand as the majority of aristocratic houses of the period of which we write.

It was a perfect wilderness of a place, and a place seldom disturbed by the presence of company.

A large number of servants, male and female, were employed at the establishment, and the only persons they had to wait upon were Lord Stretton and his son Horace.

A more gloomy brooding specimen of humanity never existed than Lord Stretton.

Married to an estimable lady many years previous to the opening of this romance, he had had one child by her—this son Horace—after they had been married over six years.

The marriage was one of convenience —that is to say, Lord Stretton's wife was the daughter of a wealthy merchant who had saved and saved all through his life, on purpose to marry his daughter to a lord.

His daughter should have a title — that was all he troubled about.

This wealthy man by some means or other got introduced to Lord Stretton, who at that time was certainly as poor as any church mouse.

They got into conversation ; the merchant advanced Stretton money— Stretton did not repay it, but borrowed more, and when he owed a large sum, the merchant boldly proposed that he should lead his daughter to the altar.

"And," he said, "I will settle upon her the sum of one hundred thousand pounds. And in the event of her death the money will be divided between you and any children of the marriage."

Lord Stretton jumped at the offer as eagerly as a hungry hound would jump at a bone.

He was at once introduced to the daughter, who, he was delighted to find, was not the ugly female he expected, but a very beautiful and, for her position, highly accomplished young lady.

The unfortunate merchant's daughter loved and was beloved by the worthy son of a worthy London citizen. The merchant knew it, but when he had Stretton ready and willing to lead his daughter to the altar, he laughed at what he was pleased to term his daughter's idiotic folly, and declared that he would curse and disown her if she did not conform to his wishes.

In the end the marriage took place, and from the first hour the pair mutually disliked each other.

Seldom did they meet in any of the rooms of the gigantic mansion in Pall Mall.

If they did meet they passed each other with a cold formal bow.

This was the result of a marriage *a la mode.*

Lord Stretton was nearly always absent from home.

The hundred thousand pounds settled upon his wife, he handled, and handled pretty freely too.

But by-and-by a word dropped here and a word dropped there, caused him to become suspicious of his wife.

Though he loved her not, and he knew she did not care one straw for him, he was, nevertheless, jealous that she should be spoken tenderly to by any man, and least of all by the citizen we have spoken of.

This young man was welcomed by the unfortunate victim of a father's craze— the Lady Stretton—welcomed with open arms.

Love between them had undoubtedly been effectually stifled, but warm staunch friendship had taken the place of love.

The upright honest young citizen pitied Lady Stretton from the bottom of his heart, though in her presence he tried, for her sake, to put on a cheerful countenance ; yet, when alone, he shed bitter tears over this poor beautiful flower, so slowly but surely withering away in the prime of her womanhood.

This young citizen's visits became frequent and yet more frequent, and the news was carried to Lord Stretton by his servants and by others.

Stretton, naturally of a jealous disposition, flew into a fearful rage.

He sought his wife's chamber, and then and there, before her maid, he dared his wife ever to allow such a " low, base-born scoundrel " to darken the doors of his house.

But he found that, though hope was dead within that gentle breast, that though despair was gradually usurping its place, her spirit had not quite deserted her.

Never did Stretton forget the look on

his wife's lovely face as she drew herself erect, fixed her flashing eyes upon his, and threw back, with majestic scorn, the insults he had heaped upon her.

She defied him to prove his charges.

"And," she added, standing up before him and clenching her white hands until the nails were imbedded in the flesh, "remember that though *sold* to you, I am not yet your *slave*. You may be *master* here, but by Heaven, I am *mistress*, and mistress will I remain until the quiet grave I have so long wished for shuts me out from you and the world! Remember, my lord, that this house is as much mine as it is yours, having been purchased with my father's money. I shall invite whom I please, and I *dare* you to stay me."

Stretton found that his wife's words were not idle.

She *did* invite whom she pleased, and the principal visitor was the young citizen.

He had not heard of the quarrel between Stretton and his wife, and therefore he continued to come and go, having no fear, having no suspicion that he was walking blindly to his fate, having no suspicion that a pitfall was being prepared for him—a pitfall into which he would certainly stumble.

But so it was. One night, two hours after his visit to Lady Stretton, he was found in Birdcage Walk, St. James's Park, quite dead, a dagger being buried to the hilt in the brave sympathising young heart.

Oh, it was a cruel crime!

But who was the assassin?

Oh, he was not far to seek.

The brand of Cain was upon Stretton's brow.

If the public did not see it, Lady Stretton did.

Directly she saw her husband after the awful news reached her, she pointed her trembling finger at him, and in low tones—tones which sank deep into his guilty soul—she said—

"*You*, Stretton, *are his murderer!* Yea, 'tis so, for I see 'guilty' plainly written on your face. Oh, my lord, what a deed—what a deed!" she said in agonised tones; "but it will recoil upon yourself, it will recoil *upon your child*. In a few short hours I shall give birth to your child—and it *is* your child, I take

Heaven to witness that!—and I pray God that that child is a boy. He will be your punishment, he will be your anxiety, your sorrow. I shall never live to leave the room where your child is born! *You*, Stretton, have broken my heart! *you* have made me the wretched, wretched woman I am now! *you*, Stretton, have caused me to long to be laid in the cold ground! *you*, I say, have blasted my young life, and not content with that, you have brutally murdered the only friend I could trust in the wide world."

Stretton essayed to reply, but the poor young lady tottered to her room, heeding not his cry of, "Come back, Esther, come back, I beg of you."

It was the last time he saw her alive.

She gave birth to a boy within twenty-four hours.

She lingered on for four days, when she died.

Her father had been ailing for some time, and he, strangely enough, survived the daughter he had sold by one day only.

Father and daughter were buried side by side.

The merchant's will was afterwards read, and it was found that he had left all his immense wealth to his daughter, or in the event of her death to her husband.

So, at one stroke, Stretton got rid of his wife and inherited an enormous fortune.

Within a month of his wife's death he set himself to work to endeavour to win the beautiful Lady Portsdown, whom he had long worshipped.

But he found the task hopeless, for Lady Portsdown loved and was beloved by the Earl of Rothburn, who very soon led Lady Portsdown to the altar.

Stretton's jealousy did not cease here.

He pursued Rothburn like a shadow.

His revenge was slow but sure.

Soon after the birth of the first-born —a son—it was stolen from the house, and about a month after that, the earl was found murdered in one of the card-rooms at Clivedon House in St. James's Street.

By whose hand he had fallen was not known, though guessed at.

Stretton, by many persons, was strongly suspected of the foul deed, but nothing could be brought against him.

Murders were not investigated in such a thorough manner at that time as they are, fortunately, at the present day.

The murder of the noble, generous, and faithful courtier, of the kind and loving husband—the Earl of Rothburn—was a mystery, and truly it seemed as though it would ever remain a mystery.

Soon after the murder of the earl, Lord Stretton disappeared in a strange manner, but it was only for a short period.

He soon turned up again, and with all his old audacity again offered his hand to the forlorn and almost heart-broken countess, who, however, treated his advances with the supreme scorn and contempt they merited.

And so years passed.

Lady Stretton's curse brought its fruits undoubtedly.

If ever men were cursed, then those men were Lord Stretton and his son Horace.

Nothing they did came right, except it was villainy—that alone seemed to prosper with them.

With all sorts of abandoned, God-forsaken people they mixed themselves up, and they were very frequently the guiding stars of the villains with whom our readers are already acquainted — *The Bravos of Alsatia.*

Among them young Stretton was known as "Master Melton," and our readers will remember that we have, more than once, mentioned the name.

Master Melton was reckless, daring, and profligate.

Not a particle of his angelic mother's gentle spirit pervaded *his* body; on the contrary, he had inherited all his father's cunning and cruelty, and he had no more respect for a man's life than he would have for a dog's.

Such was Master Melton, one of the most important characters in this our romance.

*   *   *   *   *

Lord Stretton and his son were seated before a blazing fire in his lordship's library.

My lord's head rested upon his hand, and his eyes were fixed upon the blazing wood on the huge hearth.

Horace, however, was *not* in a thoughtful mood.

Beside his chair lay two ponderous and ugly-looking bloodhounds, their heads resting upon their forepaws.

Now and then Lord Stretton, without moving his head, directed a piercing glance at his son, either for the purpose of watching the ever-changing expression upon his cunning countenance, or to ascertain whether he was about to make any effort to break the silence which, for such a long time, had remained unbroken.

At last he said, in tones which had anything but a pleased ring in them—

"You appear to have an enormous amount to think about."

"I have," smiled Horace; "and you, my lord, also appear to have an enormous amount to think of. So, too, do the dogs, for you observe——"

"Silence, for Heaven's sake, silence ! When will you cease to talk nonsense ? We have a host of most important things to think of—things which will occupy all the time we——"

"You say *we*," interrupted Horace.

"Aye, *we*. Important things concerning *me* should be deemed important by *you*."

"Hem ! No doubt. But you see, your lordship, I have, for so many years, devoted such a large amount of time to your affairs, that——"

"It is false !" interrupted Lord Stretton, knitting his brows fiercely together ; "all your time has, and is, devoted to the disgraceful pursuit of pleasure, for which I have to pay—and heavily, too."

"Well, you have not much to complain of. What has *your* time been devoted to ? The *pursuit of a shadow*—ha, ha !"

"Laugh at me again, Horace," said Lord Stretton, in cold, determined tones, "laugh at me again, I say, and I will blow your brains out. I *will*, so help me Heaven !"

So ominous and imperious were these words that even the very hounds raised their sleepy heads and looked at the speaker.

Horace smiled, but the smile was a sickly one.

"You would not dare to reach one of those pistols from the wall," he said.

"Would I not—eh ? And why ?"

"My hounds are too well trained."

"What do you mean ?"

"That they would prevent you from

reaching a pistol, did I but give the word."

"Great Heaven!" cried Stretton, "and do you mean to sit there and say that you would set your hounds at *me?*"

"Certainly, if you offered violence to me."

"And yet I am your *father!*" gasped Stretton.

"Aye, and yet I am your *son*," sneered Horace; "and I have as much right to threaten you with certain death as you have to threaten *me*."

And he thereupon rose.

"Resume your seat," said Stretton; "I have something important to say."

"Good; pray proceed," said Horace, again seating himself.

"The remark you made just now — that is to say, that I was pursuing a shadow—had reference to the Countess of Rothburn?"

Horace nodded.

"Hem! Well, on second thoughts, the definition is happily put. It has really been the pursuit of a shadow for years—oh, *accursed* fate!—for years and years!"

"Why accursed fate? Why wish to *bind* yourself to a woman? Bah!"

"But," resumed Stretton, without noticing his son's expression of disgust, "the pursuit of the shadow is ended."

"What?" cried Horace, joyfully.

"I have said it is ended. Yes; all is over between us. At last my eyes are opened, and I see how hopeless it is for me to ever again solicit her hand."

"Why this change, my lord? Why this sudden change. Have her rebukes been of a more emphatic character lately? For that she always *has* rebuked you you have indirectly admitted."

Stretton slowly shook his head.

"Well," said Horace, "has—— Ah! I can guess—you have a rival."

Stretton nodded.

"A *successful* rival!"

Again Stretton nodded.

May I ask his name, for of course at present I am hopelessly in the dark?"

"Lord Clinton," answered Stretton, in deep, low tones, as though it wrung his very heart—if he had one—to utter the name.

Horace, for some few seconds, looked hard at his father.

He was wondering whether he had really heard aright.

"Lord Clinton?" he said. "Clinton the grand—Clinton the handsome—Clinton the graceful—Clinton the royal favourite—Clinton the——"

"Silence!" roared Stretton; "silence, if you would not drive me insane."

"I must express my feelings. I am so intensely surprised. And yet, when I come to think of it, I need not be so."

"Have you ever seen anything between them?"

"I have watched them meet on more than one occasion, my lord—that is all."

"Well, what did you remark?"

"I remarked how different was her greeting of Clinton to you. When the countess and you have suddenly met, the look on the beautiful countess's face was one of—what shall I say? I know so little of women—ho, ho!—well, it was a look of hatred, terror, scorn, and defiance combined. Was it not so?"

"How the deuce should *I* know? But go on."

"When she met Clinton, her face wore an expression of welcome and pleasure. It was a look——"

"Enough—enough! Listen. Henceforth Clinton and I are deadly enemies."

"Naturally," was Horace's calm reply.

"And the Countess of Rothburn will find me a terrible foe."

"No doubt. I would not spare her. By Heaven, father, I would make her suffer!"

"Aye, I shall—I shall; fear it not."

"How did you get to know this?"

"I came upon the pair suddenly."

"In her own house?"

"Aye, in her own house."

"Oh, I see—your terrible wound, about which you would not tell me. You, my lord, quarrelled with Clinton?"

"I did."

"And fought?"

"Yes."

"Where?"

"In the countess's library."

"Good gracious! Well, you have to thank your lucky stars that you are here alive at this moment. Clinton, as many persons with whom I am acquainted are able to testify, is a most expert swordsman. If I had to deal with him—— Ha, ha!"

Here Horace laughed immoderately.

"Yes, yes. Had you to deal with him?"

"I should come on him *from behind*. Ha, ha! Ho, ho!"

"Ah, you were always a coward, I am sorry to say, Horace."

"Sometimes it is safer to meet a swordsman *behind* than in front. Besides, I never care to exhibit my skill as a swordsman before a lot of people."

"Probably because you have no skill to exhibit. Well, I have said that Clinton and I are deadly enemies."

"You have."

"What follows?"

"Oh, simple enough. Clinton dies!"

"Certainly."

"*Suddenly?*"

"No! I say *no!* A thousand times no! Think you that his sudden death would satisfy my revengful feelings? No!"

"What would you, then? If you hate a man and you wish for his death, I should think that the sooner the affair is finished the better."

"Not so fast. This is what I intend to have done. Clinton shall be seized and conveyed to Vauxhall—White assisting us. He shall be confined there until we can bring the countess to witness his punishment. Or we might capture them together."

"What will be the punishment?"

"Death—but by torture?"

"You would gloat over his agony?"

"I would; and I would witness the agony of the Countess of Rothburn, for she shall be a witness of the torture he shall surely undergo."

"Hem! a horrible idea, but worthy of you. Ha, ha! I suppose that you would not risk another fight with him?"

"It would give me no satisfaction."

"Then you, of course, wish me to assist you in effecting the capture of Clinton?"

"Assist *me*? No. You will effect his capture yourself."

"You will remain entirely in the background?"

"Yes, entirely," said Stretton.

"And am I to be assisted by the bravos only?"

"Certainly. By all the fiends! who else would you have? You will find the bravos quite sufficient for your purpose. I could suggest no one so suitable as Captain White and his crew. You are

well known to all of them, and they obey you blindly."

"Yes, that is true; but why do they obey me? Because I am free with my money!"

"Pardon me! *my* money!"

"Ha, ha! Well, well—yours. And that reminds me that I am at this present moment in great need of money."

"A week ago you received a large sum from me—a sum sufficient to last even an extravagant man a month. What have you done with it?"

"Lost it," replied Horace.

"In what way?"

"Dice!"

"Ha! Well, let me assure you that I have not the remotest intention of supplying you with money to satisfy your gambling debts. This evening if you come to me I will give you a sum of money, but it will be a far smaller amount than the last."

"Thank you!"

"To-night, I shall have finally arranged everything for Clinton's capture."

"Which shall be effected as speedily as possible."

"Yes, it must be quickly carried out."

"Of course the particulars of the recovery of the countess's necklace have reached you."

"I have heard a great deal," replied Stretton, "but can arrive at nothing definite."

"Fancy a youth like this goldsmith's boy——"

"Master Walker has no son."

"I mean his assistant."

"Yes; go on."

"I say, fancy him—— But you, of course, heard about him being set upon by the bravos, who captured and took him to Alsatia."

Stretton shook his head.

Whether Horace believed his father knew nothing about the adventures of our hero or not, we do not know.

However, he proceeded to give him a very fair account of the extraordinary adventures of our hero and the necklace.

"And the name of this clever youth?" asked Stretton, unconcernedly.

"Let me see—er—*Felix Ferdinand.*"

"What!" shouted Stretton, starting from his chair white and trembling;

"do I hear aright ? Repeat the name—quick ! "

"Wait a moment—wait a moment," drawled Horace, daintily waving his ruffled-bedecked jewelled hand ; "if you go on like that I shall begin to think you are mad. Besides, these sudden jumps and howls make me feel nervous, and my hounds——"

"Confound your hounds ! " raved Stretton. "I say, repeat the name."

"Felix Ferdinand."

"Felix Ferdinand ! " gasped Stretton ; "it is the same—it *must* be the same."

And he paced the apartment with rapid strides.

Horace watched him for a few seconds, a disdainful smile on his face.

At last he, too, arose.

"When you have done tramping about, my lord," he said, "perhaps you will be good enough to tell me why it is that the name—Felix Ferdinand—has affected you to this great extent."

"Yes, I will tell you," replied Stretton, turning swiftly, "for I intend to take you more into my confidence than ever."

"Thank you," said Horace, with just the ghost of a sneer.

"Know, then," continued Stretton, hoarsely, "that *Felix Ferdinand is the son—the lawful son of the Countess of Rothburn.*"

Horace expressed no surprise.

"You mean the stolen infant ? "

"I do."

"That you said was lost after the death of the man you appointed his guardian."

"Yes."

"Pooh ! You do not know it is the same."

"There is hardly a doubt about it. I found that he started to London to seek his fortune."

"Or his death. Ha, ha ! Well, if it *is* the same he is by this time dead."

"What do you mean ? " cried Stretton, seizing his son by the arm and looking fiercely into his face.

"The bravos attacked the goldsmith's house not so many hours ago."

"Go on."

"I am at this very moment expecting a letter from Captain White, who promised to give me particulars."

"What interest have you in this matter ? "

"The goldsmith's daughter."

"Ha, villain ! you will disgrace me yet. I will go off to the blackguard White and get him to——"

At this moment a knock came upon the door, and, the footman entering, handed a heavily-sealed letter to Horace.

It was addressed—

"MASTER MELTON.
"(*Private Communication*),
"C.W.C.I.C."

These letters signified — "Captain White, Commander-in-Chief."

The handwriting was heavy and laboured, and looked as if it had been written with a poker or a whitewash-brush.

"Is that the expected communication ? " asked Stretton.

"It is," replied Horace, proceeding to break the seal.

"Who brought this ? " asked Stretton of the footman.

"A man, your lordship—a quiet-looking sort of——"

"It is Pearman," whispered Horace.

"Show the man in here," said his lordship.

The footman bowed and withdrew.

Horace spread out the "letter."

"Shall I read it aloud ? " he said.

"If it pleases you so to do."

"Here it is—

"'HONOURED SIR,—All entirely successful at the *House*. Got a large booty. Compelled, in self-defence, to destroy the porter and the goldsmith. All others except the girl escaped. Several of ours killed, others maimed. We have the girl safe enough, and she is yours directly the sum agreed upon is paid. Will give fuller particulars when I have the honour to see you. Please send *your messenger* to calm the girl.—Ever your humble servant,

"THE CAPTAIN.'"

"A very precious document, certainly," said Stretton. "And who does he mean by 'your messenger'? "

"My valet, Clipton."

"What can he do to calm the girl ? "

"Oh, he has his own methods. One of them is to dress himself up as a woman."

"Well ? "

"Then he can assume a woman's voice."

"Hum! He has acted for you before?"

"Many times."

"Successfully?"

"Entirely."

"Ah, he will find that the goldsmith's daughter is not to be imposed upon. Her father killed? By Heaven, unless I am mistaken, it will now go hard with the Alsatians, for the goldsmith was an especial favourite of King James!"

"That they must chance. As you are aware, they well know how to take care of themselves. But here is Pearman."

Pearman walked into the room, in what he intended to be a slow and impressive manner.

But it would not do.

He was the worse for the enormous quantity of intoxicating liquors he had consumed, and his gait was "rickety."

"Well, you intoxicated beast," said Stretton with unmistakable disgust, "and so you are the bearer of this letter?"

"From my honoured chief."

"You scoundrel!" cried Stretton; "do not try to thrust your foolery down *my* throat?"

"I am dumb!"

"It would be a good job if you were."

"Especially for you."

"Eh?"

"I could not then tell what——"

"Silence!" interrupted Horace; "his lordship is not in a very good temper to-day. Silence, you fool, or by Heaven, I will set my hounds on you, and have you torn limb from limb."

Pearman drew back with a start.

"Now listen. I have read this letter, and I am very pleased that the girl is awaiting my pleasure," said Horace.

"*Beautiful* creature!" ejaculated Pearman.

"What?"

"*Sweet* creature!" grined the ruffian.

His mincing tones made Stretton's blood boil.

"Tell the captain," said Horace, "that I will at once dispatch my messenger."

"Can he return with me?"

"Let me see—yes, he shall return with you."

"Good! excellent! A fine fellow is Clipton, and wonderfully clever. He will console her. Ha, ha!"

"And tell Captain White that I shall see him to-night."

"Good! I shall not forget, never fear."

"And—whisper this—his lordship will accompany me."

Pearman opened wide his eyes in astonishment, but he made no reply.

Turning to Horace, he said—

"And the money?"

"That I will bring with me."

"Good—good! Everything is very satisfactory."

"How did the goldsmith come by his death?" asked Stretton.

"Pardon me, I don't understand."

"You hypocrite! Who killed him?"

"I didn't."

"Who *did?*"

"Well, you see, Captain White used his butts, and Sharpley—know Sharpley, your lordship?" he leered.

"I have heard of the wretch?"

"Estimable man — *Sharp* man!—well, he used his dagger."

Murderer as we have seen Stretton really was, he fairly shuddered at the cool way the man spoke.

"Enough," he said huskily; "enough! And now what amount of property did you take?"

"Don't know."

"What!—you don't know?"

"Well, I don't choose to *tell* you. Perhaps that answer will suit your lordship much better than the other. I don't ask your lordship how much property *you* have plundered."

Stretton gnashed his teeth with rage.

"After all," said Horace, "that matter does not concern either of us; and as for the girl—well, she concerns *me* only."

With this he rang a silver bell by the fire-place.

The footman appeared, and was directed to tell Clipton he was wanted.

This individual—Horace's valet—soon made his appearance.

He was a man of about fifty years of age, tall and thin, and very effeminate in appearance.

His face bore not the slightest sign of hair, which on his head was very long, dark, and wavy.

On entering the apartment he bowed, and slyly winked at Pearman.

"'SAFE! HEAVEN BE THANKED FOR THIS!' CRIED ABLISS."——(See No. 8).

"You are wanted, Clipton," said Horace.

Clipton bowed.

"You will attire yourself in the satin dress and etceteras."

Again Clipton bowed.

"And you will then accompany this person to Alsatia. Understand?"

"Perfectly," replied Clipton.

"Do you feel competent?"

"Your worship may see at a glance that I am in good condition."

This reply was spoken in an entirely different voice.

The change was certainly remarkable, for the tones were now as clear, as sweet, and as musical as a woman's.

"Good," said Horace. "Now all you have to do is to keep away from the drink. Only then can you perform the task. You are to go through the *usual* ceremony—say that I am a noble lord who has taken a fancy to her, and intend to marry her, and,—and, so forth."

Clipton grinned and bowed.

"Very pretty, I must say," said Stretton, sardonically; "wonderfully edifying, and very amusing, Horace."

"My lord!"

"You have dared to give these, your vile instructions, before *me*—your *father*."

"Well, my lord—and the reason? Did you not say but a short time ago that you were about to let me more into your confidence? Soh! I cannot but return this great compliment—consequently, my lord, I do you the honour to let *you* into *my* confidence."

"Heaven help him if you did!" muttered the valet.

Stretton turned impatiently away, and Horace, waving his hand, said—

"Go—and remember!"

The valet, nudging Pearman, turned and left the room.

Pearman, with much "*hem*-ing," and "*ah*-ing," ceremoniously gathered his cloak about him.

Then he bowed curiously, and waving his hat fan-wise, with more "*hem*-ing" and "*ah*-ing," bowed himself with extraordinary rapidity to the door.

But, not turning to see where he was going, he bumped against the door-post with such violence that he was pitched forward on to his face.

The hounds, with a low growl, instantly darted upon him, and probably they would have left the marks of their teeth on him, had not Horace called them off.

"Pick yourself up," said Horace, "and be off. As I live, I believe you get a bigger fool every day."

Pearman was about to deliver himself of a short speech, but the hounds frightened him.

Turning swiftly, he left the apartment without a word.

"My lord," said Horace, "to-night!"

"Aye, to-night."

"Till then, adieu."

And waving his frilled hand the aristocratic, cunning, brutal, and profligate young scamp called to his hounds, and strode from the room.

Stretton, with a deep groan, turned and looked blankly into the fire.

* * * *

Clipton, the valet, was undoubtedly a clever man—or, perhaps, we shall be more correct if we say he was a clever scoundrel.

He spoke several languages, was a versatile mimic, and when he liked had a very superior address.

At the period of which we write, stage-plays were rapidly finding favour with everyone, and the beauties of Shakespeare's works were beginning to be appreciated.

So Clipton, had he chosen, could, with all his extraordinary and singular talents —the female parts in various plays at that time being performed by men—have been very successful on the stage.

The few managers there were, would have snapped him up very quickly.

But Clipton's talents were counterbalanced by drink.

He was never so happy as when in a state of partial intoxication.

Then he made an idiot of himself, and frequently got into serious troubles—troubles which his master, with all his cunning, had great difficulty in extricating him from.

Pearman accompanied Clipton to his chamber.

There the valet in a very short time attired himself as a lady—putting on everything a lady usually wears, including a pair of satin shoes.

All the articles were of an expensive make, especially the dress, which was a really handsome satin one.

During the—to Pearman—highly interesting and amusing ceremony of fitting himself out, Clipton was regaled with brandy from Pearman's flask.

All being finished, the pair left the house by a back way, and with all the effrontery and assurance in the world proceeded to Westminster Stairs to take a boat to Alsatia.

Clipton looked a really fine woman.

The haughty curl he gave to his lips when anyone eyed him too closely was a source of infinite diversion to Pearman.

Clipton, in his anxiety for drink, forgot a most important fact—that is to say, that well-dressed ladies were not in the habit of frequenting houses of refreshment.

So as often as Pearman asked him to drink, as often was the invitation accepted.

Under these circumstances our readers will readily believe that long before Westminster Stairs were reached, Clipton and Pearman were pretty well "gone."

Nevertheless, Clipton walked steadily, yet his movements were often impeded by his companion, who persisted in bumping his portly person against him.

Almost every person turned and looked at the couple.

What their thoughts were we hardly know, but perhaps they were well expressed by their peals of laughter.

The laughing, grinning, and remarks of the passers-by had its effect on Clipton at last.

At the top of Westminster Stairs two gentlemen—court gallants evidently—were standing.

As Clipton and Pearman approached, one said—

"Look at this drunken man! This is one of our national disgraces."

"Aye," replied the other, staring hard at Clipton; "and the woman is as bad, and so well attired too!"

Instantly Clipton turned, and raising his hand he dealt the gentleman such a stunning smack on the face that he was sent spinning down the long flight of stairs.

"How *dare* you insult a respectable lady!" shrieked Clipton in feminine tones; "how *dare* you, I say!"

A crowd soon collected, and on Clipton telling the people that the gentleman had called him (her, of course) a drunkard, the crowd threatened them with violence, and the two rash courtiers turned and fled, the one who had been knocked down the stairs having the front of his rich dress spoiled by the blood which was rushing from his nose and mouth.

In the meantime Pearman had secured a boat, in which he seated himself.

The waterman assisted "the lady" in, and soon they reached the Temple Stairs.

* * * *

We must now return to the unfortunate heroine of our romance—Rosamund Walker.

Our readers will, of course, remember that she was caught in the arms of Pearman, who soon had several of the rascally Alsatians to his assistance.

She was thereupon passed down the stairs, gagged and bound, covered with an enormous piece of baize, which was torn down from its position over a doorway, and borne away by two of the bravos.

By Pearman's instructions—and his word, in some things, was considered as good as Captain White's—she was at once conveyed to the residence of Mercutio Merrywell, who was known as "the Miser of Sword Alley."

Mercutio was a Polish Jew—though he never actually admitted it—and at the time of our story was about eighty years of age.

He was short and thin—nothing, in fact, but a "bag o' bones," and he was invariably clothed in nothing but a mass of filthy rags.

He looked considerably shorter than he really was, owing to the fact that age had bent his back in the shape of a bow.

His little eyes were sunk far back in their sockets, but, nevertheless, they were still sharp and penetrating, and capable of expressing anger or pleasure.

The most remarkable thing about Mercutio Merrywell was his hair and beard.

Both were of a snowy whiteness, and of enormous—some might say ridiculous—length.

His hair and beard served one purpose, at any rate, and that was to show off the shrivelled parchment-like nature of his face, which never looked so repulsive as when agitated by the mention of the—to him—magic name of "Money!"

Mercutio's residence was situated at the back of "The Fountain of Life."

It was in the corner of a small yard, and looked as if it had been *thrown* there with a "Here, get out of it!"

To look at the dilapidated miserable-looking habitation, one might think that the interior was very small.

But it was not so.

The rooms, especially those *under ground*, were large though not lofty.

Like many other rooms we have had the honour to introduce to the reader, it abounded with trap-doors, false fireplaces, secret staircases, and so on.

There was no doubt about the fact that Mercutio Merrywell was a miser.

His actions alone showed that.

The old villain was possessed of sufficient money to buy up the whole of "Filthy Alsatia," had the vile den or dens ever been offered for sale.

Where he *kept* his money, however, was a profound mystery.

It was a secret locked in his own skinny breast—a secret which could not have been wrung from him.

His only companion was his daughter, a maiden of some fifty years of age, named Parthena, a person whose ugliness could not have been matched in London.

Yet this dear and virtuous creature still cherished the hope of being one day led to the altar.

Parthena had, like other females, her likes and dislikes.

The principal thing she *liked* was a bony cat, the friend of her loneliness; the principal thing she *dis*liked was *beautiful women*.

And it was in the hands of Parthena that Rosamund was first placed.

All was profoundly dark when the bravos reached the Jew's residence with their lovely and insensible burden, but a light burned dimly in the topmost garret.

This light showed that the Jew was awake and—so the bravos thought—amusing himself by counting some of his hoarded gold.

The bravos rapped on the door, and their rapping was instantaneously answered by, first, a shrill whistle, which seemed to proceed from the bowels of the earth, and secondly, by a loud clanking, as if a number of chains had been dropped.

At the same moment the light in the garret disappeared.

In another few seconds a squeaky voice said—

"Who is there?"

"Friends, old parchment!" was the reply.

"Ee, friends! Ee—dessay! But all right, I can hear who it is."

Several chains, bolts, and bars were removed—for Mercutio would not trust an Alsatian if it were to save his life—and the door was drawn slowly back.

On the threshold appeared Mercutio, and behind him, holding aloft a smoky oil-lamp, was his daughter.

"Ah, what have you there?" asked the miser, starting back. "A dead body? If so, let me tell you this is no charnel-house."

"Silence!" cried one of the bravos, sternly; "let us enter with our burden."

"Nay, nay, not till you tell me what it is. Not till——"

"It is a lady, then!"

"A lady?" said Parthena, pressing forward, "a lady?—of rank?"

"Of rank!" mimicked the bravo; "how should we know whether she is of rank? She is the goldsmith's daughter!"

"What goldsmith?"

"Master Walker, of Temple Bar."

"My gracious!" almost shrieked Parthena. "Rosamund Walker *here?* Impossible!"

"'Tis not impossible, you infernal fool!" cried the bravo, impatiently. "This *is* Master Walker's daughter, I tell you, and——"

"Who told you to bring her here?"

"Pearman."

"Ha!" said Mercutio, at once guessing the expedition of the bravos this night. "Ha! I see—I see; and the goldsmith?"

"Dead."

"Murdered," said Parthena.

"I never said *murdered*," said the bravo, sharply; "I said *dead*, and how he came by his death—at whose hands, and so on, is nothing to do with you, ugly Parthena, or you, old parchment;

so just do as you are told, or it will be the worse for you."

"Yes, let us do as we are told, my dear," whined the Jew as he took the lamp from his daughter's hand; "let us do as we are told, by all means. We are but the humble servants of——"

"Shut up your mouth, will you!" roared the bravo. "Here, Parthena, you dear creature!—ho, ho!—er—show us to your chamber, will you? There we will deposit our precious burden. She will be claimed before many hours are over her head."

"By whom?"

"Would you like to know?"

"Much," replied Parthena, eagerly.

"Ha, no doubt. Well, you see we don't know for certain, but we can guess for whom she is taken."

"Go on."

"Master Melton."

As the bravo uttered this name the miser almost jumped from the floor.

"Ah," he said, "you must be mistaken. He is mistaken, Parthena; isn't he, my dear?"

"How should I know? I have heard Master Melton, as he is called here, express his intense admiration for the goldsmith's daughter more than once, and so have you."

"Ah, perhaps I have—perhaps I have; but my memory is so bad."

"Especially where money is concerned, you withered-up old villain," cried one of the men, as he roughly pushed the Jew aside.

"If Master Melton intends to adopt the goldsmith's daughter," said Parthena, "he will want more money."

"Will he?" shrieked Mercutio, "will he? By all the incarnate fiends he shall not have one oat—not one oat!"

"We shall see," muttered Parthena, as she led the way up the rickety stairs.

Mercutio stood at the door until the bravos descended and took their departure.

When they had gone, he saw to the door, and ascended to his daughter's chamber.

He found Parthena standing by the bedside.

She had taken a lamp from the table and raised it aloft so that its sickly rays fell upon the pale, but beautiful features of Rosamund Walker who lay upon the bed.

Beautiful, we said.

Ah, words cannot express how lovely, how angelic she looked!

So quiet and still did she lie, that verily one might have taken her to be dead.

Yet a close inspection would have revealed the fact that her bosom rose and fell, though irregularly.

The expression upon the hideous face of Parthena Merrywell was savage in the extreme.

Her teeth were firmly set—she seemed to be breathing a curse upon the lovely creature before her.

"Well," growled Mercutio impatiently, "what are you staring at?"

"*Her!*" replied Parthena, pointing her bony finger at the insensible girl.

"What for—what good will that do you?"

"What for? I am comparing *her* beauty with *my* face and figure!"

"He, he! Ho, ho!" screamed the Jew; "a nice comparison, my dear—excellent!"

"Why should she be so beautiful and I so ugly?" continued Parthena bitterly.

"Goodness knows—it's fate—*fate!*"

"You are so ugly—my mother was so ugly."

"Likely—likely! You have said the same thing a million times. But look here, my dear, my money balances my ugliness."

"Confound your money and *you!*"

"And *you*, you vixen!" screamed Mercutio; "confound *you*, I say. But Parthena!"

"Aye, what is it?"

"Will you listen to me?"

"I generally do as you bid me."

"Yes, yes; so you do—so you do. You are a good *girl*, a *very* good girl, and some day you will get your reward. Well, now, get the girl round first. I wonder if she has got any money about her?"

"Since she has no dress on, I should say 'tis hardly likely she can have money."

"Well, what is that about her neck?"

"A gold chain."

"Take it off—take it off and hand it to me, my dear; it will pay for a drop of brandy for her. Give it to me, quick ? "

Parthena quickly took from Rosamund's neck a gold chain, to which was attached a cross, also of that worshipped metal, gold.

These articles Parthena handed to her father, whose tallons seized upon them with the eagerness of a vulture descending on its prey.

" Nice gold ! " he chuckled, as he held the glittering articles near his wicked eyes. " And now, my dear, the brandy. 'Tis in my bedroom ; lift up the flap of the window, my dear."

Parthena departed to procure the brandy, while Mercutio, approaching the bed, looked at Rosamund's wrists and ears, in the hopes of finding either bracelets or earrings.

But he was disappointed, and he gave vent to his disappointment.

Oh, a shockingly depraved old wretch was Mercutio Merrywell !

Tottering on the verge of the grave as he was, he yet had not a single thought as to how near he was to that day when he would have to answer for the terrible deeds he had committed, and for the vile oaths he was constantly uttering. Neither did he have a thought as to the probable manner in which he would die.

For years he had lived among these blood-thirsty Alsatians, lending them money, and taking the interest.

On her return with the brandy, Parthena poured out a glassful, and while her father held Rosamund's head up, she forced some between her lips.

The effect of the powerful spirit was soon apparent.

Again the glass was placed to her lips and emptied.

With a low gasping cry, and a violent struggle for breath, Rosamund recovered from the trance-like state in which, for so long a time, she had remained.

" Where am I ? " she asked, turning her beautiful large eyes on Parthena.

As Rosamund looked upon the grim ugly face of the miser's daughter, a shudder passed through her frame.

" I know her not," she thought ; " who can she be ? And that old man with the long white hair ? "

" Are you better ? " whined Mercutio in tones which he meant to be very

soothing, but which, in reality, meant, " Now then, no more of this nonsense ! "

" I am better," muttered Rosamund, struggling hard to collect her scattered thoughts ; " yes, yes, I am getting better. Oh, Heaven, I remember—I remember ! My father—murdered ; my mother—where is she ? Felix—Alice— oh, where are they ? Say, old man, where am I ? "

Mercutio slowly shook his head.

His hands toyed restlessly with the chain and the cross.

Rosamund caught sight of them, felt her neck, then saw that the articles in the miser's hand were hers.

" I must be in the hands of thieves ! " she thought, " in some vile den, perhaps. I repeat," she said aloud, " where am I ? Will *you* tell me ? " she asked Parthena, in sweet, silvery, pleading tones.

In striking contrast to her voice was Parthena's, as she answered :

" That is our business, not *yours !* "

The words fell upon Rosamund's ears like the hiss of a serpent—they fell upon her innocent heart like a bar of heated iron.

" Not *my* business ? " replied Rosamund ; " not *my* business ? It *is* my business," she cried, leaping up. " Old man "—and here she leapt from the bed to the floor in her excitement, not to say terror ; " old man, tell me where I am ? "

Again Mercutio shook his head.

" Oh, Heaven ! " groaned Rosamund, placing her hand upon her wildly beating heart ; " why this mystery ? *Why* —but for some evil purpose ? Oh, old man, you—*you* would not injure me—*you* could have no interest in that. Oh, tell me the truth—the truth. Do not lie to me—for remember, old man, your days are numbered, and you may be suddenly called away to answer for the falsehoods you might tell me.

" Oh, look, look ! " she cried, in tones which would have wrung the very heart of an ordinary man, as she threw herself at the miser's feet ; " look, old man, —on my knees I beg, I entreat you to tell me where I am ! "

But Mercutio spurned the beautiful girl with his half-clad foot.

" Away ! " he shrieked, in his high falsetto-like tones ; " away ! I will *not* tell you where you are. My days are numbered, you say ! " and here he stamped his foot wildly and savagely upon the floor; "thou liest! wretch—worm! My days are *not* numbered. I am to live—to live—until—until——"

He stopped, gasping for breath, but the rapid movements of his eyes, his mouth, and hands, showed the passions working within his breast.

Parthena pushed him into a rickety chair, and handed him the bottle, saying—

"Fool that you are, to take notice of a chit of a girl like this!"

Turning to Rosamund, she said—

"You are in a house from which you could not escape, even if you wished. You are, in fact, *trapped!*"

"Yes, yes," chuckled Mercutio; "trapped—that's it, my dear—trapped!"

"But in Heaven's name, how have I offended anyone that I should be treated like this? Oh, I should be pitied!" she cried, rising and bursting into tears, "for my father has been murdered and robbed by the Alsatians, and for aught I know my mother also may be dead."

"That concerns us not at all," said Parthena, coldly; "*we* had no hand in that matter. All we have to do is to obey orders——"

"Whose?"

"That is *our* business, not yours. You will, no doubt, remain in this trap until a better one—a gilded trap with plenty of servants to wait upon you—is provided for you."

Instantly Rosamund guessed what she meant.

She shuddered, but made no reply.

"I will still trust in Heaven," she thought; "God will never forsake me—no, no!"

During the day Rosamund was visited by Captain White and Pearman, after which the former wrote the letter, and, as we have seen, sent Pearman with it to Horace.

*　　*　　*　　*

The day wore on.

Rosamund had no means of telling how the time was passing.

Somewhere below, she could hear the slow measured tick, tick, of a clock, and now and then, the wind wafted to her ears the echoes of the deep-toned bells of the clock in the tower of Old St. Paul's.

The door of the apartment in which she was, was securely barred and bolted, and thick iron bars protected the window, which was painted a dull red, so that it was useless for her to attempt to find out what was below the window.

No sounds reached her ears, save the opening and shutting of heavy doors, the distant echo of a voice or the clanking of chains.

But suddenly a shrill whistle fell upon her ears.

So peculiar, so unearthly, and so near did its piercing shriek sound, that Rosamund started up in terror.

In a few moments a hasty footstep was heard on the stairs.

Then came another, and in less time than it takes to write, the room door was opened, and Parthena, in low surly tones, said—

"A lady of title to see you."

She then stepped aside, and in walked —the valet Clipton!

On arriving in Alsatia, he had to some extent "brushed himself up," and had partaken of a "pick-me-up," but that compound, whatever it was, had not had the desired effect.

His gait was decidedly unsteady, his face flushed, his eyes dull, and he did not gather up his skirts in anything like the manner befitting a lady.

Directly he had entered, Parthena closed the door with an impatient exclamation, and descended the stairs.

Thus the two were alone.

Despite the fact that Clipton was unsteady on his legs, consequent upon the enormous amount of liquids he had, in company with Pearman, partaken of, the falsetto in which he pitched his voice was undoubtedly perfection itself.

Rosamund surveyed her visitor with wonder, not unmixed with consternation.

Who was this tall, fashionably—nay, gaudily-attired creature?

"My brief stay in this place," she considered, "has at least taught me to be on my guard."

"Well, my dear," said Clipton—who gazed with admiration upon the beautiful figure before him, "and how are you by this time?"

"Madame," replied Rosamund, "I understand you not."

"I ask you, my dear, how you are. When you recovered consciousness, you were no doubt terrified to behold yourself in a strange place. I hope that feeling has now entirely left you?"

"You hope wrong—it has not left me. But who are you, madame?"

"I—er—my dear—why, I am a lady of title. I am sister to a noble lord, who——"

"Yes, yes, pray do not stop—proceed."

"Who has taken a great fancy to you."

Clipton received his answer in the shape of a scornful curve of Rosamund's lips.

"And," continued Clipton, "when you see him, you will, I am certain, take a great fancy to him."

"Ah! And was it this noble lord who authorised my father's murder?"

"Certainly not."

"Nor gave instructions that I should be brought to this horrid place—wherever it is?"

"Certainly not, my love. Perish the thought!"

"*Then how did he know I was here?*"

This was a poser for Clipton.

"I haven't the least idea," replied Clipton; "but let me assure you——"

"Stop!" cried Rosamund, sternly, as she drew herself erect, and fixed her flashing eyes upon this audacious fellow; "stop! You *lie!* Hear me—you *lie!* Great Heaven! what am I brought here for?" she gasped—"what for? Villain! you are a wolf in sheep's clothing. I have penetrated your disguise—you have indeed betrayed *yourself*, for you, a moment ago, used your *natural* voice and not the one you have had the audacity to *assume!* You are a man—and not a woman—a *man*, I say! And, oh, you are one of the *lowest* of your kind. The dastardly assassin is far higher in the social scale, *far* more entitled to respect than the villain who dons the attire of the opposite sex to deceive a poor girl. Go, coward, from from my sight—go!"

Clipton, to speak the truth, was considerably more than startled at this emphatic outburst.

In his state of semi-intoxication he had not noticed that he had made the mistake of changing his voice.

"It is all over," he thought; "I am fairly found out this time. But I will have my revenge. I will have one kiss before I go."

"Go!" repeated Rosamund, pointing to the door.

"One moment," replied Clipton, advancing. "I must admit that what you have just said is correct, but, believe me, your beauty is to blame for it. The noble lord I have spoken of is in love with you, and who could help being in love with you? Bestow upon me one kiss—one!"

Ere Rosamund could prevent him, he had thrown his arms around her.

To shriek for help Rosamund knew would be useless.

Unaided, she must attempt to baffle the monster.

Exerting all her strength, she flung Clipton off, and then, rushing to the table, snatched from off it the knife which had been supplied with the only meal she had that day partaken of—and scanty and poor enough it had been.

Holding it dagger-wise in her hand, she said in passionate, yet determined tones—

"Attempt to approach me again, and by Heaven you will make me forget my sex! For I swear by all I hold most sacred, that I will attempt to bury this dagger in your cowardly heart!"

This threat, so far from awing the villain, caused him to laugh outright.

"Excellent fooling!" he said; "most excellent. I swear I am——"

He paused, for footsteps were heard ascending the stairs.

"Someone comes, my dear," he said; "one kiss, and then I will——"

He again advanced, and raising his arms he was about to embrace Rosamund, when our heroine, with a suppressed shriek, stepped back a pace, raised the glittering knife on high, and the next instant it was buried to the white haft in Clipton's breast.

A loud terrible yell left his lips as he staggered back, the blood rushing down the splendid satin dress.

He tried to seize something to prevent himself from falling, but nothing was in the way, and with a crash he fell close against the door.

Rosamund, shuddering at the sight, covered her face with her hands.

Another moment, and the door was flung open, and Parthena, with the miser, Pearman, and Captain White, appeared on the threshold.

An exclamation of horror escaped the lips of the latter three, as their eyes rested upon Clipton.

But Parthena was as firm, as stern, as free from emotion as if nothing out of the common had occurred.

"By Jupiter!" cried White, "what is this we see?"

"It's Clipton," whispered Pearman.

"Yes, it is Clipton," replied White, pushing Pearman aside, "and with a knife buried in his bosom. So it is evident that the girl was clever enough to penetrate his disguise. Soh! Well, perhaps Master Melton will not put so much faith in disguised messengers for the future. Now!" he shouted, turning to Rosamund, and fixing his bloodshot eye upon her, "now, *now*, what do you think will happen to you?"

"Yes," screamed Mercutio, "what do you think will happen to you, vixen? *You* who have turned my daughter's bedroom into a room for murder?"

"Silence!" cried White; "it is my business to interrogate her. Now then —speak up. What do you think is going to happen to you, *murderess!*"

"I neither know nor care!" replied Rosamund, boldly.

"Is he dead, Pearman?" asked the villain White.

"Aye, he's dead."

"Take the knife from his body," whined the miser; "take the knife out, Parthena, I say. It is my knife— *mine!*"

"Then take it out yourself," said White; "do you hear? If you want it, take it out yourself, you shrivelled-up old wretch."

"Parthena, Parthena!" continued Mercutio, "take it out of his body—do, there's a *good* creature, or someone will take it and keep it."

"I shall not touch it," replied Parthena, grimly. "Let the one who put it in take it out."

"Listen to me," said White to Rosamund; "the man you have killed was the principal servant to Master Melton, of whom perhaps you have heard."

"Ah!" gasped Rosamund; "Lord Stretton's infamous son?"

"Oh, you know him, do you? Well, it is a matter of indifference to me. Now——"

"Hand me over to the officers of justice, wretch," cried Rosamund; "I am willing to be tried for what I have done. I defended my honour, and a jury of my countrymen would applaud me for what I have done in my defence, and not find me guilty."

"Oh, indeed," sneered White; "you have a strange idea of your countrymen, let me tell you. But it is not necessary to hand you over to the officers of justice. We have laws here of our own, and——"

"Ah," interrupted Rosamund, "now I know where I am—I am in Alsatia!"

"You are; it is unnecessary to deny it. And you will find, my pretty maid, that we have some strong laws here. However, here you will be kept until tonight, when Master Melton will arrive. We will consult with him as to what should be done with you, for after what has occurred, I expect he will have nothing to do with you."

"Pray Heaven it may be so," replied Rosamund.

"So beautiful, and yet such a fiendish temper!" exclaimed Pearman, raising his eyes and hands to the ceiling. "Who, to look at her, would think it? Alas, alas! what are we——"

"Shut your mouth!" cried White, as he delivered a sound smack on Pearman's face.

Rosamund, taking a few hasty steps forward, looked hard into the face of Captain White.

"Well," said the wretch, as he burst out into a demoniacal laugh, "what are you looking at?"

"At you, villain," replied Rosamund —"at *you*, monster! What of my father?"

"He's dead, as you know," answered White, as he coolly folded his arms and stretched his legs apart; "and your mother too, for aught I know."

"Oh," exclaimed Rosamund, "does there breathe in all London such a terrible monster as you?"

"I hope not," was the reply, "for I have always *endeavoured* to take the lead."

"A day of retribution will come," said Rosamund, "aye, and it cannot be far off. Oh, that I were free!"

"That you will *never* be," answered White, "for let me tell you if Master Melton will not have you, after what has occurred, I will."

Rosamund recoiled from him in disgust.

"Pearman," cried White, "lend a hand here."

"What are you going to do?"

"Remove this body."

"Whither?"

"You will see. Take hold of his head. Now, Mercutio, the trap on the stairs."

"But, one moment," replied Mercutio; "would not Master Melton like to see the body?"

"Fool! what for? See the body? No. Quick! the trap."

"Well," persisted the miser, "isn't it a pity to let him down the trap with all these nice clothes on?"

"What would you?"

"Take them off. I could sell them, perhaps," whined the miser.

"Then you won't. We have now plenty of money, thanks to the goldsmith, and so we do not require to make a few paltry pence by the sale of the clothes. Go on—the trap!"

Mercutio shuffled off to the landing, and his daughter holding the light, he went upon his knees and pulled up a trap-door.

Then Captain White and Pearman, who was so much the worse for what he had partaken of that he had the greatest difficulty in the world to keep straight on his legs, seized hold of the body of Clipton, and carried him to the side of the dark aperture.

"Here is your knife, miser!" cried White, as he caught hold of the handle, pulled it from the body, and hurled it at the miser's feet; "take it, and may it one day be used in *your* body."

"Villain!" screamed Parthena, "how dare you utter such a wish in my presence."

"*Your* presence! Hum! and who are you, I should like to know?"

"You already know. And let me tell you if you dare repeat the wish you have just uttered, I will throw myself upon you and tear you to pieces!"

White laughed, but it was a very hollow laugh.

He knew only too well what a temper Parthena possessed when roused.

"Lift, Pearman," he said.

The man lifted up one end, and White the other, and the next instant the body was flung down the hole.

The trap was then closed, and Mercutio stamped upon it to see that it was properly fastened.

Rosamund had watched these proceedings with horror.

"Alas!" she thought, "all I have heard of Alsatia is only too true. Holy Virgin! how strange it is that such a place is permitted to exist! Oh, Felix, Felix! have you escaped? Oh, if you have, may Heaven send you to my rescue!"

"Now," said White, "come, Pearman, and let us partake of a meal—a meal which by my soul we have well earned! Farewell for the nonce, my exquisite maid! Anon, you shall again be honoured with our presence!"

Down the stairs went White, followed by Pearman.

When they had left the house, Mercutio saw to the door, while Parthena again locked our heroine in the room.

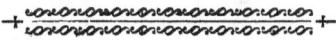

CHAPTER IX.

OF THE GATHERING OF THE TEMPLARS AND THE APPRENTICES, AND OF THE START FOR THE GATES OF ALSATIA—OF THE VISIT OF LORD STRETTON AND HIS SON, AND WHAT PASSED BETWEEN THE LATTER AND ROSAMUND—OF THE ASSAULT ON THE GATE, AND OF THE ATTACK ON ALSATIA.

AND now we must return to Felix.

As soon as morning dawned, Master Fillipy Fallory awoke.

After vigorously rubbing his eyes, he rose, stretched himself, opened the window, took a draught of wine, and then proceeded to light the fire.

This operation being performed, he

placed his weapon aside, opened the bed-room door, and said, in a deep theatrical tone of voice—

"Felix, Felix Firebrand—I beg pardon, Ferdinand—awake. Time is up; the cock crows—at least, there's no doubt he would if he were anywhere near. Felix——"

"I am awake, my kind friend," answered Felix, leaping from the small but remarkably comfortable bed.

"That's well," said Fillipy; but you do not look as if you had been asleep."

"I have not."

"Egad! that will——"

"I had too much to think off; too many dreadful thoughts were uppermost in my mind. I found it impossible to sleep. I closed my eyes and that was all."

"Hum! Well, my young friend, let me tell you that I went sound asleep; I am a fairly good slumberer, Master Ferdinand. But when I don't feel drowsy, and yet want to sleep, I sit down to a few law books, and over those musty records, my eyelids soon close, and I fall into the arms of Morpheus—I beg pardon, I fall on the table. But now come forth; a small nip of wine——"

"I thank you, but would rather not drink wine at this hour."

"Eh?" cried Fillipy, opening wide his eyes in astonishment; "not drink? Why, my young friend, it will put fresh life into your body; it will make you——"

"Nevertheless," interrupted Felix, "I assure you I would rather not partake of it."

"As you will. But since that does not meet with your approval, will you choose to drink a basin of the compound called tea?"

"I have no objection to that."

"So be it. But 'tis vile stuff, according to my thinking."

The tea being placed upon the table, Fillipy set in front of Felix part of a chicken, a small loaf, and a few other articles; but our hero could not have swallowed a mouthful for a handful of gold-pieces.

He drank the tea, however, and felt considerably refreshed.

"And now," said Fillipy, "let us consider what is best to be done."

"I told the girl," said Felix, "that it was not likely I should see her, but dur-ing the night I have considered that it would be advisable to say a few words to her."

"As you will, my young friend," replied Fillipy.

"I have thought of a most important matter. You are aware of the fact, Master Fillory, that the apprentices do not bear the Alsatians any goodwill."

"Yes, I am perfectly aware of the fact. They are, like we templars, deadly enemies. Indeed on many occasions they have greatly assisted us. But what is the important matter you have thought of?"

"You have heard, no doubt, of a person of the name of Andrew Arliss."

"I should think so. Andrew Arliss is the leader of the City apprentices, and a fine young fellow he is. He is in the employment of Sir Thomas Gateby, the watchmaker."

"Quite right. I have not yet had the pleasure of seeing him, but I know that he is Alice's lover."

"What, the maid below?"

"Exactly."

"Then, by all means, speak to her at once. If I can get the Templars to assist, and the maid, by speaking to Andrew, can get the apprentices, we stand a fair chance of rescuing Mistress Walker, and also of recapturing some part of the treasure taken from the goldsmith. It would first, however, be advisable for us to visit the house—eh?"

"Nay, rather let us speak to the girl first."

"Very good."

Off down the stairs went Fillipy.

He returned in a few moments, escort-ing Alice, who, poor girl, looked more fit to be in bed than anywhere else.

Ghastly pale she was, and her eyes showed that she must have been weeping for hours.

Felix placed a chair for her, and tenderly assisted her to it.

"You have passed a bad night, Alice," said Felix.

"Aye, indeed," was the sad reply; "and you—you have been unable to sleep?"

"Quite."

"Ah, my poor mistress! What can have become of her? At this moment she may be dead—or if not, she may have been subjected to indignities which are far worse than death."

"'FLY, FLY, MASTER MELTON! NO TIME IS TO BE LOST!' CRIED THE JEW."

"Very true," said Master Fallory; "very true indeed. These Alsatians are not very particular, I do assure you. But just listen to me for a moment. I want to ask you a question—one which you, as this young lady's maid, should be able to answer. It is, has your young mistress been pestered with the attentions of anyone?"

"Yes," replied Alice, promptly.

"Ah, who—what was his name?"

"His name was Master Melton."

Fillipy commenced a rapid promenade of the room.

Pausing abruptly, he said—

"By Heaven's mercy! she could not have been pestered by a greater blackguard than this same Master Melton, who, however, has no more right to that name than have I. His right name is Horace — the *Honourable* Horace Stretton, only son of Lord Stretton, of Stretton House, Pall Mall. Have you not heard this before?"

"I have, indirectly. But the goldsmith hated the man as much as did his daughter, who could never bear to hear his name mentioned."

"Well, my dear maid, you can now guess the reason that your mistress is in Alsatia."

"I can, I can!" replied Alice, wringing her hands.

"And unless a rescue is attempted to-night, at the latest—for an attack in the daytime would be useless—to-night, I say, at the latest, and your young mistress rescued, she will certainly be removed to a house which Master Melton will select. And she will not be the first by a good many."

"I pray Heaven I may meet this man face to face!" said Felix, fervently.

"Well, you may to-night, in Alsatia. He is more frequently in Alsatia than anywhere else. He and his father, Lord Stretton, than whom no more treacherous and depraved lord surely ever existed—he and his father, I say, give these Alsatians plenty to do. But now, my dear—excuse me, I am in the habit of calling every female — not excepting Mother Clap-trap—ahem! 'my dear'—but now, I say, Master Felix tells me that you, like other young ladies, have a lover, and that that lover is no less a person than Andrew Arliss."

Alice coloured up as she replied—

"Yes, sir, that is my lover's name. Do you know him?"

"Right well."

"I trust, sir, you know nothing wrong of him?"

"Wrong? *Wrong?* Bless me, no! I know everything that is good of him. He is a fine, handsome, brave young fellow, and I assure you I am proud to call him my friend. Under Sir Thomas Gateby, the watchmaker, your lover will rise in the world if he *watches* it. He is young yet, and so there is plenty of *time* before him. Well, now, Alice, your good lover, Andrew Arliss, is the acknowledged leader of the City apprentices."

"So I have heard, sir."

"And he has but to give the word for a couple of hundred apprentices to follow him?"

"I am proud to know that he is so highly esteemed."

"And," continued Fillipy, warming with his subject, "I have hardly a doubt but that I can get a large number of the Templars to join in so necessary a work. Now, my dear, will you just scribble a note to Andrew if I get someone to take it?"

"Willingly, sir."

"Then pray do so at once. Here," he said, as he went and opened the cupboard, "here we have pens, ink, and paper—that is, if the mice have not eaten them, for really, I have not had the pleasure of using the articles for some time. Ah, here you have pens, ink, and paper!"

Alice seated herself at the table and wrote a few words, urging her lover to "follow the bearer" with all speed.

The note being ready, Fillipy went to the head of the stairs and whistled.

"Aye, aye," cried a shrill voice, "whose chamber?"

"Master Fallory's," was the reply, "and hurry, or there will not a whole bone left in your carcase."

In a few seconds a rapid pattering of feet was heard on the stairs, and soon a short, shock-headed, grimy little urchin appeared.

"Our errand lad," said Fillipy. "Now, Mark——"

"Sir!" screamed the urchin.

"Hold your tongue, sirrah. Listen to me, Mark—in fact, *Mark* well what I am about to say.   You know Sir Thomas Gateby's shop at Ludgate?"

"Quite well."

"Do you know Andrew Arliss there?"

"Quite well."

"Sure?"

"Quite *well!*"

"Then take this note to him. Be careful it is not seen by anyone else. And here are a few pence for yourself. Don't let the apprentices' 'What d'ye lack?' tempt you to stop on the road. Be off!   And—here, Andrew Arliss will return with you."

"Right."

"Don't stop on the road."

"No, sir."

"Or I'll break every blessed bone in your little carcass."

"Yes, sir."

Away went the urchin, and at such a pace down the stairs that it was a mercy he did not fall and break his neck.

Patiently our hero and Alice waited the appearance of Andrew.

Fillipy endeavoured to make the time appear as short as possible to them by retailing various anecdotes, grave and gay.

He possessed the remarkable and most valuable gift of entertaining persons, no matter who they were.

But the thoughts of our hero and Alice were otherwhere.

They listened, but they heard not.

An hour passed.

Fillipy, for the fiftieth time, had consulted his watch, and was about to return it somewhat impatiently to his pocket, when he heard the street-door closed with a crash.

"Here you are!" he cried; "that was Mark closing the door, I'll be sworn."

He was right.

A light quick tread was heard on the stairs.

Alice, her face suffused with blushes, started up as Fillipy flung open the door and admitted a tall, stout, muscular youth of about our hero's age.

It was Andrew Arliss, the recognised chief of the City apprentices.

And a noble-looking young chief he was, certainly.

Alice, ignoring the presence of our hero and Fillipy, threw herself into her lover's arms.

"Safe!" cried Andrew.   "Heaven be thanked for this!   For hours and hours I have been nearly distraught.   For——"

"The news of what has happened is all over the city, Andrew—eh?" said Fillipy.

"The *City*, sir.   The whole of *London* is ringing with it.   I have but just returned from my hunt after you, Alice, and hence the reason of the delay. Safe, safe!   It seems hardly possible, my beloved Alice, that I hold you in my arms again!"

"You have to thank that young man," replied Alice, pointing to Felix, "had he not persisted in making me accompany him, no doubt I should have been killed, or worse might have happened to me."

"Ah!" exclaimed Andrew, "his name?"

"Master Felix Ferdinand."

"I have heard of him," said Andrew, advancing to Felix, and taking his hand, which he warmly pressed. "Master Felix Ferdinand, I thank you from the bottom of my heart."

"You have also to thank that young gentleman," said Felix, pointing to Fillipy, "for he kindly provided us with shelter."

"Oh, I pray you do not return *me* any thanks," exclaimed Fillipy; "I am not deserving of any.   What I did was only a duty.   Besides, I ought really to thank them for coming to my miserable garret-fire for once in the way.   But now to business, or in other words, to discuss the many important matters before us."

But Andrew persisted in first learning all the particulars of what had occurred at the goldsmith's.

When Felix had finished his narrative, Andrew said—

"And now let me supplement your narrative by giving you some good news, which not long ago I learnt. Alice, your young mistress's mother is at the mansion of the Countess of Rothburn."

"Oh!" exclaimed Alice, clasping her hands, "that knowledge is indeed a heavy load off my mind.   Is she safe?" she asked in eager tones.

"Safe?   You mean was she injured? She was—most greviously.   Poor lady, it is very doubtful whether she can recover!   All the bodies have been removed from the house in Fleet Street, and taken to the public mortuary except the goldsmith's, and that is in the charge of my master, Sir Thomas Gateby, who, learning what had occurred, organised a search-party, who went into every part of the premises."

"Did you accompany them?" asked Felix.

"I did."

"And what did you notice?"

"That the place was, in the manner of speaking, absolutely wrecked. The dastardly Alsatians, too, have carried off everything they could lay their hands upon. Huge iron safes have been wrenched open, secret doors searched out —in fact, the whole place is in an awful state."

"May Heaven's most bitter curse descend upon them!" cried Felix; "they have slain Rosamund's father, nearly killed her mother, and robbed them of their fortune. Oh, time!" he cried in a voice of agony, "hurry, hurry, hurry!"

"Why do you say that?" asked Andrew.

"Because, until darkness sets in, we cannot attempt to rescue Rosamund."

"Most true. And now to draw up a plan."

"I was thinking," said Fillipy, "that the best plan would be to summon the apprentices."

"They will rise at a single word from me!" said Andrew, proudly; "but you, Master Fallory, you will endeavour to get the Templars?"

"Most assuredly. Let no further time be lost. Listen to me, Master Andrew. What number of apprentices do you propose to summon?"

"Two hundred of the best."

"A goodly number! Well, I fancy I can obtain a hundred Templars—that will make three hundred altogether. Good! What arms will the apprentices have?"

"Nothing but clubs."

"Clubs to the Alsatians!" cried Fillipy in amazement.

"The apprentices," said Andrew calmly, "can handle clubs and staves better than any other weapons, and you may take my word for it, that if they engage with the Alsatians, those beauties will find that they have need for a cartload of sticking-plaster. Another thing, Master Fallory; you, as a law student, should know that the apprentices are not allowed to carry such weapons as a sword or pistol."

"That is true. But you, as the leader of them—you will never come armed only with a club?"

"I shall carry a sword, and, probably, a pair of pistols."

"Do, by all means. These Alsatians, as you are well aware, are a desperate lot. Captain White appears to get more ferocious than ever. I understand he has placed a cannon behind The Fountain of Life, ready for use. He has been heard to swear that if attacked in Alsatia by a large number of persons—king's troops, or anyone else—he will use it in defence of the place."

"An idle threat, I should say," said Andrew.

"Nay, I think not, he generally carries out what he says, or as more often the case, gets someone else to do it. Still, one cannon, nor a dozen, will not frighten either the Templars or the apprentices."

"You say right," said Andrew. "We will fight the villains to a man."

"Once let me get into Alsatia," said Felix, "once let me find out in what particular spot Rosamund is, and I swear that I would go to her rescue, were it raining fire!"

"Pray Heaven your efforts may be crowned with success!" cried Alice, fervently.

In a short time Andrew departed to the City, while Felix set out with Master Fillipy Fallory.

Alice was left in charge of Mother "Clap-trap," as Fillipy was pleased to call her.

* * * *

The snow-storm had passed entirely away, but the frost held the piles of snow, firm and crisp, upon the ground.

Night came round, and a bright moon threw her rays upon the old City of London, making it look absolutely beautiful.

The clock struck eight, and hardly had the echoes died away ere two youths, attired in short jerkins, and wearing flat caps set jauntily upon their heads, passed the watchman on duty at the Fleet Street gate of the Temple, and turned into Pump Court.

Their movements were rapid in the extreme.

Two minutes passed, and then two

more youths, similarly attired, passed through the gates; another minute, and down came two more.

All walked rapidly, and not a word was passed between them.

Every moment brought more, until, before an hour had passed, *nearly two hundred youths* must have turned into Pump Court.

The London Apprentices were gathering, armed. Aye, and for a purpose.

Now, what was most extraordinary was the fact that, although so many youths had turned into Pump Court, not a sign of one was to be seen.

All had disappeared.

Where?

Into the chambers of the Templars.

Everything was being done so quietly and so secretly that there was no chance of the Alsatians getting an inkling of what was being done.

Ten o'clock came round.

The silence of the grave seemed to prevail in Pump Court.

But suddenly a light blue flame lit up the gloomy-looking brick buildings.

It seemed like a sudden flash of lightning. This was, of course, a signal.

In a few moments the court became almost full of apprentices, and Templars, who poured out of every house.

The apprentices were armed with clubs, while the Templars carried rapiers, and some of them pistols.

Andrew Arliss was armed with sword and pistol, as also was Felix.

Andrew took command of one hundred apprentices, Felix of another hundred, and a young Templar, named Meekin, with Fillipy to assist him, assumed command of the Templars.

They were soon placed in order, yet without making much noise; and the word being given, away they went to the Temple Gate leading to Alsatia—the gate, our readers will remember, through which Felix rushed in his flight ere he plunged into the Thames.

*   *   *   *

To return to Lord Stretton and his evil son.

At nine o'clock horses were ordered, and the pair, well muffled up and well armed, set off for Alsatia.

Though they rode side by side, and though, through not being able to travel fast in consequence of the state of the streets, they rode close together, hardly a word was exchanged between them.

Thoughts of being terribly avenged on Lord Clinton and on the countess kept Stretton silent.

Horace did not attempt to interrupt him.

He had nothing in particular to think of (except the fair Rosamund).

At last Whitefriars was reached.

After some considerable delay, during which Stretton relieved himself with several volleys of choice imprecations, much to the diversion of Horace, who laughed heartily, the "friars" on "duty" admitted them.

Horace, without a word or the least hesitation, at once led the way to The Fountain of Life.

Directly their arrival was announced, a tremendous commotion was caused both inside and outside the infamous tavern; a visit from Lord Stretton (who, it may be remarked, was erroneously supposed to have great influence at court) being considered a matter of great importance.

The horses were placed in charge of two men, with instructions that they were to be fed and watered where they stood.

In a few moments father and son— the latter leading the way—were in the captain's reception-room, which had been "put to rights" in anticipation of this visit.

Lord Stretton found the captain seated in his chair at the head of the table, the villain Pearman at his side.

As Stretton entered, White rose and bowed, while his bloodshot eye blinked rapidly.

"Your lordship is right welcome," he said. "It is not often we have the pleasure of welcoming you to our—ahem!— our palace."

"Your den of infamy, would sound much better," replied Stretton, looking disdainfully at the score or so men around the table.

"Yes," said Pearman, "he is quite welcome—more than welcome. Good men like ourselves are happy to greet others——"

"Silence!" yelled White.

"Don't mention it," was the reply.

"Your lordship wishes to see me on *business?*" said White.

"I do," was the surly reply.

"Good. I am at your service in a few moments. Master Melton—ahem—er——"

"None of your 'ahems!' Captain White," interrupted Horace, sharply. "I have often told you that one of your confounded 'ahems!' is quite sufficient for the night."

"No offence is intended. I——"

"If no offence is intended, it is conveyed; so don't forget, Captain White. I feel certain that you have no inclination to lose your other eye."

"You are quite right. And I have no inclination to be insulted, that's another thing. Look here, Master Melton, I have serious news for you."

"Indeed? What is the nature of the news? Proceed, for I am anxious to be off to——"

"I understand. Well, sir, Clipton, your favourite is no more."

"What!" roared Horace, starting as though he had been shot.

"He is no more, I repeat."

"Do you mean to tell me that my valet is *dead?*"

"Precisely. You have hit it. He is, I repeat, no more."

"What cursed villainy have you been practising on him?" said Stretton.

"Clipton dead!" said Horace, in hoarse tones. "Explain—quick!"

"In the first place," said Stretton, "tell us if he was murdered?"

"He was."

"By whom?"

"By Mistress Rosamund Walker."

And the captain surveyed Master Melton with a twinkle in his eye.

Had a thunderbolt fallen at the feet of Stretton's infamous son, he certainly would not have been more startled.

"Killed by Rosamund Walker!" he gasped. "Impossible. You are deceiving me; you——"

"Oh, well," interrupted White, "if you don't believe *me*, there's the girl herself. She will not conceal from you or from anyone else the fact that she slew him."

"Tell us all," said Horace.

Thereupon the captain told him all the particulars of the death of Clipton.

"And," concluded White, "I can assure you that the thrust she gave would have killed any man."

"She is beautiful," said Pearman, "lovely—exquisite—entrancing—splendacious! but by all the saints, much too strong for a female!"

"I will at once repair to her," said Horace; "she needs a lesson at my hands."

"You had better be careful," sneered Stretton, "for she may have another knife concealed about her person."

"Where is she confined," asked Horace.

"I will send a man with you to the spot," replied White; "but no doubt you know the house well enough. She is in charge of the mi——"

At a warning look from Horace, Captain White paused.

But Stretton had observed his son's look.

"Proceed," he said, in authoritative tones. "What were you about to say?"

"Nothing, my lord —nothing."

"Proceed, I say. At whose house is this girl confined?"

"At the house of Mercutio Merrywell, your lordship; quite a respectable wealthy citizen."

"Soh!" muttered Stretton. "At the miser's house. Ah!"

Turning suddenly to Horace, he said in low tones—

"What business transactions have you had with this miser?"

"My lord!"

"It is not necessary for me to repeat the question. You understand me perfectly well."

"I don't understand you in the least."

"What money have you borrowed of this man?"

"Well, to tell the truth, I have 'borrowed' sums, but from that you are not to conclude that he has advanced all I could wish."

"How much has he advanced?"

"About a thousand."

"Ah! On what security?"

"Note of hand."

"It is false!" hissed Stretton. "I know Mercutio Merrywell. He would not advance a penny on note of hand. I repeat, what security has he had?"

"Pray calm yourself; I do assure you——"

"Horace," whispered Stretton, in low impassioned tones, "you have been to my strong-box. Ha! you start. Your face betrays you. What did you take? Answer me instantly."

"Well, my lord," said Horace, "I will not deny it. It was on the impulse of the moment. I had to satisfy a debt of honour. I took the deeds which relate to your property in Pall Mall."

Lord Stretton reeled as though from a fearful blow.

"Villain!" he hissed. "For one thousand pounds you have deposited in the hands of Mercutio Merrywell property worth at least *twenty* thousand!"

"Well, I am exceedingly sorry. Were it possible I would instantly recover the deeds, and place them in your hands."

"Were it possible, you say. It *shall* be possible!"

"Well, I will try to get them. Is your lordship prepared to repay the money advanced, together with interest?"

This question Horace asked with remarkable coolness and composure.

"No," was the reply; "I have not such a sum at hand."

"Well, I must try to recover them without the money. Though I should like to know how that is to be done," he muttered.

"Away, then, to the miser!"

"Aye," said Horace, at once leaving the room. "I shall shortly return, my lord."

"Are you now at liberty to consult with me relative to the business you came about, my lord?" asked White.

"Yes; lead the way to a private room."

"Pray follow me," said White, rising. "Pearman, to your care I leave my *chickens.*"

"Good. I will see that they do not *crow* too loud."

But, in defiance of this assurance, the "chickens" crowed so loud that the captain and Stretton could hardly hear themselves speak.

Horace, accompanied by one of the men—who went with him, not to show him the way, but to prevent him from being attacked by any of the "villains" who might mistake him for a stranger—went round to the miser's house.

The man then left him, and Horace knocked.

A whistle, which sounded close to him, was the immediate response.

In a few moments Parthena appeared at one of the upper windows.

"Well?" she queried.

"Master Melton," was the reply.

"Who—who?" squeaked the voice of the miser, who was behind his daughter.

"Master Melton."

"Ah—oh! Say I'm coming—I'm coming!"

Thereupon the miser hurried back to his room, scrambled up a lot of gold pieces and goldsmiths' notes off the table, and placed them down a trap beside it, the door of which stood open.

Securing this, he took a lamp and descended the stairs.

Master Melton had been a borrower to a large amount, and Mercutio was, no doubt, under the impression that he had come, not only for the girl, but to repay the money, or, at least, the interest on the money he had borrowed.

He did not know "Master Melton" thoroughly.

After the usual preliminary rattling of bars, bolts, and chains, the miser drew back the door.

"Ah, ah!" he chuckled, "Master Melton! He, he! I am *de*-lighted to see you, Master Melton—he, he!"

"Then let me tell you that I am not *de*-lighted to see *you,*" replied Horace.

"And why—and why?"

"That's my business."

"Well — well — well," answered the miser uneasily, for the thought suddenly struck him that Master Melton, instead of having come to pay money, had come to borrow some.

"His lordship has discovered the loss of the deeds."

"Well," sneered the miser. "And what of it?"

"What of it! I will tell you what of it. You must accept my note of hand and return me the deeds!"

"What?" shrieked Mercutio. "*What? return* the deeds — *return* them? I would see you in Hades first! I would see you—— I would see you—I——"

"Father, father!" said Parthena, from the top of the stairs. "Father, what are you exciting yourself about now!"

"What do you think, Parthena? What do you think?" whined Mercutio. "This Master Melton——"

"I hope you are not going to excite yourself over such a contemptible wretch as Master Melton," interrupted Parthena in her cold hard tones.

"Contemptible wretch!" said Horace excitedly.

"Well, well," replied Mercutio, "she is generally *correct*—generally correct."

"Then you agree with her, you old rascal?"

"He cannot *help* it," said Parthena. "I can produce *instant* proof."

"Oh, where?"

"*Upstairs.*"

"What does she mean, Master Merrywell?"

"I mean," said Parthena, "I mean the girl Rosamund Walker! Is not the fact of her being confined here a proof that you are a contemptible wretch?"

"Not so strong, my dear—not so strong!" cried Mercutio; but as Horace passed in he chuckled. "Clever girl is Parthena — though she's ugly. Nice clever girl. Like her mother, only her nails are somewhat sharper. Get her reward some day! Clever girl—he, he! Very Clever—ho, ho!"

The top of the stairs having been reached, Horace said—

"Master Merrywell, of course by this time you have come to the conclusion that what I said in reference to the deeds was only—er——"

"To try me," put in the miser.

"Precisely."

"I *thought* you were jesting, Master Melton," replied Mercutio, as shading the lamp with his long hand, he looked cunningly into Horace's face. "Yes, yes, I thought you were jesting, for you couldn't be such a fool as to think that *I* would take a note of hand—eh?"

"Of course not."

"No; it would——"

"But you are not forgetting the *value* of the deed?"

"By no means. But what value do you place on it? I don't remember that you placed any——"

"My father has put a price on it."

"Oh! Well, what was it."

"Twenty thousand pounds."

"Ah,—oh, indeed! Why, I thought it was worth more—much more."

"In the name of all that's wonderful, you wretched skinflint!" said Horace angrily, "what do you want for a paltry thousand?"

"As much as I can get, my dear—as much as I can get," chuckled Mercutio; "but now you want the pretty Rosamund. She's very pretty, but dangerous. Mind she hasn't anything dangerous about her— a dagger or some weapon that will kill," he whispered. "Be careful, for she might pick up anything. No doubt you have heard all about how she killed the clever individual you sent here, and tried to make love to her. Ha, ha!"

"I have."

"Hem! Look out then, she *might* fly at you."

"I will take care of that."

"I am anxious, you see," sneered Mercutio; "because, if you happen to be killed I should have to press the matter of the deed you see."

Horace made no reply to this.

"Open the door of the apartment in which the girl is confined," he said sternly, "and then leave us. I will tame her."

"Don't you think Parthena had better stay outside the door?"

"Curse Parthena, and you too!"

"He, he!—ho, ho! What a bold man you are. Well, here is the room. My daughter's bed-chamber. But we are going to call it the room of death in future, in memory of the dreadful deed committed to-day."

"Call it what you like," was the reply Horace made, as pushing Mercutio aside, he entered the chamber in which was poor undefended Rosamund.

She did not look up on his entry.

Rosamund was seated near the fireplace, her face buried in her arms, which rested on the back of the chair.

Horace was not able to make her out as distinctly as he would have wished, for the chamber was only lighted by one candle, and that was so thin that it appeared to shiver with the cold.

Advancing a few paces, and endeavouring to put a tender tone into his voice, the dissipated young villain said—

"Rosamund—fair Rosamund! Look up, I pray you."

No reply.

"Rosamund—dear Rosamund! *Do* listen to me. I am hear to assure you that I deeply sympathize with you in the great misfortune which has overtaken you and your parents."

"Hark to the villain!" whispered the Jew, who, with his daughter had secreted themselves near, and consequently could overhear all that was said. "Parthena, my dear, he will always be a rascal. Hark to him again."

Parthena remained silent.

"Rosamund," continued Horace, "you have been told that it was I who authorised your capture. If so it is a falsehood. Rosamund, I am here to offer you my hand. If you accept this offer, I can at once effect your release. I can assure you I am not angry with you for killing the man who came to you in disguise. Far from it. No doubt he was a villain, and you resented his advances."

"As I resent yours!" cried Rosamund, starting to her feet, and confronting the young villain with flashing eyes. "Monster! *You* offer me your hand? *You*—but I cannot find words sufficiently strong in which to express my intense loathing of you. Accursed son of a villainous lord that you are, I would sooner be subjected to the most horrible torture than be joined to you! Yet, think not that I do not know, when you say you offer me your hand that you offer nothing of the kind. I know you too well for that, Master Melton, as you choose to call yourself. You are a miserable villain! Begone!"

Horace smiled, but it was a very ghastly smile indeed.

"Hark to her! She's got a temper, Parthena—eh?" whispered the miser.

"No doubt of it," answered Parthena; "and she has also got his character to perfection."

"Begone!" repeated Rosamund.

"Listen to me, dear Rosamund," said Horace; "if you will not consent to become mine, and leave this place with me, here you shall remain, and in this very room be married to me. We have a registered parson not far from here."

"You cannot terrify me," replied Rosamund, firmly. "I defy you!"

"You shall be mine by your own free will, or by force, very quickly."

"Never!"

"I swear you shall. Not another moment will I give you, girl. You will find that in me you——"

"Hark!" cried the Jew to his daughter; "what is that. Hark!"

At this instant a loud roar, as from a multitude at a distance, was heard.

Then followed another and another,

and then was heard the unmistakeable sound of the striking of hammers and axes on wood and iron.

Horace turned as pale as death.

Down the stairs rushed the miser and his daughter, and they reached the threshold just as Lord Stretton hurried up.

A few rapid words were exchanged, and the miser ran back.

Pushing open the door of the room in which were Horace and Rosamund, the miser shrieked—

"Fly, fly, Master Melton! No time is to be lost. Your father is below. He says the horses are at hand—fly, or murder will be done in this house!"

"What has happened?" gasped Horace.

"An attack is being made on the place. The apprentices and the Templars have joined themselves together, and are at this moment at the Temple Gate. Mercy on us! we shall all be killed."

Horace calling out, "Lock her in! lock her in! Do not let her escape!" rushed from the room and down the stairs.

"An attack!" said Rosamund; "a rescue! Felix—Felix!" she cried frantically. "'Tis he who has come to save me! Stand away—stand out of my path, old man!" she said, as, seizing a bar of iron, she rushed forward.

"No—no!" cried Mercutio; "no! You shall not move from here! You are my prisoner."

"May Heaven pardon me," said Rosamund, "but if you do not move I will strike you down! Away!" she said, now maddened at the thought of being kept a prisoner while a rescue was being attempted. "Away! Felix—Felix! This way! Help!"

Brandishing the iron bar over her head, she rushed on, but, ere she had gone far, she stopped, with a low bitter wail of anguish.

There, on the threshold of the door, stood the upright figure of the miser's daughter.

Her outstretched right hand grasped a pistol, the glittering barrel of which was exactly on a level with Rosamund's breast.

"Stay where you are!" said Parthena in cold hard tones. "Advance but another step, girl, and I fire!"

"Heaven pity me!" sobbed Rosamund, falling on her knees.

*   *   *   *

The apprentices and the Templars—only about a fourth being present, for the remainder of the students were absent from the Temple—reached the Temple Gate in comparative silence.

In the manner of speaking, "they crept upon the enemy unawares."

Andrew, Felix, and the student Meekin, thought that the Alsatians might have omitted to bar and bolt the gate.

But there was not much fear of their neglecting so important a matter.

The gate really belonged to the Templars, who had placed it there to keep the Alsatians from their precincts; but when the Alsatians had found that the Templars had barred and bolted them out, they at once placed bars and bolts on *their* side, and so kept the Templars from Alsatia.

Felix was the first to advance to the gate.

He gently pushed it, but it yielded not.

Though but a faint sound was caused by pushing the gate, it was heard.

The wicket in it was slowly pushed aside, and a villainous-looking face appeared behind the bars.

Of course, the man, owing to the darkness, could not see very distinctly who was behind the gate.

"Who's there?" he growled.

"A friend," answered Felix.

"Oh, a friend—eh?—a friend? You are on the wrong side to be a friend. But what is the password? Ah, you can't give it—eh? No! Be off, or you will repent it!"

Crash went the wicket.

"Light up," whispered Andrew.

The word was passed, and in a few seconds a couple of dozen links were lighted and held aloft.

The reflection of them alarmed the man at the gate, who thinking that a fire had broken out, again pushed back the wicket.

As his eyes rested upon the crowd of apprentices and Templars, his capacious mouth opened to its fullest extent.

"By all that's evil," he muttered, "where can they have sprung from?"

"Open the gate," said Felix; "open the gate instantly, or your life shall answer for it!"

The man returned no answer.

Shutting the wicket, he seized an enormous rattle which hung near him, and, holding it in his two hands, sent it swiftly round and round.

The noise it made was tremendous.

The rattle was at once answered.

Windows flew up in every direction, and the Alsatians, men, women, and children, appeared at them, and on the balconies.

Those of the men who had rattles in their possession swung them, and those who had not shouted lustily, and in this they were joined by the women and children.

Louder and louder rose the howls and screams, until it was evident that the whole of Alsatia was alarmed.

Lights appeared in dark, deserted-looking corners, as if by magic.

As the noise increased, indeed, flaming links appeared on the very tops of the houses.

But the most striking object was the figure of a man perched on the top of a stool or tub on the roof of "The Fountain of Life."

He had nothing on him but a pair of ragged breeches, and an equally ragged shirt.

Round his shoulders was placed a broad leathern belt, and attached to that was a drum.

The links held out at the windows below him, served to bring out the figure of this man with wonderful distinctness.

This man was the "Alsatian Drummer," specially kept at "The Fountain of Life" to give the alarm from White himself.

The drum was never beaten except by White's orders.

The order was very quickly given when the news was conveyed to the captain as to who were on the other side of the gate.

Then the man commenced his tattoo, and a wild unearthly tattoo it was.

As he beat the drum, he screamed at the top of his voice.

"Arm — arm! Tipstaff! Bailiffs! Arm—arm! Turn out! Fight for your lives! Turn out—turn out!"

"Open the gate!" cried Felix.

Hardly had the words left his lips ere the wicket was hastily pushed aside and the muzzle of a pistol thrust through the bars.

Andrew struck it up with his sword just as the trigger was pulled, so that the bullet did no harm.

But alas for the man who fired it!

Felix instantly pulled a pistol from his belt and fired.

The bullet penetrated the man's cheek, and, with a wild unearthly scream, he fell to rise no more.

But by this time he had been joined by many more Alsatians, and the wicket was again, though with difficulty, closed.

"Hammers and axes," cried Felix. "Down with the gate; let nothing stay our progress!"

"Aye—aye," cried Andrew. "Forward, apprentices! Forward, lads! Hammers and axes! Hurrah!"

Thereupon a score of young fellows, blacksmiths' apprentices, came forward.

Each carried a hammer or an axe over his shoulder.

These they brought to bear upon the gate.

Truly the youthful blacksmiths showed that they could ring as merry a peal on a gate as they could on their anvils.

The din they caused almost drowned the cries of the Alsatians.

Captain White soon "ran out" his chief men to take command.

The principal "officers" (save the mark!) and men—hardly one of whom was properly dressed — hastened, as a matter of course, to the Temple Gate.

There Captain White, after seeing that Lord Stretton had gone after his son, followed them.

"Hold! Without there!" roared White. "Hold, I say! Hold your confounded hammers and let us know what you want."

"Hist!" cried Felix, "that was White's voice."

"Aye, that it was," said Fillipy, who carried the heavy rusty blade we have before spoken of. "I could recognise his voice out of ten thousand. Better stop a moment."

Andrew gave the word, and the apprentices stayed their hands.

"Now," repeated White, "what do you want?"

"Open the wicket," cried young Meekin, "and we will tell you."

"Ho, ho!• A likely thing! What do you take us for?"

"Thieves and murderers."

"No doubt. Ahem! Very good. What do you want, I say?"

"The whole of the property stolen from the goldsmith's residence," shouted Felix, "the person of Rosamund, his daughter, and lastly yourself, villain."

Captain White burst into a roar of laughter, in which he was joined by his men.

"And if we do not have what we want at once," continued Felix, "we will force an entry, and then look to your lives, rascals."

Captain White secretly gave orders to a few of the men near him.

"Get two or three ladders," he said, "mount them, and fire at the person speaking."

"Oh, you'll force an entry, will you?" he shouted. "Well, I must have a few moments to consider what I shall do."

As he said this, Captain White drew back the wicket just enough to look through.

A shout of surprise left his lips as he saw the host of apprentices and Templars.

"By all the powers!" he said hoarsely, "the place is *alive* with apprentices and Templars armed to the teeth. And Stoddart" (the man who had had charge of the gate) "Stoddart shot dead. Ha, this looks like business. Hark ye, you fighting crew," he roared, "if you do not disperse instantly, it will be death for you all."

Felix heard him.

"Friends, on again with the hammers," he cried.

"Aye, aye, my lads!" cried Andrew. "Work with a will this time. It cannot long withstand a determined attack of the City lads."

"Master Fallory," said Felix, "do you keep an eye upon the top of the gate. These wretches may attempt to steal a march on us that way."

"Don't fear it," replied Fallory, as he pulled out a gigantic pistol and cocked it. "Here my friends," he added to three or four Templars, "watch the top of the gate, and if you see any heads appear, fire!"

"'HOLD! PAUSE ERE IT IS TOO LATE!' CRIED PARTHENA."

Hardly had Fallory spoken, ere three or four heads appeared.

Fallory at once fired at the nearest and with so true an aim that the ball penetrated the man's brain.

The Templars fired at the others, who retreated in hot haste.

Our readers will bear in mind that during these incidents the man on the top of The Fountain of Life had continued to beat his drum in the most frantic manner, and to howl as loud as he was able.

Occasionally he "refreshed" himself from a bottle of brandy, which was handed to him through the roof.

There being no opportunity of firing on the apprentices and Templars, Captain White, his sword in one hand, and a pistol in the other, stood, backed by a hundred howling Alsatians, watching the effect of the blows upon the gate.

There can be no doubt that he was under the impression that it would not yield, for the bars and bolts were of the most ponderous description.

But the one-eyed villain was mistaken.

Though the bolts and bars remained in their position, the woodwork every few seconds showed signs of giving way.

Presently, amid a roar of delight on one side, and a howl of dismay on the other, a large piece of the wood was crashed out.

"Stand back!" said Felix. "Make a lane between you—quick!"

The order, though hurriedly given, was instantly obeyed.

But not too quickly, for some of the Alsatians, perceiving their chance, raised their pistols, and fired.

The result was that a young Templar was shot dead.

This, however, was the only mishap.

The fire was returned with interest, and from the huddled condition in which the Alsatians stood, many of them were hit.

"Stand to your posts, my men!" shouted the villain White. "Give them shot for shot! Cut them down! You won't allow yourselves to be beaten by a lot of boys, will you?"

An angry roar in the negative was the reply to this.

"Stand here," continued White, as he seized one of his men by the collar, and placed him on the proper spot, "and let your pistol do some work. *I am going to run out the cannon!* It is the first time I have had a chance of using it, and I now intend to try its effect. What ho! my men," he yelled, "keep to it but a few moments, and we will clear the whole lot away with the cannon."

A great cheer was the reply.

"Follow me," said White to three or four of his men.

With this he set off at a run.

The whole place was now in a terrible state.

Men armed with swords, pistols, pikes, and in fact every other kind of weapon, continued to hurry up to the Temple Gate.

As White hurried along, he paused at every public-house, and shouted out to the host to keep the men well supplied with refreshments, for which he would pay.

When White arrived in front of The Fountain of Life, he was surprised to see Lord Stretton and his son there.

Both were mounted.

"I thought you had gone," said White.

"Nay," answered Stretton, "we are going to see the result of the fight, and whether honest men or villains win the day."

White shrugged his shoulders.

"If either of you are shot," he said, "it will not be my fault. Master Melton, why don't you take the girl and be off? The amount *due* can be paid at some other time."

"His lordship will not allow me," said Horace.

"Nay," said Stretton, "my son shall carry out no foolery while I am near."

"Well, your lordship," said White with a hideous grin, "you will not have to wait long to see the result of this impudent attack on our sanctuary. Come, my men."

"What does he intend to do?" asked Stretton.

"I haven't the least idea," was Horace's reply "something monstrous, I'll be sworn."

In a few moments a wild cry rose on the air.

"Stand back! Stand back!"

Lord Stretton and his son backed their horses, as with a thundering rushing sound, a fairly good-sized cannon was run out from a passage at the side of The Fountain of Life.

It was drawn by half-a-dozen men and three or four brawny women.

All being maddened with drink and excitement the yelling and screaming were something truly awful.

Even Stretton shuddered as he looked upon these fiends, and thought of what they might do with such a weapon.

Captain White walked by the side of the touch-hole.

His naked sword was still in his right hand, in his left he carried a large piece of lighted tarred rope.

On either side of him were a couple of women, carrying a long lighted link in each hand.

The carriage on which the cannon was mounted was a lumbering but very strongly constructed affair, the wheels being of enormous width.

Underneath was a strong box, with an iron lid.

In this was stored sufficient ammunition to fire about half-a-dozen rounds.

" One moment, Captain White," cried Lord Stretton. " What do you intend to do with that ? "

" Fire it, and kill as many of the Templars and apprentice lads as I can ! " roared White.

" I warn you that——"

" I do not require your warning," interrupted White; " not I."

" If you fire that, and it comes to the knowledge of the King, nothing can save you from the rope."

" Can't it ? " sneered White. " What do I care for the King ? I am king *here*; and—but there ! I am only wasting time. On, my men—on with the cannon ! "

Away through the narrow lane rushed the men and women dragging the cannon.

The sight of the weapon seemed to put fresh life into the men at the Temple Gate.

" Hurrah ! hurrah ! " came in shouts from the villainous crew.

A terrific struggle had been raging there.

The young blacksmiths had nearly smashed the gate to atoms.

And in the meantime firing had been kept up on both sides.

Many Alsatians lay dead or greviously wounded, while several Templars, and

one or two apprentices, had also been wounded.

On the open space to the left of the gate, some of the apprentices had piled the pieces of wood, as they had been knocked out of the gate, and had set light to them.

The dry but heavy oak burned furiously, and threw a weird light not only over the opposing parties, but it also lit up the gloomy Temple buildings.

Anyone on the River Thames must have thought that a large fire was in progress.

Just as Captain White came up with the cannon, the centre-bar—a ponderous piece of iron—gave way at the rivets, and Felix, waving his sword, shouted—

" On, comrades ! Show the rascals no mercy ; and remember we intend to carry out what we commenced ! "

" Hurrah ! "

The Templars and apprentices, with a lond shout, dashed forward.

Felix was to the front, Andrew Arliss was on his right, while the student Meekin was on his left, and Fallory immediately behind him.

Poor Meekin !

He had not taken a dozen steps, ere a shot struck him in the breast, and he fell dead without a single cry.

But Fallory avenged his sudden death.

He had noticed the man who fired, and, pushing his way towards him, he cut him down with his blade, which, though old-fashioned and rusty, proved itself to be of true steel in so brave a hand.

Captain White, you may depend upon it, noticed the onward rush of the Templars and apprentices.

He was undoubtedly under the impression that they had not seen the cannon, and he was chuckling at the way they would run when the weapon was disclosed to them.

But Felix and Andrew had observed it.

White kept it, as he thought, concealed from view, by the aid of his men, who stood in front, while he adjusted the swivel.

This being ready he shouted to his men to draw aside.

Just as they obeyed this order, Felix dashed forward, followed by the apprentices and Templars, and cut down all who opposed them.

With a shout Captain White raised his flaming tarred rope, but at the very same moment, Felix at the risk of being blown to atoms, seized the muzzle and gave it a violent push.

The swivel instantly acted.

The cannon swerved to the right.

The powder at the touch-hole was ignited.

A tremendous explosion followed—an explosion of so violent a nature that every house in Alsatia was shaken, and hundreds of windows in the Temple shivered.

The explosion was followed by screams and yells.

The weapon had been loaded to the muzzle, and dealt death and destruction, not on the persons for whom they were intended, but on the Alsatians themselves!

In the manner of speaking, Captain White had dug a pit, and his men had fallen into it.

For some few seconds an awful pause occurred.

Captain White, who had turned pale, stood still, his bloodshot eyes glaring at the spot where his men lay.

"Vengeance on the apprentices," roared some of his men.

The word broke the spell.

"Aye, vengeance!" cried White. "Stick to me, my men, and not many of this Templar and apprentice crew shall leave Alsatia this night alive!"

They were idle words, and no one knew that better than Captain White.

Felix called on the Templars and the apprentices, and in less time than it takes to write, a hand-to-hand fight was commenced.

The apprentices armed as they were with their City clubs, did great execution, owing, no doubt, to the fact that the Alsatians found no opportunity of firing their pistols, having plenty of work to ward off the blows aimed at their heads by the lads.

Brave Felix, as our readers may suppose, tried hard again and again to reach the villainous captain of the villainous crew.

But he found it impossible.

Captain White, seeing that the fight was terminating in favour of the young but determined Templars and City lads, did what he *always* did when he found himself being worsted—that is to say he sneaked towards the rear, and urged his men forward in the fight.

Assisted by some of his men, White wheeled the cannon across the lane.

Barely was this accomplished, ere Felix ran forward.

White instantly drew a pistol and fired at him, saying: "Ah, I have you now." But, fortunately, the ball went wide of its mark.

Shouting out to his brave companions to follow him, Felix clambered up on the gun.

"I thought I had hit you!" cried White. "By the fiends, I will be even with you—but not now; it is death to those that fight on my side."

Turning, Captain White ran away as fast as his legs would carry him.

Pearman, who was near White, attempted to follow, but he was too late!

Jumping from the cannon, Felix seized him by the collar, flung him round, and holding the point of his sword to his throat, said—

"Villain, your time has come!"

"Oh, spare me—spare me!" whined the villain, sinking on his knees. "I am quite innocent. I am the——"

"Wretch!" interrupted Felix sternly. "I know who and what you are."

"Spare my life! Don't slay me. Spare me!"

"I will, on one condition."

"Oh, name it—name it!"

"Where is the goldsmith's daughter."

"I—I assure you——"

"Tell me," cried Felix; "tell me the truth, or, as sure as I stand here, I will plunge this weapon into your dastardly carcass."

"She is at the miser's."

"Where is that?"

"At the back of The Fountain of Life."

"This is true."

"Yes."

Felix called to two of the apprentices:

"Watch this man," he said; "on no account let him go."

"Never fear it," replied the apprentices, as seizing the man by the collar, they flung him against a wall.

Felix, calling upon Andrew and Fallory to follow him, went on.

* * * *

Lord Stretton and his son saw the onward rush.

"The Alsatians have many of their men killed, and think they are beaten," said Stretton.

"There's not much doubt of it," answered Horace ; "and it will be just as well that we are not seen. Let us escape or hide."

"Truly. Back your horse under this arch. It will answer two purposes. We shall not be recognised, and shall not stand a chance of being hit by the bullets which are flying about."

Accordingly, father and son drew back under an arch, nearly opposite The Fountain of Life.

CHAPTER X.

OF THE RESCUE OF ROSAMUND—HOW HORACE ATTEMPTS TO CUT FELIX DOWN —HOW HE IS DRAGGED FROM HIS HORSE, ON WHICH FELIX AND ROSAMUND ARE QUICKLY MOUNTED—HOW STRETTON STARTS IN PURSUIT, AND BY WHOM HE WAS CONFRONTED AT LEICESTER FIELDS.

THE thoughts of Felix Ferdinand, as may be supposed, were fixed on pretty Rosamund, and even if he had noticed the two horsemen under the archway, it is doubtful whether he would have thought who they might be.

Andrew Arliss was perfectly acquainted with the whereabouts of the miser's house, and he quickly led our hero to the spot.

They were followed by a large number of Templars and apprentices.

During the time the attack on the gate and the fight had been in progress, neither the miser nor his daughter had crossed the threshold of the house.

The miser was too fearful of receiving a stray shot, and Parthena considered the affair a matter of the utmost indifference to *her.*

The reports of the pistol-shots, the clash of weapons, the cries of the men, women, and children, did not cause this extraordinary creature to betray the slightest alarm.

Nay, not even the tremendous report of the cannon, which shook their miserable dwelling to its foundation, caused her any anxiety.

But the noise had a great effect upon the miser.

From cellar to cellar, from room to room, the wretched man ran, wringing his hands in despair, as he thought it likely that he might be plundered of his ill-gotten gold.

Every moment he vowed vengeance on Rosamund, for he declared that she was the cause of Alsatia being invaded.

He would have released Rosamund had it not been for his daughter.

Parthena stood outside the door, and dared her father to attempt to enter the room.

"But we shall all be killed ! " screamed Mercutio. " And all my money—all the nice broad gold pieces I have been saving for so many years will be stolen. Yea—yea ! I shall be plundered."

"You have not been robbed yet," replied Parthena coldly. "It is time enough to complain when you are *being* ill-treated."

"I *am* ill-treated, I tell you," whined the miser.

"By whom ? "

"By you—*you,* my daughter—who should shield and protect me ! "

"I have protected you for years. Had it not been for me, who has been your shield for years, you would, long ere this, have been rotting in your grave."

"In my grave, daughter ? "

"And," continued Parthena in freezing tones, "and what have you saved your gold pieces for—eh ? What for, I say but to pander to the tastes of such unhanged scoundrels as Master Melton ! "

"Oh, my dear, you wrong him—you wrong him. He is the essence of—of——"

"All that is good—eh ? " sneered Parthena. "Ah, it is useless to try to deceive me. I have lived too long in Alsatia."

"Since you hate Master Melton so much, why don't you let the girl go ? "

"Why ? She is beautiful, isn't she ? "

"Beautiful?" cried the miser, stamping his feet. "How should I know? And what if she is?"

"You know I hate beautiful women!"

"You have often said so."

"Well, in my opinion, I have a right to *destroy* beauty in woman whenever and wherever I may chance to see it."

"Kill the girl, then!" said Mercutio eagerly. "Kill her, and let us drop her down the trap."

"I do not mean that *I* should kill beauty exactly. I mean that I should be the *means* of——"

"Oh," interrupted Mercutio, "you are a *fool*—a fool! Ah, the shots are becoming nearer! Oh, Moses, I shall lose all my treasures!"

"A good thing too. What use are your treasures to you?"

"Haven't I promised you——"

"Pah!" interrupted Parthena with a look of disgust. "What notice do *I* take of your promises! There—hist! What is that?"

"A knocking at the door!" cried the wretched miser, now thoroughly alarmed. "Hark, Parthena! Don't you hear? They will smash the door down."

"Let them smash it, then."

"Parthena, Parthena, don't be so indifferent!" cried Mercutio, bursting into a passion. "Oh, Parthena, they will have all my money! Save it—help me to save it!"

'How is it possible?"

"Release the girl—do—quick. Perhaps if we give up the girl they may go away."

"No fear of that. Whoever they are, they know that you are worth an enormous sum of money, and they will not go away without some of it."

Seeing that his appeals to his marble-hearted daughter were in vain, Mercutio, with a loud cry of anguish, ran to one of the windows which looked out on the front.

It will be observed that Mercutio devoted not one thought as to whether his *life* was in danger.

Not at all.

To him, his gold was far dearer than his life, or his daughter's life.

Throwing up the window he leaned out.

He was amazed to see every inch of ground alive with armed persons.

The glitter of the scores of weapons filled him with dismay, for he saw that the persons surrounding the house were not Alsatians, and therefore he could come to no other conclusion than that they were the invaders.

Mercutio gave vent to a series of groans of despair.

Leaning still farther out of the window, he saw (for the glare of the torches made everyone fairly distinct) Felix, Andrew, and Fallory standing by the door, with drawn swords in their hands.

Certainly the sight of the young but determined Templars, and the powerful and no less determined apprentices, armed as they were, and led by three persons whose attitude meant "business," would have caused a stronger and more courageous man than the miser considerably more than a moment's uneasiness.

As the miser looked he was observed by the apprentices and Templars, who greeted him with three significant groans.

Felix stepped back and looked up.

"What want ye, my masters?" asked Mercutio in tremulous tones.

"You are well aware what we want," replied Felix sternly.

"I don't know—I don't indeed," was the reply. "I am but a poor man—a very poor man, and so gentle that I would not harm a living soul."

"Wouldn't you!" mimicked Fallory; "we know you better than that. We have come for the young lady, Rosamund Walker, whom by orders of Captain White, who, no doubt, took his instructions from the infamous Master Melton, you have concealed in your house."

"Hear you that," said Lord Stretton from his place of concealment.

"I hear, my Lord," answered Horace uneasily.

"Who was that who spoke?"

"I know not. But I can tell who it is who is bent upon the rescue of the girl!"

"Ha. Who?"

"Felix Ferdinand, the youth who was the hero of the Countess of—— I beg pardon! Who was the hero of the jewels his *mother* lost."

"Sneer not. You can't tell yet that it is the same youth."

"Pshaw! Put one thing and the

other together, and you could arrive at no other conclusion."

"I should like to see the youth. A few questions put to him would soon settle the matter as to whether he is the youth I placed with Nicholas Fielding when an infant. Well, well, I must wait."

"Answer us !" roared Felix. "Answer us, if you value your life !"

"Say that she is here if you *dare !*" hissed Parthena, who had crept up behind her father. "You have thought of your gold, have you not? Swear to them that she is not here, and they will go peacefully away."

Between two such fires, what was the miser to do.

He knew not. He was now in a terrible state.

Great drops of perspiration rolled down his face as he thought that he really might lose his gold if any of the individuals before him obtained admittance.

"We have no young lady here of the name of Rosamund Walker," said Mercutio. "We haven't indeed ! I can swear to it !"

"Your swearing will avail you naught," answered Felix. "Come down and open the door instantly, or we will burst it open."

"Oh, gentlemen, don't be so hard on a poor harmless old man like me !" whined Mercutio.

The answer to this was a loud burst of derisive laughter.

"As the wretch will not open the door," said Andrew, "why, we must, of course, break it open !"

"Certainly," replied Felix. "Come, my friends, down with the door !"

The apprentices with the axes and hammers came forward, and began to work with a will on the door, the woodwork of which, being old and wormeaten, soon showed signs of giving way.

The miser remained for some few moments at the window, alternately imploring and cursing ; but at last Parthena pulled him away, and closed and barred the window.

"Go," she said, "and leave *me* to deal with these wretches. They shall not have the girl, for I will rather slay her with my own hand."

"But what good will that do you ?"

answered the old man, who trembled so violently that he could scarcely keep on his legs.

"I hate her !" answered Parthena, fiercely.

"She never harmed you."

"She is beautiful—I am not."

"Oh !" screamed the miser ; "that is what you have said dozens of times.

"Yes," he continued, "she *is* beautiful ! And you are ugly—ugly—you are a vixen—a——"

"Go, I tell you !"

"Yes, yes ; I am going. Oh, Moses ! hark to the thundering noise ! Oh !" he said, in a voice resembling the whining of a fretful child ; "oh, the blessed house will soon fall about our ears."

"The *cursed* house, you mean," said Parthena.

Mercutio made no reply.

Off he went wringing his hands.

Parthena lit a fresh lamp, opened the front of her dress, and took out a pistol.

From the careful way she examined it, it was evident she was quite familiar with the handling of these deadly weapons.

"Rosamund Walker, the pride of the City !" she muttered, as a demoniacal smile lit up her hard features. "Faugh ! a *heroine !* Yes, a heroine, as well as one of the most beautiful girls. By Heaven ! if I slew her, *I* should be brought into notice. Yes, yes, all London would ring with my name. Ah, as I live they have entered !"

Such was the case.

The door had at last given way before the tremendous blows of the apprentices, and they and the Templars, with Felix, Andrew, and Fillipy at their head, rushed into the passage.

All the doors on the ground floor were locked, so, without hesitation, up the stairs ran Felix, Andrew and Fallory keeping close to his side.

The first door that Felix saw was ajar he pushed open.

He now stood on the threshold of the room in which was Rosamund.

The sight that met his eyes, and the eyes of those who accompanied him, was one which was never forgotten.

Near the fireplace knelt Rosamund Walker, her hands raised as if begging for her life.

Beside her, a lamp in her left hand

and the pistol in her right, stood Parthena.

"Rosamund!" cried Felix, advancing.

"Hold!" cried Parthena, pointing the pistol at Rosamund—"hold! *I* am here. Pause, ere it is too late!"

"Great Heaven!" cried Felix, who, of course, was at a loss to comprehend the meaning of this. "What do you mean, woman? Put down that pistol!"

"Certainly not," answered Parthena, in tones remarkable for their coolness. "And let me caution you against addressing me in such——"

"Rosamund!" interrupted Felix, appalled by the look on Rosamund's face; "Rosamund, answer me——"

"She cannot answer you," interrupted Parthena.

"*Cannot?*"

"*Dare* not, then, if that will suit you better. I have warned her that if she attempts to speak, or if she attempts to move before you and your ruffians quit this house I will kill her."

"In what way has she injured you?"

"That is *my* business, and not yours!" replied Parthena, grimly.

"I will throw her off her guard," said Fillipy in so low a tone that Felix alone heard him, "and then *act.*"

"I will see the miser," said Felix.

"My father has retired to his own room," replied Parthena; "and even if he had not, he would take no heed of what you said. I call on you to leave this house—you, who I see is the leader, and your dastardly crew."

During this speech Fallory had contrived to possess himself of a large shell which stood on a slab near him, and, getting behind Andrew, he, unseen by Parthena, flung it at an ornament on the mantelpiece.

The article was smashed to pieces.

Involuntarily, Parthena turned her head, and of this movement Felix instantly took advantage, for, darting forward, he struck up the muzzle of the pistol with the back of his sword.

At the same moment Parthena pulled the trigger, and the charge exploded with a tremendous report, the bullet crashing through the rotten plaster of the ceiling, and calling forth a series of awful screams from the miser, who was in the room above.

Rosamund leapt to her feet as Felix, sheathing his sword, caught Parthena by the wrist, and snatched the pistol from her grasp.

"Thou fiend!" said Felix, sternly; "aye, *fiend* in the garb of a woman! If I had the time, I would hand you over to justice, and you should stand on your trial for attempted murder."

"Aye," replied Parthena, "and a time may come when I will have that girl arrested *for* murder, for this *very day* she committed murder in this very room."

"She raves," said Fillipy. "Look at her face. Any fool can see she is mad."

"Nay, I am not mad," said Parthena. "Ask her if I have not spoken the truth."

"If it is murder to slay a villain who attempts to—" commenced Rosamund.

"I understand her," said Fillipy; "was the person you did *justice* on called Master Melton?"

"Nay," answered Rosamund; "but it was a man in his pay who came here disguised as a woman."

"You shall tell me all about it at a more convenient time," said Felix; "at present all that is to be done is to remove you from vile Alsatia. Come, Rosamund."

Rosamund, with difficulty stifling a sob of joy, gave Felix her hand, and our hero proudly led her from the room.

Parthena muttering curses "not loud but deep," would have followed, but Fillipy, gracefully waving his hand, said—

"Depart, my friends. In other words, leave the room. As to *you* madam" (here he bowed in a style which was simply *par excellence*), "we will trouble you to remain. Your miserly father can let you out—when he can find the key."

With this Fillipy blew out the lamp, banged the door to, locked it, and put the key into the lining of his hat.

Felix led trembling but delighted Rosamund down the stairs, which were lined on both sides by apprentices and Templars.

The young fellows would have greeted the pair with loud cheers, but having in their minds the calamity which had overtaken Rosamund's parents, their greeting was one of respectful silence.

"Now, Master Ferdinand," said Fallory, as he joined our hero, "your next duty is to see Mistress Rosamund to a place of safety."

"I cannot leave you and Andrew and our brave friends until——"

"Tush, tush!" interrupted Fillipy. "Leave the arrangement of everything to us. It is of the utmost importance that you get Mistress Rosamund to a place of safety as rapidly as possible. If you do not, let me tell you that you will require a lot of skill to save her life."

Felix started and looked at Rosamund.

He could see how the poor girl was struggling to retain her self-possession ; but the death-like pallor of her features warned him that nature would soon assert its sway.

"Yes, yes," said Andrew ; "delay not another moment. Will you take her to——"

"She can go to the Temple," interrupted Fallory, "where her maid awaits her."

"My mother," moaned Rosamund ; "what of her ? Oh, what of her ?"

"She is lying seriously ill at the residence of the Countess of Rothburn," said Andrew.

"Ah," said Felix, "'tis there I will take her. Yes, to the Countess of Rothburn. Come, dear Rosamund—come!"

"Alice shall attend upon her within a few hours," said Andrew.

"Get her into Fleet-street," said Fallory ; "a few of the Templars will accompany you, and see you safely within a litter."

"But you, and Andrew, and all these brave young fellows ?" said Felix.

"Oh," answered Fillipy, as he lightly touched his huge sword, "we will remain here a little while in order to see whether there is any chance of recovering any of the property stolen from the goldsmith, and if possible to give Captain White a lesson he will not easily forget. We had better thrash him within an inch of his life, then hand him over to the officers of justice."

"Let us meet to-morrow at the residence af the Countess of Rothburn," said Felix.

"Good !" was Fillipy's reply. "Say to-morrow night. And now, away with you !"

Felix led Rosamund forth.

"Look there, you see they have obtained posession of the girl," said Lord Stretton.

"By Heaven, yes !" answered Horace. "But they shall not retain her without a struggle on my part to——"

"Horace !" interrupted his lordship, "you are a fool to risk your life now! Do you imagine that you, single-handed, could take that girl from these determined youths ?"

"Yes."

"Try it, and lose your life, fool."

To this Horace made no reply. Clenching his teeth, he drew his sword, and spurring his horse through the crowd, reached Felix.

"Release that girl !" he cried, waving his sword over his head.

"Ah !" exclaimed Rosamund, as she clutched her lover for support. "Felix, 'tis Master Melton—he who——"

Her voice was drowned by the cries of the apprentices and Templars.

"Master Melton !" they shouted. "Master Melton ! Down with him !"

"I'll down with you, you cubs !" hissed Horace, spurring still more towards Felix. "Yield up that girl !"

"Rascal, stand aside !" answered Felix.

Horace lifted his sword and was about to cut Felix down, when a young apprentice, leaping up, dealt him a tremendous blow on the arm with his club.

The sword fell from his grasp, and his arm dropped powerless at his side.

He attempted to snatch a pistol from his holster, but at a cry from Andrew he was instantly surrounded by the apprentices, dragged from his horse, and hurled to the ground.

Lord Stretton witnessed this, and he frantically endeavoured to urge his horse to the scene.

But the way was now too much blocked, and though he shouted as loud as he was able, his voice was completely lost in the shouts of Templars, apprentices, and Alsatians.

"Mount, Felix," cried Andrew. "Mount ! We'll hand the girl to you. Mount quickly !"

Felix jumped into the saddle.

Andrew and Fillipy handed Rosamund up, and Felix held her in front of him.

"Farewell, brave friends, for the time !" cried Felix.

"Farewell," was the answer. "A safe journey to you!"

Felix now gave the animal the rein, and away he dashed towards Blackfriars.

This was not the way Felix wanted to go, but the road was clearer.

Lord Stretton had watched what had been done, and directly the horse dashed away Stretton was after him, with sword and pistol ready for use.

The Templars, now recognising who he was, sent a few shots after him, but Stretton still went on, and it was evident that they did not take effect.

On went our hero.

Until Blackfriars was reached, he was not aware that he was being pursued.

His attention was divided between controlling the horse, which, having been nearly frightened to death, had become almost unmanageable, and tore madly along, and soothing Rosamund who clung to him as though he was now the only one left whom she could love and cling to for support.

But as he reached the gate at Blackfriars, which, neglected by the "friars," was fortunately open, Rosamund drew his attention to the fact that they were followed.

"By the dress of the rider," she said, "he must be a person of some importance. I should not wonder if he is the father of Master Melton."

"Lord Stretton?"

"Aye."

"Let us take no notice of him. Let me but reach Fleet Street, and we will try who has the best horse. Cling to me, Rosamund."

"Fear it not, Felix, But—ah! Your hand is on your pistol!"

"True, Rosamund."

"Oh, I pray you, no more bloodshed this dreadful night!"

At this moment Lord Stretton shouted—

"Halt, halt! I tell you, or I will fire!"

"You hear him?" said Felix. "If we do not halt, he will fire. Well, then let him fire! The shot must pass through my body ere it can reach you, my love. If he fires, you may depend upon it that it will be shot for shot. I must protect you at any cost!"

On flew horse and riders, and at a most remarkable pace considering the depth of snow on the ground.

Just as they reached Temple Bar, Lord Stretton, raising himself in the stirrups, fired.

But the shot did not take effect.

Felix turned and fired, but he did not aim at Stretton, thinking that a warning would be sufficient.

Stretton, who now began to regret having left his son, repeatedly plunged his spurs into the smoking flanks of his horse, but the poor beast could not do more than he was doing.

His son's horse, if it was not the fleetest of the two, was certainly the more powerful, and therefore was enabled to get over the snow-covered ground at a quicker pace than his own.

At length, as Felix turned into Leicester Fields—now Leicester Square —Lord Stretton suddenly disappeared.

"Thank Heaven," said Rosamund, "our pursuer has given up the chase!"

"Which he found fruitless," replied Felix. "Thank goodness, we are near St. James's Park. In a short time, Rosamund, I hope to see you clasped in your mother's arms."

"Oh, how I long for the—— Ha!" Rosamund suddenly exclaimed; "our pursuer has *not* given up the chase. See —see!"

Rosamund pointed to a space on the left of the fields, across which a horseman was galloping.

It was Stretton, who had taken a nearer cut—a cut Felix was totally unacquainted with.

With a pistol in his outstretched right hand, Stretton rode furiously towards Felix.

"I have you now! Yield!" he cried, "yield —thou accursed cub, yield!"

"Who are you who calls upon me to yield?" demanded Felix.

"That I will not tell you, boy."

"The father of Master Melton," whispered Rosamund.

"Aye, I know," replied Felix.

"Yield," repeated Stretton, grinding his teeth in his rage; "yield, or I will send a ball through your brain!"

Felix placed his hand on his pistol, but Stretton saw the movement.

"Attempt to draw a weapon," he said. "and I swear I will fire. It is useless to attempt to defy me. You have now no rascally apprentices to assist you."

"But he has a *friend*, nevertheless!" exclaimed a deep, firm voice.

Ere Stretton could turn his head, his wrist was grasped by a hand of iron, and his pistol snatched from him.

"Lord Clinton!" said Felix in astonishment.

"Aye, 'tis Lord Clinton," was the reply, "and fortunately for you, Felix, I happened to be near this clump of trees."

"Clinton!" hissed Stretton, now white with rage, "again I am foiled by you!"

"Aye, again, and maybe yet again. Felix, resume your journey with your fair charge. Leave this man to me. I can guess your destination. Adieu!"

Raising his hat, Clinton bowed as Felix again went on.

"This, my Lord Clinton," said Stretton, savagely, "is an insult which I will wipe out with other scores."

"When and wherever you please, my lord," answered Clinton coolly, "but if I may be allowed to suggest a time and place, it is now and on this spot."

"You mean that we may fight a duel here?"

"Precisely, that is just what I do mean."

"I should not think of again crossing swords with you. I do not mean," he said hastily, "that I am *afraid* of you——"

"What, then, is your reason for declining to fight? But perhaps you require time for arranging your *family affairs*."

There was a bitter sneer in this remark.

"Nay," said Stretton, hoarse with passion, "that is not my reason. Thank Heaven, I was never much troubled with family affairs."

"Well, perhaps your lordship will think proper to tell me your reason."

"Suppose we *did* fight? There is a chance of your being killed, is there not?"

"Of course," smiled Clinton.

"Good. Then if you were killed, I should not have the opportunity of *carrying out my ideas in respect to you, and for which I have arranged*."

"Thank you—you are very kind. Pray proceed, I am much interested."

"That is all, except that if I happened to be killed the result would be the same—my arrangements would fall to the ground."

"May I be allowed to ask the nature of your kind ideas in respect to me?"

"You will know all in time—you and the Countess of Rothburn shall both feel my vengeance!"

"Faugh!" exclaimed Clinton contemptuously. "Who would pay heed to such a depraved wretch as you?"

"My lord," said Stretton, fiercely, "beware how you further insult me."

"Ha, ha!" replied Clinton with provoking coolness, "you have your remedy. You have your sword at your side Dismount and fight."

"I refuse."

"So do all cowards."

"Trusting to your swordmanship, you can afford to throw insults on all sides of you."

"I do *not* do so, my lord, and you know it. My reason for urging you to fight is to settle the quarrel existing between us—to settle it away from the presence of a *lady*."

"I refuse to cross swords with you."

"As you please. I will, however, circulate the news of this meeting."

"It will not affect me—ha, ha!"

"Well, you are right," answered Clinton; "one cannot ruin the character of a man whose character is *already* blasted. So, you are at liberty to go."

"At *liberty*!"

"Yes, at liberty. By this time the persons you were in pursuit of are out of your reach, were they not, I should not allow you to proceed one step. So, farewell."

Stretton watched him for some few seconds, then rode slowly back towards Alsatia.

With this Clinton, gathering his cloak around him, departed.

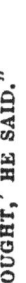

"'AS I THOUGHT,' HE SAID."

CHAPTER XI.

SHOWS A MEETING BETWEEN MOTHER AND SON, WHO, HOWEVER, ARE "STRANGERS YET"—OF HOW LORD CLINTON AND THE COUNTESS OF ROTHBURN WERE STOPPED ON THE WINDSOR ROAD, TAKEN PRISONERS, AND CONVEYED TO THE "OLD MILL," AND OF WHAT TRANSPIRED THERE.

WE would willingly give a description of the meeting between Rosamund and her mother, but that we feel it would become us better to draw a veil over a picture at once so pathetic and heartrending.

The countess, notwithstanding the hour at which Felix and Rosamund reached her house, was up, and, with two or three of her servants, in constant attendance on the unfortunate goldsmith's wife, and she herself received the pair.

And surely no affectionate parent could have received them with more tenderness or more compassion.

The first outburst of joy over, tears of sorrow for the cruel death of Master Walker followed, and Felix did not feel ashamed to shed *his* tears in sorrow for the loss of a kind and affectionate friend.

In the house of the countess he was enabled to think calmly over what had occurred, to fully realise the loss of this valuable friend.

"Surely," he thought, "there can be no more unfortunate person in the world than me. At one moment fortune smiles on me, the next she frowns. Oh, would that I had died when Nicholas Fielding perished!"

"Why do you express such a wish?" asked a low sweet voice.

Felix looked up and saw before him the splendid figure of the countess.

"Ask me not, madam," replied Felix; "ask me not!"

"'Tis my duty to ask you," answered the countess gravely, yet oh, so kindly; "for the wish you have unknowingly uttered aloud is a dreadful one. Answer me, my son—answer me."

"*My son!*"

The words caused our hero to tremble—with what he knew not.

"I cannot, your grace—that is I have no wish to inflict upon you——"

"Whatever you may say I will listen attentively to. Lord Clinton has told me all about you, and I need hardly tell you that I have taken a great interest in you. I seem drawn towards you, as it were," she said in a quick agitated tone; "for your voice—your figure—your very face remind me of——"

She paused and placed her hand upon her heaving breast.

"I remind you, madam—of whom?" asked Felix with great interest.

"Of my late husband."

"Did he die recently?"

"Nay—many, many years ago. But let me proceed. Clinton told me something of your history, and I can feel for you because I had a son—a——"

"You had a son—yes?"

"Aye, he was my only child. He was stolen when but an infant."

"How sad! And did you never recover your son?"

"Never, never!" answered the countess. "Never! God gave, and man—relentless man—took away!"

"I do not quite understand you. Do you mean that an enemy of yours, wishing to do you an injury, stole the child?"

"Yes."

"Have you no suspicion of who that enemy was."

"I have. But I have no direct evidence. Yet the man I suspect has told me to my face my son lives!"

"Great Heaven! then why do you not compel this man to tell you?"

"It is impossible. I can only wait—wait as I have waited for years. The man who could tell me where my child is—and I believe he speaks the truth—is a man I hate and despise—he is now my most bitter enemy!"

"You have great trouble!"

"True!"

"It is no business of mine, else I would ask you who this enemy might be."

"Oh, I need not hide it from anyone. The enemy is Lord Stretton."

Felix started violently.

"The same who pursued us," muttered Felix. "The father of Master Melton."

"The same," said the countess. "And since you are so interested, Master Felix, you have my permission to ask Lord Clinton to give you all particulars."

Felix bowed.

"And do not forget my words, Felix Ferdinand. Live on in hope, as I do. One day you may find your parents; one day Providence may permit *me* to clasp to my heart the son *I* have lost."

"In my prayers," said Felix fervently, "I will not forget to repeat your hopes to Heaven!"

"Nor will I forget your desires," answered the countess.

And so these two—mother and son—so strangely brought together, parted for the time, each in ignorance of the relationship one bore to the other.

In the evening a coach drove up the avenue leading to the countess's residence.

When it reached the door there alighted from it Alice, Andrew, and Fillipy.

Felix was instantly summoned, and, hastening to the door, he was met by Fillipy.

"You did not expect this, I know," said Fallory, "but at my suggestion Andrew has had the body of the poor goldsmith placed in a coffin, and removed from his master's house."

"The body is here then?"

"Aye, in the coach. I trust it will not inconvenience the noble lady who——"

"Not at all, my friends," interrupted the countess, who had joined the group. "You have done quite right. It will be a great satisfaction, although a melancholy one, for the widow of the poor goldsmith to be near the body of her unfortunate husband. Felix, what is this gentleman's name?"

Felix introduced Fallory—who at any other time and under different circumstances would have considered this introduction as of vast importance—as also Andrew and Alice.

Previously, he had of course, told the countess of all our readers know.

The countess directed one of her servants to at once conduct Alice to her mistress, and in a few moments the faithful maid was clasped in Rosamund's arms.

And now, carefully and reverently, the coffin containing the remains of the poor goldsmith was taken from the coach by Felix, Andrew, and Fillipy, carried into the hall, and, at the farther end, placed on a pair of trestles.

Hardly had this been done, ere Rosamund, with a wild bitter cry of anguish, ran forward.

Without a word Felix lifted the lid, and stood on one side, as did the others, until Rosamund's first outburst of grief was over.

Andrew's master had done his duty towards his fellow-citizen, for the coffin was beautifully furnished.

Rosamund's mother, owing to her condition, was not able to walk from her room to look upon all that remained of her loving husband, and as it had been considered advisable that she should not see it for a day or two, the countess gave orders for it to remain where it was.

Refreshments were placed before Fillipy and Andrew, and during their discussion, Felix was made acquainted with what had transpired in Alsatia after his departure.

"Master Melton," said Fillipy, "was, no doubt, taken in charge by some of the Alsatians. At any rate, he disappeared. The Alsatians had received quite sufficient punishment at our hands, and though we showed ourselves quite ready to renew the fight, they declined to have anything further to do with us.

"We had serious thoughts of burning the place down, and so ridding London altogether of the filthy hole; but then we thought of the number of women and children we should place in danger, and so we refrained from so doing.

"So it was decided that we should gain an entry into Captain White's reception-room.

"We found this by no means a difficult matter. The Alsatians were completely cowed by what they had suffered, for they had lost a good number of men, and they offered no resistance, neither did the host of The Fountain of Life or his crew.

"We swarmed into the infamous den, and searched it from top to bottom, but, I am sorry to say, not a vestige of the treasure taken from the goldsmith could be seen.

"Well, we treated Captain White's goods as he and his men had treated the goldsmith's—that is to say we smashed everything we could lay our hands on, and left the place a perfect wreck.

"And now Andrew has something to tell you."

"Yes," said Andrew, gravely, "something of importance. I have discovered the wretch who slew the goldsmith—that is, I have discovered his name.

"One of the Alsatians who had been shot and mortally wounded during the fight, had crept into a cellar near the reception-room, as it is ironically called, to die.

"The man's moans attracted my attention and I went to him. I could see at a glance that he was dying fast, and I told him so.

"Well, he was not surprised. He asked me for a dram of brandy, and this one of the Templars gave him.

"Thinking that perhaps he might be able to tell us what had become of the treasure, I said : 'Ere you die you may be able to do an act of justice, and if you can, and will, fear it not that Heaven will give you your reward.'

"For some moments the man looked hard at me as if not fully comprehending my meaning, then he said :

"'What act of justice could I do ?'"

"I said, 'Tell us where the treasure is which was taken from the goldsmith's house.'

"A grim smile lit up his swarthy features ; he shook his head as he said :

"'Captain White and Pearman alone could tell you that. But I can tell you who slew the goldsmith, if that will be of any service, for the wretch deserves to die like me.'

"'Who was it ?' I eagerly asked.

"'Why, Sharpley Sharp,' was the reply ; 'and it was he who killed the editor of the *Morning Gazette*—of course by the captain's orders. The editor was thrown down the trap in Sharpley's shaving-room.'

"I thanked the man for the information, and he was rejoiced to know that speedy vengeance would fall on Sharpley.

"But the man hoped that Captain White would not be touched.

"'It's his living, you know,' he said with a ghastly grin, 'and it I'd lived he would have given me a fair share of what he got at the goldsmith's, no doubt.'

"We made no reply to this, but left the miserable wretch to die."

"You know this man Sharpley, I suppose ?" asked Felix.

"Oh, quite well. So does Fillipy. He is one of the greatest rogues who ever walked the City, and has long been suspected as a murderer. His business as a barber is simply a blind, for he is undoubtedly one of the principal assistants of Captain White."

"I suggest," said Felix, "that we capture him and hand him over to justice. A rope will assuredly be his portion."

"Yes, that is the best way to act," said Fillipy ; "and I think I know enough law to assist counsel in prosecuting the assassin."

While the three were in conversation Lord Clinton was announced.

His lordship was at once ushered into the presence of the countess, to whom he gave a description as to what passed between him and Stretton, but this, of course, Felix had already told her.

"I need not hope, Clinton," said the countess sadly—"I need not hope that you bring me any news as to my son ? "

"Alas ! I wish I did. But as you know, the search has commenced. Secret agents are at work, and ere long they may worm the secret from Stretton."

"Ah, Clinton," replied the countess, shaking her head, "I fear *that* is out of all question ! "

"Well, hope on. I shall leave no stone unturned, you may depend upon it, for," he said tenderly, as he took the white hand of the countess and pressed it to his lips, "have I not a great deal to gain if my quest proves successful ? "

The countess sighed.

"I wonder if happiness will ever again be mine ? " she said.

"Yes," was Clinton's reply ; "yes—a thousand times yes ! And now for some startling intelligence. My dear countess, you must prepare to depart with me."

"Where ? " exclaimed the countess, much startled.

"To Windsor. I have laid the whole matter before the king, who, strange to say, evinces great interest in the affair. I have told him all—everything—including that you have consented to be mine directly your son is found."

"Yes, yes ! "

"His majesty requested me to bring you to the Castle to-night. In the morning, first thing, he will see us, the strange tale will be repeated, and the king will give us his good advice and assistance, which, as you are fully aware, is not *always* to be despised."

"But," answered the countess, considerably agitated, "how can I leave the house when I have here——"

"My dear countess, you *must*! The house for a day or two must be left in charge of—in charge of—— Ah, I have it! Felix is still here?"

"He is."

"Why not leave the house in his charge?"

"Your suggestions are not only rapid, Clinton," said the countess, "but what is more, they are valuable. I *will* leave the place in the charge of Felix Ferdinand. Though so very young he has the sense of many men twice his age. I feel that I can fully trust the young fellow, so it shall be as you wish, Clinton."

"Good. Pray Heaven the journey proves useful to both of us!"

"Amen to that, Clinton!" answered the beautiful countess, fervently.

"My coach shall be here at eight." said Clinton. "And you will be ready?"

"And waiting," replied the countess.

"I have business of pressing importance, or I would stay and speak to Master Ferdinand—to whom, like yourself, I fell warmly attached—and to his friends, and more especially to the unfortunate mother and daughter of the man I so highly valued—Master Walker. But I can safely leave you to speak on my behalf. Until to-night, then, adieu."

"Adieu, Clinton."

The countess, with a deep sigh, held out her hand.

Clinton took it, and raised it as if about to press it to his lips, but looking up, his eyes encountered those of the countess.

The look spoke volumes.

In one instant the hand was dropped, and the next, the countess was folded to Clinton's breast.

*   *   *   *

Just after eight o'clock Lord Clinton's coach drew up before the front entrance of the countess's residence.

Her ladyship wrapped from head to foot in costly furs, awaited him on the threshold, where, on either side of her, stood a footman holding aloft a flaming link, these lighting up her lovely but now pale features.

At her side stood Felix, and beside him Rosamund; at the back of Rosamund stood Andrew and Fillipy.

Lord Clinton stepped from the vehicle, and raising his hat, said with a smile—

"I see that you are punctual."

"Yes," replied the countess, gravely; "for I am getting anxious."

"Anxious! About what?"

"I don't know exactly; but during the last hour I have felt that—that—Oh, I cannot describe it."

"You have felt that some danger was ahead?"

"Aye."

"Dismiss the feeling, my dear countess. For no danger can—— What was that?"

At this instant a low laugh fell upon the ears of those assembled, and a dark form glided swiftly through the trees and was lost to sight.

The countess trembled.

"Some drunken fool—no doubt of it," said Clinton. "Come."

The countess gave him her hand, and having bidden her guests adieu, Clinton escorted her to the coach.

"Your lordship," whispered Felix, "if aught should happen—if you *should* get into any danger, you will send for me?"

"I will, if it is possible, my lad," replied Clinton, pressing our hero's hand. "But do not trouble yourself about our getting into danger. I generally keep my eyes about me."

"But you cannot be too careful."

"True—true! I am well armed."

"You have a determined enemy in Lord Stretton."

"I fear him not, Felix."

"But there is also his son."

"Aye, I fear neither father nor son. Despite his threats, I believe that Stretton would hesitate to do me any harm."

"He has the Bravos of Alsatia at his beck and call remember."

"You taught them one lesson; I may teach them the next. However, I will not forget to let you know should any danger threaten me."

"It would have been better, your lordship, had you allowed a few of the guard to accompany you."

" I thought of it, but I dismissed the idea because it might be inferred that I was afraid of robbers. So now adieu, Felix."

" Adieu, your lordship! Heaven watch over you and the countess!"

Clinton leapt into the coach, the door was pulled to, the outriders cracked their whips, and away rolled the vehicle.

Felix and Rosamund, hand-in-hand, watched it until it disappeared in the darkness, and as Rosamund turned, she said—

" I know not how it is, dear Felix, but I must confess to the same uneasy feeling as the countess."

" As to myself, Rosamund," replied Felix, " I must say that I did not think so much about it until I heard that strange laugh, and saw that dark figure flit through the trees. Thank Heaven, Clinton is well armed, and is able to defend both himself and the countess."

* * * *

That night Felix, Andrew, and Fallory drew up a plan for the capture of the bloodthirsty wretch, Sharpley Sharp.

Little did either of them think that it was Sharpley Sharp's laugh they heard when the coach was about to move off, or that it was Sharpley Sharp's figure they saw disappear in the darkness.

Directly the coach had gone, Sharpley hurried as fast as he was able towards Vauxhall.

Near the edge of the river there stood a large wooden flour-mill, which had fallen into disuse long before the time at which our story commences.

The mill and grounds had for generations been the property of the Strettons.

The last tenant was a man who was mad enough to meddle with State affairs.

He mixed himself up with a lot of conspirators, and allowed them to use his mill for their meetings.

Lord Stretton— through his son—got scent of it, gave information, and one night the whole lot of conspirators were entrapped and captured.

They were executed, and Stretton claimed and obtained the reward.

The *informer*, Lord Stretton, turned the place into a meeting-place for *himself*, and though the meetings had no reference to " State affairs," they were always of a most lawless character.

Crossing several fields, Sharpley paused before a small gate, looked eagerly around him, and then gave a peculiar whistle.

In less than two seconds a brilliant light appeared at one of the upper windows.

It burnt steadily for half a minute, and then vanished.

" Hum!" cried Sharpley, " all is right. I am glad they are here, for now I shall get what is due. But if they had not arrived I should not have waited for them —no fear!"

Opening the gate, Sharpley walked up to the principal door, on the threshold of which stood the figure of a man.

It was a figure which once seen was never forgotten.

The figure of Pearman.

" Ah, my dear boy," he said, " I am glad you are not late. How have things progressed. How——"

" Hold your tongue!" interrupted Sharpley. " Give me a dram of brandy."

" Hist, my dear boy," said Pearman, elevating his eyebrows. " Here is a little brandy. Drink, and welcome."

And the villain handed Sharpley a brandy-flask, in which there was the veriest drain of brandy.

Pearman generally carried two flasks in his enormous coat-tail-pockets—one for his own use, and one to offer a friend.

Having just wetted his lips, Pearman said—

" Now come! his lordship awaits you."

" Is Lord Stretton himself here?" asked Sharpley in amazement.

" He is."

" I thought it was his son who was going to carry out the business?"

" So it is—so it is! And Lord Stretton will wait here until the return."

" All are here, then?"

" Aye—everyone. Come."

Sharpley entered, and Pearman shut the door.

Pearman took a link from a bracket, and beckoning Sharpley to follow, led the way up the stairs, which were so worm-eaten and rotten, that it was a wonder they bore any weight at all.

Halting on the first floor Pearman pushed open a small door, and ushered

Sharpley into the presence of Lord Stretton.

The room was not a particularly large one, with a remarkably low ceiling, from which hung two or three lamps.

Several small circular apertures did duty for windows, but on this occasion they were carefully filled up with sacks.

In every recess of the room were huge pieces of timber, piles of heavy chains, old mill-stones, pieces of iron, pulleys, and other articles which had been used by the late unfortunate tenant-owner of the mill.

Seated at a rude wooden table was Lord Stretton, with a map of England before him.

On his right sat his son, on his left the villain White, and at the back of him were a dozen Alsatians armed to the teeth.

"Sharpley Sharp," grinned Pearman, "and he brings good news."

"That's lucky for him," growled White, "for if he didn't—well, he knows what would have happened."

"Now to see whether your lordship is right," said Horace.

Addressing Sharpley he said—

"You saw the coach?"

"I did."

"How near did you get?"

"Why, within a short distance."

"Then you saw Lord Clinton and the countess?" asked Stretton eagerly.

"I did," was the reply; "I saw Lord Clinton hand the lady into the coach."

"Did you catch the order given to the postillions?"

"Aye—Windsor. Halt once at the—let me see—— Hum! I've forgotten."

"Think!" said Stretton, impatiently.

"If he doesn't," said White, "he knows what to expect."

"I have it," said Sharpley, "halt at The Crown Inn for water—that was all."

"Did you hear whether they intended to change horses?"

"No."

"They will not change on so short a journey," said Horace. "You may depend upon it that Clinton has taken the best horses in his stable. I will warrant they are the dashing greys."

"You are right," said Sharpley; "the four horses are greys."

"Then," said Horace, "if they are to be intercepted, a move had better be made at once."

"I'm ready," replied White.

Turning to a man at his side, he said—"Horses."

Away went the man to bring out the horses, which had been stowed away in a barn belonging to the mill.

Sharpley gave Stretton particulars of all he had seen, and knowing that Stretton was madly jealous of Lord Clinton, he gave a highly-coloured account as to the "loving" manner in which Clinton and the countess behaved one to the other.

Though Stretton did not interrupt him, his description caused him to bite his lips with rage.

When Sharpley had finished, he said as he placed his finger on a particular part of the map—

"Here is the Windsor road. About here is the Crown; a little farther on to the right is Love-lane—you can't mistake this place, because you will see a large stone cross exactly opposite it. The coach will cross the lane, and then—then will be the time to make the attack. Keep the men concealed until the right moment, then——"

"Leave all that to me," interrupted Horace; "you may depend upon it that I will see everything properly carried out."

"With my assistance," put in White.

"Of course with your assistance."

"I and my men will have to do the dirty work."

"What makes you say that?" asked Stretton, sharply.

"What makes me? Why, because we always do the dirty work."

"In this case," said Horace, "there will be no dirty work, or what you call dirty work, for there will be no bloodshed."

Captain White smiled grimly.

"So you think," he said, "but you ought to know Lord Clinton better than to imagine that he will allow himself to be taken without a struggle."

"Your duty," said Stretton, "is to surprise them—to pounce upon them ere Clinton can have time to draw his sword or defend himself."

"All very well," growled White—"all very well. Lord Clinton I happen to know, and so does your lordship—ho—ho! I happen to know that Lord Clinton is very quick in his movements. Your lordship may take my word that if Clinton is quick enough to attack either me or my men, we shall defend ourselves, and defend ourselves to some tune. There has been quite enough of us killed lately," he said significantly. "Another thing is, I don't do this to gain anything. I only do it now because your lordship has thought fit to threaten me—to—to—in fact, to use your influence against me as an *informer*."

This was said with such a sneer that Stretton fairly winced.

He knew well enough what White meant, and was totally at a loss what to reply.

Horace came to his rescue.

"Let us set out," he said; "we have a long and a hard ride before us. Clinton has a good start. Come, White, see to your men and your arms. What of this fellow?" pointing to Sharpley.

"Fellow?" said Sharpley; "*fellow?* Captain White, do you hear?"

"Yes, and you will return to your shop," said White; "you cannot ride."

"Nay," said Sharpley; "I cannot ride, it is true, but I can easily pocket the money due to me."

"Your lordship owes him ten crowns," said White.

"Here they are then," replied Stretton, as with an oath he flung them at Sharpley's feet.

The murderous little barber picked them up, and pocketed them with a grin.

"Any other commands your lordship may have for me," he said, "shall be faithfully——"

"Be off, rascal!" thundered Stretton. Sharpley bowed.

"Wait for orders in Gunpowder Alley," said White; "and in the meantime, try and get rid of your vixenish wife. Kill her, if you like; if you don't she will hang you sooner or latter."

"Perhaps I will take your advice," said Sharpley with a hideous leer. "There is a comfort in the knowledge that it I do get rid of her, there are a dozen damsels ready to throw themselves into my arms."

"Well," said Pearman, "do not forget that I am at your service. Get rid of your present vixen, and I will soon join you to the other dozen for a small fee—for a small fee."

Having again bowed mockingly to Stretton and leered and blinked at White and the bravos, Sharpley turned and departed.

Horace and White, followed by Pearman and the bravos, descended the stairs.

In front of the mill the horses—very powerful animals, which had been provided by Stretton—were drawn up.

The whole party were quickly mounted.

Horace gave the word, and away they went at a trot, the trot being increased to a gallop as soon as the open country was reached.

Lord Stretton, with folded arms, watched them from the window until they had disappeared from view.

As he turned away he muttered—

"The time is coming, Clinton—the time is coming. And you, proud countess—*you*—shall, on your bended knees, sue to me for mercy!

"Oh, how I long for the moment—that moment, which, to me, will be one of supreme happiness!

"Shall I slay Clinton?" he mused as he fiercely paced the apartment, the boards of which creaked and groaned beneath the stamping of his gold spurred feet; "shall I slay him? Yea! Once in my grasp he must never escape. If I allow him to escape, my life would soon pay the forfeit of such folly. He must die!

"Then, after Clinton, comes this youth—this Felix Ferdinand. Little does he think that *I* gave him that name!

"In his own mother's house! Ho, ho! It seems too much like romance to be true. Mother and son, and yet they know it not. Nay, nor ever will. I hold the connecting link, and by Heaven I will supply it only when he is dying before her eyes."

Again his lordship laughed, and loudly too, and the many rooms echoed the laugh with startling distinctness.

His lordship's laugh was the laugh of a fiend—a fiend gloating over anticipated vengeance.

* * * *

It is not necessary for us to follow Lord Clinton's coach on the way to Windsor Castle.

Though, in consequence of the snow, the roads were very heavy, the coach proceeded at a rapid rate, being drawn by four of Clinton's most powerful horses.

Nothing of any importance occurred until they arrived almost within sight of The Crown Inn.

One of the leading horses, alarmed at something by the roadside, became frightened, plunged and kicked violently, and before he could be restrained a trace was broken.

This circumstance necessitated a longer stay at The Crown than was contemplated.

However, by this time the fears of the countess had worn off, and she was as chatty and as lively as a lady could possibly be.

Clinton was delighted, and he did all in his power to prevent her ladyship's spirits from flagging.

But this delay was all in favour of Horace and his murderers.

Horace and his party arrived at the stone cross at Love-lane just as the coach was leaving The Crown.

"Now," said Horace, as he raised himself in his stirrups, and looked around him, "are we in time?"

"A question easily answered," growled White.

"Well, answer it," replied Horace, sharply.

"You can answer it yourself," grinned White; "look at the snow."

"I am looking at the snow. What then?"

"It hasn't been snowing for some hours now, has it?"

"Not that I am aware of."

"Very well. If you look you will see that the snow is perfectly smooth and undisturbed. That proves that no vehicle has been past here."

Pearman chuckled, and this was the signal for the bravos to laugh.

"I must admit you are right," said Horace, considerably annoyed by the laughter of the men. "I should have thought of it myself, only I have already so much to think of."

"I hope you are thinking of what is due to me," said White.

"Well, at the present moment I am not. But I should have thought that you got enough from the goldsmith's to last you your lifetime."

"That, Master Melton, is *my* business," answered White, sternly.

"Well, well," said Horace, who was far from wishing to quarrel with White, "either now or at any other time, I will pay you what is due directly this affair is over. His lordship's revenge satisfied——"

"Yours will follow?" interrupted White.

"Yes, you are right—mine will follow. If I can be revenged on the cub who rescued Rosamund, I shall be satisfied. By all the fiends! I swear I would give up all I ever hope for to get him within my clutches!"

"Hark!" said White; "I hear something approaching. Now, my men, get ready!"

Instantly each man took from his hat a mask, and put it on.

White took two from his holster.

One he handed to Horace, who put it on, and the other he donned himself.

The whole party then withdrew behind some large trees.

There they stood for some time.

Horace and White alone conversed, but it was in whispers.

At last the rapid cracking of a whip was heard.

"They come!" said White.

"Aye," said Horace; "I can see the coach."

"Now, listen to me," said White. "As soon as the coach is on a level with us, all will dash forward and surround it. You, Master Melton, will go to the coach window, I presume?"

"Nay," said Horace; "I think it would be better if I kept out of the way of the window."

"But you cannot be recognised, since you wear a mask."

"True, but I——"

"You are afraid of a stray shot, Master Melton—eh?" sneered the Pearman. "Well, it is but natural."

"Pearman will go to the window," said Horace.

"*De*—clined with thanks!" returned Pearman with a mock bow. "You see *I* am a man of peace. And, besides, I got sufficiently ill-treated during the attack on Alsatia to last me a few months or so."

"*I* will go to the window," said White with a grand swagger. "Now, don't make a mistake, for here is the coach. All of you dash forward and surround it."

Nearer and nearer came the coach.

The snow so deadened the sound of the wheels, that Lord Clinton's voice could plainly be heard.

When on a level with the bravos, White said—

"Comrades, forward!"

Away dashed the whole party of ruffians, and in the twinkling of an eye the coach was surrounded.

The outriders, with a great shout of alarm, drew up their horses.

The countess, uttering a loud cry of terror, fell back on the cushions, trembling violently.

Clinton, without waiting to ask who had stopped the coach, drew a pistol and fired at the man nearest him—Captain White.

The ball, however, struck one of the men at his side.

It pierced his breast, and he at once dropped from the saddle.

Captain White, with an oath, seized Clinton's wrist.

"Surrender," he said in assumed tones, as he pulled a pistol from his holster and pointed it at Clinton's head. "Surrender, or I will have your life! This is no time for foolery, if——"

"Let go my hand, blackguard!" roared Clinton, as he wrested his hand free, and with the other burst open the coach door.

White's finger was on the trigger, and, in defiance of Stretton's orders, he would have fired, had he not seen that, if he did so, he would probably hurt the countess.

Clinton's sword flashed from its sheath.

"Villains!" he cried, in passionate tones. "What means this outrage? You are not robbers—that I can see at a glance. Who—— Ah, by heaven, I have it! This is Stretton's work—yes, it is Stretton's work! For *you*"—here he pointed at White—" you I recognise, despite your assumed voice—despite the mask you wear—I recognise you as the villainous Captain White of Alsatia!"

"Perhaps I am, and perhaps I am not," replied White. "Anyhow, you will be wise if you put that sword down. If you do not, I shall be compelled to put a ball through your heart."

And again he raised his pistol.

"Fire!" shouted Clinton; "fire you

accursed coward! for I will never yield to you or your dastardly crew."

"Beware how you speak of *gentlemen*," said White.

During this conversation, Horace had dismounted on the other side of the coach, and creeping round, tried to approach Clinton unawares.

But his movements were observed by the countess.

Springing from the coach, she threw herself by Clinton's side.

"Beware!" she said; "beware. We are surrounded by *treacherous* and brutal ruffians. Look at this man!"

And she pointed to Horace.

Clinton stepped back a pace, surveyed Horace an instant, and then, ere he could get out of the way, he darted forward and tore the mask from his face.

"As I thought," he said. "These are Stretton's orders, and his son assists in carrying them out. Scoundrel, defend yourself!"

Horace snatched his blade from its sheath—to ward off the thrust Clinton made at him.

But White and the bravos drew close in, watching their opportunity to aim a blow at Clinton.

His lordship was, however, guarded by the countess, who placed her beautiful figure before him.

"Clinton," she said, with a bitter cry, "resistance is useless. For my sake, sheath your sword!"

"Oh, that you were not present!" said Clinton; "I swear that I would teach these villians a lesson. Oh, what degradation to be captured by a lot of Alsatian bravos!"

"Fear it not, Clinton," answered the countess; "your time will come."

Horace smiled maliciously.

His grin was observed by Clinton, who, a sudden thought striking him, turned to White.

"Captain White," he said, "I am forced to give in; I——"

"I am glad your lordship acknowledges it," answered White with a chuckle; "it saves a vast amount of trouble. Your lordship will doubtless favour me with your sword."

"One moment. I have a proposal to make."

"Hum! A proposal. Hem! No doubt your proposal is to the effect that

I will permit the countess "—here the one-eyed wretch raised his hat—"to resume her journey without further molestation. Hem! I am sorry to say that that is out of the question. My instructions are to bring both you and the countess to London."

"Nay," replied Clinton; "my proposal is very different."

"Even if the scoundrel said I would be allowed to proceed," said the countess, drawing her fine figure erect, "I would not go. Where you go, Clinton, there I go also."

"Nobly said, fair lady," said Pearman, with a leer. "My own wife—if I had one—ahem!—could not have delivered—"

"Silence!" shouted White, dealing Pearman such a stunning blow on the mouth that he nearly rolled off his saddle. "Silence! and let us hear what the proposal is."

"It is this," cried Clinton. "You are aware of the fact, Captain White, that I am a rich man?"

"Ha—hem—I am."

"Very well. Perhaps you have also heard that I am a person of my word."

"Well—er—I believe you are."

"Good! Now I make you a fair offer. I swear that the countess and myself shall accompany you quietly to London, to whatever part we are to be taken, and I will give you an order which will enable you to obtain a thousand pounds in my name, on condition that you stand aside while I fight a duel with this villain."

And he pointed to Horace.

Horace, with a cry, started back.

Captain White saw the effect this startling and unexpected proposal had on Stretton's son, and he thoroughly enjoyed it.

The captain stroked his chin reflectively.

"Accept his terms," whispered Pearman. "A thousand pounds is not always so easily obtained."

"Have I not already *many* thousands stored up!" replied White. "Besides, there are many other reasons why it is impossible to agree to such a proposal. You are aware of the fact that Clinton is a deadly enemy of the Alsatians, are you not? Stretton wants to get hold of him, to torture him, and do away with him. So while he satisfying *his own*

desire for revenge, he is removing an enemy from *our* path."

"Your answer?" cried Clinton.

"He does not *dare* to accept your terms!" cried Horace.

"Don't be too sure," sneered White. "I dare anything."

Horace trembled.

He knew well enough that if Clinton was allowed to attack him, he would be a dead man in but a few short moments.

"Your answer?" repeated Clinton, eagerly.

"It is out of all question, my lord," answered White. "In the first place, a delay——"

"No delay shall occur, I assure you," interrupted Clinton.

"A delay would take place," continued White; "and besides that, I have made a solemn promise to——"

He paused abruptly,

"To Lord Stretton, you would say," said Clinton, bitterly. "Well, you refuse; but a time will come for me—a time will come. There is my sword, villains!" he cried, flinging it violently at Horace's head, and narrowly missing it. "Take it, and may Heaven's curse rest upon you all!"

Several of the bravos dismounted.

One produced two or three stout pieces of rope, and commenced to disentangle them.

"Do you mean to say," said Clinton, "that I am to suffer the indignity of being pinioned?"

"Well, I think we can dispense with that," replied White, "if your lordship will give your word of honour that you will neither attempt to escape, nor offer any violence towards any of us."

"You *cannot* dispense with it," thundered Horace, who, now that Clinton was no longer in possession of a weapon, had become very brave; "you *dare* not dispense with it!"

"Oh," said White; "and why not, pray?"

"Because it is my orders that he be pinioned; and not only that he be pinioned, but that the countess be pinioned also."

A frenzied cry left Clinton's lips, as, throwing off the arm of the countess, laid so lovingly on his own, he dashed upon Horace, tore the sword from his grasp, and fastened his muscular fingers on his throat.

"WITH A BOUND HE WAS UPON HORACE, ERE HE COULD PULL THE TRIGGER."

" You cur!" hissed Clinton; " you vile wretch! I will rend your carcass into pieces! I will——"

" Hold!" roared White. " Hold, I say!"

Clinton, now thoroughly roused, paid not the slightest attention to the shouts.

With one hand he held Horace by the throat, with the other he seized him by the waistband, and exerting all the strength in his herculean frame, he raised Horace over his head and dashed him against the coach-wheel.

With a heavy thud he fell to the ground.

" I think he has killed him," said Pearman.

" He has not killed him, don't fear," said White; " he'll meet with a worse end than that, or I am much mistaken. Here, boys," he shouted, " take this flask of brandy. turn him over, and pour some down his throat. Your lordship has made a mistake," he added as he turned to Clinton; " suppose you had killed him?"

" In that case," replied Clinton, " a future task would be spared to me."

" Well, I don't know what your future arrangements are," said White, " but I can tell you that whatever arrangements you may have made are, in consequence of us taking you prisoners, rendered null and void."

" For the time being—yes."

" No! For ever!"

So emphatically did White say this, that Clinton at once saw that he had good grounds for so expressing himself.

" Let us trust to Heaven, Clinton," said the countess in low, earnest tones.

" Aye," answered Clinton, bitterly; " but remember, my dear, that I have not your patience."

" Captain White," said Horace in hoarse tones, as the men assisted him to rise; " Captain White, are your prisoners bound?"

White was about to return him a saucy answer, but, seeing the state he was in— his face completely covered with blood which issued from a deep wound in his head, caused by its coming violently in contact with the wheel—he refrained, and said—

" I have given orders that his lordship is to be pinioned. Now then, my men, see that it is done."

Resistance was useless.

With a groan of despair Clinton allowed his arms to be pinioned behind his back.

" Now the countess," said Horace.

" No, that be hanged!" said White. " I can't manage that. My men, like myself, know better manners than to pinion the arms of such a lovely creature."

And once more the ugly one-eyed wretch raised his hat.

" A rope," said Horace; " I will pinion her arms myself."

" Do you dare?" said the countess.

" Yes, I *dare!*" replied Horace.

" Proceed then," said the countess, scornfully; " proceed, wretch, and be quick, or perchance your courage may fail you."

" Your sneers will not affect me, countess," said Horace, " for let me tell you that I have not one spark of respect for you."

" Vile worm!" answered the countess, whose eyes filled with tears at this insult. " Vile worm—for whom have you respect? Oh, Heaven! what have I done that I should be so treated?"

" Were it possible, countess," said Clinton, " I would make him suffer for the insult on the spot."

" I know it, Clinton," returned the countess; " I know it well! But calm yourself—for my sake, calm yourself."

Then she added to Horace, who had been handed a piece of rope—

" Proceed with your outrage!"

" Faugh!" muttered Horace, as he proceeded to tie the countess's arms behind her back. " I do not consider it an outrage."

The pinioning process was soon completed.

Horace pulled the rope as tight as he was able, but his cruelty drew not a single cry from the countess.

But Clinton saw, from the quivering of her lips, the agony she was enduring.

" Bear up," he said tenderly, " your trials will soon end."

" Yes," said Horace; " from what I can at present see of it, both your trials will soon commence, and end with your deaths."

Horace placed his hand to his aching brow, and said--

" Be good enough to dismount, Pearman, and tie this kerchief around my head."

"Your pate you should have said," replied Pearman as he carefully slid off the saddle, " your *cracked* pate. It not only sounds more refined but it is true. Are you much injured ?" he asked, as he looked at the wound.

"Listen to me," said Horace severely, in low tones. "You are becoming too familiar. I warn you that——"

"Too *familiar?*" interrupted Pearman with a stare of astonishment. "You surprise me! I am aware that you are the son of a lord, but what of that? You are as great a blackguard as any of us, are you not? You choose to mix with us, and therefore——"

"Silence, you hypocrite! Take this kerchief and tie my head up. Lord! how it throbs!" he groaned.

"No doubt," replied Pearman; "but I don't think you have lost anything except a little blood. I have looked near the coach-wheel, *and don't see any brains.*"

Captain White overheard this, and he laughed loudly.

"I presume we are to ride together in the coach?" asked Lord Clinton.

"You must since there is no other way of conveying you to London," replied White.

"There is another way," said Horace.

"Oh," said White, " there is — is there? And pray, what is the other way!"

"One of your men was shot dead, so there is a spare horse. Let Lord Clinton be strapped to it, his face towards the horse's tail."

"Captain White," said Clinton in low determined tones, " let me tell you that I will not be subjected to further outrage. If I so chose I could easily snap the chords which bind my hands. And if I did so, by Heaven, someone would suffer ! "

"Do not trouble yourself, your lordship," said White. "You will go in the coach. We have been quite long enough over this job," he whispered, drawing up beside Horace, "and further delay will be dangerous. Besides, mounted on horseback, his lordship could shout for assistance at the very first opportunity."

"What of it—what if he did? I should say that he was a State prisoner."

"And his lordship would call upon you to produce your warrant. What would you do then?"

"Ah, well—into the coach with them."

"This way, countess," said Pearman with a leer, as he raised his hat; "this way. I know the fact of your arms being bound will not inconvenience you to any great extent."

"If you could *bind your tongue,* so that it be not heard on the journey, I could easily put up with the inconvenience occasioned by my arms being bound," answered the countess haughtily.

Pearman grinned, and held open the coach door with the remark, "*Pray* enter."

Clinton stood on one side his head bowed upon his breast.

The countess being seated, Pearman addressed himself to Clinton.

"*Pray* enter," he said.

Clinton bestowed upon him a look of disgust.

"Ho ! " cried White, who by this time, like his men, had taken off his mask. "Ho ! where the deuce is the other outrider ! There is only one now."

"He has escaped," said the outrider, who had been too closely watched to get away.

"Escaped ! " cried White, turning to his men. "Then where were your eyes. Confound him. May he fall into a ditch and break his neck. Which way did he go, sirrah ?"

The outrider did not reply.

"Which way did he go ? " thundered White.

"Towards the castle," was the reluctant reply.

This was untrue, for the man had gone off in the direction of London.

"I will warn the youth at the countess's residence," he had said ; " Felix Ferdinand."

"Oh, to the castle, has he ? " growled White.

"In that case the sooner we are off the better," said Pearman.

"Since one outrider only is left," said White ; "why we must do with one only. So now are you all ready ? Are you all right, Master Melton ? "

"Yes," was the surly reply.

"I hope you are both perfectly comfortable?" said Pearman, poking his face into the coach.

There was no answer.

"Yes," said the ruffian; "they say they are very comfortable indeed."

"Mount, then," cried White.

All being in readiness the party went o ff.

The Alsatian who had been shot dead by Clinton was left at the side of a clump of trees.

Every article of value had been taken away from him by his comrades, so that when found he would be taken as a victim of highway robbery.

It was the rule among the Alsatians to rob friend as well as foe, and it was a rule rarely, if ever, forgotten.

* * * *

Hour after hour passed, and still Lord Stretton paced the apartment in the old mill.

Occasionally he looked from the window, his restless gaze wandering over the broad fields, covered with snow, or upon the broad bosom of the Thames, or upon the banks, now white and crisp with snow and ice.

Not a boat of any description moved either up or down the Thames, and he could see nothing move on land, except it was the black leafless trees, which seemed to bow gravely before every blast of wind.

At last the clock in the belfry of the tower of Westminster Abbey proclaimed the hour of one.

"One of the clock," muttered Stretton, impatiently; "and still no signs of them! I should not wonder if my confounded luck is once more against me! Perhaps there has been a fight, and——"

He paused abruptly.

He was thinking that if there had been a fight, perhaps his son might be one of the slain.

"But no, no," he muttered, as a grim smile lit up his ferocious face; "that would not be. Ha, ha! If Horace saw danger ahead he would take to flight. Yes, yes; I know him too well to fancy he would stand his ground. Oh, I feel as though I cannot contain myself much longer. If they *have* captured them they must be near at hand."

Suddenly a shrill whistle rang out.

Stretton started.

"That was White," he muttered, "but it must have come from the opposite side."

He listened intently.

Again came the whistle, this time louder and more prolonged.

It was decidedly on the opposite side of the mill.

Stretton snatched up a lamp, and hurried from the room, across the landing, to the opposite window.

By the merest chance he missed a trap-door which had been left open.

Had he fallen through it he would certainly have broken his neck.

Pausing a moment he flung the heavy trap-door down.

Reaching the window, or rather let us say aperture, he held up the lamp and waved it backwards and forwards for a moment.

Then looking out he saw the party slowly approaching.

As soon as he made out the coach he uttered a wild exultant cry.

"Captured! captured!" he cried. "My revenge is close at hand!"

Presently one of the men rode forward.

Stretton recognised him.

It was Pearman.

Stretton hurried down the stairs and met him.

A few words passed, and then Stretton said—

"What made White come that way?"

"To avoid being seen as much as possible," replied Pearman. "Once or twice we were asked 'Whose coach?'"

"Well, well, and what answer did you give?"

"Oh, we said it was Lord Stallimore's coach. Ha, ha!"

"Very good. Take this lamp and light the party up. By the party I mean Master Melton, Captain White, the *two prisoners*, and yourself. The men may remain here. I suppose Lord Clinton is pinioned?"

"He is, and so is the countess."

"The countess?" cried Stretton in astonishment. "What scoundrel was it who tied her hands?"

"*Your scoundrel son!*" chuckled Pearman as he stood on one side.

Stretton had clapped his hand to his sword, but seeing that the party was now so close, he contented himself with directing a fierce look at the insolent ruffian, and then ascended the rotten stairs.

In a few moments the coach was drawn up before the mill-entrance.

Pearman stepped up to it, and opened the door.

Holding the lamp aloft, he said—

"*Pray* descend. At last your lordship and your countess-ship have reached your destination."

Clinton stepped from the coach, turned, bowed to the countess, and stood aside while the beautiful but unlucky lady descended.

"Alas, my dear Clinton, what changes are effected in a few short hours!" she said.

Clinton bowed, but he made no other reply.

His heart was full to overflowing at the sight of the tear-stained and pale face of the countess.

With one hand Pearman held the lamp aloft, and with the other he pointed to the gloomy entrance.

By this time Horace and Captain White had dismounted, and had reached the doorway.

As soon as Clinton saw Horace, he said—

"Are you not going to release this lady's arms?"

"In a few moments I will consider the matter," was Horace's sneering reply.

"Wretch!" cried Clinton; "you shall be repaid your insults a thousand-fold!"

Horace bowed mockingly.

"Clinton," said the countess, pausing on the first stair, "can you tell me where we are?"

"Oh, yes," was the reply. "I know well enough, though from their conversation these men were evidently under the impression that I know not in what part of the country we are. This is the old mill at Vauxhall. Your ladyship must have heard of it."

"I have indeed," answered the countess with a shudder. "And we are to be confined here, I presume, until Lord Stretton thinks proper to release us?"

"*Death* will soon release you!" said Horace.

"Proceed!" cried White impatiently. "You are keeping us waiting. Show them up, Pearman, and be hanged to you!"

In less than a minute the countess stood in the apartment in which was Stretton.

He stood on the opposite side of the table, his arms folded across his breast, his looks fierce and revengeful.

The countess, uttering a low cry, recoiled as Stretton hissed—

"Face to face once more!"

The countess drew her fine figure proudly erect.

"*You* here?" she said in low tones.

"Aye, I am here," was the answer.

"Monster!"

Stretton, with the smile of a demon, bowed ironically, and as he bowed, Clinton stood on the threshold.

Directly he saw Stretton, he started violently.

A wild cry left his lips, he half bent his body, and with a powerful wrench, snapped in twain the chords which bound him.

"Hell-hound!" he roared, making a bound towards Stretton, who had plucked his sword from his scabbard, "let me but get at you, and——"

"Not so fast!" said White, as he seized one of Clinton's arms.

"Not so *rapid!*" said Pearman, as he seized the other.

"Let me go," shouted Clinton, let me go, or I will dash your brains out against this wall."

"Move an inch," cried Horace, as he held a pistol within an inch of Clinton's face—"and I fire."

"Desist, Clinton," said the countess; "for my sake! Have but a little patience. Let us hear what the villain has to say."

"Whom do you call villain?" asked Stretton.

"You—*you*, vile depraved wretch!"

"Hum! I thank you."

"Shocking language for such a lovely being to use," smirked Pearman.

"Captain White," said Stretton, "remove that lady's bonds."

"You wish me," said White, "to give *instructions* to that effect. Hum! I am in the habit of *giving* orders, not carrying them out myself. Pearman, remove that lady's bonds."

"Certainly," replied Pearman, who thereupon untied the cords and handed them to Horace.

"The rope," he said, gravely.

"I don't require it," said Horace, haughtily; "keep it."

"I will," muttered the ruffian in tones loud enough to reach Horace's ears; "I sell all my old rope to the hangman. On this *I will place your name.*"

Clinton was quiet now.

With folded arms he stood surveying Stretton with a look of hatred.

Stretton picked up a pen, and while still standing, wrote these words on a slip of paper.

"Send Pearman down to bring up half-a-dozen of the men. Let him also bring in a heavy chain and padlock which he will find in the adjoining room."

This he handed to White, who having closely inspected it with his one eye, handed it to Pearman, who at once went off.

"Stand where you are, Horace," said Stretton, "and fire if I give you the word."

"Listen to me," said Clinton, hoarsely, "tell us why we are brought here. I warn you that I will not be trifled with much longer. One pistol nor ten will presently prevent me from——"

"Clinton, Clinton!" cried the countess, "have patience."

Stretton, after bestowing a withering look upon the countess, said—

"I will tell you why you have been brought here. I will say naught about you, Lord Clinton, regaining your liberty, for I have an account to settle with you. But the Countess of Rothburn shall go hence in one day if she agree to my terms."

"Name them," said Clinton.

"Aye, name them!" repeated the countess.

"That you leave this house *as my wife!*"

"Never!" cried the countess; "never, monster! I would never consent to so degrade myself! As Heaven is my judge, I would sooner be thrown in the vilest dungeon than live to be called *your* wife!"

"Well spoken, countess!" said Clinton. "For those words I thank you."

"Reserve your thanks, then," sneered Stretton, "for a more fitting occasion."

"For a more fitting occasion?" said Horace. "From what your lordship has led me to understand, an opportunity for thanks or anything else will never occur."

Stretton smiled faintly.

"You are right," he said.

Turning once more to the countess, he said—

"I again make you aware of my terms. Think a few moments ere you again reject them."

"Were I to think for ten years," was the scornful reply, "my answer could never be anything but what it is now."

"Hum! Well, then, let me tell you —that you shall be married to me *against* your will!"

"Against my will? Never!"

"Never? Remember that you are in my power."

"True. But Heaven will not forsake either Clinton or myself."

"We shall see," sneered Stretton.

"Abominable, vile coward," cried the countess, "treacherous wretch that you are, you would not stand before Clinton when he had a chance to defend himself. You must employ your wretched son and a number of bravos to assist you in wreaking your vengeance on the man of whom you are afraid."

"And now tell me," said Clinton, "in what way do you propose to wreak your vengeance upon me?"

"I do not choose to gratify your curiosity," replied Stretton. "You will learn quite soon enough."

"Fool! Do you imagine that you can treat me as a child? I will no longer submit to this treatment. Thus do I show you what I—single-handed —am able to do!"

With a bound he was upon Horace ere he could step back or draw the trigger of his pistol.

Down upon the floor with a terrible crash he went.

A portion of the rotten flooring gave way with a loud cracking sound, and down through the aperture into the inky blackness below went Clinton and Horace, Clinton's hands being firmly fixed round the neck of the infamous son of Lord Stretton.

CHAPTER XII.

WHEREIN IT IS SEEN HOW FELIX AND HIS TWO FRIENDS PROCEED TO THE HOUSE
OF THE MURDEROUS BARBER, OF WHAT HAPPENED THERE AND SHOWS HOW
SHARPLEY SHARP FALLS INTO THE TRAP HE HAS SO LONG USED FOR THE
DESTRUCTION OF OTHERS.

On fully discussing the matter, it was decided between Felix, Andrew, and Fallory that nothing should be said to Rosamund or her mother respecting their intention of going to the house of the infamous barber.

"It will only cause both of them anxiety," said Felix, and at present it is absolutely necessary that they should get as much rest as is possible."

"I quite agree with you," said Fallory; "and that puts me in mind of the fact that I also require rest."

"And I," said Andrew. "And so do you, Master Felix."

"Very true; but I will seek rest at a more suitable time."

"For my part," said Fillipy, "although I require rest, I do not mean to seek it until that villain Sharpley is in the hands of the officers of justice."

"Nor I," said Andrew.

The three waited until midnight, and then Felix, having assured himself that Rosamund and her mother had retired for the night, informed the night-porters that he was about to leave the house on business.

Having well armed themselves, and provided with a whistle, Felix, Andrew, and Fillipy set out.

It was a most unfortunate thing that something did not cause them to be detained for another half-hour.

For at the expiration of that time the outrider who had escaped from the bravos reached the countess's residence.

When the outrider heard from one of the porters that our hero had gone out, and that it was uncertain when he would return, he fell with a groan on the threshold of the house, wringing his hands and crying:

"All is lost then! It will be too late—too late!"

Our business, however, is not now with this man, but with Felix.

On went the three at a good pace.

They found the streets nearly deserted, and that is not to be wondered at, considering what a bitter night it was.

Temple bar being reached, a number of people were observed congregated about it and at the entrance to the Temple.

"Come this side," said Fillipy, "for I can tell that a large number of Alsatians are about."

"Yes," said Andrew, "they are evidently trying to get all their friends together. I should not be at all surprised if they attacked the Temple when the Templars least expect it."

"I pray Heaven it may not be so!" said Fillipy. "When they make the attack—that is, if they contemplate such a thing—may I be there to assist in receiving them."

"Let us draw our cloaks closely about us," said Andrew, "and our hats well over our brows."

"And above all see that your swords are loose in their scabbards," said Felix. "We may be suddenly attacked by the blackguard White and some of his men, for you may depend upon it they will keep good watch for us."

"Aye," said Fillipy, "and so will Lord Stretton and his son."

"So that we meet them face to face, and have an opportunity of drawing our weapons," said Felix, "we have little to fear."

Ah, little did either of them dream what Stretton, his son, and Captain White were doing at that moment!

But not a soul interfered with them.

As the three turned into Gunpowder Alley, however, sounds of revelry fell upon their ears.

"I should not wonder if we find that the filthy little barber and his friends are making a night of it," said Andrew.

"Do you think that Captain White is present?" asked Felix.

"Well, I should not be at all surprised. But why do you ask?"

"I long to meet him."

"No doubt your opportunity will come at a future time. But hark!"

The three paused within a few paces of the barber's dwelling.

They listened, and heard a voice which said—

"Here's to the brave bravos! May they never want. And here's to myself the bravest barber in the whole City! Here's also to Captain White; may he never have the luck to lose the other eye."

A loud roar, and a tremendous clatter of tankards was the response to this toast.

"There can be no mistaking that voice," said Andrew. "It belongs to the barber. And now—— But stay, he is about to say something else."

"Once more, my friends," continued the voice, which certainly belonged to Sharpley. "This is a toast in the drinking of which you will all feel considerable satisfaction. Here's to Master Melton and the goldsmith's daughter, who, however, for the time being, has slipped through his clutches, but who, nevertheless he will soon have in his possession once more. The goldsmith's daughter, I say. Here's also to Lord Stretton, and his lovely *intended bride*, the Countess of Rothburn!"

"By Heaven!" hissed Felix, "if I once get the wretch within my power I shall not feel inclined to let the officers of justice get possession of him."

"Hist!" said Fillipy. "The blackguard! I would I had him at the point of my sword!"

But if what the barber had just said caused the trio such indignation, what must the next words have caused them?

These were the words, and they were in answer to a question to one of the guests, whose voice, however, our friends could not hear—

"Yes, there can be no doubt that by this time Lord Clinton and his precious countess—the lady he thought to snatch from Stretton—horses, riders, coach, and all, are in the possession of the brave captain, the boys, and—and—Master Melton. Therefore you ought all to be thankful that you are not with the noble captain on this particular night."

Felix, Fillipy, and Andrew looked askance at each other.

"My friends," said Fillipy, "we have made a great mistake in leaving the residence of the Countess of Rothburn."

"Not so," replied Felix in hoarse tones. "Had we not come here we should not have discovered that Clinton had been intercepted. Alas, the fears of the countess were not without reason!"

"We must know more," said Andrew, "and from this wretch himself!"

"Look here," said Felix, pointing to a low wall at the side of the house, "lift me up. No doubt we shall be able to effect an entrance this way without alarming the blackguards."

Andrew and Fillipy lifted up our hero, who, after a look round, said—

"I will get over, and do you follow me, Andrew. Master Fallory, will you stay near the door, and so prevent escape from that way?"

"Certainly," replied Fallory, "I will guard the door. Do you see an opportunity of gaining the inside of the house that way?"

"Yes; there is a ladder over here, leaning against a window which is open."

"Then over you go, and may good luck attend you?"

Felix was over the wall in an instant, and Andrew, being assisted by Fillipy, soon followed him.

Fillipy, drawing his sword, and having his hand upon his pistol, stood by the door.

With cautious steps Felix and Andrew crept along the wall until they came to the ladder our hero had spoken of.

It stood against what was evidently a landing window, and this, as Felix had said, was open.

Felix commenced to ascend it, and Andrew kept close behind him.

The window being reached, the pair glided through.

In another moment they stood on the first landing.

They were in almost total darkness.

The loud shouts of revelry continued.

Felix was just about to place his foot on the first stair when a door almost by the side of him opened, and a woman, carrying a small lamp, appeared.

It was the barber's wife.

That she was considerably the worse for drink could be seen by her unsteady carriage.

For one moment, surprise at suddenly encountering two strangers with drawn swords held her speechless, the next, however, she opened her lips to give utterance to a loud shriek of alarm.

But ere she could cry out, Andrew was upon her.

He clutched her firmly by the throat, and at the same moment Felix snatched the lamp from her hand.

Mistress Sharp was a woman possessed of fairly good strength, though she could not boast of much flesh, and she commenced to struggle violently.

Andrew placed his sword between his teeth, and pressed the woman to the ground.

Felix placed the lamp down, and came to his assistance.

"One moment," he said, as he entered the room and caught up a sheet; "we must gag her. If she uttered one cry our plans would be spoilt."

"Quite true," said Andrew; "and we must also bind her, or by some means she will give the alarm."

The sheet was quickly placed about her head, and firmly secured.

Despite her frantic struggles, Felix and Andrew dragged her into the room, and with the cord of the bed-curtains they fastened her firmly, hands and feet, to the bedpost.

Leaving the lamp burning in a corner of the landing, the pair descended the stairs.

The "entertainment" which the barber was giving to his friends—a dozen of the Bravos of Alsatia—was taking place in the very apartment where the unfortunate Stephen Fantenoy, and many others, had been so foully murdered.

Waiting until a loud roar of laughter drowned the sound of their movements, Felix advanced to the door, which was ajar, and flung it wide open.

Had a bomb been thrown into their midst, the blackguards collected together in that room could not have moved with greater rapidity than they did when Felix and Andrew stood on the threshold.

"Hold!" Felix cried; "it is useless for you to draw your weapons. The house is surrounded!"

A cry of consternation left the men's lips.

Felix took his whistle from his pocket and blew a loud blast upon it.

"Listen," he said.

The signal was immediately answered by Fillipy blowing his whistle.

The looks of consternation changed to looks of terror.

"Deliver up your weapons," said Felix, "and surrender yourselves. Do this quietly, and you may not be severely dealt with."

Felix had thought that it would be a fine stroke if he could succeed in confining these men in the apartment until the officers of justice could be fetched.

But the bravos were not the sort of men to be caged without making an effort to escape.

They were well aware of the fact that if brought to trial there was no hope for them.

In the meantime, the barber had gradually slunk back.

It was, of course, his intention to try and make his escape, whatever the others might do.

But Andrew saw his movement.

"Stay where you are, Sharpley Sharp!" he cried; "we came here principally for you. Stop where you are, I tell you, or as sure as I stand here I will send a bullet through your body."

"What have I done that I should be thus attacked in my own house?" whined the barber who was now considerably whiter than the sheet which had been bound about his wife's head.

Before Andrew could reply to him, the bravos made a frantic rush towards the shop.

One of them smashed a window and looked out.

Instantaneously Fillipy raised his pistol and fired, but the shot did not strike the man.

Uttering loud howls of vengeance, the bravos rushed back.

At the same moment Felix and Andrew darted from the doorway and seized the barber, who had succeeded in getting up the window.

Through the doorway and up the stairs flew the terrified bravos.

Many of them did not wait to descend by the ladder, but they leapt clean through the window into the yard.

Felix and Andrew, as well as the barber, heard the loud thuds as their bodies touched the ground.

Not daring to approach the front, the villains made off as fast as they were able by the back way, pulling down every obstruction in their path, in order to facilitate their escape from what they though a court full of officers of justice.

Sharpley Sharp, now thoroughly alive to the fact that unless he made a bold dash for liberty his capture was certain, struggled violently to release himself.

After a tussel of some moments' duration, he actually succeeded in slipping from the grasp of Felix and Andrew.

Rushing to one side of the room, he snatched a dagger from his pocket, and, waving it aloft, cried out—

"Dare to approach me, and I will stab you to your hearts! Away!"

"Let us have no more, villain!" said Felix, pointing his pistol at his head. "Put down that dagger, wretch! Put down that dagger, I say, and tell us what has happened to Lord Clinton and the Countess of Rothburn!"

Sharpley lowered his dagger, and stared hard at our hero.

"Will you let me go," he said, "if I tell you all about it?"

"I will think of it."

"Well, if you'll promise to spare me I'll tell you all I know."

As he said this the cunning wretch had gradually shifted his position to near the fireplace.

Not being acquainted with the many secrets of the place, neither Felix nor Andrew took any notice of his movements, or if they did they attributed it to his uneasiness.

"We know you have had to do with the matter," said Felix sternly, "for we happened to overhear what you said. Now, for your life, speak—quick!"

Hardly had the word "quick" left his lips ere a loud sharp click rang out, a portion of the wainscoting by the fireplace moved rapidly inwards, and instantly Sharpley disappeared.

All this was done much more quickly than we can write.

Felix and Andrew, of course, at once rushed to the spot, but before their hands could prevent it, the door resumed its former position.

Just at this moment Fillipy appeared.

To him Felix explained what had occurred.

"I have heard a great deal of the place," said Fillipy, "but I have never before been here. From what I can see of it I should think the murderer has escaped."

"There is one thing," said Felix; "we must find out where it leads to."

"What do you suggest?" asked Andrew.

"I suggest that we smash this door down, and that we follow the passage."

"It is risky," said Fillipy, "for this looks the very place for secret traps and staircases, where, in a moment, one may fall and break one's neck. However, since your suggestion is the best way out of the difficulty, let us at once set about our task. Here is a heavy stool. That will do for the purpose. And, hallo! what have we here?"

Pushing the table on one side, he placed his hand in the iron ring of the trap-door—that trap with which the reader is so well acquainted—and pulled it up.

The stench which emanated from the black filthy hole was almost overpowering.

"Heavens!" said Felix, recoiling, "what a fearful hole! In the name of all that is most wonderful, where does it lead to?"

"That, judging from its position," said Andrew, "is exactly over the Fleet Ditch."

"Let us leave the trap open," said Felix; "there is no telling whether, after traversing a number of passages, the barber may not appear here."

"Well by all the books of the law!" cried Fillipy, as he fixed his eyes on a steel rod by the side of the wall, "what can this be?"

There was a small handle attached to this rod, and, of course, Fillipy at once pulled it.

The result was extraordinary.

A loud grating noise was heard, and a trap-door, fixed in the ceiling above, dropped down.

It was at once apparent to Felix and his friends, how, could he only get them into his clutches, Sharpley Sharp had in his power those he intended to destroy.

"Let these traps remain as they are," said Felix, "so that we shall not forget to show the proper authorities what a den of infamy has for years been existing in their very midst. Master Fillipy, lend me the stool."

Fillipy handed Felix the heavy stool, and our hero set to work on the door.

"It is to be hoped that during our delay the wretch has not managed to escape," he said.

"You may depend upon it," replied Fillipy, "that this door communicates with passages inside the house, and not with the street."

With all the strength at his command, Felix brought down the stool again and again on the secret door.

The woodwork proved to be very weak, for, after a few heavy blows, a large piece of the wood was crushed in.

Felix then searched for the secret spring, as also did Andrew and Fillipy, but they were quite unable to discover it.

The only thing to be done was to totally demolish the woodwork, and this was accomplished after a few more tremendous blows.

There were two lamps in the room, and Felix seized one, and blew the other out.

The three men proceeded along the passage, which was so narrow that they found the greatest difficulty in advancing.

Of course, even had the passage been of a good width, their progress would have been slow, for it was necessary to pause every moment to examine the floor and the walls.

They soon became aware of the fact that the passage was occupied—by rats; large fellows they were, too, whose head-quarters were no doubt the Fleet Ditch.

But no barber could they see.

Still, on they went, and every step they took they became more and more amazed at the singular construction of the place.

It was certain that the passage had not been made after the house was built, but while the building of it was in progress, and they were undoubtedly of a most ingenoius character.

Suddenly they found themselves in a small vaulted apartment, entirely destitute of furniture.

There was a small oak door at the farther end which appeared to be securely fastened.

"Be careful!" cried Felix, as he sounded the floor with his feet; "there may be some accursed hidden machinery here."

"Look!" Andrew suddenly shouted, "yon door moves."

But Felix had already noticed it.

As swiftly as an arrow from a bow, he darted forward and pushed the door wide open.

As he did so the figure of a man with a lighted link in his hand rushed across his path and vanished through a small door on his left.

Before it had time to close, Felix hurled his body against it, and the door flew back so suddenly that ere Felix could recover his balance he fell with a crash to the floor.

A wild yell instantly followed the fall, and at the same moment the bright glitter of steel was seen in the rays of the torch.

It was the barber—he had raised a dagger aloft.

Andrew saw it, and recognising the danger Felix was in, he levelled his pistol and fired.

The torch was extinguished, and when the smoke had raised itself, the barber had again vanished.

"By the Virgin!" cried Fillipy, who looked the very picture of amazement, "this accursed barber must be as active as the fiend himself!"

"You are not hurt, Felix?" asked Andrew.

"Nay," answered our hero, as he raised himself, "only slightly bruised."

"Certainly 'tis a wonder there was not some accursed trap where you fell," said Fillipy; "the place seems as full of traps as it does of rats."

"Come, follow me!" cried Felix, as holding his sword firmly in his hand, he entered the passage through which the barber had passed.

Swiftly up this passage ran the three, until a flight of stairs were reached.

To mount these were but the work of an instant.

Felix saw now that he was upon a landing.

A window was before him, and looking out, he saw that it was above the yard, and that it was the second floor of the building.

He moved towards the window, and once more the figure of the barber crossed his path.

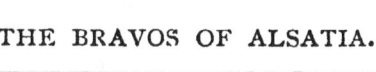

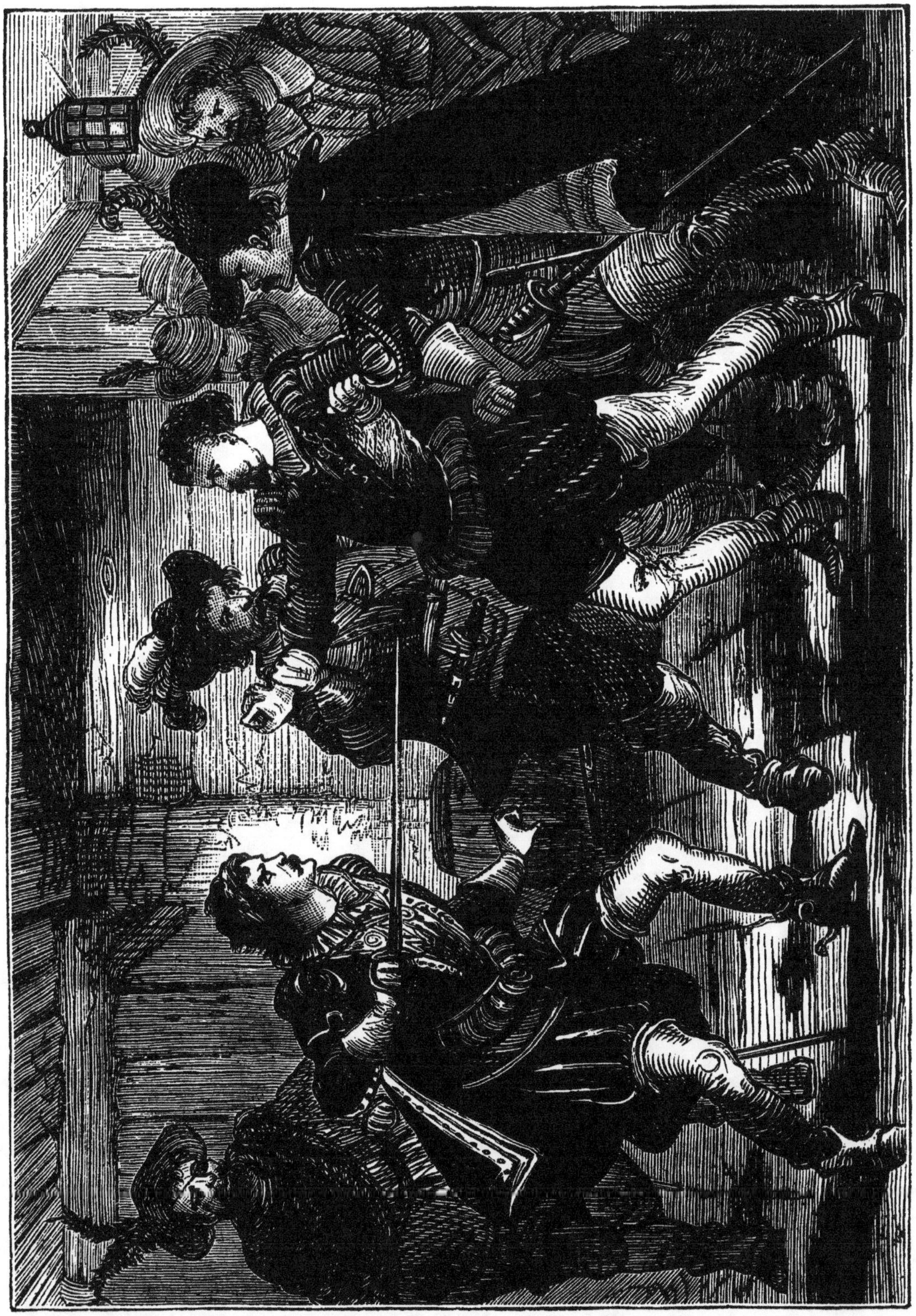

"'HOLD HIM! BY THE FOUL FIEND I WILL CLEAVE A PASSAGE THROUGH HIS BODY!' CRIED HORACE."

Sharpley had concealed himself in the shadow of one of the window curtains, no doubt with the intention of eventually gaining the roof.

"Hold, villain!" shouted Felix, "hold, and surrender yourself!"

But there was no fear of Sharpley Sharp doing this.

Terror had now obtained a complete mastery over him.

With extraordinary swiftness he bounded forward, and commenced to descend the stairs.

"Don't fire!" cried Felix, "we shall have him in a moment."

Down the stairs, two at a time, went the barber, and in a few moments the bedroom was reached.

Now, by some means the barber's wife had wriggled herself free from the bedstead.

Though her hands were still securely bound, and though the cord still dangled at her feet, she had sufficiently loosened it to be able to move herself, and she had contrived to reach the door of the room.

The little lamp threw its rays upon her sheet-covered head, and altogether she presented such a ghostly and horrible appearance that the barber, directly he beheld her, uttered an ear-piercing scream.

His yell fell upon the ears of his wife, and she answered him with a series of rapid grunts.

The door of the room opposite was open, and the faint rays of the lamp showed the barber that the trap was open.

How it came to be open, however, he did not pause to consider.

Instantaneously the thought flashed through his mind that if he could reach the room below his escape would be assured.

Therefore he dashed towards the trap.

As he ran, Felix shouted to him to stop, but all to no purpose.

Without waiting to fall upon his knees and drop into the room below, Sharpley gave a jump, and flashed out of sight.

The earthly career of this bloodthirsty wretch was thus ended, for the trap below, and which was in connection with the Fleet Ditch, had been left open, and thus *the barber had fallen through both!*

"Ho," cried Felix as he took the lamp, and ran down the other stairs into the room below, "he has certainly killed himself."

Down on his knees went our hero, and placed the lamp over the black filthy hole.

But nothing was to be seen, not a sound was heard.

Our hero was soon joined by Fillipy and Andrew.

"Never more will he be beheld," said Andrew. "The rushing stream, fifty feet below, has even now carried him a long distance off. Anon his body will be shot out into the Thames, and no doubt it will never be recovered. If it is, it will be quite unrecognisable."

"I would to heaven that Captain White had gone with him!" said Felix.

"Perhaps a worse fate awaits him," said Fillipy.

"Nothing can be done here," said Felix, rising, "so we had better at once depart. Had we only learned what had happened to the countess and Lord Clinton, I should have been satisfied."

"No doubt we shall soon get to know something about it," replied Fillipy. "Let us return with all speed to St. James's Park."

"What is to be done with the barber's wife?" asked Andrew.

"I think we had better release her," replied Felix, "and let her know her husband's fate."

Forthwith up the stairs went the three.

In the meantime, Mistress Sharp, in an endeavour to descend the stairs, had toppled over, and Felix found her stretched full length across the topmost stair.

He at once released her, and lifted her to a sitting posture.

For some few seconds the hideous old woman looked first at one and then at the other.

Having discovered that she really was at liberty, she gave utterance to a piercing yell.

This was quickly followed by another, and no doubt another would have followed that had not Felix shouted out—

"Silence! and listen to me, or we will again gag you, and leave you here!"

"Murderers!" shrieked out the old woman.

"Silence!" repeated Felix.

"Oh, villains!" continued Mistress Sharp.

"Your husband is no more, woman!" cried Fillipy, who was thoroughly disgusted with the wretch.

"No more! What do you mean?" replied the woman.

"Your husband is *dead!*" said Felix, solemnly.

"It serves him right!" was the reply. "When did he die?"

"But a few minutes ago."

"Did you kill him?"

"No; he——"

"Then it was not you who has rendered me a service. Who was it? Let me know, that I may thank him."

"She means that she is glad her husband is dead," said Andrew.

"Of course I am!" cried the old woman, emphatically. "Didn't he say he was about to kill me?"

"How should we know what he said" replied Felix.

"Well, he did say so," said Mistress Sharp, "and had you not entered the house I should have been dead by now. The bravos he had with him below were going to assist him. I heard them say so. Sharp said that it was Captain White's orders that I should die."

"Come," said Felix, "let us hasten away. Old woman, listen, in his attempt to escape from us your husband jumped through the trap-door below. If you want to find his body the Fleet Ditch must be searched."

"I should be a fool to let anyone take the trouble!" howled the old woman.

Felix did not reply.

Followed by Fillipy and Andrew he left the house in disgust, and the three took their way at a rapid pace in the direction of St. James's.

CHAPTER XIII.

WHEREIN OUR READERS ARE ONCE MORE CONDUCTED TO THE OLD MILL AT VAUXHALL.

OUR readers will remember that Lord Clinton and Horace, locked in a deadly embrace, fell through the flooring of the old mill into the apartment below.

This room communicated with the flap through which the bags of flour used to be drawn.

It was called the "Flour Room."

A long, long time had elapsed since it had been used for the purposes of trade.

Now, instead of it containing such things as bags or barrels of flour, it held a large quantity of *arms* of all descriptions, and in a corner, by the door, were piled eight or nine black-looking kegs.

On each of these, in flaming letters of red, was written the word "Brandy," But no such liquor did these kegs contain.

They were crammed with *gunpowder.*

That Lord Stretton intended to use it at some time or the other was certain, and that Captain White occasionally had a couple of kegs from the old mill was equally certain.

We have drawn attention to these kegs, as we shall have reason to refer to them anon.

Just as Lord Clinton and Horace fell,

Pearman hurried up with the men and the chain required.

The countess stood—pale, it is true, but nevertheless firm.

"Hurry, Captain White," cried Stretton hoarsely; "hurry, and see what has become of them. And mark it, spare not his lordship. If it is necessary in order to save my son, to slay him, why then slay him as you would slay a dog!"

Down rushed Captain White, Pearman and the bravos at his heels.

Stretton looked fiercely at the countess.

A grim smile played about her mouth.

"You do not seem much concerned," said Stretton.

"True," answered the countess. "I have little fear as to the result of this encounter if Lord Clinton is allowed sufficient time."

"You hope he kills my son?"

"Aye, that I certainly do!" replied the countess, in tones which showed she meant what she said.

"Fiend!" hissed Stretton.

"Nay," replied the countess calmly, "'tis yourself, my lord, who is the fiend; I am only one of your victims. Oh," she said, as she clasped her hands fervently together; "oh, that Heaven would send us succour! If Clinton could but get free——"

"Silence!" shouted Stretton fiercely; "he shall never be free. "Never—I swear it!"

At this moment Stretton snatched up a lantern, and holding it over the hole in the flooring, looked below.

* * * *

To return to Lord Clinton.

He fell on the top of Horace, who, had he been a little nearer the door, would have fallen upon the kegs and probably he would have broken his back.

Not for an instant did Clinton release his hold on Horace's throat.

"Release me!" gasped Horace; "release me!"

Grasping his pistol by the muzzle, he dealt Clinton a terrific blow on the head.

But before he could repeat it, Clinton snatched the pistol from his grasp and hurled it away.

"Caitiff!" he said, "I will strangle you! If I am to be assassinated in this vile den, I will at least die with the knowledge that I have put you beyond the power of injuring others. You shall die."

"Mercy!" gasped Horace.

His cry was so low that Clinton scarcely heard it.

"Mercy!" replied his lordship contemptuously; "you cry 'mercy'—you who can practise your brutality on a defenceless woman? Coward, your time has come!"

It was at this moment that the door was burst open and Captain White appeared.

"Forward, men, and drag him off!" he shouted.

The bravos were instantly upon Lord Clinton, and with little ceremony they dragged him off the nearly strangled Horace.

Directly the villain was lifted to his feet, he snatched Captain White's sword from his hand, and shortening it, cried—

"Hold him! By the foul fiend, I will cleave a passage through his body!"

Stretton, who had placed his head through the aperture above, saw the movement.

"Hold!" he cried; "hold! Since you have him so securely, spare him for a while. You shall be amply avenged, Horace. Chain him, and then bring him up for torture."

"Captain White," said Clinton, "let me go free—for it is in your power to free me—and I will pay you the sum of ten thousand pounds."

But the offer of this enormous sum did not now tempt the one-eyed wretch.

And why?

Because he had the money and jewels stolen from the goldsmith, and the amount of that he did not know himself.

"I couldn't do it," he said; "no, not for twice the sum. I am under a bond to obey Lord Stretton."

In a brief space Clinton's hands and feet were securely fastened with a heavy chain, and in that condition he was conducted once more to the room above.

The blow from Horace's pistol had made a deep wound in his head, from which the blood slowly trickled down his face.

As the countess beheld him, chained and bleeding, she burst into tears.

"Do not weep." said Clinton, looking pityingly at the unfortunate lady; "a day of reckoning will surely come for these villains."

"Your day of reckoning has arrived!" said Stretton.

"Wretched mockery of a man!" said Clinton with disgust, "talk not to me again. If I am to be confined or murdered, let me be removed at once from your presence."

"Aye," said the countess; "and let me also be removed."

"Promise to do as he asks," whispered Clinton, "and you will be treated with more consideration."

"I can never promise to be his wife," returned the countess—"not for any amount of consideration."

"They are muttering one to the other," cried Stretton; "but I will soon put a stop to that. Captain White, see that this *man* is placed in the cellar at the edge of the wharf."

"Where?" cried White, opening his one eye to its fullest extent.

"In the cellar at the edge of the wharf. Here is the key."

"Well," said White, "if he is to be placed there, you had better let his lordship say good-bye to the countess."

"Begone!" replied Stretton sternly, as he pointed to the door.

"He will not live a dozen hours!" persisted White.

"Fool! Begone, I say."

"He will live long enough to undergo the torture we shall apply to him," said Horace, "and for the countess to be a witness to it."

"Come along, your lordship," said White, as he tapped Clinton on the shoulder.

Clinton turned to the countess.

To raise his hand was out of the question, since he was so firmly chained.

"Farewell, my love!" he said, in broken tones; "may heaven watch over you!"

With a wild passionate cry the countess bounded towards him, threw her arms about his neck, and kissed him again and again.

Stretton, with a terrible oath, strode forward, seized the countess by the arm, and flung her aside.

"Remember, you are in my power!" he said, as he gnashed his teeth with rage.

But, in defiance of Stretton, the countess again rushed to Clinton.

"My love," whispered Clinton, "if I die—as I have no doubt I soon shall—you will avenge my death."

"Aye, Clinton, if that fiend puts you to death, I swear to avenge you if I live! I will leave no stone unturned. But bear up, Clinton—for my sake, bear up."

"My love," said Clinton, hastily, "if you see a chance of bribing any of Stretton's varlets, neglect it not. If Felix Ferdinand could be communicated with, our escape would be certain."

"Away with him!" roared Stretton, stamping his feet with rage. "Away with him, I say! Captain White, to you I look for—— But no—no matter. Horace, will you see that Clinton is properly secured?"

"Certainly, my lord."

"It is a long time since I visited the cellar near the wharf, but, if I remember rightly, on one side there is a large iron ring, which it is impossible a man, or a dozen men, could break. Let him be fastened to that."

"Cruel monster!" cried the countess, passionately clenching her little hands. "Will you so degrade his lordship?"

"Most assuredly I will," was the answer. "He shall be chained there until you have consented to be my wife."

"Until the ceremony is carried out," suggested Pearman. "Promises are like piecrust with ladies."

"Aye, until the ceremony is carried out," replied Stretton.

"And that can be here, in this very apartment, if so be your lordship wishes it," continued Pearman.

Clinton was now led away.

Captain White and Pearman went first; Clinton, surrounded by the bravos, four of whom carried links, came next; and Horace, his sword in one hand, and his pistol in the other, brought up the rear.

Down several flights of stairs went the party, until the vaults below the mill were reached.

The mill being, as we have stated, at the edge of the river, our readers can just imagine what they must have been like.

Many of the walls dividing the various vaults were rotten.

Time and the action of the water from the river had made many a breach in them.

Some of the vaults, in fact, were, at high tide, flooded with water, which, on receding, left behind a lot of foul mud.

The apartment which Stretton had called a cellar was nearer the river than any of the others, and consequently was the worst of the lot.

The mill was built of wood; this cellar was constructed almost entirely of brick.

It was quite evident from the way in which Captain White led the party, that he was perfectly acquainted with the whole of the vile den or dens, and he chuckled as he muttered to Pearman—

"Stretton makes a mistake if he fancies that Clinton will live in this cellar for any length of time. He will defeat his purpose, and death will soon rob him of his vengeance."

Pearman smiled.

"This confinement in this cellar is no doubt Stretton's idea of torture—eh?"

"I should imagine so. My impression is that he intends to confine Clinton here, and starve him. Occasionally he will bring the countess to look at him."

"Unless she consents to become his wife?"

"Just so."

" And if she does consent, he would marry her here ? "

" No doubt of it."

" And then—eh ? "

" What do you mean ? "

"After that, what about his lordship ? "

" Oh, he would let him remain there until the judgment day."

" But I was under the impression that the youth, Felix Ferdinand, was to be captured and brought here."

" So he is, unless the countess consents to be Stretton's wife."

" Then it is certain that this Felix *is* the long-lost son of the countess ? "

" The stolen child—yes."

" And yet the countess does not know it ? "

" Not yet."

" What is your impression of the whole affair ? Do you think the countess will consent to become Lady Stretton ? "

" She may promise—that is all."

" What, do you think that if she saw Clinton dying inch by inch of starvation, and if she was aware of the fact that by becoming the wife of Stretton she would put an end to his suffering—do you think, I say, that she would not marry Stretton ? "

" No ! "

" *Hum!* " ejaculated Pearman emphatically.

" You see," said White, " Stretton would bring her to the cellar to look at Clinton, and every time he did that Clinton would urge the countess to disregard his (Clinton's) sufferings, and still to remain firm in her refusal of Stretton's offer."

" Ah," muttered Pearman, " time will show. There is one very important thing I would observe. It is this : if this Felix Ferdinand discovers the whereabouts of Clinton and the countess, no mill, nor fifty mills, would ever hold them for long."

" Why do you say that ? " said the captain fiercely.

" I am remembering what happened at Alsatia. It is quite evident that Felix Ferdinand is a daring youth, and that, with a hundred Templars and apprentices at his back, he would pause at nothing."

" Let me get him ! " replied White, grinding his teeth, (or, we should say, the tusk-like stumps of what at one time of his existence had been teeth); " let me get him and by all the fiends, I will pay him with interest what I owe him ! But there is no chance of his discovering their whereabouts."

" What of the outrider ? "

" Well, *what* of him ? He only knows that the coach was stopped by a party of men he, no doubt, took for robbers, and——"

" I don't mean that one. I refer to the other."

" Ah, of course ! I had forgotten him. But he is safe enough. He will be kept at the mill. But here we are. Halt ! "

The party halted, and Horace came forward.

Captain White produced the key, and unlocked a low narrow door.

It was a door which a strong man could have burst open with his fists, so rotten was it.

Horace shook his head as he beheld it.

" Such a door as this," he whispered, " will never hold Clinton for any length of time."

"Pah ! " answered White, " you forget, Master Melton, the ring your father spoke of. A man chained to that could never reach this door."

With this he pushed the door wide open, and the men bearing the torches entered.

The light from the links revealed an apartment twelve feet by eight.

The walls were of brick, so also was the ceiling.

There were no windows, the only ventilation obtained was through the cracks in the doorway.

Whether the flooring was of brick, stone, or wood it would have been difficult for anyone to have given an immediate answer, but, no doubt, it was simply the same substance as what constituted the bed of the river—that is to say, mud and sand.

" There is the ring," said White, pointing to a ring fixed in the wall.

It was a ponderous affair weighing about a hundredweight, and, though rusty, it would have withstood the strain of a couple of furious lions, let alone a man.

Clinton's face betrayed no surprise as he looked at it.

"Thrust him in," said Horace, "and quickly. Let the royal favourite, the chosen lover of the proud Countess of Rothburn, learn what it is to lie and rot in this foul dungeon. Anon his howls for mercy will be heard."

"Liar!" thundered Clinton, drawing himself as erect as his chains would permit; "were I being eaten alive by the vermin which, beyond doubt, abound here, I would not give utterance to one cry for mercy. I might as well cry for mercy to a stone wall as to you or your infamous father."

"Your lordship is quite right," answered Horace calmly. "We have had some difficulty with you, but our hour of triumph has at last arrived."

"The day of retribution is not far distant," said Clinton.

"So you may think. You, however, will never live to see daylight again."

"I feel that," said Clinton; "but I can easily make my peace with Heaven, for I have never knowingly injured man or woman."

"Neither has Master Melton," chuckled Pearman.

"Silence, you hound!" cried Horace, "Now, quick—the lock, and hand me the key!"

In a few moments Clinton was securely fastened to the ring, the chain being placed round his ankles only.

Horace and the whole party now drew back.

"Here, your lordship," sneered Horace, "you can give utterance to your feelings entirely unchecked; no one will venture here to interrupt you."

"Oh, thou abandoned wretches!" exclaimed Clinton. "What hearts must you—your father—these men possess, when you can so calmly contemplate the sufferings of a fellow-being."

"For my part," said White, with a hoarse laugh, "I never possessed a heart —at least, so my wife said. Don't you remember, Pearman?"

"Which wife do you mean?" asked Pearman.

"The one I killed."

This the captain said in the most indifferent tones it is possible to imagine.

"You killed two to my knowledge," said Pearman! "so that——"

"Peace!" cried Horace. "Let us leave this hole, for I swear that my limbs are becoming quite numbed with the cold. Farewell, your lordship!" he sneered, as he made a mock bow. "When I visit you, I trust you will be able to assure me that you have got quite used to your quarters."

But his lordship made no reply.

Folding his arms across his broad chest, he fixed a terrible look on the wretch.

Yet it was not a look of hate—nay, it was a look of horror and pity combined.

With loud laughter at some remark Pearman had made, the blackguards departed, White locking the door, and handing the key to Horace.

So Lord Clinton, who never before in his life had been a prisoner—who had always been surrounded with every luxury money could purchase, was left alone in this furnitureless, muddy, and foul-smelling hole.

And yet he did not despair.

Something seemed to tell him that anon the silver lining in the black cloud would show itself.

"So," said Stretton to his son as soon as he appeared—"so you have made him secure?"

"We have," was the reply, "and no doubt very comfortable. Of a surety, my lord, you choose the vilest place in the whole mill."

"Aye," said White. "His lordship knows which best suits his enemies."

Lord Stretton took this as a compliment.

"Yes," he replied with a fiendish grin; "I flatter myself that I am fairly conversant with the likes and dislikes of the generality of people."

"My lord," said the countess, "how much longer am I to continue in your hateful presence?"

"Listen to me, countess," said Stretton. "If you will take my advice you will scatter your haughty and contemptuous demeanour to the four winds of Heaven. You will gain absolutely nothing by continuing to defy me, so that——"

"Pshaw!" interrupted the countess. "What have I to fear from you?"

"Everything!"

"Mark me, my lord," said the countess in impressive tones, "I shall *continue* to defy you—you, your son, and the villains under your and his direction. I have nothing whatever to fear. Think you I fear *death?* No, no! Welcome, death—right welcome death, rather than the outrage to which you would submit me! Inhuman monster, vile kidnapper, and *murderer*, as anon you will be proved to be, I defy you! And I will continue to defy you, I repeat, so long as my heart beats within my bosom! I hate you—loathe you; and I love Clinton with all my heart and soul! I am passionately devoted to him, and were you at this moment to plunge your dagger into my breast, the last cry I should utter would be, 'I love you, Clinton—I love you!'"

During this speech, delivered as it was in most passionate tones, Stretton became almost white with rage.

"There is more than one cellar below," said Horace significantly. "No doubt a confinement of some hours in an apartment similiar to the one in which Clinton has been placed would be of some service in bringing the countess to her senses."

"Fool!" replied the countess, directing a look of contempt upon him; "I am *already* in possession of my senses."

"Nothing can be done with her at present," thought Stretton. "She is too full of Clinton—curse him! But probably, after a few hours' confinement, she will alter her tone. Strange how she hates me so much! Do I still love her? No! All the love I ever had for her I have torn from my bosom; but I will marry her, because that will be the best punishment for her."

"What is to be done with the countess?" asked Horace impatiently.

"She is to be taken to the miller's room."

"Hem!" said White. "That is the best apartment in the mill."

"I know it. She is to be taken there and placed under lock and key until arrangements can be made for our marriage."

"Good!" said White; "very good. Then after that is done we are at liberty to depart?"

"Yes, but you must not remain long away. We will, however, talk that over in a moment. Away with the countess."

Pearman tapped her ladyship on the shoulder.

"*Pray* follow," he said in mincing tones.

"Touch me not, thou beast!" exclaimed the countess, as she shrank from his touch.

Pearman grinned, and bowed almost to the very ground.

Placing his hand on his heart—at least where his heart should have been—he said—

"Your ladyship—I beg your pardon—your countess-ship's orders shall be obeyed to the letter."

"*Let—her* be, then!" chuckled White.

"Do not make your vile puns in my presence," said Stretton; "do as you are bid, and hold your peace."

"I for one will do as you order," replied Pearman, "because I am a man of *peace.*"

"A very bulky *piece*," said White. "But the keys, my lord."

"Here they are. The largest is the key of the room in which the countess is to be placed."

"Follow me, your ladyship," said White, pushing Pearman out of the way, and taking his place.

The miller's room, as its name implies, was formerly the private apartment of the tenant of the mill.

It was on the top floor, and the window of it looked out upon the waterwheel. Close by the window was a high steel handle.

This was the lever of the water-wheel, and it only required a strong pull to set the machinery in motion.

The apartment contained a mouldy couch, a mouldy piece of carpet, and an equally mouldy chair, a few pictures, a cranky table, and in various parts of the room several business ledgers, which smelt as if they had been buried for a few years and then dug up again.

The window we have referred to was small, but a man could have got his body through, no doubt.

But it would have been out of all question for a woman to try and get out of it.

So the countess saw that escape from the window was impossible.

"The place is secure enough," she thought.

"Here is your room, countess," said Horace, "and I hope you will be pleased with it. If you could see the cellar in which Clinton is placed, your ladyship would agree that this room is a palace compared to it."

The countess did not reply.

"Her ladyship has lost her tongue," said White.

"She may find it by the time we come again," said Pearman, "and use it to a better advantage than she has just done."

"I don't know what his lordship will order regarding refreshments," said Horace, "but if your ladyship likes I will mention the matter to him."

Still the countess made no reply.

Turning to the window she looked out upon the swift little stream which, after turning the wheel when it was in motion —which it never was now on account of it having no flour to grind, and because it made too much noise—after turning the wheel, we say, assisted to swell the waters of the Thames.

Finding that the countess would not reply, Horace gave the word, and the party left the room, the door of which White carefully locked.

"And now," said Stretton, "let the outrider be brought before me. It was a cursed nuisance that you allowed the other man to make good his escape. Still, no doubt, nothing will come of it."

The outrider, who had been kept closely watched, was brought forward.

"We do not intend to do you any harm," said Stretton, "but for various reasons you must remain here for the present. You will be placed under lock and key, but you will not be treated as a prisoner. You will be well supplied with refreshments, and although we cannot accommodate you with a bed, you may have the cushions from the coach, as well as a number of sacks."

"And a good bed, too, for an outrider," said White; "he don't deserve anything of the kind. You would have got away if you could, wouldn't you, sirrah?"

"Certainly I should," replied the outrider, a young and powerful fellow, who had been a sailor.

"If you behave yourself," said Stretton. "I will enrol you in my service."

The outrider laughed in his lordship's face.

"I would not serve you," he said, "if you paid me twice as much as my master, Lord Clinton."

"And why, varlet?"

"The reasons are too numerous to mention."

"You are a saucy knave."

The outrider was about to give a suitable reply, but thinking better of it, he merely turned up his nose.

"Let him be taken to the 'Round Room,'" said Stretton, "and let him have the cushions and refreshments."

"Eatables and drinkables?" asked Pearman.

"No, drinkables only," replied Stretton. "Had he kept a civil tongue in his head he might have had eatables, but as he did not, he will go without them until I think proper to see him supplied with them. I will give you the wine in a moment."

The outrider was conducted to the Round Room, a circular apartment which was immediately under that in which the countess had been placed.

This had one window, and, like the room, it was of a circular shape.

Beyond a rickety old chair, a table, and a stool, the apartment contained no furniture.

On one side stood a pile of sacks.

In a short time the coach-cushions were thrown in by White.

Then a bottle of wine was brought by Pearman, who placed it on the table with the remark that it was from his lordship, and much too good for an outrider.

"Where is the lamp?" asked the outrider.

"Lamp?" cried White; "you will get no lamp, my friend! You don't think his lordship wants the mill burned down, do you?"

With this Captain White banged the door to and locked it.

Returning to Stretton, he said—

"Does your lordship mean to let that man go at any time?"

"Certainly not!" was the immediate reply; "he will be found dead before many hours have passed."

"Your lordship means that you have poisoned the wine?"

"Certainly. But let no one know— not even Pearman."

"Hem! I thought your lordship was too wise to release the fellow. Really it is astonishing how devoted everyone is to Lord Clinton."

To this Stretton made no reply.

"What is to be done now?" asked Horace.

"We now leave the mill. Captain White and his men return to Alsatia, where they will remain until to-morrow at midnight. As for us, we go to Lambeth."

"To-morrow at midnight," said White. "I shall not forget. And no doubt your lordship will not forget the money which——"

"No, I will not forget," interrupted Stretton sharply.

"The business we shall next be upon," said White, "is, of course, the capture of Felix Ferdinand?"

"It is," replied Stretton.

"And the girl, Rosamund Walker," said Horace. "They are both at the countess's residence, and can be easily captured."

"Would it not be better to leave the girl for some other and more fitting occasion?" said Stretton.

"I fancy not," was Horace's reply. "We may just as well kill two birds with one stone."

"As you will. It is no concern of mine."

"Your lordship will please *make* it so," said Horace insolently.

"Eh—what mean you?"

"One good turn deserves another. I interested myself in the countess; you will interest yourself in Rosamund Walker."

"Is it your intention to marry her?"

"That I will consider."

"Very well. When you have considered let me know the result. Now prepare for departure, Captain White; let your most trustworthy man remain here to watch the building."

"Do you think *one* will be enough?" asked Horace.

"Aye, quite enough. No one knows what has taken place here; therefore we have nothing to fear. Prepare!"

One of the bravos, a tall, awkward, ugly-looking wretch, named Hooper, was left in charge.

He was provided with a bottle of wine, and Stretton gave him twenty crowns, which more than satisfied him.

The coach and horses were placed in one of the outhouses, and all being in readiness, the whole party set off.

Captain White and his myrmidons towards Alsatia, and Lord Stretton and his son in the direction of Lambeth, where Stretton owned a house.

CHAPTER XIV.

SHOWS HOW THE OUTRIDER EFFECTS HIS ESCAPE, HOW THE COUNTESS IS MADE AWARE OF IT.—HOW FELIX IS WARNED, AND HOW OUR HERO AND HIS FRIENDS ACT.

THE outrider, by name Fleet, who had been placed in the Round Room, as we have before observed, had been a sailor, having seen some ten years or so in the service.

We have also remarked that he was young and powerful.

He was, and, as young sailors generally are, remarkably active.

Also he was possessed of a light heart, and was altogether an individual whose constant cry would be "Never despair!"

For a long time after Captain White had locked the door on him, the outrider surveyed the scene from the window.

Little could he see through them, however, on account of their filthiness.

The snow, however, was plainly seen, as was also the stream which fed the water-mill.

While studying the prospect without, the outrider saw the whole party leave the mill.

"By my soul!" muttered the outrider, "I do not often wish a person any harm, but I do hope and trust that that one-eyed villain, White, Lord Stretton, and and his son, and that scamp who calls himself Pearman, may fall and break their necks!"

He watched them until they were out of sight, then he left the window and turned to the table, on which he could just make out the outline of the bottle containing the wine—wine our readers will remember hearing Stretton say was *poisoned*.

He raised the bottle and smelt it.

"One man is left," he muttered; "and only one."

Here Fleet burst into a low prolonged laugh.

"He, he!" he chuckled, "the whole lot of them must be consummate fools if they fancy that I will not have a try—and a good try—to escape!"

The bottle was raised to his lips.

The next instant he lowered the bottle, and replaced it on the table.

Slowly he shook his head.

"No," he muttered; "I will not touch it. No; that was supplied by Stretton himself! The villain's very breath is poison, and no doubt this is poison as well as wine. Ugh! the thought makes me shudder. Now, I heard them say they would all return to-morrow at midnight—good! I have, therefore, plenty of time for sleep. If I manage to rest myself a little, I shall be in the proper condition to attempt to escape."

Fleet, therefore, arranged the cushions and sacks to his satisfaction, threw himself upon them, and was soon fast asleep.

Hour after hour he slumbered on.

But, alas! what of the poor countess?

What of poor Lord Clinton in the foul black cellar!

How long must the hours have seemed to them?

At last Fleet awoke with a start.

Leaping to his feet, he peered from the window.

A somewhat thick fog hung over the river, and enveloped the old mill.

He listened, but for some moments no sound did he hear.

Suddenly, however, the deep-toned bell of Westminster Abbey began to chime.

Fleet pressed his ear close to the window.

The hour bell tolled, and he counted four.

"Four!" he muttered in astonishment. "Why, that must be four of the clock in the afternoon! Certainly it is. Heaven, I had no idea that I had slept so long! To work—to work! Thank goodness, there is a thick fog about, and that will effectually screen me from observation. Ha, what was that?"

Pausing in the middle of the room, he listened.

He heard a slow measured tramping overhead, as if someone were pacing backwards and forwards.

Our readers will understand that, though the outrider knew the countess was confined in the mill, he had no idea as to what particular part.

For some few moments the sound troubled him somewhat; at last, however, he thought—

"The man watching the premises is below, surely?"

We may here observe that he was, and about as drunk as a man could well be, for after drinking what had been provided for him, he had searched for and found the cupboard in which Lord Stretton kept the liquors, and without hesitation he broke it open, and took what he wanted.

Fleet fell upon his knees, and placed his ear to the crack below the door.

He heard a deep hoarse voice chanting some drinking-song.

"That is the man who was left in charge," thought Fleet. "Then the person above—— By Heaven, it must be none other than the countess! If I could only communicate with her? Would to Heaven I carried a strong dagger! Can I do anything with this?"

And from his pocket he took a clasp-knife.

It was short, but very strong and sharp.

After contemplating it for some moments, he jumped upon the table.

Pressing his hand upon the ceiling he picked out what he considered was the weakest part, and with the knife commenced to dig at it.

The ceiling proved to be quite as rotten as any other part of the mill, and the plaster descended in showers.

Very soon a large hole was made, revealing the laths.

A few of these Fleet soon pulled from their position.

The boards above were disclosed.

With the handle of his knife he rapped loudly at them.

Instantly the monotonous tramping ceased.

Fleet now inserted the blade of his knife in one of the cracks, and wriggled it to and fro.

"WHEN I VISIT YOU AGAIN, I TRUST YOU WILL BE ABLE TO ASSURE ME THAT YOU HAVE GOT USED TO YOUR QUARTERS!" CRIED HORACE."—(See No. 12).

A startled cry above was heard.

Evidently the countess had observed the knife.

Drawing it out of the crack Fleet said—

"My lady—my lady! Fear nothing. I am Fleet, one of Lord Clinton's outriders!"

Uttering a loud cry of joy the countess fell upon her knees, and placed her ear to the crack.

"Speak!" she gasped. "Speak! You say you are one of Clinton's outriders?"

"Yes, yes!"

"How came you there?"

"I have been confined here by Lord Stretton's orders, of course—so that I should not give information. I have been here hours, but have been asleep. I had no idea until just now that you, my lady, were above. Place your eye to the crack, and try whether you can see me."

The countess did as desired.

"Yes," she said, in tones of deep emotion, "I can just see you. Alas, our trouble has brought trouble upon you!"

"Oh," replied Fleet, "don't think I am afraid, my lady. Thank goodness I have been able to communicate with you. My lady, all the party will return at midnight, and from what I can glean I should fancy that something terrible would then take place. But if all goes well they will find the tables reversed."

"What mean you?" asked the countess hastily.

"I mean that I intend to escape and give the alarm to Felix Ferdinand."

"Oh, that such a thing were possible!" cried the countess, clasping her hands.

"I'll make it possible, my lady, never fear," cried the young man. "So keep a brave heart, and I'll soon bring help for you and my noble master."

The outrider laughed softly.

"My lady, I have been a sailor," he said.

"Yes—yes?"

"And I have got out of worse scrapes than this, for——"

"But how can you attempt to escape?" she cried.

"By the window," replied the man.

"Have you a rope?"

"Nay, but I can soon make one. There are here a large number of sacks,

and with the assistance of my knife I will soon make a rope."

"May Heaven further your efforts!" cried the countess fervently. "If you escape and give the warning which will lead to our timely rescue, you shall receive a large reward."

"I thank you, my lady. Reward, however is a secondary consideration."

"What sort of window have you?"

"Circular. It is not very large, but I shall be able to get out all right."

"Surely it is not unfastened?"

"Not likely, my lady."

"Then how do you propose to unfasten it?"

"With a bar of iron I have here. If I don't smash it to pieces, I'm no man!"

"But is there no one left to guard the premises?"

"One man only, my lady, and from what I can hear, I conclude that he is drunk. If he hears the noise he will take no heed of it."

"Proceed then, and delay not a moment, my friend."

Jumping from the table, Fleet picked up a rusty piece of iron, and, raising it aloft, brought it down again and again on the window.

In a few moments it was smashed to atoms.

Not a bit of the framework was left.

"On what does your window look?" asked the countess.

"On a water-wheel, my lady."

"As also does mine. From my window, when you are ready, I will watch your movements and pray for your safety."

"It will take me three or four hours to make the rope, I am afraid," said Fleet, as pulling out the sacks he at once set to work on them.

A lot of the stuff he cut up had to be discarded on account of its rottenness.

Now and again the countess cheered him considerably by her sweet voice.

Strange as it may seem, not a sound was heard, either outside or inside the mill, during the whole of the time Fleet was weaving his ropes.

The reason that no sound was heard inside was probably owing to the fact that the man in charge, having drunk as much as ever he possibly could, was now lying on the floor quite insensible.

Fleet could have worked much quicker

had he not been hindered by the darkness, which deepened every moment.

As darkness crept over the country, however, Fleet noticed with considerable satisfaction that the fog gradually lifted itself.

The window being out, he could hear most distinctly the chiming of the Abbey clock.

Just after the hour of seven had struck, the moon, bursting through a mass of black clouds, quickly dispersed what remained of the fog, and threw her rays over the country, showing up a part of the ice-bound river, the snow-clad fields, and one part of the mill; but, fortunately, it left that part by the water-wheel in comparative darkness.

At last the rope, forty feet in length, was finished.

"I am ready, my lady," said Fleet.

"Fly, then, my friend," was the answer, "and may heaven watch over you! I trust you have made the rope strong enough."

"I think so—nay, I am sure of it. It would bear twice my weight. For awhile, my lady, I bid you farewell. Do not forget this. When help has reached you, you will, if you be watching from your window, observe the flight of a rocket. Do not forget. Again farewell !"

"Farewell, my friend."

With the assistance of the bar of iron and the table, Fleet managed to secure one end of the rope, then throwing the other end out he saw that it touched the water-wheel.

Clambering up he was quickly on the other side of the window, and fearlessly he commenced the descent.

Oh, with what a wildly beating heart did the unfortunate Countess of Rothburn watch that descent.

And when Fleet reached the end, stood on the water-wheel, and waved his hand, she felt as if she must cry for joy.

She covered her face with her hands and breathed a prayer of thankfulness to Heaven.

When she again looked the outrider had disappeared.

"Felix Ferdinand will be warned !" cried the countess, as she excitedly paced the gloomy apartment; "but will it be in time ? Yes, yes. At midnight Stretton will be here, so that—— But

what if Stretton should change his mind and come here earlier than he intended ? Oh, I pray Heaven it may not be so ? "

*   *   *   *

When Felix, Andrew, and Fillipy, after the tragic death of Sharpley Sharp, arrived at the willows, the residence of the countess, they found the whole place in a state of uproar, for we cannot put it in a milder light.

Every servant, male and female had risen from their beds, and they had been joined by a large number of servants from Lord Clinton's house.

The large servants'-hall was crowded with these excited individuals, and nothing that Rosamund (already nearly distracted at Felix's absence) could say would quiet them.

Of course this excitement had been caused by the outrider who had escaped from the coach when it was stopped on the Windsor road.

His version of the affair was, as may be supposed, that the coach had been stopped by robbers.

But as all the servants knew of the hatred existing between Clinton and Lord Stretton, they would not believe anything but that Stretton had been the one to stop Lord Clinton and the countess.

Directly Felix appeared, Rosamund, with a cry of joy, threw herself into his arms, and hastily she told him of what had occurred, and what were the servants opinions of the affair.

"They are right," said Felix gravely : "there can be no doubt that his lordship and the countess were stopped by Lord Stretton, his son, and Captain White, with some of his blackguards. So it was in the Windsor road. Master Fallory, let us mount, and at once set off. We must scour the road from end to end, and make enquiries in every direction."

"Aye, that is the best way," replied Fillipy.

And Andrew agreed.

"Felix," cried Rosamund, "you will not set out upon this journey without taking with you some assistance ? "

"Nay, my love, I will not. A dozen of the best men shall be picked from among the servants."

At this nearly every man rushed forward to volunteer.

Felix picked out a dozen strong fellows from amongst them, and told them to bring horses from Lord Clinton's and the countess's stables.

These, including horses for Felix, Andrew, and Fillipy, were soon procured and brought round, and Felix armed the servant's from the countess's armoury.

In a remarkably short space of time the whole party were ready to move.

"Rosamund," said Felix tenderly, "there is no telling what the result of this journey may be. To-day is the day fixed for the funeral of your poor father. Must it be delayed?"

"Nay, nay," replied poor Rosamund. "I will arrange all that."

"If we do not return in time, the ceremony must take place without us, I fear."

"Oh, yes, for the body must remain here no longer. Trouble not yourself about that, dear Felix, though I should have liked you to have been present when all that was left of my——"

Here the poor girl broke down and burst into tears.

"Bear up, dear Rosamund," said Felix, whose eyes, however, were wet with tears; "my thoughts will be with you."

"Delay no longer, but away, and may Heaven bring you success, and punish those wretched men, Lord Stretton and his son!"

The whole party, led by the outrider, set out upon what proved to be a "wild-goose chase."

Our readers would not be much interested in a description of that journey, and of the search that was made.

We need only say that it was continued in every direction until Windsor Castle was reached.

There Felix obtained an audience of the Lord High Chancellor, and to him explained all that had occurred.

The facts were communicated to the king, who had been terribly annoyed because Lord Clinton and the countess had not obeyed his orders as he thought.

"Stretton again!" said King James; "we will get haud of this traitor, my lords! He shall answer for this conduct! By my halidame, the axe shall be his portion! Scour the country, scour it from end to end, my lords."

"If Lord Stretton is discovered, your majesty, what is to be done with him?"

"Lodge him in the Tower? Away with ye; nae mair need be said!"

Again the country was scoured but nothing came of it.

A body of soldiers, with the Duke of Buckingham at their head, then returned to London with Felix and his party, and proceeded to Pall Mall.

There of course they gained no information; the servants had heard nothing of Lord Stretton or his son for hours and hours, and as to when it was likely they would return, they knew no more than a stone wall.

The duke and his troops returned to Windsor in order to consult with his majesty respecting the serious state of affairs, and Felix, Fillipy, and Andrew, exhausted and sick at heart, returned with the servants to St. James's.

They reached the residence of the Countess of Rothburn precisely *at the very moment* that the daring outrider was descending the rope at the old mill.

During the day the melancholy task of conveying the goldsmith to his last home had been performed.

Poor Mistress Walker was still too ill to leave her room, consequently the whole of the sad business had devolved upon poor Rosamund.

Accompanied by her maid and a troop of servants, Rosamund followed the coffin to the graveyard, and behaved with great fortitude until the ceremony was over.

The Templars and apprentices lined the route, and a striking and never-to-be-forgotten sight they presented as they stood with bowed uncovered heads.

So in the little churchyard of St. Mary's, in the shadow of the Abbey, the goldsmith was laid.

Many were the muttered vows of vengeance on the Alsatians, as the coffin was lowered into the cold ground.

Rosamund, clothed in deep black (which sombre material, however, became her admirably), and surrounded by a host of servants, male and female, met Felix and his friends on the threshold.

She saw at once, from our hero's dejected look, that the journey had been a fruitless one.

She was quickly made acquainted with all the particulars.

"Alas!" said Rosamund as she clasped

her hands convulsively together, "what terrible fate hath overtaken them?"

"Heaven knows!" replied Felix. "Oh, this fearful suspense! If no tidings are gained of them in a short time, I verily believe I shall go mad."

Both Fillipy and Andrew, who, like our hero, were completely tired out, were looking remarkably serious.

"What is best to be done now, dear Felix?" asked Rosamund.

Singularly enough, all the servants were under the impression that our hero was the only person qualified to advise, and they anxiously awaited his answer.

"My idea is," said Felix, "that refreshments should be provided for and partaken of by the men without dismounting."

"A capital suggestion," said Fillipy, "One never knows. Some definite information may reach us at any moment."

The question was put to the men, and, tired though they were they unanimously agreed to remain upon their horses until ordered by Felix to dismount.

Accordingly, refreshments were provided for them and for the horses.

Barely had the thirsty men drained their tankards of ale and the horses their pails, when a rushing sound was heard in the avenue.

In a few seconds the outrider Fleet, mud-splashed and bathed in perspiration, dashed up to the door.

His appearance was greeted with loud shouts of wonder, and he was instantly surrounded by the whole of the servants.

Tankards and flasks were thrust into his face, but Fleet put them from him.

Rosamund, seeing the condition he was in, seized the kerchief from her bosom, plunged it into a pail of water, and bathed the poor fellow's face.

Felix then shouted for brandy.

"He brings us the news!" our hero cried joyfully. "I see it in his face. But first let him recover himself."

A draught of brandy put fresh life into the outrider, who said—

"Yes, I bring you the news, and bad news you will find it, my masters—very bad news, indeed. There——"

"One moment," interrupted Felix hastily. "Both still alive?"

"Aye, they both still live, at least so far as I am aware. But you shall hear all."

The outrider then, amid the most profound silence, gave a full account of all that had occurred, and with which our readers are perfectly acquainted.

No sooner had he concluded ere a mighty shout arose on the night air—

"A rescue! A rescue!"

"Aye," said Felix sternly, "and vengeance on all who took part in their disgraceful capture. Poor Lord Clinton! what terrible sufferings he has undergone!"

"Let us at once prepare," said Andrew. "Us three, with the men servants to assist us, will be quite sufficient, for no doubt Stretton will have no more bravos at his call than he had before."

In a few moments all was in readiness for departure.

"Master Ferdinand," said the outrider, as he took a packet from his breast, "place this on your saddle-bow; I shall want it when we reach the old mill."

"What is that, my friend?"

"A rocket which I purchased as I came along. Her ladyship, you may depend upon it, is eagerly watching for its flight. It will prove to her that help is nigh, and will give her fresh courage."

"True. Now, my men," said Felix. "Oh, but you," he added to the outrider, "had better lead us to the old mill in a roundabout direction, for though Stretton said he would be there again at midnight he might be there before—nay, he might be there at this very moment. So on!"

Felix's thought that Stretton might be at the old mill before midnight was right.

His lordship *was* there!

CHAPTER XV.

IS A CHAPTER FULL OF STARTLING AND MOST EXTRAORDINARY INCIDENTS.

IF our readers have fancied that Lord Stretton, when he reached the house which was part of his property at Lambeth, at once sought rest, they are mistaken.

Horace, after partaking of plenty of spirits, sought a couch, and in a short time he fell into a sound sleep.

And soundly he slept for many hours—hours of fearful length to his lordship, who, his mind fixed upon the old mill and its occupants, could not have slept for any amount.

"I will marry the countess," he thought, "and that ere many hours have passed. Oh, that the hour was already here! Shall I force Clinton to witness the ceremony? Yes, yes! And then—then I will slay him—or cause him to be slain before her eyes. Then I will cause her son to be captured, and—— But let that wait—let that wait."

Hour after hour went by, and at last two of the clock in the afternoon came round.

Our readers know that a thick fog hung over the City.

Gloomy in the extreme everything looked; but the gloom interfered not with Stretton.

On the contrary, it tallied with his own gloomy and revengeful, not to say diabolical thoughts.

Still Horace stirred not.

"He sleeps like a child," muttered Stretton. "One would fancy that he has nothing of any importance on his mind. Aye, he sleeps; and I—I pace the apartments backwards and forwards, forwards and backwards! And there are hours—many hours, ere midnight again comes round. I cannot wait. Nay, I *will* not wait. I will arouse him. We will set out for Alsatia and summon White.

Forthwith, Stretton strode off to the apartment in which Horace slept.

There, stretched at full length on the floor, he found his son, for he had fallen off the couch, no doubt in his anxiety to reach the brandy bottle, which was tightly clutched in his hand.

His attire was disarranged, as also was his hair, and the wounds he had received had evidently opened afresh, for blood was on the side of his head.

Lord Stretton surveyed his son with a shudder, and more than once a deep groan escaped his lips.

This was his only son—his heir!

It was horrible to think of!

But as he looked a voice seemed to whisper in his ear—

"*Like father like son!*"

Stooping suddenly, Stretton snatched the bottle from his son's hand, and with a bitter curse flung it to the other end of the apartment, and it was smashed to a thousand pieces.

The crash awoke Horace, who at once started up and laid his hand on his sword.

But recognising his father he sheathed the half-drawn weapon, and burst into a loud drunken laugh.

Stretton surveyed him in silence for some seconds.

At last he said—

"It is well that I found you."

"Ah!—and why?"

"Had a servant discovered you, your condition would have——"

"Don't talk to me about condition!" interrupted Horace with a snap of his fingers. "What do I care for condition? What do either of us care for condition? Pah! Since we have forfeited our positions, what can conditions——"

"What mean you?" interrupted Stretton.

"I speak plainly, my lord, do I not?"

"Remarkably so as a rule; but not now. You said, 'since we have forfeited our positions.' Explain that."

Again Horace laughed.

"Is it possible—is it really possible, I say, that your lordship is not aware of the fact that what we have done within the past twenty-four hours has caused us to forfeit our positions?"

"Nay!"

"Nay? Do I hear aright. Nay? May the Virgin bless your ignorance! Why, what we have done within the last twenty-four hours is sufficient to get your lordship a very close acquaintanceship with the axe and the block. You have outraged the king's own favourite. What crime can be worse than that?"

"That is all very well. But what proof has the king, or anyone else, that I have outraged his favourite?"

"The proof will not long be wanting. Directly the king misses Clinton—and since he is almost always with him that will be soon—he will cause the whole country to be searched. But your lordship knows that well enough, or you would have gone to Pall Mall, *instead of coming here!*"

"I will not argue with you, but I will add that though you speak of the punishment which may be in store for *me*, you never hint at what would be *your* punishment."

"I can prove that I am your *tool.*"

"Tool? You are my *son*—unfortunately!"

"Unfortunately? Ha, ha! ho, ho! Well, as I said, I am your tool—like Captain White, or——"

"Listen!" thundered Stretton; "you say you could prove you were my tool?"

"Precisely."

"How?"

"How? Well, I presume by the same means as other people prove matters."

"You mean *this!* That supposing I were to be arrested you would give evidence against me?"

"Providing I could save my own neck. Yes, that is just it," replied Horace, with remarkable coolness.

Stretton turned quite pale.

He looked at his son as if it was impossible he could have heard aright.

At last he said in hoarse tones—

"No, no, I cannot—*cannot* believe what you say. Scoundrel though you have proved yourself, you are still my son, and——"

"Scoundrel!" said, or rather shouted, Horace. "Scoundrel! In the name of the foul fiend, if I am a *scoundrel*, what is your lordship?"

"Silence! Do not provoke me. Beware, or your jeers and your taunts may make me forget than I am your father."

"I am always ready to defend myself!" was Horace's answer, as his fingers fastened fiercely round his sword-hilt.

"You are not yourself at present," said Stretton; "the cursed demon Drink has got hold of your brains. Come, I have something important to say."

Stretton turned and strode away, followed by Horace.

When in the principal room, where a large fire burned, Stretton pointed to a chair.

But Horace, shrugging his shoulders, refused to sit down.

"Is there nothing to eat?" he asked

"How can there be anything to eat when there is no one to procure it?" was the answer.

"I will go myself," said Horace.

"That you certainly will not! If I let you leave this house I should not behold you again for days."

"If I cannot eat I must drink."

"The brandy is on the sideboard yonder. Drink if you think proper, but you will only drive yourself mad."

"No fear!" laughed Horace. "My brain is not so sensitive as your lordship's."

Walking to the sideboard he filled himself a goodly-sized tumbler of the fiery liquor, and, turning to his father, wished him happiness with the countess.

"Now listen to me," said Stretton. "During the hours you have been lying in a drunken sleep I have been awake."

"I have not the least doubt of it. You have been brooding, as usual. You have been thinking which would be the most horrible torture you can apply to Clinton."

"I have been thinking of nothing of the kind. No torture I could think of would be worse than that which, at the present moment, he is undergoing. No, this is what I have thought of. That to remain away from the old mill until midnight will be too long."

"That is just what I have thought."

"I propose that we take our departure from this house at once."

"The proposal is excellent. It entirely agrees with my views."

"Yes; we had better leave here, and proceed by water to Alsatia. Our horses can remain here. If we go by water there will not be so much chance of our being recognised. Arrived in Alsatia, we can disguise ourselves——"

"And what—to *me*, at least—is of more importance," interrupted Horace, "we can partake of some refreshment. You, my lord, I must say, are one man out of ten thousand; but if you are under the impression that *every* man can keep up and transact business (or pleasure for the matter of that) without food, you are most grievously mistaken."

"Arrived at Alsatia," said Stretton, "you can devour whatsoever you fancy."

"Then we leave here at once?"

"Aye, at once. But first you had better see whether you cannot rearrange your dress, and——"

"With your permission, that can be done in Alsatia. I am fearfully anxious to leave this hole. The rearrangement of my dress is a matter of little importance to me."

"Well, the fog will effectually conceal you from observation—that is quite certain, so prepare for instant departure."

"I am quite ready."

"Come, then."

Lord Stretton left the room and descended the stairs.

Horace followed him as soon as he had filled his flask.

A full brandy-flask was to him quite as important a matter as the carrying of a sword.

In a few moments the house at Lambeth was once more empty.

The fog, which seemed to be getting denser, was of great assistance to these two precious scoundrels, for it hid them from observation.

Arriving at Lambeth Stairs, Stretton paused.

"Why do you stop?" asked Horace.

"I am trying to make out the outline of the old mill."

"Curse the mill!"

"I shall do nothing of the kind. My curses are devoted to the occupants."

"As you will. Only let us get on. As to seeing the outline of the mill—well, you could not do so if you possessed the eyes of a cat, which is supposed to see in the dark (a supposition which however, I much doubt). The outline of the rotten old mill is not of so much importance to you or me at this moment as the outline of a boat."

"I see not the ghost of a boat," said Stretton, looking about on all sides of him.

"What ho!" yelled Horace. "Sculler —sculler! Whoa! Sculler! Treble fare—treble fare. Sculler! sculler!"

Ere the echoes of his voice had died away, a boat shot suddenly out of the fog.

"Hallo!" said a hoarse voice, "who cries sculler! Who said treble fare?"

"Here, my man," answered Horace; "draw up here—quick!"

The waterman pulled closer in.

"How am I to know that you can pay treble fare?" he asked.

"You impertinent scoundrel!" exclaimed Horace, furiously, "we can pay twenty times the fare if we felt so disposed. Let me inform you that we are——"

"Silence!" whispered Stretton, "our names must not be given. Draw in, my man," he said to the waterman, "and before you take us to our destination I will pay you your fare."

"That is much better," answered the waterman; "but let me tell you, whoever you are, that I am no scoundrel. Where do you want to go?"

"To the Temple Stairs."

"Good. That is not such a great distance, and treble fare is nothing out of the common for such weather as this. I will take you for treble fare and welcome, but I hope both of you can swim."

"Eh?" replied Horace, "swim? Why do you say that?"

"Simply because, not only is the fog dangerous, but the river is crowded with huge pieces of ice."

"We must risk both," said Stretton; "here is your fare. Danger or no danger I will not brook delay."

The boatman laughed, and said—

"Thank you, your worship. Get in, but carefully."

The waterman attached a link to the bow of the boat, lit it, and asked Stretton and his son to shout out if they saw a boat approaching, or if they saw any pieces of ice.

They saw both, but not near enough to do them any harm.

In half an hour the boat touched the Temple Stairs, and Stretton and Horace sprang ashore and soon disappeared.

On the spot where the Temple Gate had stood, half-a-dozen Alsatians were collected.

They challenged his lordship and his son, and receiving their names instead of a password, they allowed them to proceed, first, however, begging a crown "to assist in building a new gate," as they said, but which in reality was wanted to pay for refreshments at The Fountain of Life.

Captain White was discovered in his reception room, or rather, what remained of it, for the Templars and apprentices, when they attacked Alsatia, had transformed the place into a perfect wreck, which Captain White had never taken the trouble to repair.

He had his reasons, and good reasons they were.

The goldsmith's money had never been shared.

Pearman and the bravos were under the impression that the whole of the money and jewellery was safely stowed away below the flooring of this reception-room, and that the noble captain was only awaiting a convenient opportunity to divide it.

Never was Pearman or the bravos more grievously mistaken.

Secretly, little by little, the cunning one-eyed beast had taken away every fraction, every jewel, to Mercutio Merrywell, who had placed it where no one could find it except his daughter.

White held receipts for it, but he did not know where it had been placed.

His reason for taking away the property was because he had made up his mind to fly the country.

The miser had said that if he joined his money to his (the miser's) he could marry his daughter—they had not, however, consulted Parthena in the matter —and at his death Captain White would become the proud owner of the lot.

"And you can both live abroad under another name," said the miser, "and not be recognised. My death may occur at any time."

Captain White chuckled as he thought that if he *did* marry Parthena the miser would not live long after.

But, as will be seen, Captain White never lived to carry out either of his plans.

As Stretton entered the room, Pearman, standing on a barrel turned bottom up, was singing, or growling, the words of a ribald song, very much to the diver-

sion of White and his rascally companions.

As soon as the visitors were perceived silence ensued.

White rose and delivered himself of a couple of elaborate bows.

"An unexpected pleasure," he said. "Pray take seats. You are quite welcome."

"I am in no need of a seat," replied Stretton, haughtily.

"I am," said Horace; "and, Captain White, will you do me the favour to procure me something to eat? I have not partaken of any solid food for hours."

"Don't mention it," replied White. "Here we never go short. Whatever our larder can afford, Master Melton is quite welcome to, and so is—is his lordship."

"I require none of your filthy food," said Stretton.

"Filthy!" cried White. "Your lordship shall see that we do not consume anything filthy here. Pearman, the viands!"

"The *what?*"

"The *viands!* and be hanged!"

"The *viands!*" chuckled Pearman, as he moved off. "The viands—certainly."

In less than five minutes a really splendid cold collation was placed before Horace.

There were some cold ox-tongues, some huge slices from a splendid baron of beef, a cold venison-pie, some tempting-looking pickled trout, and several other articles.

After fasting for so many hours Horace was absolutely ravenous.

Never before had he enjoyed a meal so much.

Well, eat, *for 'tis the last meal thou wilt ever partake of in this world!*

Stretton had been longer without food than his son, but he could not have eaten a crust to save his life.

His vile heart was full to overflowing with thoughts of revenge.

Haughtily ignoring White and Pearman's offers of wine, his lordship folded his arms, leaned back against the wall, and moodily watched his son at his meal.

When it was finished he spoke.

"Captain White," he said, "provide my son and I with disguises."

"Certainly, my lord."

"We are going to the mill, and you are to accompany us with your men, as before."

White bowed.

"I think you have wisely resolved," he said; "we had better transact all *business* at the mill before midnight. My lord, you have been at Lambeth since we left the mill."

"Both of us."

"Then you have heard nothing, of course?"

"What do you mean?" asked Stretton eagerly.

"That Felix Ferdinand has been at work again. He and those who take part with him, seem determined to have revenge. Sharpley Sharp, the barber, who took a good share in the goldsmith's affair——"

"But not of the *money*," interrupted Pearman.

"Keep your tongue still!" was White's fierce reply. "In the goldsmith's affair, I say, has been killed. Some of my men were at his place when this Ferdinand, with a companion who was present at the attack here, suddenly made their appearance, armed to the teeth. The whole of Gunpowder Alley, so my men say, was full of officers of justice. By a bold dash my men escaped; but Sharpley was killed and flung down his own trap."

"I shall shortly, perhaps, have an opportunity of meeting him," said Horace, "and I will make short work of him."

"If you *do* meet him," said Pearman, "do not forget that he is no coward, and not likely to show the white feather, like some people I could mention."

Horace was about to reply to him, when Stretton called upon White to supply the disguises without further delay.

"I would suggest that low slouched hats and long cloaks would be quite sufficient. What with those, and the fact that the fog is very thick, it is out of all question that you can be recognised."

"Very well; provide us with the articles you mention; and remember, let your men be well armed."

"Don't mention it," grinned White. "I never knew a bravo to leave Alsatia without being well armed."

With this Captain White went forth, his men following.

In a short time he returned with the disguises, and the same men who had accompanied him when Lord Clinton was captured.

Each had had several hours' rest, but owing to the fact that not one among the lot had washed himself, all of them presented a very sleepy and dissipated appearance.

It was certainly most extraordinary, but nevertheless a positive fact, that Captain White, wherever he went, was accompanied by the dirtiest and most repulsive looking men to be found in the precincts of Whitefriars.

And besides being the dirtiest, they were the most drunken—if any difference *could* be found in that respect.

Perhaps it was because they were confirmed drunkards that Captain White chose them, for these men were easily put off with plenty of liquor and promises.

"Now then," cried White, "boot and saddle—and quick!"

"Nothing of the kind," said Stretton; "we are going by water."

"*Water?*" echoed White, his one eye opening to its fullest extent in great astonishment; "*water?* Never!"

"Such is my intention."

"Why not have told me before," said Horace. "I understood you to say that you were only going to Alsatia by water."

"Do as you are bid!" interrupted Stretton, sternly. "You will accompany me, by water, to the old mill."

"I don't like water," said White, "especially in weather such as this. Besides, there would be the greatest difficulty in getting a barge sufficiently large to hold all of us."

"Try for one. Search everywhere. By water I will go, for there is not so much chance of being seen."

"But, your lordship——" commenced White.

"Do as you are told," cried Stretton, impatiently.

Pearman was dispatched in search of a barge, but though two lay off Black-friars, no waterman could be found anywhere.

Seven of the clock came round, but as no waterman appeared, and as Stretton persisted in proceeding by water, a couple of the bravos were dispatched with instructions to cut the moorings of the best barge, and bring it to the steps opposite The Fountain of Life.

This order was at once carried out, and Captain White, his men, Stretton, and Horace having taken their places, the barge left Alsatia for Vauxhall.

The bravos were considerably more unskilful with the oars than they were with the sword, and it was a wonder that the barge, ere it had proceeded a mile, was not swamped.

It was no fault of the Alsatians that it was *not* swamped, for it seemed as if they wilfully steered the vessel against every piece of ice in the river.

A deep sigh of relief escaped the lips of Captain White and Pearman when the black outline of the old mill came in sight.

"Take the links," said Stretton, "and follow quietly. One man may remain and take charge of the barge."

Before starting for the mill entrance, Stretton took a good look around.

But he was not able to see far ahead.

Though the fog had lifted, and the moon peeped forth, an inky-black cloud occasionally obscured it.

As the party reached the entrance to the mill, the abbey clock struck eight.

"Ere we enter," said Stretton to White, "look around the mill."

"Let us summon the man I left in charge," said White.

"Not yet."

White slowly examined the exterior of of the mill.

Presently he came to the water-wheel.

As he stood beside the stream the moon threw her rays over it, and White caught sight of the end of the rope by which the outrider had escaped.

Wonderingly, he picked it up and shook it, and he watched the vibration far up.

"By all the foul fiends," he yelled, "look at this!"

A great rush was made to where he stood, Stretton being first.

"Look here," cried White, "look at this rope! It hangs from the window of the 'Round Room.' Look closely at it—it has been made out of some old sacking. As sure as my name is White, that outrider has escaped!"

"Impossible!" cried Stretton.

"Impossible, is it? It is quite possible—nay, it is certain!"

"Follow me!" roared Stretton.

The men with the links hastened to the front.

Stretton and Horace, having drawn their swords, dashed into the mill.

As they did so, the man who had been left in charge staggered towards them.

His lordship instantly seized him by the throat.

"Where is the outrider?" roared Stretton; "where is the man we placed in the Round Room?"

"He's—he's managed to get—get away!" gasped the wretch, now terrified into soberness. "I not long since went up and looked under the crack of the door. I—I saw that the window had been smashed, and that the man—the man—oh! you are cho—choking me—I—the man, I say, had gone, and——"

"Dastard!" yelled Stretton, "drunken fool—die!"

Saying this, he flung the man from him, and ere he could fall he plunged his sword to the hilt in his heart.

With cries resembling those of a wild beast, Stretton tore up the stairs, followed by Horace, White, and the whole of the bravos, who up to the present had not considered whether their comrade had deserved the death he had received.

The door of the Round Room was flung open.

"The outrider has escaped!" groaned Stretton.

"A man who could have made a rope out of this material," said White, pointing to the pieces of sacking with which the floor was strewed, "must have been a clever fellow."

"Ah," said Pearman, "it has been well done! He was a clever man. I shouldn't be at all surprised if the countess has escaped with him."

This, since the door was locked, was, of course, out of all character, as Stretton would have seen had he paused a moment.

But his mind was now in such a terrible state, that he could on no account have calmly considered anything.

Turning to Horace, he shouted—

"Follow me!"

And up he rushed to the room in which was the Countess of Rothburn.

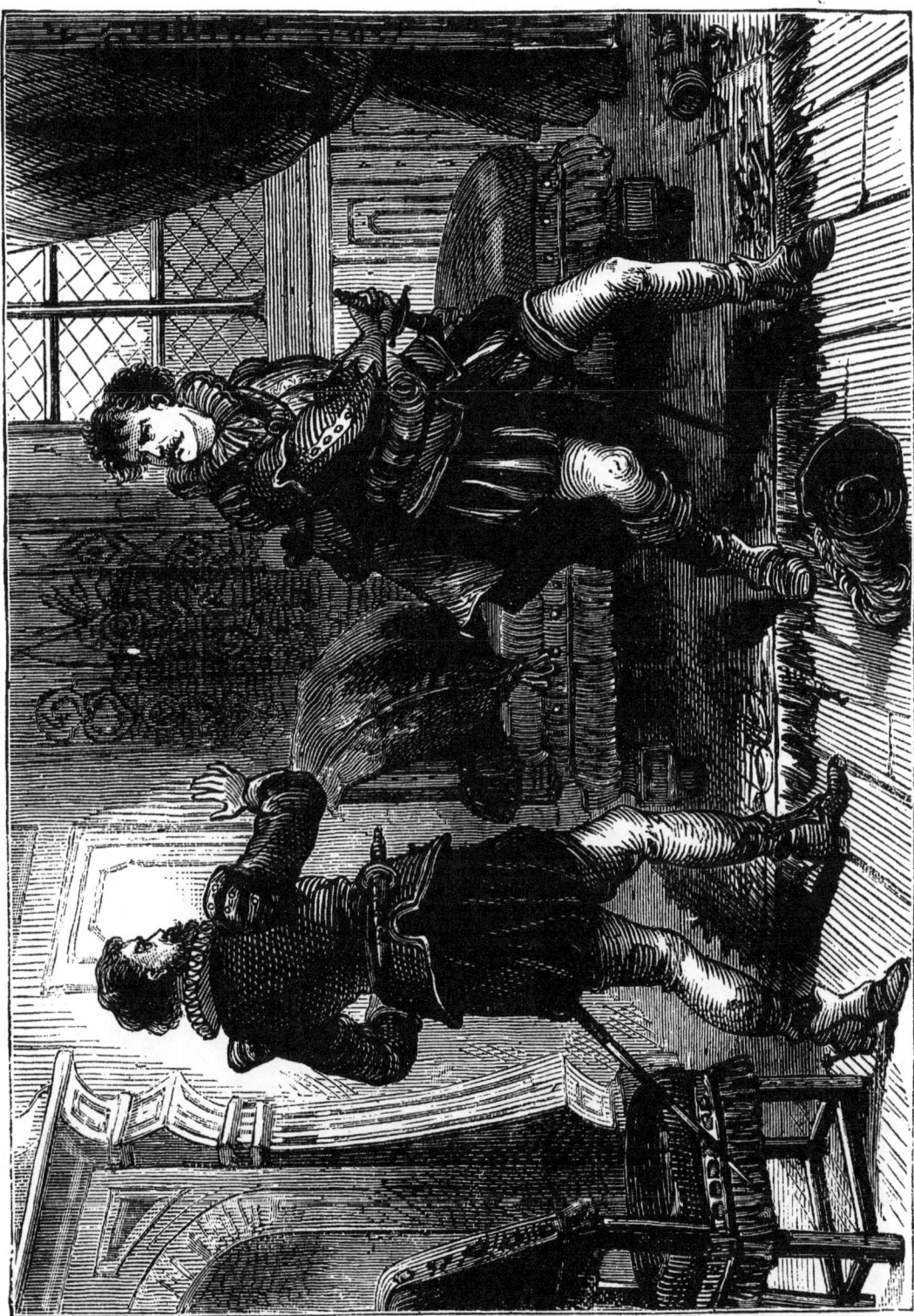

"'I AM ALWAYS READY TO DEFEND MYSELF,' CRIED HORACE."—(See No. 13.)

White and the bravos were close at his heels.

But not so Pearman.

His eyes had caught sight of *the bottle on the table.*

Watching his opportunity, he seized upon it.

"He, he," he chuckled, "the fool has left the whole of it! His attention was too much occupied with his escape. Ha, ha! Wine, wine! And from his lordship's own cupboard—it is certain to be most excellent. My Lord Stretton, here is your health! And here, Master Melton, is yours. And here, my noble captain, is yours!"

With this the wretch placed the neck of the bottle to his thick lips, and took a huge draught.

Suddenly, however, he snatched the bottle from his mouth, and hurled it away from him.

For a moment he stood stock still, his staring eyes, the entire expression of his face, showing that a horrible thought had rushed through his brain.

In that brief space he was completely transformed.

A terrible object he looked as he stood in the centre of that room, the moon's rays bringing out his distorted features with ghastly distinctness.

Presently a prolonged, a mighty shriek left his lips.

"Help!" he yelled. "Murder! Murder! Help! Help! I'm poisoned!"

And with the assistance of the wall and the table he endeavoured to reach the door.

His cries were heard above.

Stretton, who had unlocked the door of the countess's room, hastily relocked it and descended the stairs, followed by the whole of the men, who thought that the mill must be attacked.

"What is it, fool?" cried White. "What do you howl for, you——" By all the fiends, what have you done?"

Pearman, his eyes seeming as if about to start from their sockets, was pointing to the broken bottle.

It was evident that he could not speak.

White instantly saw what had happened.

"Do you mean to say you drank some of that wine?" he roared.

Pearman, with fearful groans, nodded.

"Then you are a dead man, Pearman!" said White, "*for the wine was poisoned!*"

"Aye, and it contained a most deadly poison," said Stretton, "a poison for which there is no antidote. Thou greedy drunken beast! Thou hast forfeited thy life for drink at last!"

Thrusting forth his arms, Pearman staggered forward as if to implore them to save him.

But Horace gave him a brutal push, which sent him reeling backwards.

"No one asked you to drink the wine," he said savagely, "you pleased yourself. Mark it well, my men," he added, turning to the bravos. "Do not forget that Pearman committed suicide!"

"Yes, yes," chuckled White; "committed suicide—so he did!"

Aside, the wretch added—

"He will never again speak of the goldsmith's treasure. Ho, ho!"

"Shut the door on him," said Stretton, "and follow me."

The poisoned man was left alone to die.

Once more the room above was opened, and Stretton, calling upon the men to raise their links, stalked in.

The poor countess was standing at a few paces distant from the window.

As Stretton entered, she neither spoke nor moved.

"I am here once more," said Stretton, fiercely. "It was my intention to have come here at midnight, and not before; but I could not rest. I so longed to feast my eyes on your beauteous form," he sneered, "that form which has so captivated the heart of the wretch in the cellar near the river—the wretch who ere long will be put to death—if he is not dead already."

"Which is more than probable," said Horace.

Yet, though the rapid rising and falling of her bosom showed how much the poor lady was affected, she made no movement nor reply.

Her eyes seemed to be fixed upon the heavens.

"I should not be surprised if her reason has left her," said White.

"Pshaw?" was Stretton's reply; "there is not much fear of that. Turn, countess, and listen to me."

The countess moved not one-twentieth part of an inch.

"Turn !" thundered Stretton, stamping his feet with rage.

"What can she be looking at ?" said White. "I see nothing to——— Ha !"

At this very instant a bright clear flash was seen, and then a brilliant light shot straight up into the heavens and burst with a loud report, scuttling myriads of sparks in all directions.

Uttering a cry of joy the countess clasped her hands.

"Saved !" she muttered.

"A rocket !" cried White ; "a rocket, as I live ! 'Tis a signal ! Aye, I see it, your lordship ! The outrider, ere he escaped, communicated with her ladyship through these boards. See them ? He, no doubt, told her that he would bring assistance, and that, when it arrived, a rocket would be the signal."

"Saved," cried Stretton, as he advanced and seized the countess savagely by the wrist ; "saved, you say. Nay, nay ! You will not be saved Were the mill at this moment surrounded by thousands of the king's troops, you should not be saved. Nay, for I would slay you before their eyes !"

"Inhuman monster !" cried the countess, as she vainly endeavoured to break away from the vice-like grip ; "unhand me instantly !"

"Never ! Come—come with me. To the Round Room, Horace—the Round Room !"

"If the flight of that rocket is really a signal," said Horace, "we had better leave the mill at once."

"Not yet."

"Do you imagine that I am going to stay here to be caught like a rat in a trap."

"Stay but a little while, my son," said Stretton. "White may be wrong—the rocket may be only a signal from one vessel to another."

"My impression is that Captain White is right," said Horace, "so let's away."

"Coward, you shall stay. Come !" shouted Stretton, turning to the countess, and pulling her violently along. "Come, assist me, White—assist me ! If the mill is attacked, by all the saints ! we will defend it to the last !"

Assisted by the bravos, the countess was dragged down the stairs and thrust into the Round Room.

As Stretton pushed her from him, she nearly fell over the body of Pearman, now quite dead.

"Remain there !" said Stretton, "and mark this—if your friends—my curse on them !—if your friends attack this place, and if they succeed in overpowering us, I will fire the mill—hear it ?—I will fire the mill, and you know what your fate will be !"

The countess, without making a reply, shrank back against the wall, fell upon her knees, and covered her face with her hands.

"Remember," said Horace, "that a rope dangles from the window."

"What of it ?" replied Stretton ; "she could never escape by it. Now then, for her friends, if they are here. No doubt the outrider has warned Felix Ferdinand. Listen to me, Captain White—listen to me, my men, all of you. Stand by me, and ere you leave me after this affair is over you shall each have enough money to last you your lifetime. The hour of my revenge is here, assist me in it. Hark ! what was that ?"

"It was a sound like the clash of arms," replied Horace.

"Secure all the doors !" cried Stretton ; "quick !"

In a few moments the outer doors were securely fastened by oak beams being driven into the staples.

Stretton then divided the men. Some went into one room, some into another, and with drawn swords and pistols they awaited the attack, if such there was to be.

They could not see far ahead, for again the moon was obscured by heavy dense black clouds, which now appeared to be quite stationary.

To return to Felix.

Arrived within sight of the old mill, the horses were secured to several trees in a field, where it was hardly likely on such a night as this, that they would be observed.

The whole party then cautiously approached.

Felix was the first to catch sight of the lights moving to and fro within the mill.

Holding up his hand, the party halted.

"It is as I thought," said Felix ; "Stretton is there !"

"Yes," said Fillipy ; "there can be hardly a doubt of it. What say you, Andrew ?"

"I am sure of it."

"Listen to me," said Felix; "the outrider and I will go round to the back, and do you cautiously approach the front. You must keep in the shadow until you see an opportunity of making a bold dash. If the opportunity arrives, seize it, dash into the mill, and endeavour to secure all within it."

Fillipy and Andrew promised that their movements should be cautious, and Felix, telling the outrider to proceed, left them.

The outrider, Fleet, took our hero to the very spot where White had observed the rope dangling from the window of the Round Room.

"It was from yonder window I escaped," said Fleet; "you can see the rope still hanging down, and from that I conclude that neither Stretton nor the wretches with him have observed it."

"If they have," replied Felix, "they have not considered it worth the trouble of cutting it down. Oh, that the poor countess could see us! All her hopes, which must now have given way, would be revived. Fire the rocket!"

The outrider did as desired and as soon as its lightning-like flash, and its myriads of sparks, had died away, they heard sounds of a struggle above.

This was, of course, Stretton dragging the countess out of the room in which she had been placed, to the one below.

The listeners, after a painful pause, heard the door closed with a crash, and they recognised Stretton's voice, though they could not distinguish what was said.

"The rocket has alarmed Stretton and his men," said Felix, "and they are putting the mill in a state of defence. Alas! if we cannot get admittance, the poor countess and Lord Clinton will surely lose their lives."

"Admittance is sure," said the outrider, as he pointed to the rope; "for from what I can make out, I judge all who are in the mill to be now in the front, and fortunately, our party will attract their attention. If I steady the rope, will you ascend? I swear that the rope is sufficiently strong to bear twice your weight."

Felix did not hesitate one instant. Catching hold of the rope he commenced the ascent, the outrider putting all his weight on the end and thus steadying it.

It was a slow—very slow journey, for the rope, though strong, was not very thick, and it hurt his hands.

At last the window was reached.

Slightly swinging himself, Felix landed upon the sill, and in another moment was inside the room.

The countess, with a slight scream, was about to rush forward.

For an instant Felix, who, of course, imagined her to be in the room above, was speechless with surprise.

Quickly recovering himself, he said—

"Make no noise, my lady, if you value your life. Keep still, I——"

But it was impossible that she could keep still.

Though she suppressed a cry of joy which, on recognising Felix rose to her lips, she threw her arms about his neck.

"May Heaven's most precious blessing rest upon you, Felix," she said. "You have come to save us! For myself I care not, for I have no fear of death; but Clinton—oh, save him, save him!"

"You are a brave and noble lady, indeed," said Felix with much emotion. "But I and my friends are here to save both of you. Aye, we will save you, or perish in the attempt."

At this moment the outrider, with the agility of a monkey, clambered in.

Barely had he reached the floor ere the sharp crack of a pistol was heard below.

This was immediately followed by at least a dozen shots.

Then loud shouts and cries rose on the air, and a thundering at the front door of the mill showed that Fillipy and Andrew were attempting to gain admittance.

Above the noise, which every second became louder, Stretton and Horace could be heard urging on the men.

"They are in the front," said Felix. "Fleet get your sword ready! You, my lady, at the present moment must not hesitate to defend yourself if necessary. Take this pistol, which is fully charged. If you are attacked, let your aim be low and steady. Follow me."

Felix went first, Fleet next, and the countess, who held the pistol firmly, last.

Silently, like dark shadows, they descended the rickety stairs, which creaked and groaned dismally, but the sound was lost amid the fearful noise below.

The Flour Room was at last reached.

At the side of the door a link was burning in a bracket, and this Felix took down.

"We must not enter this room until an opportunity occurs of making a dash for it," said Felix, "or of being assisted by our friends without."

The countess was now in a fainting state.

"If I had a flask of brandy with me," said Felix, "I should——" Here his eyes rested upon the kegs near the door. "Ah," he said, "here is brandy."

Raising a heavy stone, he brought it down with all his force on the head of the keg, breaking it in.

What Felix saw caused him to turn quite pale.

Truly all had had a most narrow escape of their lives, for the kegs contained *powder*, and Felix had been holding the torch right over them.

Had a spark dropped the mill and everyone within must have been blown to atoms.

Fortunately the countess had not noticed the circumstance, or no doubt her terror would have increased.

The firing of the shots continued with startling rapidity.

Occasionally a fearful shriek of mortal agony showed that some one had received his death-wound.

The sound as of heavy blows on the front door also continued, and presently a far louder cry than all was heard.

The clatter of feet, the clash of arms, shots, oaths, and yells showed that at last the door had yielded to the persistent and determined attack made on it, and that the two parties had met.

"Come!" cried Felix. "Stand by me, Fleet! Both of us must cover the countess. Now——"

But ere they could cross the threshold of the door, Stretton and Horace emerged from the sulphurous smoke, and dashed towards them.

Neither had the slightest idea that anyone had gained admittance from the back.

When, therefore, they saw Felix and the outrider, sword and pistol in hand, and the countess at the back of them, a loud yell of rage left their lips.

Felix and the outrider would have attacked them with fury, but they saw White and several of his men close at hand.

They therefore backed into the doorway, and Felix, again seizing the torch, pointed his pistol at Stretton's breast.

"Advance one step," he said, "and you are a dead man! Take this torch, countess. You have a pistol—defend yourself. If they attempt to attack you, *hurl your torch into yonder barrel of powder!* Better die thus than fall into the hands of the foul monsters who are known as Lord Stretton and his son!"

The countess, who was now firm and determined, took the torch, and, pistol in hand, stationed herself by the keg of powder.

Stretton and his son, speechless with passion, backed out slowly.

They were now attacked with great fury by Felix and the outrider.

Andrew and Fillipy, who had begun to get uneasy respecting our hero and the outrider, now made out their figures, and they increased their endeavours to get near them.

Captain White saw that both he and his men stood a good chance of losing their lives unless they managed to cut their way to the door, and he tried as hard as he was able to do so.

In the midst of the fight, which was now something dreadful, since no quarter was asked for or given, Stretton became separated from his son.

He was hotly engaged with the outrider, who seemed determined to have his revenge for what he had suffered.

But looking back he saw that Horace and Felix were far more hotly engaged than himself.

Yes, at last our hero had managed to reach Horace, and he determined that he would not leave him until one of them fell.

For some few moments after crossing swords with our hero, Horace was under the impression that he would make short work of him.

But he was most woefully mistaken.

Our readers know well enough that Felix was a remarkably skilful swordsman, and so Horace soon found.

His pistols were in his belt, but as he placed his hand upon one he remembered that having discharged them, they were both unloaded.

Felix saw the movement, and in tones of bitter contempt he said—

"You cur! You have not drawn your pistols, and that proves that they are not loaded. I have a pistol in my belt—loaded! But I will not draw it, while you face me with your sword."

Closely he pressed Horace, who gradually receded towards the stairs.

He had become ghastly white.

Ere he reached the stairs he had received two wounds from our hero, one in the right arm, the other in the breast.

Both were slight, it is true, but to Horace they were only the forerunners of what would be a fatal thrust.

Suddenly Horace's heels touched the stairs, and with a wild unearthly yell, he turned and fled up them like the wind.

Felix drew his pistol, aimed at his retreating figure, and fired.

Owing, however, to the bend in the stairs, Horace was not hit.

Seeing the door of the Round Room open, he dashed in, banged the door to, and locked it.

But Felix did not mean him to get out of his clutches so easily.

He was quickly up the stairs after him.

Again and again he hurled himself against the door, which, though it trembled violently as each blow was given, did not give way.

Meantime, Horace, on rushing to the window, saw the rope.

A great cry of joy left his lips.

"Saved!" he cried; "saved! This rope will help me. Once on the water-wheel, I can escape. Ha, ha! I have baffled him after all! Yes, I will escape —and then let him beware. When next I meet him face to face, I will take care that I have a dozen bravos at my back!"

Placing his sword between his teeth, he mounted the sill, dropped over, and commenced to descend the rope.

Finding that the door did not yield to his repeated blows, Felix bethought him of the room above, and he at once ascended to it, and looked out.

The rays of the moon, now at the full, enabled him to see Horace rapidly descending the rope.

"By Heaven!" he cried. "As I thought, he has taken advantage of the rope! And my pistol is not loaded! Then he escapes me after all! Ha! What is this?"

He had caught sight of *the high steel handle by the window*, which, as our readers will remember, communicated with the water-wheel.

Our hero knew what it was, for he had seen several while living in Essex.

Without hesitation, he seized the handle, and watching Horace as he dropped upon the water-wheel, he exerted all his strength, pulled back the handle, and fixed the lever!

A great creaking of pulleys and chains was heard, and slowly the wheel commenced to move.

As Horace saw this, a series of horrible shrieks escaped him.

His cries for mercy must have reached the ears of everyone in that mill!

He flung himself down, and grasped the woodwork, but nothing now could have stopped the wheel in time to save him.

Increasing in speed as the volume of water from the stream rushed into it, the wheel carried Horace to the frame above, and dashed him to pieces.

His mangled and lifeless body for a moment caused the wheel really to stop, but the tons of water pressing upon it, soon set it in motion again, and the next turn sent Horace's body into the stream.

Once there, the current immediately commenced to carry it to the river, from whence, if it was not interrupted by any obstruction, or picked up by the occupants of some boat, it would be carried to the ocean.

Felix darted out of the room and down the stairs.

He found that the fight was over.

The struggle had been a deadly one, for the floor and the passages told a shocking tale.

"Where is the villain Stretton?" cried Felix.

"Escaped with Captain White," replied Andrew; "how they managed it I know not. They must have made their exit by some secret passage."

"Where is Fillipy?"

"Watching over the safety of the countess. Poor Fillipy! I much fear me he is seriously injured."

"Ha, say you so."

"He received a shot from an Alsatian

which struck him near the temple, causing a large wound, but immediately afterwards I pinned the wretch to the wall with my dagger. Both Stretton and White have received some severe wounds."

At this moment Fillipy came forward.

The poor fellow was as pale as death, and trembled from loss of blood.

The brave countess had torn a piece of linen from her rich clothing, and had bound it about his head, though it did not seem as if it had stopped the bleeding.

Felix, grasping his hand, said in a voice of emotion.

"Heaven knows, Master Fallory, how exceedingly sorry I am that this misfortune has overtaken you!"

Fillipy smiled, but painfully.

As he returned the pressure of our hero's hand, he said—

"Whoever engages in battle, Felix, must expect a wound. Though I am injured—and I am afraid seriously—I trust you have not been hurt?"

"Nay. I——"

"That is well. Andrew has been wounded, but fortunately they are but mere scratches. So I am glad both of you have escaped. Did any fatal *accident* happen to either of you, you would be mourned for by those who love you, and with whom, when you have righted yourself, you will be happy. As for me, I have no one to——"

"Hist! speak not so, I implore you!" interrupted Felix; "fear it not, Fillipy, when all comes right you shall be a sharer of our happiness."

"He shall, indeed," said the countess, who now joined the group, "for he has more than once proved himself a gallant gentleman."

"To hear those words from your lips, my lady," said Fillipy, "more than compensates me for all the pain I am suffering."

"I hope not many of our men were dangerously wounded?" said Felix.

"Four were shot dead!" replied Andrew, gravely, "and all the rest, I am sorry to say, are more or less wounded. But they bear themselves bravely, for they know that they have accomplished our object. All that remains to be done now is to rescue Lord Clinton. One of the bravos was secured. He was one of those who accompanied Captain White when his lordship was placed in the foul dungeon to which Stretton consigned him. He will show us the way. What ho! bring hither your prisoner!"

Thereupon the men brought forward one of the bravos, the only man left, and a most hideous object he looked.

"Can you lead us to Lord Clinton's dungeon, sirrah?" cried Felix.

"I can if I so choose," was the surly reply.

"Choose then," returned Felix.

"What compensation shall I get if I lead the way?"

"Compensation? Rascal! Does not the knowledge that your life is spared sufficiently compensate you?"

"No!"

"Do you mean that you will refuse to lead us to the dungeon unless we pay you a sum of money?"

"Precisely," replied the bravo with an insolent swagger.

"Then let me tell you this," said Felix, "we will find out what we want to know without your assistance. But it may be interesting to you to know that we will, ere we depart, lock you in yonder room, where there are a number of barrels of gunpowder. Before we leave the mill we shall set it on fire, so you may easily guess what your fate will be."

A cry of horror left the bravo's lips.

His assumed bravado instantly vanished, and he said in whining tones—

"I will do as you wish, your worship; but of course you will afterwards allow me to depart."

"Of course I shall do nothing of the kind!" was Felix's stern reply; "my intention is to hand you over to the proper authorities, and I pray heaven I live to see you dangling in chains, a grim warning to your rascally associates. So you may choose which alternative you will select."

For a few moments the bravo hesitated.

Whichever he chose, certain death awaited him.

Still, he considered that death by being blown to atoms, a quick death, was preferable to being placed in a dock, tried, sentenced, hung till he was dead, and perhaps before even he was dead placed in chains, there to remain until he rotted away piece by piece.

He would have elected to remain in the mill had he thought what Felix had said was only a threat, and again, he *might* have an opportunity of escaping.

There was just a chance of that.

"Since there is no help for it," he said, "I will conduct you to the place. I have no desire to be blown to pieces."

"Lead the way then, rascal," said Felix. "Andrew, do you go with him, and do not lose sight of him an instant. We will join you as soon as the whole of our men are placed outside."

"The coach and horses are still in the shed," said the outrider, who had been one of the fortunate ones, having received only a very slight wound.

"They will be used by its master," Felix said, "and the Countess of Rothburn."

"And I, thank Heaven, I am alive to cross the leading horse once more!" said the outrider, binding up the wound in his arm.

The dead and wounded men-servants having been safely brought out of the mill and laid upon a heap of straw, a man was despatched to the nearest inn for a waggon.

Then the whole party moved off towards the dungeon in which Clinton had been thrown.

Our readers are familiar with the approaches to it, so that we have no need to describe them again.

The countess was implored to remain at the mill until Felix should return.

But no.

The anxiety of the brave lady for the safety of the noble-hearted Clinton to whom she had given her love was too great.

She took one of the links, and holding it aloft, fearlessly followed the party.

The deep pools of water which were encountered did not cause her to pause, neither did the occasional rush of the huge water rats wring a terrified cry from her lips.

She was indeed a woman worthy the love of the bravest and the best.

Andrew walked beside the villainous bravo, while Felix strode behind him, carrying a pistol ready for use.

Just before the cellar door was reached the man paused.

"Why do you halt?" asked Felix, sternly, grasping his pistol.

"Well, you see," was the hesitating reply, "it has just struck me that if I made an earnest appeal to you, you would re-consider——"

"It would be useless to make any appeal to me," interrupted Felix; "it is my intention to hunt every Alsatian to the scaffold, and, if Heaven spares me, I will certainly carry out my intention."

Uttering a deep groan of despair, the man again went forward.

He had some difficulty in recognising the place, for the only time he had been there was when Clinton was taken to the dungeon.

At last, however, the rotten door was reached.

The bravo pointed to it.

"Are you certain this is the place?" asked Felix.

"Aye," was the reply; "and there can be no doubt that his lordship is dead, and perhaps partly eaten by the rats."

A cry of horror escaped the countess's lips.

"Haste, Felix," she implored, "or my heart will break!"

"Stand back!" cried our hero, as, raising his axe, he brought it down with terrific force upon the door.

That one blow was quite enough.

Instantly the door fell back.

Andrew raised his torch as Felix started forward.

There kneeling in the attitude of prayer, was Lord Clinton!

With a wild cry of joy, the countess would have flung herself upon him.

But Andrew raised his hand.

"Stop!" he said.

"The time has come, then," cried Clinton, without altering his position, the time has come! Strike! strike!" he said, touching his breast; "strike— here—for I am now to die, and so be released from this agony."

"His mind has gone," exclaimed Felix.

"Nay, nay; say not so—oh, say not so!" cried the countess, bounding forward with extended arms. "Clinton, Clinton! Oh, my love—my love! Look, 'tis I—your own—your own. Clinton, Clinton! Oh, God!" she shrieked in tones of terrible agony, "remove from his face that vacant stare. In mercy, remove it! Clinton, oh say—say you recognise me."

And with a wild hysterical cry she flung herself upon her knees, placed her arms about Clinton, and pressed his head to her throbbing breast.

And now for some few moments no sound was heard but the low words of endearment the countess addressed to his lordship.

The silence of the grave had fallen upon all; all were anxiously watching the touching scene before them—all, we should say, *but the bravo!* His blood-shot eyes were watching Felix for revenge or escape.

Seeing that all were within the dungeon, he determined to make a dash for liberty.

Bracing himself up, he suddenly turned, rushed from the cellar and disappeared in the darkness.

Felix snatched a torch from a man at his side, and instantly hurried after him.

But the bravo had but little idea of the inns and outs of the place.

"Hold!" roared Felix. "Hold, villain, I say! Hold, or I fire!"

Raising his torch, its light showed him the retreating figure of the bravo.

Felix stopped, knelt down, and took careful aim.

But ere he could pull the trigger, the bravo, with a wild unearthly shriek, disappeared.

Down he fell.

Felix went carefully forward.

A moment's examination showed him that the bravo had fallen down a sort of well, which was nearly full of thick black water.

Felix held his torch over the place for a few seconds.

But he saw nothing.

The bravo had entirely disappeared.

Feeling quite sick at heart, Felix returned.

He found Clinton standing erect, while two men were filing through the monstrous chain which encircled his waist.

That he had somewhat recovered was evident from the way he smiled at the countess.

As our hero, entered, the countess said—

"He is here, Clinton."

"I recognise him," replied his lordship,

holding forth his hand. "Come hither, Felix; let me—— But no. No words I could utter would express my gratitude."

"I pray you, your lordship, say nothing at present," answered Felix; "you are too exhausted to speak. I thank Heaven we have not arrived too late!"

Clinton was, after some hard work, released from the ring, but he was much too weak too walk.

His body, supported by the men, and the countess raising his head, he was carried out of the dungeon.

As Felix turned from the place, he said—

"My regret is that I have not Stretton to place in this dungeon, in place of Lord Clinton."

"The exchange would be most just," said the countess.

"Well, it is of little moment which way retribution overtakes him," said our hero fiercely; "but overtake him it will very shortly."

In a short time, Lord Clinton was placed in his own coach, and the countess was at his side supporting him.

The countess implored our hero to join them in the coach, but that Felix declined to do.

A waggon was procured and brought round.

The bodies of the dead on Felix's side were tenderly placed in it, and Fillipy and Andrew then mounted.

The whole party moved over to a distance of about two hundred yards, and Felix, standing by the threshold of the mill, called to them to halt.

Entering the mill, he remained there for some few moments: then he returned, and mounting his horse, joined the party, which again moved slowly off.

Another two hundred yards were covered, and again our hero gave the word to halt.

Looking back at the mill, a dim light was observed to be burning near the door.

Gradually it increased, and in a few seconds a dense volume of smoke rushed forth, encircling the mill in huge fantastic wreaths.

"Ha!" cried the countess; "the mill is on fire! Your work, Felix!"

"Aye, mine. No doubt that home of many mysteries has been the scene of many tragedies. In but a short time it will have ceased to exist. Let the coach be brought round, so that his lordship may the better behold what is happening to Lord Stretton's secret place of murder."

The coach was brought round, and from the window Clinton and the countess watched the progress of the fire, which, in a short space of time, had taken a firm hold of the whole of the lower portion of the premises.

As the party watched, Felix, in a voice loud enough to be heard by all, gave the correct account of the awful death of Horace.

" I always thought something terrible would happen to him," said Lord Clinton. " My only wonder is that he did not meet with a sudden and violent death long, long ago. He was a worthy follower in the footsteps of his father, who, if he did not teach him most of his horrible and lawless practices, certainly never disapproved of them. I would the punishment of the father was reserved for me, that I could meet him sword to sword ! "

"That cannot be, my lord," replied Felix; " my intention is to hunt his lordship and Captain White down at once. Vengeance must be swift, or both will escape it by the simple plan of leaving the country."

In the meantime the mill was burning furiously, the roaring and hissing of the flames being distinctly heard by all.

In every direction the long tongues of flame shot out, writhing and twisting after the manner of a serpent darting hither and thither as if to seize a victim.

The bright flames lit up the surrounding country for miles, and the effect of the reflection of the fire on the snow and the ice was certainly grand in the extreme, and the effect was considerably heightened by the showers of sparks which fell in all directions.

In the midst of all this the waterwheel, by which Horace had lost his life, continued to turn, though the flames had caught the side of it.

And now not a word was uttered by either of the party.

All knew that very soon the flames would seize upon the barrels of powder

Higher and higher rose the bright flames with a rush and a roar, as if frantically struggling to reach the clouds above.

Suddenly one fearful crash rang out.

The flames had fired the powder.

The report was like the discharge of a score of the heaviest pieces of ordnance.

The blazing mill was instantly scattered in every direction, many huge pieces of flaming timber flying over the heads of the party.

Another moment, and nothing remained of the old mill save its burning timbers.

Of the dead left in the mill—including the body of the villainous Pearman—not a vestige was ever discovered.

"It is an awful sight," said the countess with a shudder.

"It is indeed," said Clinton; " but a better fate could not have been selected for such a place, and so the king will say when I lay all before him."

"Lord Stretton's days are numbered." said Felix, grimly; " he will assuredly fall soon."

" Retribution has overtaken his son," said the countess, " and, as Felix says, it will soon overtake the father; but oh, I pray Heaven ere he dies he may reveal the secret which I believe he has kept for many, many long years."

"It is through him," said Clinton, " that I have not been able to pursue my enquiries."

By this time the party was again in motion, and in due time it arrived at St. James's Park.

Their astonishment was great when they found the countess's residence surrounded by some hundreds of persons.

In the mansion were a large number of apprentices and Templars, anxious for news.

A lane was made for the party, which was greeted with loud and prolonged cheers.

Felix told the story of what had taken place, and while cries of vengeance on Stretton and the one-eyed Captain White were heard on all sides, they did not drown the expressions of admiration for and approval of our hero's gallant conduct.

Tired and exhausted as he was, oh,

what a feeling of thankfulness and joy filled our hero's breast when, on dismounting, Rosamund ran forward and threw herself into his arms, and, forget-ful of the crowd of onlookers, addressed him in words of rapturous endearment.

It was the crowning reward of his labours.

CHAPTER XVI.

IN WHICH OUR READERS ARE ONCE MORE, AND FOR THE LAST TIME, CONDUCTED TO ALSATIA.—THE FATE OF CAPTAIN WHITE AND LORD STRETTON.

AFTER Lord Stretton and Captain White escaped from the old mill, they made for the barge, jumped into it, and assisted by the man who had been left in charge, pulled away with all speed to White-friars.

So fearful were they that a boat would be put off in pursuit of them that they pulled away for dear life.

Never in all their lives had his lordship or Captain White so exerted themselves.

Of course there was no time for conversation, yet his lordship was anxious to say something respecting his son, as to whose fate he and White were in entire ignorance.

Finding they were not pursued, they, as soon as they arrived within easy distance of Alsatia, threw down their oars.

"Give me your flask if you have one," said White, in husky tones.

"I haven't such a thing," was the reply.

"Nor have I," said Stretton. "Would that I had! My tongue is cloven to the roof of my mouth. I could drink the black water from the river."

"Don't attempt it," sneered White, "if you do, you might, like Pearman—rest his soul (if he had one!), commit suicide."

"Captain White," groaned Stretton. "That boy Felix has again beaten us!"

"He has," replied White through his clenched teeth. "Oh, that I had him here. Curse him, I would wring his neck."

"He will release Clinton as well as the countess."

"Of course he will. But you must not be too sure that he will release Clinton in time to save his life."

"If he does, and Clinton recovers, I am lost."

"Pah! You are lost without."

"Silence—silence! I am not thinking of myself now, but of my son."

The bravo was apparently watching the movements of a ghostly-looking vessel on the opposite side of the river, but suddenly a startled exclamation left his lips.

White was suddenly struck by his companion on the shoulder.

"What's the matter with you, fool?" he growled.

"Look yonder," was the answer; "see what a bright light there is in the sky!"

White started up.

"It's a fire," he said—"a house on fire. Lord, how it burns! And it seems it is in the direction of Vauxhall!"

"What!" cried Stretton; "in the direction of Vauxhall?"

"Yes, it is so. A thousand crowns to one they have fired the old mill."

Stretton uttered a dismal groan.

"If they have—— But no," he said, "I don't think they would do that. They would be afraid to do it."

"Afraid of *what*? Pooh, this accursed Felix Ferdinand is afraid of nothing. But you will very soon learn whether it is or is not the old mill. You will not require a messenger to bring you the intelligence."

"What mean you?"

"Why, the *powder*!"

"Ah, that I had forgotten!" cried Stretton, clasping his hands together. "I pray that my son may not be within it when the powder explodes—that is, if it is the mill which is on fire. See—look—the flames are going down—the—— Heavens!"

At this moment, a mighty roar burst upon their ears, and they saw a rush of —as it seemed to them—one vast sheet of flame and millions of sparks towards the heavens.

"MERCUTIO TOOK THE LAMP FROM HIS DAUGHTER'S HAND AND RAISED IT."

Another moment, and the reflection above had entirely disappeared.

"I am right again!" said White; "the old mill has disappeared for ever."

"Haste, haste!" cried Stretton, now terribly excited; "let us land, take horse, and endeavour to learn what has become of my son."

"Not if I know it," replied White; "I have already risked my neck enough for your lordship. I will never do it again for——"

"What, will you turn traitor?"

"Turn traitor? What good would that do me?" sneered White. "No, I will not turn traitor, but I will wash my hands altogether of your lordship's affairs."

"I see. Now that all has gone against me, and you fancy there is no chance of any more money, you will——"

"Money!" interrupted White. "Listen to me." Here he leaned over and whispered in Stretton's ear. "What you owe me I will never claim. I am in possession of an enormous amount of money, and very soon I intend to leave the country. But here are the steps. Now land, your lordship, and come with me."

"Do you intend to go to The Fountain of Life?" asked Lord Stretton, after a somewhat long and painful pause.

"No; never again. I intend to take up my residence at the house of Mercutio Merrywell, and there, if you like, you can stay with me until you have decided what to do next."

"Good. I have no alternative but to consent."

Turning to the bravo, White said—

"Here are twenty crowns for you, and I will give you more if you do as I tell you. Go to the Fountain and spin a good story as to how we were attacked by two hundred of the king's troops, how many of us were killed, and so on; and——"

"But you, captain?"

"Say I will join them within twenty-four hours. But don't mention where I am at present, and don't say that his lordship is with me."

"Good," grinned the man; "I will do exactly as you say."

So, while the bravo went off to unfold his parcel of lies, Captain White led his lordship to a shed near the steps.

Taking a key from his pocket he opened the door.

"Now catch hold of me," he said, "and be careful you don't fall."

"Where does this lead?" asked Stretton, fearful of treachery.

"To the miser's house," was the answer; "but if you have any doubts about me, stay behind."

"No, no; go on—go on."

Down a flight of steps they went, and along a narrow zigzag passage.

At the end of this a flight of steps was ascended, and White, using the same key, opened another door, and the pair the next moment were by the side of the miser's house.

The darkness prevented their movements being seen.

* * * *

A few moments before this, Mercutio Merrywell was engaged in a most important task—a task, however, he had set himself.

He was in one of the vaults counting, not his own money, but the money which had been entrusted to his keeping by Captain White.

The vault in which the old miser knelt was a cellar beneath a cellar.

The entrance to it was from the cellar above, in the floor of which was a trap-door.

Captain White's plunder from the goldsmith's (to which he had added more taken from various places) was placed in two large heavy boxes, and White held the keys.

Mercutio had bought from one place and the other some scores of keys, and among them he had at last discovered a couple to fit.

There upon his knees he was bending over the boxes; his left hand held a small lamp, while his other shaded his eyes.

In the cellar above stood his daughter Parthena.

Erect, grim, and stern, this curious creature watched the movements of her father with interest though the curl of her lips showed how disgusted she was.

"Parthena!" cried Mercutio in low tones—tones which trembled with suppressed excitement; "Parthena, look—oh, look! I implore you—look!"

"I am looking."

"What see you—eh—eh?"

"An old man—a man whose right foot is already in the grave—who——"

"Ha, stop!" whined Mercutio in piping childlike tones. "I mean what do you—can't you see into the box?"

"Nay; neither do I want to."

"Descend, the trap is safe."

"Descend! Not I!"

"Well, look—look here, Parthena," and the old man plunged his hand into the box, and then held it up; "look—listen—listen, my daughter! There—there—oh, there! Hark to the music of the gold!"

And slowly he let fall a little glittering shower of gold, which fell on more gold within the box with a merry musical rattle.

Mercutio looked up with a rapturous chuckle.

"What think ye of them?" he asked.

"Nothing whatever," was the cold reply.

"Thou fool—thou thrice accursed fool! Know ye not their value? How would those diamonds look round thy neck—eh—eh?"

"Round *my* neck?" replied Parthena, with a derisive laugh. "About as foolish as a golden bracelet would look about a dog's neck. Diamonds look well when they are placed where they *can* look well—not without. Fancy placing a string of glittering diamonds about the skinny neck of Parthena Merrywell!"

And Parthena laughed bitterly.

"Oh, thou foolish child!" groaned the miser. "I have been trying to teach you the value of these things for years, and even now you do not fully appreciate them. Yet you know that money brings happiness, Parthena — much happiness."

"And much misery. If it brings happiness, which I doubt not, why don't *you* buy it?"

"Parthena! Daughter!"

"Father!"

"All in these two boxes belongs to Captain White."

"'Tis false!"

"To whom, then?"

"To Rosamund Walker."

"Bah! Ah, you mean *legally?*"

"I do."

"Then let me tell you that she will never legally recover the treasure—never! Parthena, if you married White,

you—you might wear a necklace of these diamonds, and——"

"Silence!" interrupted Parthena sternly; "silence! Do not dare to again mention that subject to me, or I may forget that you are my father *and fling back this trap-door* upon you, so that you should never see the light again. I marry Captain White? Heavens—never! Never would I allow myself to come in contact with such a vile wretch—the villain with untold murders on his soul!

"That wretch has a great deal to answer for in respect of *your* proceedings. Oh, if I could live to see Captain White dead and in chains, I should consider myself revenged! Once more I warn you—— Ah, White's knock, quick!"

At this instant rapping above fell upon their ears.

Instantly the miser relocked the boxes, and, assisted by Parthena, came out of the hole.

"'Tis White!" said Mercutio, whose exertions had taken nearly all the breath out of his attenuated carcass. "Now listen, Parthena; if White asks you, you know nothing of the whereabouts of this treasure."

Parthena nodded grimly.

She then assisted the old man up the stairs, she herself going to the door, on which White was now dealing some thundering blows.

"Open!" he growled. "Open, curse you! You know my knock well enough. Open, I say."

"We will admit you if you will have patience," replied Parthena in cold tones; "if not, we will let you remain where you are."

"Oh, it's you, is it?" growled White. "I have often said that Mercutio only was to admit me."

"Whatever you may say," was Parthena's reply as she opened the door, "will meet with but little attention at my hands. But who is with you?"

"A friend."

"I cannot admit him."

"What!" hissed White savagely. "You cannot admit him? Stand aside, or I will——"

He shook his clenched fist fiercely in her face, but it did not cause her to quail.

On the contrary, the menace brought

a dangerous light into her eyes, and a red flush to her thin lips.

"Put down your fist, you fool!" she said, 'or perhaps you will have good cause to regret having threatened me. Do you think that I am terrified by your ugly face or your threats of blood?"

Mercutio, who had reached a room above, once more descended.

"What is it—what is it, Parthena?" he whined. "What do the gentlemen want? Who are they—eh?"

"Captain White and a friend," replied Parthena; but, of course, Mercutio knew well enough.

"A friend, eh—a friend?"

Mercutio took the lamp from his daughter's hand and raised it.

A strange terrified expression rested upon his face as he said—

"Lord Stretton!"

"Yes, it is Lord Stretton!" mimicked White.

"I did not think he would have recognised me so quickly," said Stretton; "but he need not hesitate about admitting me. I promise I will not claim my papers."

"With all respect to your lordship," replied Mercutio, "it would be all the same if you did. But, Captain White, why do you bring Lord Stretton here—and at this hour?"

"His lordship wants to conceal himself."

"Hum! Well, if my humble abode is acceptable, and my terms——"

"Let us talk about these little matters afterwards," interrupted White.

"Enter," said Mercutio, "and my daughter shall show you——"

"Nothing," cried Parthena from the top of the stairs; "since you choose to invite your visitors, you shall see to their proper accommodation."

Thereupon Parthena slammed her door to with a crash.

After much whining, Mercutio conducted Lord Stretton to a room at the very top of the house.

Asked by the miser what he would require, his lordship said—

"Nothing save some paper, pens, and ink."

And these were quickly supplied.

The miser conducted White to his own room.

He locked the door, and placed what refreshments he had before the captain, who evidently intended to make himself at home.

When the repast was finished, White requested to be shown to a bedroom.

"Oh," said Mercutio, "I am very sorry, you may depend upon it; but a bedroom is out of all question."

"Is it? Listen to me, Mercutio Merrywell. I am tired, and I am sleepy, and I must rest, even if others have to be inconvenienced. Therefore be good enough to order your daughter to quit her room, so that I may occupy it."

"No—no. Don't disturb her on any account. She keeps three or four loaded pistols in her room. I am getting quite afraid of her."

"I should say so!" chuckled White; "and this is the lady you propose I should marry! He, he! ho, ho! Why, Mercutio Merrywell, I would see you hanged before I would marry your vixenish daughter!"

A singular expression passed over the miser's parchmenty face as White said this; but it was unobserved.

"You shall have my bedroom," said the miser; "it is not elaborately furnished, but——"

"No doubt I shall sleep—eh? No doubt. Well then, conduct me to *your* bedroom. But mark me, Mercutio, no foul play."

"No—no, no foul play!" repeated the miser. "No foul play, of course. I respect you, I—I have too much consideration for a man of your wealth, captain. Yes—yes. Come, and tread softly lest you wake Parthena. She is so restless of late—so very restless," he whined, as he shook his grey locks; "she makes me feel nervous."

Captain White in a few moments was in the miser's bedroom.

* * * *

We will, for a short time leave the miser and Captain White, and return to Felix and his friends.

Before an hour had passed, a splendid collation had been served and partaken of, and another half-hour saw every person in his or her bed—nay not every person—all retired save Felix.

For though our hero retired to the room set apart for him, he could not rest.

His brain was filled with the desire

for speedy vengeance on Captain White and Lord Stretton.

For some time he restlessly paced the room, but at last he made up his mind to seek the pair.

"It is, perhaps, *now* or *never*," he thought; "if I allow a day or two to elapse, they might leave the country. Let me see; they escaped together! Then it is almost certain that for some time they would remain together. And where would they stay? Where but Alsatia? Aye, that is where they will be found. By Heaven! I will seek them—and alone!"

Having thus decided, he saw that his sword and pistols were all right, and left the house.

At a rapid pace our hero traversed the streets, and at length reached Fleet Street.

After passing through Temple Bar, he walked slowly, for he wanted to find, if possible, some stray Alsatian.

He was not long in finding such an individual.

Just after passing the "Devil" tavern, one of the bravos came towards him.

Felix immediately recognised him by his swagger.

Observing Felix, the fellow paused, and leered insolently into his face.

"Well fool," said Felix, "do you intend to insult me?"

"And why not?" was the reply.

"Well, if so, my steel is handy."

"Then pick your teeth with it, friend," chuckled the bravo; "I am no fighter."

"Drink is more to your taste—eh?"

"Aye; have you any, friend, to spare?"

"Nay; but I have the money."

"Ha! that is of quite as much consequence."

"And you shall have a handful of money, friend, if you will do me a service."

"Hum! What is the service? To cut——"

"To cut nothing," interrupted Felix. "Listen. I have a big thing for Captain White, but I heard he has been, and was likely to remain absent for months."

"It is a lie!" replied the bravo.

But quickly correcting himself, he said—

"At least—that is to say—er—how am I to know to whom I am speaking! As we say in Alsatia—

"You may be a friend, you may be a foe,
  The former my hand, the latter my toe!

If you are a friend, why, *dub up!* In other words, before I give information, I like to be paid for it."

"Quite right, too," replied Felix; "here, my friend, is a purse containing fifty crowns—count them."

The bravo, whose hands now trembled with excitement, seized upon the purse as a vulture would seize upon its prey, opened it, and looked at the contents.

"You are a gentleman, every inch of you, and I will believe what you say," replied the bravo; "so I need not count. And now for the service."

"I want you to tell me whether Captain White has arrived."

"He has, with a friend of his, whose name I do not know. They have gone to the miser's house for the present; but of course you do not know the miser's house?"

"I know it when I see it. Now I want you to conduct me to the miser's house, for my business with Captain White is of the utmost importance."

The bravo hereupon drew a long face.

"That is risky," he said; "for since the attack on Alsatia the guard has been doubled. However, I will chance it. Follow me, and pass the guard quickly."

The guards, however, were too drowsy to eye Felix closely.

As the password was given they simply grunted.

Through the narrow dirty lanes went the bravo, followed closely by our hero, and at last the miser's dwelling was reached.

"If you want me again," said the bravo, "you will find me at The Fountain of Life."

Thereupon he withdrew, and left our hero to himself.

In the shadow of the opposite premises, Felix surveyed the miser's house.

He could see one light above, but that was all.

Was it possible to gain admittance? he thought.

Crossing over he carefully examined the shutters.

Shaky enough they looked, but whether there was any chance of gaining admittance through them he could not tell.

However, he determined to try.

Unsheathing his dagger, he at once commenced to attack the woodwork.

After some little time he made a hole large enough to insert his hand.

After feeling about, he found the knob of a bolt.

Without hesitation he pulled it, and instantly the shutter, at which he had been picking, shot *upward* with wonderful velocity and with a sharp click.

The noise apparently attracted no attention.

Felix looked into the aperture.

He could see nothing, for all was profoundly dark.

Sheathing his dagger, he drew his sword, and with the point of it felt about the aperture to find whether it was solid, or whether it was simply a trap.

The point of the weapon touched wood, and this circumstance satisfied our hero that so far he was safe.

Therefore he entered, but as he could not manage to find out how the shutter was to be restored to its position, he was bound to let it remain as it was.

Sheathing his sword, he dropped upon his knees, and in this attitude he commenced to grope his way forward.

* * * *

Now, to return to the miser.

Returning to the room, he placed his lamp upon the table, locked the door, and for some few seconds stood in an attitude of deep thought.

Presently he advanced once more to the table, unlocked a drawer, and took out a dagger—a long glittering Spanish blade.

"He does not mean to marry Parthena," muttered Mercutio; "but it would be all the same if he did. He will claim the treasure. Yes, yes, and I should have to give it up! And, oh, I cannot do that—I cannot do that! Never were my eyes so feasted! They must be mine—they *must!*

"I should die if they were to leave me. I can make them mine by slaying *him!*

"And would it be a crime to kill him? No, no; I should be doing London a service.

"Yes, yes, I will kill him. Parthena hates him, and she would approve of what I had done. He will be fast asleep

directly, and then I will kill him. My arm is weak, but the dagger is sharp."

With the dagger firmly clutched in his long bony hand, the old man waited near the door—waited until White slept.

Ten minutes passed.

Then he crept cautiously out, and crossed to White's room.

Listening at the door, he heard White's heavy breathing.

"He sleeps!" he muttered, as he turned the handle of the door, and noiselessly crept in; "he sleeps! And now let me strike hard—hard, and in the right place!"

With a step like a cat, he drew near the bed.

But luck was against him. Close by the bedside the captain had placed his long boots—all he had taken off—and against these the miser knocked.

Though the noise made was but slight, it awoke the captain.

With a most horrible oath, he started up, and seized a pistol he had placed handy.

Mercutio, now almost dead with fright, hastened from the room.

White, cocking his pistol, hurried after him.

He had not recognised the intruder, but was determined to kill him whoever he was, so he stopped to take steady aim with his pistol.

The lamp from the opposite room served to show him the dim outline of a figure, and he was about to fire, when there was a swift rush of footsteps, and ere the captain could draw back, a dagger was buried to the hilt in his body.

The hand which struck the blow was not the miser's—nay, it was the steel-like hand of Parthena Merrywell; who, unseen by the miser, had been watching her father's footsteps.

The pistol fell from the captain's hand, and exploded on the floor.

Back staggered White—back—back—into the room, his right hand upon the hilt of the weapon, fixed so firmly in his body—back, until he touched the woodwork of the bedstead, and then a prolonged terrible shriek left his lips.

Not knowing what he was doing, he wildly commenced to pull out the dagger.

But before many seconds had passed, the "Chief" of the Alsatians fell back a corpse upon the miser's bed.

With folded arms, Parthena stood erect and as firm as a solid piece of marble on the threshold of the door.

"You die," she hissed, "like a dog! And by my hand above all others. Fiend, bloody-minded wretch! I do not regret the crime one instant that robs the world of such a monster!"

Turning, Parthena called out—

"Father, come hither—come hither!"

She was not answered. The opposite room was empty.

Parthena was about to search for him when she heard a hurried tread descending the stairs.

In a few moments Lord Stretton, lamp and naked sword in hand, was on the landing.

His pale face and the convulsive twitching of his lips showed how terrified he was.

"What is it?" he asked; "what has happened? I heard loud voices—the report of a pistol-shot, the——"

Parthena checked him by pointing to the bedstead.

"Look there," she said hoarsely; "there lies your principal accomplice—at least, your principal with the exception of your son."

"Slain!" gasped Stretton.

"Aye, slain. I slew him, or he would have slain my father!"

"Heavens!" groaned Stretton, "what horrible proceedings! I will at once leave the house."

"Do so, if it so pleases you," replied Parthena coldly; "go where you like. But wherever you go you may depend upon it you will be sought for."

"He has been sought for, and is found!" cried a loud voice, and Felix, who had crept noiselessly up the stairs, bounded forward, threw back his cloak, and hurled his hat to the floor.

Parthena was startled at the sudden appearance of Felix, sword in hand.

As for Stretton, he was dumb struck.

Thus for a moment Felix and Stretton confronted each other.

Parthena never moved, but she said—

"I will not ask how you gained entrance here, but I can guess. You have sought this noble lord and Captain White? Good. In that room lies White, slain by my hand. I have punished him for the many insults he heaped on me. What you and Lord Stretton have between you I know not, but there he is."

"What seek you?" asked Stretton, hoarsely.

"Vengeance?" answered Felix; "vengeance! No words need be passed. Defend yourself, my lord, or I will run you through as you stand!"

Stretton gave vent to a loud laugh of derision.

With a contemptuous movement he raised his sword.

"Defied by a boy!" he said. "Well, I must put up with it when surrounded by hundreds, but when you dare to beard me single-handed, why I must teach you a lesson by slitting your tongue."

Felix did not reply.

The swords crossed with a loud clash.

Parthena backed to the stairs, and there she stood holding aloft the lamp.

Try all he could, Stretton could not get a single chance of inflicting the smallest injury on our hero, and this fact worked him up to a pitch of blind fury.

His defence became the defence of a madman—wild, erratic; and at last he gave Felix a chance, which was instantly seized upon.

In an instant Stretton's sword was whirled from his grasp, and our hero's sword passed through his breast.

Stretton fell with a deep groan.

"You have been slain in fair fight," said Felix, "and now I ask you, ere you die, to entrust to my keeping the secret you hold—I mean that relating to the Countess of Rothburn."

"Never!" gasped Stretton. "Never! never! Oh, Horace—my son—my son!"

"Your son is dead."

"Dead!"

"Aye, dead. He was killed at the old mill."

"And you wish for the secret—no—it shall—it shall—die—with—— Come hither," he said as he beckoned to Parthena.

That strange being approached, and bent over him.

"Promise me," whispered Stretton, "promise—me—that you will cause me to be buried in my clothes—just as I am—promise—don't let them open—my—Oh—I die—I die! My——"

He had been resting on his elbow, but here he suddenly stopped and fell upon his back.

"I can make no such promise," answered Parthena. "You die! yea, and are no better than the villain yonder!"

Again Stretton opened his mouth to speak, but instead of words a volume of blood issued trom it.

A convulsive shudder passed through his frame, and then—then the spirit of Lord Stretton had fled, to stand at the side of that of his son, both to answer for the many foul deeds of which they had been guilty.

"You search for a secret," said Parthena; "and from what he says as to being buried with his clothes on, I should imagine that the secret is concealed about him. Search, and then get you gone!"

Felix fell upon his knees and tore open his lordship's doublet.

A sealed letter met his anxious gaze—a letter addressed to Horace.

Nothing else could our hero see.

"That letter has not long been written," said Parthena; "for I recognise my father's paper. Since that is all he has, get you gone."

"But the bodies?"

"What of them."

"Let them remain here until you hear from me."

"As you will. Whether they are taken away by you or thrown into the river by the bravos my father will hire, matters not to me. Come, and quickly."

"Remember this, the property stolen from the goldsmith, and which I have reason to believe is here in this house, I shall claim on behalf of Rosamund Walker."

"It shall be handed over. That I promise you."

So Felix departed.

He did not seek out the man who had obtained him admission to Alsatia, he had the password, and he found it quite sufficient, for, unquestioned, he reached the "Devil" tavern in Fleet Street.

CHAPTER XVII.

THE FALLING OF THE CURTAIN.

PARCHED with thirst, Felix entered this noted hostelry, and calling for a bottle of wine, ensconced himself in a corner, and, bringing forth the letter, cut the silken threads, spread open the document, and prepared to read.

It was a long letter, in which Stretton—evidently not dreaming that his son was dead—deplored the condition into which they had fallen, and advised Horace to join him.

There were other matters, but of no interest to Felix.

It was the postscript which was of importance to him.

It ran thus—

"*There is no longer any doubt but that this Felix Ferdinand is the same I placed with Nicholas Fielding. He is beyond question the lawful son of the Countess of Rothburn.*"

Felix, with a wild cry, started from his seat.

Excitedly, he continued—

"*I have sworn to slay him, and slay him, I will—if spared! But should I die, Horace, you will avenge me by slaying this accursed youth, and then informing the countess who he really is. There is one thing, however, which must be done; the lodgings of this youth must be searched—for this reason: Nicholas Fielding had a lot of my letters, and he also held the counterpart of the diamond necklace with which, singular to say, this youth has been mixed up.*"

Again a wild exultant cry lett our hero's lips.

"THE LOST SECRET!" he cried. "Heavens! I see it all! The cottage shall again be searched!"

He continued the reading—

"*When it first dawned upon me that this Felix Ferdinand was none other than the Countess's son, I visited the cottage at Stratford, but learned nothing. So it is evident that this youth has the articles I require in his possession. We must have them; or he may establish his identity.*"

This was nearly all.

Placing the letter in his pocket, Felix bowed his face in his hands, and for some time was lost in deep thought.

Rousing himself at last, he called for pens, ink, and paper, and these being supplied, he wrote a letter to Clinton, saying that business of the utmost importance would cause him to be absent some hours—that he was quite safe, and that he would join them in a short time.

He concluded thus—

"Your lordship will, I know, do me a favour. It is that to-night you have the countess, Rosamund, her mother, Andrew, Fillipy, and Alice, Rosamund's maid, together in one room. Fail not, I implore your lordship."

In consideration of the payment of two crowns, one of the serving-men agreed to take this letter to St. James's Park, and we may here say that it safely arrived.

Felix ordered a horse of the host, and proceeded to Stratford.

* * * *

It was broad daylight when he reached the straggling village.

He found it just as miserable and deserted as when he had left it.

He made enquiries of the first person he met, and found that the cottage had been closed since the death of Nicholas Fielding.

Our hero thought it necessary to declare himself, and very soon he was the centre of an admiring crowd.

He announced that he had reappeared in order to make another search of the old cottage.

Several men provided themselves with pick-axes and spades, the door of the cottage was broken open, and the work of searching commenced.

Down they dug, and when three feet had been reached they stopped, assuring Felix that the search was a search after nothing.

"We can go no farther," said one, "for we are near the foundation-stones."

Felix stooped and pulled aside one of them, then another, and another.

Suddenly a loud cry left his lips, and indeed the lips of all present, for under the largest stone rested a small iron box.

Our hero seized the box and dragged it from its position.

On the lid was scratched:

"The property of my ward, Felix Ferdinand."

"I have found what I required," said Felix, as he handed over the money. "And now divide the payment among you."

Our hero looked for the lock of the box, but it was not to be seen.

The only thing to be done, therefore, was to burst it open.

Felix and a couple of the men set to work upon it.

It was old and rusty, and the lid soon yielded.

The top was filled with papers, and on our hero removing these the precious necklace was discovered!—that necklace which was the exact counterpart of the one with which Felix had been so intimately associated!

Oh, what were our hero's feelings as he replaced the papers, and strapped the box to his saddle-bow!

Mounting, he bade adieu to the villagers.

Felix rode into Bow, and was about to call at the house of his old friend, the minister, but at the gates a sexton told him that the old gentleman had been dead and buried long ago.

Felix put up at an hostelry, partook of some refreshment, and then lay down for a couple of hours.

He fell into a sound sleep, and awoke much refreshed.

A thorough rest and another meal made him look almost a different individual.

Once more mounting, our hero again set off, this time for St. James's.

The countess's residence was reached without accident.

Felix entered, and directing the servant to at once inform Lord Clinton of his arrival, he proceeded to his bedroom.

In a few moments Lord Clinton joined him.

Rushing to our hero, who was now in a state of almost uncontrollable excitement, his lordship took both his hands, pressing them warmly.

"My dear boy!" he said, "what on earth can all this mean? Until we received your letter we were all in a state of dreadful suspense and anxiety. But I thank Heaven I see you safe and sound!"

The servant who had ushered up his

lordship was about to depart, when Felix directed him to inform the countess of his safe arrival, and that they would join her in a few moments.

Then, locking the door, he bade his lordship take a seat, and rapidly he told him what had occurred since he stole out of the house, unseen and unheard.

Lord Clinton listened after the manner of a man who listens to a wild, fascinating, romantic tale, the narration of which would be broken off by a sound.

When Felix had reached that part where the necklace was found, he placed the box on the table, opened it, and brought out the glittering ornament.

Of course Clinton instantly recognised in this the counterpart of the one the countess had in her possession.

"Then you are indeed the long lost child!" cried his lordship, starting up. "The stolen child!"

"I am!" answered Felix in a voice quivering with emotion.

"How strange—how marvellously strange! All along the countess has been drawn towards you. Parental instinct. And yet, so have I. It is indeed a wonderful, startling thing!"

"My lord, the countess, my dear mother, promised you her hand if you brought her child to her."

"She did!"

"Then take me to her. You will have fulfilled your contract. That is why I informed you of all first."

"Heaven bless you, my boy!" cried Clinton fervently. "Come—come, no need for you to repeat your story. I will do that for you."

With the box under his arm Felix descended with Clinton to the magnificent drawing-room, where he found our friends assembled.

All started towards him as he entered, but of course Rosamund was the first in his arms.

"Safe and sound!" cried the countess. "Heaven be thanked!"

"Countess!" cried Clinton in exultant tones, "your hand is mine! For why? I have fulfilled my contract; nay, do not start—*behold your son!*"

And he pointed to Felix.

"My *son!*" cried the countess, starting back and clasping her hands together.

"Aye, your son. Look!" and his lordship, taking the box from Felix, brought out the necklace. "Do you not recognise this?"

A wild scream escaped the countess's lips.

"I do! I do!" she cried; "it was around my child's neck when he was stolen."

Felix stood forward, and held forth his arms.

The countess rushed forward, and mother and son—so long parted—were together again, heart to heart, lip to lip, hand to hand.

Oh, it was a joyful meeting—a most joyful reunion!

* * * *

On such a picture we are compelled to lower the curtain, but for an instant only.

Behold! it rises again.

In the centre of the room, surrounded by all the party, Clinton stands relating all that had happened since Felix left the house.

An expression of thankfulness leaves the lips of all present as they learn of the tragic death of Captain White and Lord Stretton.

The papers are then opened.

All are letters relating to Felix, but one is in the handwriting of Nicholas Fielding.

Among other things it said—

"I do not know the rank of the person who gave you into my charge, but that he is a nobleman I am certain. He says that you are the son of titled parents, but that is all. From what he has let fall from time to time, I believe that this person was the slayer of your father, but whether in fair fight or not, I cannot tell. He has told me that one day he would restore you to your mother, but I doubt it, for he is a man to be feared. He has not been near me for a long time, and if he does not come soon, I intend to search for your mother. I write this, however, in case anything should happen to me. Fear this man, Felix, and guard the necklace with your life."

"This," said Felix, "must have been written but a short time before his death. Oh, that long ago I had discovered this box!"

"Thank Heaven all is now set right!" said Clinton.

"It seems like a dream—too good to be true!" murmured the countess.

"After his many fortunes and misfortunes," smiled Clinton, "Felix, or I should say, Elric Earl of Rothburn "—a loud cheer arose as Clinton said this—" will be happy with his mother, and——"

" His *father*," smiled Felix.

"Aye, and with pretty Rosamund, whom he will marry. Mistress Walker, who, I see, is smiling through her tears, will have no objection to their union."

The old lady shook her head.

"Andrew," said Clinton, "at the same time as our marriage takes place, you and Alice will be of the party."

"With much pleasure," replied Andrew, " if Alice——"

Felix led her forward.

No words were wanted. Alice was quite satisfied.

"And you, Master Fillipy," said Clinton, " you who have shared so many perils on Felix's and our behalf."

"Oh," replied Fillipy, " I have no doubt but that in the course of time I shall find someone willing to join me in my perusal of musty law-books, and——"

"Don't talk of them, Fillipy," said Felix warmly; " I trust you and Andrew will always remain near me. I shall have enough, shall I not, mother?"

"Aye, my son, and to spare!" answered the delighted countess.

*   *   *   *

On the following day Lord Clinton laid everything before the king, and a great sensation his recital made, Felix being at once summoned before his majesty.

After the audience, Clinton, Felix (as we feel bound to continue to call him), Andrew, and Fillipy, proceeded with a large troop of soldiers to Alsatia.

The miser's dwelling being reached, admission was demanded in the name of the king.

Parthena pale, but still erect and firm, answered the door, and, in reply to Felix,

told him that two hours after he had departed, Mercutio was found at the bottom of the cellar-stairs with his neck broken, having evidently fallen in his frantic haste to escape from White.

Without any hesitation she conducted them to the place where lay the treasure taken from the goldsmith's, and it was carried away by the soldiers, as also were the bodies of Captain White and Lord Stretton.

*   *   *   *

Our romance draws to a conclusion.

Stretton was buried, without a soul to mourn him, in the family vault, and his property confiscated to the crown.

"Captain " White's body was hung in chains at Vauxhall until his flesh rotted from his bones.

In a few months Felix was granted his letters patent and acknowledged Earl of Rothburn, and with that proud title he was married to Rosamund. At the same time Clinton married the countess, and Andrew, Alice, the church being crammed with Templars and apprentices, all of whom were entertained, after the ceremony, at Lord Clinton's house, the chief of the ceremonies being Master Fallory.

Andrew was afterwards created steward to the Earl of Rothburn, while Fillipy accepted a like office under Clinton.

Thus all our characters—not forgetting dear old Mistress Walker—were nearly always together.

Parthena Merrywell had all her property secretly removed to France, and it was said she there united herself to a French gallant, who, if he did not love her, was partial to her money.

And now, in bidding adieu to our readers, we have to thank them for so closely watching the "Fortunes of Felix Ferdinand," the dark deeds of Horace, Lord Stretton, and, under the one-eyed villain, "Captain " White, the horrible proceedings of " THE BRAVOS OF ALSATIA."

THE END.